T0194339

THE
GARELOI
SOLUTION

THE GARELOI SOLUTION

DONALD E. PHILLIPSON

iUniverse

THE GARELOI SOLUTION

iUniverse books may be ordered through booksellers or by contacting:

iUniverse
1663 Liberty Drive
Bloomington, IN 47403
www.iuniverse.com
1-800-Authors (1-800-288-4677)

ISBN: 978-1-4917-8923-0 (sc)
ISBN: 978-1-4917-8924-7 (hc)
ISBN: 978-1-4917-8922-3 (e)

Library of Congress Control Number: 2016902086

Print information available on the last page.

iUniverse rev. date: 03/15/2016

To Suzanne, Laura, and all future generations

C O N T E N T S

Appendixes and Notes

LIST OF FIGURES

PREFACE

This book has been many years in the making and has called upon both my educational background—bachelor and master of science degrees in chemistry—and my professional background as a trial lawyer.

Although my practice at a large Denver law firm for more than two decades included lawsuits involving scientific subjects, those subjects were sidelights to the main legal work required for the lawsuits. In the early 1990s I felt a need to bring science back into my life. The new subjects that intrigued me at that time were the developing recognition of global atmospheric warming caused by chemical changes in the earth's atmosphere and renewable energy technologies that could use free and essentially inexhaustible energy sources.

So, with strong support from my wife Barbara, I resigned from my law firm to pursue those interests.

My science education facilitated research in climate science and renewable technologies. And my professional background as a trial lawyer helped me critique the factual evidence relating to both subjects.

Renewable energy technologies at the time were not mature enough to begin to meet the massive energy needs of modern society. A small business using those technologies without that impact did not interest me.

If global atmospheric warming was to reach a threshold where significant and harmful climate changes began to occur, what would be our response? I thought that an answer to this question could form the core of a science-based novel. So I began writing down ideas and drafting text.

Normal life soon intervened. Within a year after leaving my law firm, I returned to legal practice to earn income by working on complex civil cases for clients and law firms that could use my expertise. With this new endeavor as an independent lawyer, however, I could carve out chunks of time to continue my research, write down ideas, and draft text of a novel. Ten years later, I had a reasonably good draft of *The Gareloi Solution*, but could not find a publisher. Shelving the novel, I continued my legal practice and then embarked on another detour when I conceived some new ideas for federal tax reform. That detour, which built upon a decade-long interest in federal taxes, resulted in my book entitled *The FAST Plan for Tax Reform*. It was published by iUniverse at the end of 2013.

Encouraged by my publishing experience with iUniverse and *The FAST Plan for Tax Reform*, and having finally retired from practicing law, I returned to my novel. Updated research and actual occurrences in the decade since shelving my novel are now reflected in the final version of *The Gareloi Solution*. It is scientifically as accurate as my research and understanding could make it. I hope you enjoy reading *The Gareloi Solution*.

CHAPTER 1

GARELOI ISLAND

Paul Anderson paused as he reached the top of a small ridge on the northeast side of Gareloi Island. Usually Paul encountered mist and gray clouds, but today a bright sun made Gareloi's volcanic seaside cliffs stand out sharply against a dark blue sky.

Despite its beauty, Gareloi was ominously still on this cool and calm late September afternoon. The thousands of Aleutian terns, auklets, and other birds that had filled the air with incessant chatter and endless flights less than a month ago had all begun their southern journey away from the oncoming darkness and cold of this far northern latitude. Fat sea lions, so numerous in August, had also abandoned Gareloi's shorelines for their winter homes thousands of miles away. Those few animals that did not migrate, such as Gareloi's blue foxes, had been the subject of intense trapping and relocation efforts to neighboring islands. Except for human activity that was oddly out of place in this remote location, Gareloi was lifeless by design.

A dot of land in Alaska's Aleutian Islands chain, Gareloi was a typical volcanic island. Like its neighbors, Gareloi had been formed from thousands of years of magma eruptions caused by the collision of the Pacific and North American tectonic plates far beneath the surface of the Bering Sea. This exposed cone with a double summit, known simply as Mount Gareloi, rose a mile above sea level. Its visible base above the ocean surface was five miles in diameter. Mount Gareloi had remained active, on and off, during the past two centuries. It was this feature that had brought Paul and more than a thousand other people to this small island a year ago in the summer of 2033.

Paul had hiked along this trail every afternoon since he had returned to Gareloi two weeks ago. It was one way that he could keep himself physically fit in this remote location. Now in his late sixties, Paul looked much younger than his age despite his short gray hair. At just over six feet tall, he had an easy gait that allowed him to cover most of this undulating trail in less than an hour.

As he had done every day on this trail, Paul had taken his binoculars with him. He always hoped to get a rare view of Tanaga Island some twenty-five miles to the east. Today, that hope was a spectacular reality. Much larger than Gareloi, Tanaga had more varied terrain and a distinct bay directly facing Gareloi. Tanaga Volcano, about the same height as Mount Gareloi, dominated the northwest part of Tanaga Island. As Paul looked at Tanaga Volcano though his binoculars, he imagined that he was looking back at Mount Gareloi. He tried to visualize what Gareloi would look like from Tanaga after October 7th. He had seen drawings that suggested its transformation, but its projected change was still hard to imagine. The double summit of Mount Gareloi would be gone and many of Gareloi's green hillsides would be covered in gray ash.

Paul turned his attention to the hillside before him. He carefully scanned each clump of grass to see if any blue fox had somehow eluded the intense trapping efforts of the last month. Soon a different sort of movement attracted his attention.

Less than a mile north of Paul, a United States Navy transport boat started to leave the temporary dock on the northern side of Gareloi. Paul knew its destination and purpose. The destroyer USS Truman had set anchor that morning two hundred yards from the dock. The Truman and similar destroyers had come almost daily to transport personnel to and from Gareloi. Helicopters usually transported personnel and materials from these ships to the island, but Paul knew that helicopters would not be used today. They simply did not have the power to lift the heavy cargo brought by the Truman.

Paul sat down on a large rock, binoculars still in hand, to watch the naval transport boat rendezvous with the Truman. Fortunately, the sea was calm. When the transport boat was about ten yards from the Truman, a large crane on the Truman began to move. It turned to its right, lowered a heavy cable into the middle of the ship and then was still. After less than a minute, the cable became taut. The crane slowly lifted a steel container from the Truman's ammunition hold, straining from its weight. Even from a distance, Paul could see that the container was no larger than an ordinary automobile. Once the container was well above the deck, the crane swung the container across the deck, out over the open water, and above the transport boat. The crane gently lowered the container into a receiving device on the transport boat. The boat sank into the water from the container's weight.

Paul was so intrigued with this operation that at first he did not notice the heavily armed military personnel who stood guard over the whole operation. When he did notice them, he was surprised how many there were in this isolated place. He had counted over forty guards on the destroyer alone when he interrupted his count to watch the naval transport boat leave the Truman. He lowered his binoculars to watch it return to the landing dock. He saw six patrol boats converge adjacent to the path of the transport boat, forming a protective corridor to the dock. Paul raised his binoculars again. He followed the transport boat until it landed at the dock, then moved his binoculars left and up the hill to find Building 2 on a flat space not far from the loading dock.

Building 2 was the largest of five operations buildings constructed by the Corps of Engineers beginning just twelve months ago. A Spartan silver metal structure with only one floor and basic office and meeting room amenities, Building 2 was the island's headquarters for Project Prime, the first project of Operation Vulcan. Operation Vulcan itself was headquartered at Adak Naval Base on Adak Island, ninety miles east of Gareloi.

Operation Vulcan relied upon the most carefully but quickly assembled group of scientists with a grim international mission since the Manhattan Project of the United States in the middle of the last century. That project, organized during World War II to create the first atomic bomb, was focused on weaponry designed to win that total war. The Allies needed to create this weapon before Nazi Germany could do so and thereby threaten the Allies' upcoming victory. To achieve this goal, President Franklin Delano Roosevelt had authorized the assemblage of many top civilian scientists, especially physicists, to work in secrecy with military personnel to achieve success.

The current president, James Clark, had created Operation Vulcan using similar principles. Paul Anderson was one of the civilian scientists enlisted. Paul's professional niche, meteorology and climatology, was the heart of Operation Vulcan, just as atomic physics had been the heart of the Manhattan Project.

Even though Paul was individually very important to Operation Vulcan, he was not its director. That responsibility rested with General Wayne Meyer of the United States Air Force. Paul was glad that General Meyer was in charge because the unique methods to be used in Operation Vulcan made it unmistakably a military mission despite its civilian purpose.

Paul moved his binoculars away from Building 2 and back toward the naval transport boat. A newly constructed crane at the dock, basically a duplicate of the crane on the USS Truman, had just finished unloading the first container. The transport boat was already beginning to move away from the dock. In the next hour, the operation that Paul had observed was repeated with a second heavy steel container carried by the Truman. As he watched the second container being loaded onto the dock, Paul glanced at his cell phone. He had less than an hour before the team meeting in Building 2 that had been scheduled by General Meyer. He had better start back to allow time to gather his materials for the meeting.

Paul could see all of the operations buildings and most of the Project Prime complex as he hiked back along the trail. It was astounding that only two years ago, neither this complex, nor Project Prime, nor Operation Vulcan, had been conceived by anyone, much less created and approved at the highest levels of the United States government. Their genesis and Paul's involvement were forced by unwanted and unexpected events that even now were hard to believe.

In just nine days, at precisely 10:00 a.m. on October 7, 2034, Gareloi Island would be changed forever.

CHAPTER 2

HARBINGER

"A food shortage? In the United States?" exclaimed President Clark. He looked sternly at Bill Rand, his secretary of agriculture.

Rand had just completed a ten-day tour of farms in California, Texas, Nebraska, Illinois, Pennsylvania, and Florida. His tour had been prompted by preliminary data he had received in the middle of July 2032 about expected crop production in the United States. These data suggested that total production in every farm segment would be less than in 2031, which itself had been a poor year compared to production during the previous decade.

"Yes, a shortage," answered Rand, standing firm under President Clark's intense glare.

President Clark was an imposing man, tall and lanky with piercing dark eyes. His brown hair was just beginning to show some gray. Good looking in a stern way, James Clark could be intimidating to anyone not prepared for his intensity.

Bill Rand could not be more different in appearance than the president. Short, stocky, and now mostly bald in his sixty-second year, Rand looked like he had just come off a farm. In some ways, he had done just that, at least in his heart. He had been an independent farmer in Montana for more than two decades before entering political life, first as a senator in Montana's legislature and then as Montana's congressman. He had served in the House of Representatives for five terms before President Clark had asked him to become secretary of agriculture after Clark's election in 2028. Although a decade older than the president, Rand had become one of President Clark's closest friends and most trusted Cabinet advisors.

Bill Rand always candidly gave the president the facts. If the preliminary projections for crop production in 2032 were correct, and if the downward trend from 2031 continued, there could actually be a food shortage in the United States in 2034, or even 2033.

Still incredulous, President Clark turned to look out the south-facing windows of his Oval Office in the White House. The president collected his thoughts while looking beyond the Ellipse toward the people enjoying a hot, sunny August day on the Mall. How could there possibly be a food shortage that would affect these people? The idea was preposterous. The data Rand was relying upon must be flawed.

"Bill, I just don't see how this can be possible. Your data must be wrong."

"I thought so, too, when I first saw it," said Rand. "But Karen Lewis and her staff compiled the information. You know how rigorous she is. Remember last year? She's the one who spotted the across-the-board declines in US crop yields. Even though they were small, a year with declines in all segments of our agriculture hasn't happened before. As you know, because of her analysis, we quietly released a lot of acreage from non-production status this year just in case yields declined again. I'm sure glad now that we did it."

"I am too," replied President Clark. "Still, you must have had doubts about her data and conclusion for this year despite our increased farm acreage. Otherwise you wouldn't have taken your trip."

"I did look for exceptions to the projections that Karen was making," said Rand, "but I found none. Thank God I've made these goodwill trips regularly before now. There was very little publicity. I could ask pointed questions to many farmers with no media around."

"We don't need this problem on top of the petroleum mess," said President Clark.

Since early 2031, President Clark, the United States, and all of the world's nations had been contending with huge increases in petroleum prices. Their genesis was complex and driven by new and unexpected conditions.

Before the turn of the twenty-first century, some analysts had warned that world-wide petroleum production might peak before 2010. And a peak would mean greatly increased prices as well as potential shortages.

These analysts had based their warnings on a methodology that had been used by the geologist M. King Hubbert when studying the United States oil industry in the 1950s. Using graphical extrapolation from data on production capacity and estimates of total discoverable petroleum in the United States, in 1956 Hubbert had predicted that US production would peak in the early 1970s. Although Hubbert had been roundly criticized and ridiculed when he made his prediction, the early 1970s had proven Hubbert to be right, not his critics. US production had indeed peaked in 1970. Except for a small increase caused by petroleum from Prudhoe Bay in Alaska that had come on line in the early 1980s, US production had declined steadily after 1970 until the early part of the twenty-first century.

By the beginning of the twenty-first century, petroleum prices had risen enough to justify the use of improved and more expensive technologies to extract petroleum from shale that locked petroleum in its tiny open spaces. Especially in the United States, hydraulic fracturing and horizontal drilling had achieved petroleum production from widespread shale oil deposits. Optimism had prevailed that these deposits and technologies would produce so much petroleum for so long that any peak in world petroleum production would be many decades away. Higher prices also had encouraged expanded petroleum production from the huge Canadian tar sands that geologists had known about throughout the twentieth century.

A cycle of booms and busts had then occurred. Variable production from traditional wells had affected worldwide prices in a way that alternately encouraged or discouraged extraction of petroleum from unconventional sources such as shale oil and tar sands. Very low prices in the mid-2010s had been counterbalanced by much higher prices in the early 2020s. These cycles had affected prices, but not ultimate availability. Some economists and geologists had then questioned whether Hubbert's methodology applied to modern conditions with new extractive technologies. Many political leaders had assumed that peak oil production would occur so many years in the future, if at all, that they need not prepare for that possibility.

However, in late 2029, it had become clear that world-wide demand for petroleum was getting to be greater than both conventional and unconventional sources could physically supply. Both economists and geologists had then reevaluated Hubbert's methodology. His methodology had not been wrong, but the data upon which it depended, which had been all that had been available at the beginning of the twenty-first century, had been too elusive for its predictions to be correct. Data on production capacities of conventional oil wells were suspect because OPEC countries had controlled their production for political, price, and other reasons since the early 1970s. Thus, annual production data had not adequately reflected physical production capacity. In addition, estimates of conventional oil reserves in some petroleum-rich countries had been based as much on political decisions as geological information. Estimates of available petroleum resources also had to be expanded to include petroleum production capabilities from shale oil and Canadian tar sands as they became economically viable. These flawed or unavailable data had given incorrect predictions on when peak oil production would occur.

Whatever the reason for prediction failures, there had been no doubt by 2030 that a production peak had occurred the previous year. Nevertheless, in part because few had been prepared to deal with the consequences of a real peak, petroleum prices in 2030 had risen little beyond the highest prices experienced in the previous two decades. Optimism had remained that new discoveries and even better extraction methods would allow production to increase enough to satisfy new demands for many years. After all, the doubling of prices that had occurred in the early part of the twenty-first century had spurred those kinds of developments.

This optimism had been crushed by the end of 2031.

By then, everyone had recognized that the gap between petroleum demand and physical production capacity from both conventional and unconventional sources was so great that no reasonable estimate of new discoveries or new technologies could fill the gap in a short enough time period to prevent shortages. This recognition had jarred international markets. Nations rich with reserves and companies operating successful extraction facilities had reevaluated how they managed their resources. Both shortages and dwindling reserves had created a powerful seller's market. Beginning with sharp rises in January, petroleum prices had quadrupled during 2031.

At least in the United States, only increased prices, and not serious shortages, had occurred. Other parts of the world had been less fortunate.

Most people in developing nations simply could not afford petroleum or petroleum products at the new prices, so they faced serious shortages.

President Clark had been struggling with the consequences of these new prices since their inception. Now called "the new petroleum reality," these prices had directly and indirectly caused all sorts of economic problems for Americans and other citizens of the world. And they had influenced the president's thinking on many other subjects as well.

President Clark quickly assumed that the new petroleum reality must be causing the declines in US crop yields in 2032 that Rand was talking about. He bluntly asked Rand what he had done to investigate the effect of the new petroleum reality on American agricultural production.

"We have been looking at this impact since the middle of 2031," said Rand. "Our biggest concern has been fertilizer. Most of the fertilizer our farmers use is made from petroleum. Fertilizer prices did not rise sharply until after our farmers had already bought their supplies for the 2031 growing season. Se we think that the price increases in 2031 had no effect on the amount of fertilizer our farmers used that year."

"What about this year?" interjected President Clark, getting impatient. He wanted Rand to confirm his assumption that high petroleum prices were causing whatever decreased crop production might occur in 2032.

He was already thinking about how this would play out. American farmers must have used less fertilizer in the current year because prices were too high. That would surely decrease crop yields. Yet decreased crop yields in one year would not necessarily prevent American farmers from supplying the needs of American consumers. If crop production did decline this year, demand would push grain and other crop prices higher. Normal market forces of supply and demand would then encourage American farmers to increase their yields by using more fertilizer, despite much higher prices. They would also devote more land to farming. So there would not be any shortage of corn, or wheat, or whatever in following years. In short, any decrease in crop production would just be temporary, despite Rand's warning about 2033 and 2034.

"We can't say one way or the other," replied Rand.

"Why not?" asked the president sharply.

"Data on fertilizer usage are not available yet," Rand answered.

This was not the response President Clark was looking for. He was running for reelection this year. If American crop production became an issue in the campaign, he had to have a way to show that high petroleum prices were causing any declines. Then he could assert that free market forces would correct this temporary decline. Or he could propose economic incentives to farmers to achieve the same result. Free market forces and incentives would also assure adequate crops for the US biofuels industry, now burgeoning as a response to the new petroleum reality.

President Clark decided to get the information he wanted by delegation. He directed Rand to figure out some way to show the relationship between high petroleum prices and reduced US crop production. He said that he wanted this information by mid-September.

Rand nodded agreement. What else could he do? His intuition, and pointed questions to farmers, told him a different story. The probable decline in American crop production in 2032 was more complicated, and a lot more serious, than a temporary response to high fertilizer prices. But he was not yet ready to challenge the president's assumption. He left the president and returned immediately to his office at USDA headquarters. He had to place in action the president's demand. He could trust only one person with this sensitive assignment. He called her immediately.

Karen Lewis could tell from Rand's tone of voice that he was troubled. He asked her to come to his office right away to get a new project assigned by the president.

The president? thought Karen as she got up, left her office, and walked quickly down a corridor to Rand's office. Why would she be in line for a project from the president?

Karen had worked as a research biologist for sixteen years at Colorado State University when her daughter's graduation from high school prompted her to make a career move to the USDA. With her long and unique history at CSU, her colleagues had been surprised at this move, but nevertheless supported it.

Karen had come to CSU as a freshman from a Chicago suburb. Sporting a fine academic record, Karen had chosen CSU for an unlikely reason—to be with her boyfriend, now husband, at the college of his choice. Having no pre-conceived major, she had boldly tried a variety of courses to see what might intrigue her. One of those had been a course about issues in agriculture. Much to her surprise, she had found that she had a natural aptitude for understanding biological concepts, especially as they related to food crops. This natural aptitude had awakened both curiosity about and a strong interest in the agricultural discipline. As she had pursued a major in CSU's College of Agricultural Sciences, this short, thin African-American had stood out among her mostly male classmates both physically and academically. She had remained at CSU for graduate studies and then to work in research after receiving her PhD.

Sensing an opportunity with Karen's changed home life, her many professional friends in the USDA had encouraged her to join them. With the full support of her husband, five years ago she had joined the research section of the USDA in Washington, D.C. There, she had quickly found a niche in analyzing data on crop production. Her extensive knowledge about how plants grow and what affects that growth, especially grain crops such as corn and wheat, had allowed her to see relationships among data that other people could not discern. She had achieved assistant secretary status two years ago as the head of a newly formed analysis group. In this capacity she and her staff had compiled the troublesome preliminary data on US crop production in 2032 that had prompted Rand to take his recent tour.

Rand's office door was open. Karen walked in without hesitation. He motioned for her to close the door behind her and to sit in one of the two wooden chairs in front of his desk. He sat down in the other chair.

"The president is upset about my warning from your projections," he said, looking squarely at Karen.

"We expected that," she replied. "It's certainly not good news. What did he say?"

Rand then described in detail his meeting with President Clark. He ended by telling her that the president thought that any declines in US crop yields came from high fertilizer prices caused by the new petroleum reality. The president wanted Rand to figure out how to prove that this was so.

Hearing this, Karen was miffed. *Even if he is the president,* she thought, *how could he just order someone to concoct information that would support his assumption? Why didn't he order an investigation of all the facts?* After all, she knew that Rand did not agree with the president's assumption. Rand had already told her that during his recent trip he had found no farmers who had changed their fertilizer usage this year. Whatever limited data she had seen on fertilizer sales showed no changes either. Why didn't Rand tell the president what he really thought was going on?

Rand knew Karen well enough to anticipate and prepare for her reaction. He explained that the president was so wrapped up in the new petroleum reality that just about every negative occurrence in the American economy was to him related to escalating petroleum prices. The president knew that that the normal 2032 crop data would be compiled and made public just a month before election day. If the data revealed significant production declines, he wanted to be ready to counter any opponent's criticism of his administration for this result by blaming uncontrollable petroleum price increases.

Karen slowly relented as Rand recited his justifications for President Clark's demand. His mini-diplomacy paid off. Karen's thoughts began to focus on how best to get useful information now. When Rand finished his pitch, he waited hopefully for Karen's response.

Karen remained rigid in her chair, now staring intently at the USDA seal behind Rand as she probed for a solution. She remained quiet for an uncomfortable amount of time. At last, she spoke.

"A questionnaire," she said succinctly.

"A questionnaire?"

"That's right," said Karen slowly. "Let's take advantage of our extension offices. They are scattered all around the country. Our people in those offices know what is going on in their districts. Let's find out from them."

Of course, thought Rand. Karen had come up with a direct solution, one that could be placed in motion right away.

"The president wants his information by mid-September," said Rand.

"I think we can have a questionnaire ready by mid-August. I assume that you want this probe to be quiet with no publicity."

"Outright secrecy would be even better if you can do it."

"We'll figure out a way," said Karen confidently, as she began to think about who could best draft a useful questionnaire. It would have to be detailed, but not burdensome. Otherwise, she would not receive responses in time to reach conclusions by the mid-September deadline set by the president.

Karen began to smile inwardly as she thought more about the questionnaire. Neither President Clark nor Secretary Rand could have anticipated what she was now preparing to do with something so innocuous as a questionnaire to USDA extension offices.

CHAPTER 3

FIELDS

Walter Wyzanski parked his car in front of the USDA extension office building located in the outskirts of Lincoln, Nebraska. The sun was just beginning to peek over the eastern horizon behind him, its image reflected in the extensive front glass windows of the one-story building.

Shielding his eyes, Walter looked quickly at his printed itinerary for the day. A full schedule, he thought, as he collected his electronic tablet, an old-school clipboard with forms, a pen, and his lunch. He got out of his car, locked it, and walked to the south side lot where the USDA vehicles were parked. There was no need to go inside the office.

Walter chose the same light green pickup that he had used for the last seven years when on official USDA business. Although the chipped USDA logos on both doors revealed its age, this sturdy truck was always reliable and comfortable to drive. He unlocked the door and got into the pickup. In the sunny warmth of what would soon be a hot summer day, he lowered both side windows as he backed up slowly from the pickup's designated space.

In just a few minutes, he was speeding along a country road where the unmistakable, but faint, aroma of freshly cut hay wafted into his cab. The hay that had been growing along the side of the road was now bound up in bales that looked like giant pieces of Tootsie Roll scattered here and there along the length of the road. Very few bales for mid-August, he observed, as he approached the first farm on his itinerary.

For the last eighteen years while he had been the director of the West Lincoln USDA extension office, Walter had taken several days in the middle of every month during the summer growing season to visit a group of farmers that he had selected at the beginning of the season. This year, he had chosen twenty-four farmers. Their farms were scattered across his district. All of the six farmers on today's long itinerary had planted corn. Walter had called these farmers last week to remind them that he would be coming. They already knew what to expect. Despite his affable nature and longstanding friendship with most of these farmers, Walter was all business on these visits. He could not afford to get very far off schedule or he would run out of daylight with the last farmers on his list.

Dan Lundquist was at his barn when he spotted Walter turning onto the gravel road that stretched a quarter mile northward to his farmyard. He strode quickly back to his farmhouse nearby his barn, poured two mugs of very strong coffee, and was back outside by the time Walter parked the pickup. Within moments, the two old friends had exchanged greetings and a firm handshake. They quickly consumed Dan's coffee and proceeded to the purpose for Walter's visit.

As soon as Walter asked his first question about Dan's corn crop, Dan's frown revealed real worry. Precise measurements were not needed for Walter to see than Dan's corn was shorter and less full than in previous years. Obviously, this year's yield would be much less than in those years. Still, precise measurements are what Walter came for, so they next walked into the middle of the quarter section stand of corn north of Dan's barn.

During Walter's visit in July, he had picked out ten plants within a diameter of about fifty yards, marking each plant with a numbered bright pink plastic ribbon. He and Dan found each plant again to record the same set of information for each plant. First, Walter measured its height, excluding the tassels. Next, he counted the number of ears of corn and measured their length. Finally, he examined each plant for mold and insect infestation. After recording data from the last plant, Walter made a quick mental note of his findings. The median height was just under five feet, at least a foot shorter than normal for this time of year. The ears also were smaller and fewer per plant than even last year's mediocre crop. The only positive datum was the absence of mold or insect infestation.

Dan confirmed what Walter had learned in July about Dan's planting and care of his crops. Dan had used typical amounts of fertilizer after the corn kernels were planted. He also had used minimal insecticides because they were not necessary with this particular genetically-engineered hybrid. Dan's fields were not irrigated, so he depended entirely upon natural rainfall. Dan said that he thought that the summertime rain at his farm was definitely below normal. He was sure that this had prevented the growth he needed in July and August to get the bushels per acre yield he wanted.

Walter made quick notes before he and Dan started back out of the cornfield. Loudly rustling corn stalks made conversation impossible, but they could not impede Walter's thoughts about what he had seen. If Dan's farm was typical of other farms, clearly corn yields in his district would be less than in 2031. Maybe that would not be so bad if nationwide production also was down. A relative shortage would cause higher corn prices and maybe give normal profits to his beleaguered farmers based on the corn that they did have. The possibility of a severe national shortage did not occur to him.

Within a few minutes after leaving Dan's cornfield, Walter and Dan were standing next to the USDA pickup. Walter reminded Dan that he would come again in late September after the harvest. Then Dan would know exactly what his yields had been. Walter would then also examine selected remaining corn stalks to learn whether some now-hidden disease or insects had been involved in what surely would be disappointing yields.

Walter and Dan exchanged succinct farewells, concluded with another firm handshake. Walter waved from the pickup as he started down Dan's gravel entrance road.

The second farm Walter visited, and the third, and indeed all of the farms where corn was grown, had plants that were similar to Dan's. Walter's measurements yesterday in the two soybean fields and one sunflower field that he had visited also confirmed mediocre or low yields for the year. Walter had seen these patterns developing during his July visits. He was well aware that precipitation records at most of the weather stations in his region showed less rain than normal in July and August. Still, he had hoped that those measurements were not an accurate reflection of the conditions on all of the farms. Typically, strong downpours were scattered across the countryside in early August, so several or even most of the farms in his sampling could have had their benefits. He saw on his visits on this day that this had not occurred for any of these farms.

Walter returned to his USDA extension office just before dark. By now, everyone had gone home. Rather than going directly to his car, he entered the building to leave his notes and a few ears of corn that he had collected during the day for further examination. Once in his private office, he placed his notes in a bookcase next to his desk and the labeled ears of corn in one of several baskets on the top of the bookcase. He then looked quickly at his mail, which the office's secretary had piled neatly in the middle of his desk. On the top was a brown envelope from the Secretary of the Department of Agriculture. With his fatigue from a long day, Walter did not notice that it had come by expedited mail directly from the secretary's office.

Nothing special here, he thought, as he pondered whether to check his e-mail. Enough is enough, he concluded, glancing at his dark computer screen. He turned around, walked to the door, and left the building to go home.

The next morning, Walter arrived at his office an hour late after a badly needed night's sleep. Now refreshed, he first opened his e-mails to attend to any problems that might have been reported. None appearing, he turned to the pile of mail on his desk. He noticed for the first time that the brown envelope had been mailed just two days ago and had come directly from the secretary of agriculture. This was doubly puzzling. For a long time, nearly all communications from higher up came electronically. The few paper documents that still were sent came from the general mailing office of the USDA. Why was there a paper document, and why was it sent directly from the secretary's office by expedited delivery?

Walter opened the envelope apprehensively, wondering if somehow he had been singled out for rebuke. He was well known for his independence and unique way of conducting the USDA's affairs in his district. What he found instead was a cordial cover letter with an original signature of Secretary Rand, followed by a three page questionnaire, one page of instructions, and an envelope addressed to the secretary himself.

The cover letter was succinct. It said that the secretary was trying to find out from all extension offices whether the recent fertilizer price increases had changed the way farmers in each district had used fertilizer this year. If so, had those changes made any difference in apparent crop yields? The letter specified that the questionnaire be completed by the addressee and no one else. The letter ended by asking that the completed questionnaire be kept confidential and be physically mailed to Secretary Rand, not faxed or scanned via e-mail, by August 24th.

Simple enough, thought Walter. He turned to the questionnaire to asses how much work it would be to complete. He hoped that it would be easy, as he had plenty of other work to accomplish this week.

The first page set the pattern for all questions by categorizing the answer space according to each type of crop. The crops listed were corn, soybeans, sunflowers, wheat, and "other." Based on a small identifier at the bottom of the page, Walter concluded correctly that different crops were listed for different agricultural regions.

As he read over the questionnaire, he noted that the questions on the first page were largely background questions and neutral, but that the questions on the second page seemed to start from an assumption that high fertilizer prices had negatively affected fertilizer usage and thus crop yields. Theoretically, that assumption could be correct, he thought. But the bureaucrats in Washington did not seem to understand that farmers had major investments in equipment to support particular ways of planting and nurturing their crops. Few could quickly make major shifts in methods, even greatly reducing the use of fertilizers, without jeopardizing their yields.

The third page seemed out of place. Its questions were much broader. Some questions asked about crop yields in the district, actual for 2031 and projected for 2032. Others asked about reasons for any changes in crop yields, especially any declines. The instructions suggested numerous possible causes for changing yields. Weather conditions were listed first, including rainfall, relative temperatures, and destructive events such as hail, floods, and winds. After weather, suggestions included blight, molds, and insect infestations. These were all just possibilities, as all questions were open-ended so that any answer could be written in.

Walter thought this third page was the best. Someone, he thought, was trying to find out what really affected the farmers in his district.

Walter now knew that the secretary's questionnaire would be a challenge to answer. He set aside all day on Friday to do so. In the meantime, he wanted to complete his scheduled visits to farmers. He was not only committed to those visits, but they would also permit him to gather more information pertinent to the questionnaire.

Walter's careful measurements of crops and discussions with these additional farmers confirmed what he had seen during all of his visits to farmers that month. Corn, soybean, sunflower, and wheat yields would all be much less than normal this year. Everyone agreed on the cause. July and August had been drier than normal, although not so dramatically dry as to be considered a severe drought.

On Friday morning, Walter sat down at his desk to deal with the secretary's questionnaire. He was not accustomed to answering questionnaires, certainly none from the secretary of agriculture. He proceeded cautiously. He carefully considered each question and wrote short responses on the first two pages. He now believed that the second page was an attempt to tie any crop yield problems to the new petroleum reality that Washington and the media had been talking about. That attempt would be unsuccessful for his district. His farmers had not changed their use of fertilizer this year despite escalating prices. Although a few farmers were beginning to rethink how they could achieve profitable yields with much less fertilizer, none had yet adopted any new method.

The third page was more challenging.

To answer the question about comparative crop yields, Walter had to extract information from his records for last year. Then he did a rough calculation of projected yields for this year based on data he had collected during his recent visits to farmers. He also compared those figures against a ten-year running average that he, and all districts, had available from Washington for his district. He saw that yields in 2031 had been lower than average and that his projected yields for 2032 would be lower still. Neither year's yields were in the extremely low range typical of a severe drought.

The question about causes of changing crop yields was simpler. Walter at first wrote simply "reduced rains in July and August." As he was writing this answer, he realized that there was something odd about this fact. He remembered that the spring seemed abnormally wet. Rarely did dry summers follow a wet spring. He then checked precipitation records for Lincoln and two towns in his district. Despite the dry months of July and August, annual precipitation up to now was above normal. March and April rains had made the difference. "March rains?" he asked himself. He reflected that March is a snow month, not a rain month. Walter decided to add two sentences to his answer. They said simply:

"Precipitation records for this district will be misleading. March and April rains added to the annual total but were not repeated when needed in July and August."

The remaining questions on the third page of the questionnaire forced Walter to think beyond the obvious. One question asked whether newly genetically engineered seeds had performed differently than other seeds traditionally used in his district. Another asked about the use and effectiveness of insecticides. Walter answered these questions as best he could without any real data to rely upon.

Walter completed the secretary's questionnaire shortly after noon, earlier than he had thought he would. He made a copy for himself and sealed the original in the envelope addressed to Secretary Rand. He mailed it that afternoon.

Walter Wyzanski was not alone in this endeavor. Around the country, other extension office directors also were answering their USDA questionnaires and mailing them to Secretary Rand.

Unknown to any of these extension office directors, Bill Rand, or Karen Lewis, events were occurring thousands of miles away that would have a profound impact on understanding the changes in US crop yields that these questionnaires would reveal.

CHAPTER 4

SMER

On the same day that Walter Wyzanski was measuring corn plants at Dan Lundquist's farm in Nebraska, Nicolette Marceau took measurements of a different sort in the cold reaches of the northern North Atlantic Ocean. She looked at the readout from the electronic salinity detector in the ship's instrument room. She looked again, squinting to be sure that she had read it correctly the first time. After more than two months' experience taking sea water samples, she knew what to expect. That was definitely not what she saw.

Nicolette decided to take another reading of her sample. No change. She recounted in her mind exactly how she had collected this sample just one hour earlier. Nothing seemed amiss. What else could have affected her sample? Should she take a new sample?

A heavy rainstorm had drenched their ship last night. Water still sloshed around the deck on this cool, gray morning. Could she somehow have had rainwater in her sampling canister before she lowered it into the sea? Not likely. Even if rainwater had been present, the two-foot long canister opens at both ends to collect a sample, so the rainwater would have been flushed out long before the canister collected the sample. But then she thought that maybe the canister had not opened correctly. If so, some rainwater could have remained in the canister.

As she was trying to figure out what could have happened, Marie Leclerc, her project leader, came up behind her.

"Nicolette, you look puzzled," said Marie with her distinct Parisian accent.

"Dr. Leclerc, this sample this morning, it's, it's …" Nicolette could not even say what she had found.

"It's what?" asked Marie gently, coaxing Nicolette to finish her thought.

"It's almost fresh water!" stammered Nicolette.

"Fresh water?" exclaimed Marie. "Impossible. There must be a mistake."

"That's what I thought, too, but I checked everything over again," said Nicolette.

"Maybe your canister had some rainwater in it from last night," said Marie.

"It didn't," said Nicolette, now defensively.

Marie did not feed Nicolette's anxiety by raising her voice or challenging Nicolette's response. She instead suggested another cause for the reading.

"Maybe our salinity detector has finally cratered," said Marie. "It's pretty old by now."

"I was just going to test it with a sample I have left from yesterday," said Nicolette.

"Good idea, do that first," said Marie. "If the detector is okay, let's take another sample together. By the way, what was your sample depth?"

Five meters," said Nicolette.

Five meters thought Marie silently as she left Nicolette to go see the ship's captain. She wished that Nicolette had said something more like two hundred meters. Then a sampling or detector error would certainly be the cause of Nicolette's fresh water reading. But fresh water at just five meters depth could mean …

Marie stopped herself. No need to get carried away with possibilities. This was now her fourteenth summertime research voyage in the North Atlantic waters south of Greenland. The research pattern had remained the same for all of those years. Her team had begun each season by taking water samples near Iceland in early June, then had worked westward to the Newfoundland coast, then had sailed back and forth, completing their last samples in early September. During those previous voyages, Marie had seen anomalous readings before, although nothing as dramatic as Nicolette's. In each case, some equipment or sampling error had caused the reading. Her feared conclusion would not be proper, at least not yet. She would await Nicolette's test of the salinity detector and then resampling if the detector was functioning properly.

Marie Leclerc was a scientist employed by La Société de la Mer, known to all members simply as SMER. Based in Nantes, France, SMER had been formed in 1999 by several marine biologists who had worked for the better-known Cousteau Society. They had left the Cousteau Society because they had wanted to focus their research on the northern part of the North Atlantic Ocean, by far the most important body of water to France and most of northwestern Europe.

Their interest had been prompted by fishery collapses in the North Atlantic in the early 1990s. Their first research projects had been directed to understanding the population dynamics of each major fishery. From this research, they had hoped to be able to recommend changes that would allow the fisheries to recover and then be fished sustainably. Because of these goals, they had been able to get early funding from several fishing groups and the Canadian and French governments. Over time, many individuals had supported their work as well.

Marie Leclerc had joined SMER in 2017, just after earning her doctorate in chemistry from the Sorbonne in Paris. Although she had grown up in Paris and had lived there with her husband while pursuing her doctorate, Marie had long wanted to live by an ocean and to study ocean dynamics and marine life. SMER had been a great opportunity to realize her dream.

When Marie had come to SMER, SMER still had done research only on North Atlantic fish life cycles, food supplies, and harvesting pressures. The executive director had hired Marie because they had wanted to begin studying ocean current variations as another potential force affecting fish populations. Marie's recent doctorate had made her well suited to this task.

Just one year after Marie had come to SMER, Georges Gagnon, SMER's executive director, had received a surprise telephone call from François Duval, France's minister of agriculture. Minister Duval had wanted a secret meeting with Gagnon to discuss a possible project for SMER. Gagnon had been perplexed why the minister of agriculture, of all people, would want to talk to him. Duval's request for secrecy had added to the mystery. This secret meeting had eventually occurred at a small restaurant in a suburb of Paris. It had determined Marie's professional life at SMER since then.

As told to Marie by Gagnon, his meeting with Duval had begun innocuously. Duval had first pontificated about the greatness of

France's agricultural sector. He had said that France was not only the best producer in all of Europe, but also that much of Western Europe relied upon French agricultural products. He had even expounded with examples. Gagnon had listened politely, wondering how any of this could relate to SMER.

According to Gagnon, Duval's demeanor had then changed suddenly. He had begun speaking in a hushed tone.

Duval had said that France's agriculture depended upon relatively predictable weather over time to produce its abundance of goods. That weather, in turn, depended greatly upon the North Atlantic Drift. This warm current, which flowed northeast between Great Britain and Iceland, helped to keep Western Europe much warmer than its latitude would suggest. If the North Atlantic Drift were disrupted, much colder and unsettled growing conditions could occur in France, even in all of Western Europe. Crop failures could follow unless the changes could be foreseen early enough for farmers to make crop adjustments, assuming that good crop adjustments were even possible.

To drive home his point, Duval had described the eruption of the volcano Tambora in 1815 as a grim reminder. Even though Tambora was in Indonesia, its eruption had forced huge amounts of particles into the high atmosphere that had spread throughout the world. In turn, those particles had blocked so much sunlight from hitting the earth's surface that much colder temperatures had occurred in Europe for several years until the particles gradually fell to the ground. French crops had failed in 1816. Many French citizens had experienced civil anarchy and even famine as food supplies had become scarce.

Duval had then paused and leaned over toward Gagnon. He had begun speaking in a barely audible whisper. He had said that people in the highest levels of the French government had grave concern about the North Atlantic Drift. They had recently been told that this current could be disrupted in just a short time if atmospheric warming caused the Greenland Ice Sheet to melt quickly. Duval had added that no official believed that this disruption would cause famine or even food hardships. After all, 2018 was very different than 1816. Everyone was confident that modern international grain markets would make up for France's crop losses. Still, major losses would have severe economic consequences to France and even Western Europe.

Duval had then sat back, looking at Gagnon to assess his reaction. Normally unflappable, Gagnon had been stunned. He had needed time to regain his composure. He had then asked Duval who Duval had meant by "highest levels" of the French government and how those officials had come to this "grave concern" on a subject that normally was only in the bailiwick of scientists.

Duval had been candid. He had said that the "highest levels" included President Jacques Pointeau himself. As for how President Pointeau came to his grave concern, the story was more complex.

Duval had said that an unnamed science advisor to President Pointeau had come across a study by some American scientists first published back in the year 2000. This article had described aerial measurements of the thickness of the Greenland Ice Sheet. The Americans had flown special aircraft over the ice sheet in the 1990s, measuring ice elevations along numerous paths. When measurements taken five years apart had been compared, these scientists had discovered unexpected changes in the ice sheet. While some areas had thickened slightly, several areas at the southern edges of the ice sheet had thinned as much as ten meters. Other scientists had later calculated the amount of water lost or gained by the ice sheet in those five years. Losses had far exceeded gains.

With the thinning being the most important, the scientists had tried to figure out how this could have occurred. They had suggested that surface melt water could have penetrated to the glacial base, allowing the ice to creep downhill more quickly than normal. This process could then have accelerated ice removal, whether by calving or by melting. These ideas had only been suggestions. No one knew for sure at that time why such a large net loss of water had occurred.

Duval had also said that President Pointeau's science advisor had done some more research to see if the Americans' discoveries had just been aberrations. He had learned that later measurements using several different techniques had shown that the Greenland Ice Sheet had not only continued to thin, but that it had done so at faster rates than measured in the 1990s. Later studies on the history of the Greenland Ice Sheet had also shown that rapid reductions in the amount of its ice were possible over just a few decades.

The science advisor had mused about what would happen if the Greenland Ice Sheet were to melt much faster than the Americans and later studies had measured. Rapid melting would pour a lot of fresh water into the northern North Atlantic Ocean. The advisor had contacted an expert on ocean currents at the Université de Poitiers to learn whether this would matter. That is when he found out that a large amount of fresh water pouring into that part of the ocean could greatly reduce the North Atlantic Drift. And that event could cool France's climate, not just a little, but a lot.

According to Duval, the science advisor somehow had gotten President Pointeau's immediate attention. In a private meeting, the science advisor had told President Pointeau that France must create some kind of early detection program. Surprisingly, President Pointeau had agreed, but also had decided that the program must be secret. He had been concerned that panic, or at least confusion, could occur if the general public learned about any projected disruptions in France's climate before a plan of action could be prepared.

At first, President Pointeau had wanted to make this detection program a military project as part of national security operations. But he had recognized that this approach inevitably would involve French naval vessels spending many months just patrolling back and forth south of Greenland. People who saw those patrols would raise questions and suspicions about what France was doing. Instead, President Pointeau had decided to conduct this program through a ministry and using private contractors. When he had revealed his ideas to his cabinet of ministers, they had thought that this approach also made good sense, especially those who questioned the whole premise that a risk existed. A program run through a ministry would also be much less expensive than one run by the military. Furthermore, it would not divert military personnel from their primary task to protect France from threats by foreign enemies.

President Pointeau had decided to assign his detection program to the Ministry of Agriculture. He had explained his choice in logical terms to the French Parliament in a closed session. He had said that if the program uncovered a condition that would cause changes in the North Atlantic Drift, the Ministry of Agriculture would be the most important ministry in figuring out how to deal with those changes, so it should be the most involved in the program at the outset.

In truth, President Pointeau had chosen the Ministry of Agriculture for a different reason. Minister Duval had long been Pointeau's personal friend. Pointeau had known that Duval was the grandson of a well-known activist in the French Resistance during World War II. From his grandfather's many stories, Duval had become savvy about different ways that secret operations could be hidden by subterfuge. President Pointeau had trusted Duval to devise a way to kept France's detection program truly secret.

After reciting this history, Minister Duval had then told Gagnon why he had chosen SMER for its role. He had said that the most important part of France's new detection program would be to take measurements of conditions in the northern North Atlantic Ocean. This was so because important changes in ocean water salinity or temperatures would be expected to precede any measurable changes in the North Atlantic Drift. By having SMER take these measurements, their true purpose could be masked. They would be seen simply as one logical part of SMER's other activities in the North Atlantic Ocean. Only a few SMER personnel would have to know how to interpret the data, and fewer still would have to know the project's connection with the French government.

Duval also had told Gagnon that he knew that secret governmental designation would raise questions and maybe even hostility within SMER. He had then described his simple scheme to achieve secrecy without arousing suspicions among SMER's staff. Instead of giving the program official national secret status, he had simply asked Gagnon to treat the research results as proprietary to the French government. Some level of secrecy would then make sense within SMER because the French government would be paying for the work to be done.

Gagnon had told Marie that he had not committed SMER at that meeting with Duval. Secrecy meant that the research results could not be published. Scientists working in the program would have to accept this significant limitation, which would impede development of professional reputations. Maybe no one at SMER would be willing to work under this limitation.

Gagnon had asked Marie to direct this detection program for SMER, even though she was young and had only been with SMER for one year.

When Gagnon had asked her to take on this role, Marie at first had said no. Marie's daughter Annette had just celebrated her tenth birthday. Marie had known that SMER's new program would require her to spend her summers on a research vessel in the North Atlantic Ocean. She had not wanted to spend those months away from Annette.

But Gagnon had offered Marie an equivalent amount of time away from SMER during Annette's school year. With that extra time, Marie could be as involved as she wanted to be in Annette's school activities. This offer, the support of her husband Claude, and the challenge of learning more about North Atlantic sea dynamics and their effects on Western Europe, had then convinced Marie to take on this challenge.

At first Marie had thought that regular tracking of the North Atlantic Drift would be enough to provide the early detection that the French government wanted. Physical phenomena associated with warm ocean currents had made this possible with modern technologies. Major currents such as the North Atlantic Drift formed a bulge of warm water wherever they meandered. Precise satellite measuring devices could identify their locations by measuring the height of the ocean at numerous places. Infrared sensors also could identify differences in heat emissions from one part of the ocean to another. When mapped, these differences could show the locations of especially warm currents near the surface.

As useful as these methods were, Marie had recognized that they shared a critical flaw. They could only identify what currents such as the North Atlantic Drift had already done. They could not identify forces that would cause these currents to change in the near future. Yet knowledge of these future changes was the information most needed. Only advance knowledge of future changes would give French farmers time to try to adjust their crops to new conditions.

The one force that everyone had agreed could disrupt the North Atlantic Drift was increased annual influxes of fresh water from the Greenland Ice Sheet into the North Atlantic Ocean. The only way to identify this force was to measure ocean salinity south of Greenland. And salinity could only be measured by sampling sea water.

Marie had single-handedly created the water sampling plan that had begun in 2019. Her team was still using the same basic plan now in 2032.

SMER, or more correctly, the French government, had first bought a new two hundred foot long all-weather ship to be dedicated to this project. Eleven crew members, with eight scientists, had set out from Nantes at the beginning of the sampling season each year. The team had collected water samples from ten different depths, at least twice daily, using simple canisters and long steel cables. Samples had been taken at the same locations each year, or at least as close to the same locations as geosynchronous satellites and weather would allow. All samples had been analyzed on board and then returned to the sea.

Sampling had become routine over the years. SMER had discovered that ocean water salinity south of Greenland had varied somewhat from year to year. SMER also had discovered a general, but slight, decrease in the average salinity of sea water south of Greenland over its fourteen years of observations. The only large variations in salinity that SMER had observed had all been proven to be incorrect readings caused by faulty equipment or sampling.

Surely, Nicolette's finding that morning must also have been incorrect. Or at least that is what Marie hoped.

After speaking with the ship's captain, Marie returned to the ship's deck and stood silently looking northward toward Greenland.

Sensing that Nicolette was approaching her, Marie turned around. Nicolette was just a few feet away. She did not have to speak. Nicolette's somber face told Marie that she had bad news. SMER's salinity detector had worked fine on the sea water sample left over from yesterday.

Marie had already asked the ship's captain to return to the location where Nicolette had taken her sample now two hours ago. They would soon again be at that location.

Upon arriving there, Nicolette took a new sea water sample under the watchful eye of Marie. She first chose a different canister than the one she had used earlier. She checked to be sure that it was empty and tested its end doors to be sure that they opened and closed properly. Then she lowered the canister into the sea using the normal steel cable. In just five minutes, she had a new sample from five meters beneath the surface. She unfastened the canister, held it tightly, and walked quickly with Marie to the instrument room. Nicolette dipped the salinity detector's test tube into the canister to obtain fifty milliliters of water. She placed the test tube in the detector. Within moments, the detector's computer screen and printout gave its analysis. The results were the same as the reading from this morning's sample. The top five meters of water at this location was nearly fresh water.

Marie had already mentally prepared herself for this possibility. A fresh water incursion at this location, just seventeen kilometers offshore from Greenland, could be nothing more than a local occurrence. They had seen an abnormal number of icebergs on their approach to this location. Maybe the fresh water came from a localized ice collapse at the Greenland Ice Sheet. That could have sent many chunks of ice or even a torrent of water into the sea that had not had time to disperse.

There was only one way to know for sure. Marie devised a new sampling plan to try to determine the boundaries of this fresh water incursion. She decided not to report its discovery to SMER's headquarters until they had better knowledge of those boundaries.

Marie's plan called for samples to be taken in an expanding circle from the location where Nicolette's fresh water had been found. The regular locations that fell within this expanding circle would be included in the plan. At each location, samples would be taken at the normal range of depths, not just five meters. Everyone would work long hours to enable twice the normal number of locations to be sampled daily.

The next two weeks revealed a troubling story.

Icebergs abounded. Every sample taken south or east of Greenland revealed much fresher water than they had ever measured before Nicolette's discovery. Not until the end of these two weeks did they begin to reach the southern and eastern edges of the fresh water influx. They had no doubt what was happening. In the summer of 2032, the Greenland Ice Sheet was discharging ice and water into the North Atlantic at an unprecedented rate.

Marie made a rough calculation of the amount of fresh water they had found. It was enormous. The total was far greater than the annual fresh water discharges of any European river, and even greater than all European rivers combined. She knew of only one comparable influx of fresh water into any ocean. The Amazon River in Brazil annually discharged so much water during its flood season that the sea was fresh water up to one hundred miles out from its mouth. Marie did not know how much water the Amazon River discharged daily, nor did she yet know how much water was coming daily from Greenland, so she could not directly compare the two. But just thinking about them as comparable magnified the importance of their discovery. The time had come to report their discovery to SMER's headquarters.

CHAPTER 5

SECRECY

Late in the afternoon of August 31, Marie radioed SMER's director, Richard Pelletier, to tell him what they had found. Pelletier understood immediately its significance. He granted Marie's request to continue taking more samples. SMER's ship would remain at sea an extra week, but no more. They both knew that an extra week at the end of the ship's voyage would bring provisions close to the margin of safety designed to protect everyone on board in case bad weather impeded the ship's return to Nantes.

While Marie and her crew returned to their tasks, Pelletier devised a plan for what to do with the information that Marie had given him.

Richard Pelletier had replaced Georges Gagnon as SMER's director upon Gagnon's retirement in 2028. Gagnon had told Pelletier the history of Marie's detection program and had described his policies in dealing with each minister of agriculture during its existence. Continuing Gagnon's policy, Pelletier had already decided to deliver SMER's annual findings and data personally to the current minister of agriculture, Camille Morin, with whom he had developed good rapport.

Pelletier's plan was simple. He would first tell Minister Morin in person about Marie's findings as soon as possible. Then he would assign SMER staff to compile and make sense of Marie's data promptly upon her return to Nantes.

The next morning, Pelletier finally reached Morin after working through a phalanx of protective receptionists and administrative staff. Pelletier told her that he wanted to see her personally as soon as possible to reveal some "interesting information." Morin did not question

Pelletier's request. She knew that this information had to concern SMER's North Atlantic detection program. She invited Pelletier to come the very next day, even though her whole ministry was in mild chaos because everyone was now returning from their traditional August vacations.

After she spoke with Pelletier, Morin sat quietly in her office trying to recall exactly why something SMER had discovered would be important and urgent. She remembered that SMER's program was designed to detect changes, or more accurately, to predict upcoming changes, in the North Atlantic Drift that could adversely affect French agriculture. Morin already knew that French crop production in 2031 had been below normal. She also knew that current projections for crop production in 2032 showed further declines. Despite low production, the statistics were within the range of historic variations. If a serious problem existed in the North Atlantic, it had not yet impacted France.

What, then, could Pelletier be so anxious to tell her?

Despite annual meetings with Pelletier, it had been several years since Morin had read any part of the secret report about France's detection program conducted by SMER. She could not remember exactly how changes in the North Atlantic Drift could occur and how those changes would affect France. She decided that she needed to know how this worked before Pelletier arrived tomorrow. Otherwise, she would not be able to judge whether Pelletier's "interesting information" was important or not.

Morin got up from her chair behind her desk, walked to a tapestry hanging from ceiling to floor on the wall at the left side of her desk, and reached behind the tapestry. *Ah, there it is*, she thought. She pressed a secret button that activated an electric motor that swung the tapestry smoothly out from the wall, revealing the steel door of a safe. An old combination lock was in the middle of its door. The Ministry of Agriculture had very few top security documents, so no one had bothered to update this ancient safe. Morin twirled the dial three times to the correct numbers and opened the safe's door. The safe had three shelves. The secret report about SMER's project was on a shelf at eye level, its turquoise cover reflecting someone's clumsy attempt to connect it to the sea. She removed the report, closed the safe's door, replaced the tapestry, and returned to her desk, already beginning to glance through the report.

The table of contents alone began to remind Morin about the details of SMER's detection program. SMER's annual tasks were to take and assess salinity measurements in the northern North Atlantic Ocean near Greenland. *Not very exciting*, she mumbled to herself. *Why exactly was that so important?* Scanning the table of contents, she found the section she thought might answer this question.

Its lead sentence was terse:

"Large influxes of fresh water in the northern North Atlantic Ocean could disrupt the North Atlantic Drift."

The following text described how this could occur.

The North Atlantic Drift was a unique extension of the Gulf Stream. The Gulf Stream began in the ocean near southern Florida and extended northeast into the northern North Atlantic Ocean. It transported huge amounts of water, and more importantly, heat, eventually to Europe. A combination of forces formed and maintained the Gulf Stream, especially westerly winds and the Coriolis force caused by the earth's rotation.

The Gulf Stream split into two currents as it neared Europe. One current circulated south over the deep ocean back toward the tropics. The other current flowed northeast between Great Britain and Iceland. That current was the North Atlantic Drift. It occurred in part because waters south and east of Greenland regularly sank deep into the North Atlantic Ocean, leaving a water void that the North Atlantic Drift partly filled. This process also increased the amount of water flowing in the Gulf Stream itself, which increased the amount of heat it transported.

Fresh water influxes into the northern North Atlantic Ocean would not affect the forces that initially formed the Gulf Stream. They could, however, diminish the North Atlantic Drift in at least two different ways. One way could be by interacting directly with the Drift. The second way could be by diminishing the North Atlantic thermohaline circulation, the process that helped to sustain the Drift.

Morin thought that direct interaction with the North Atlantic Drift was easier to visualize than impacts on the thermohaline circulation.

The report said that several mechanisms for direct interaction were possible. They all revolved around a single idea—fresh water is less dense and therefore lighter than salty ocean water. Cold fresh water from melting ice in the Greenland Ice Sheet might float south over denser salty water to intersect the North Atlantic Drift. This cold fresh water could then mix with the Drift in new ways, cooling the current, changing its course, or stopping it altogether. All of these impacts would diminish the amount of heat being transferred to Europe by the current.

The report emphasized, however, that these mechanisms, although possible, were unlikely. They all depended upon an intact fresh water pool flowing south to meet up with the Drift. The fresh water pool simply had to travel too far. Most likely, it would be mixed in with salty sea water before it could reach the Drift.

This very mixing of fresh water with salty sea water, however, would lead to the second way that the North Atlantic Drift could be diminished.

In the cold Arctic winter, water in the Greenland and Norwegian seas south and east of Greenland became colder than other water in the northern North Atlantic Ocean. Because colder water is denser and therefore heavier than warmer water with the same salinity, this water sank deep into the ocean. There, this water gradually pushed bottom waters south along the ocean floor, well below all the warm surface water currents. This deep, slow current extended all the way to the southern end of the South Atlantic Ocean. This current then joined some deep ocean currents originating in the Weddell Sea at Antarctica. From there, the deep currents flowed into other oceans of the world. This whole network of deep currents was called the thermohaline circulation.

If large amounts of fresh water were discharged into the northern North Atlantic Ocean, its mixing with sea water could decrease the sea water's salinity. This decrease would make this sea water less dense, counteracting the effects of winter cooling that normally made this water denser. The net effect could be sea water that would not sink as much as previously, or maybe even not at all. Should this effect occur, the thermohaline circulation would diminish or even stop. With one driving force for the North Atlantic Drift being gone, the Drift would also diminish. A greatly weakened Gulf Stream would exist whose eastern path would be much different than the path that had existed throughout recorded history.

The report also said that if the North Atlantic thermohaline circulation ceased or decreased, the slow, but large, deep water southern current of the Atlantic Ocean would also cease or decrease. Even though North Atlantic water took hundreds of years to move through the North and South Atlantic Oceans and spread into the Pacific and Indian

Oceans, its ultimate heat exchanges influenced climates around the world. No one had any real idea what would happen in the other oceans if this deep current were to decrease significantly.

Morin stopped looking at the secret report for a minute to try to absorb what she had just read. She thought that the possibilities seemed logical, but she could not imagine either possibility actually occurring. After all, the earth's natural systems, including the Gulf Stream, North Atlantic Drift, and thermohaline circulation, were very powerful. They must have existed for millions of years. How could some fresh water from Greenland really change what had been around so long?

Morin looked back at the report's table of contents, looking for something that would confirm her doubt. She found nothing promising on the first page. As her eyes reached the middle of the second page, her hopes rose. She found a section titled "The Paleoclimatic Record." That sounded like a long time ago. This section surely would show how robust and long lasting these natural systems were.

She began reading this section, but soon realized that she had to readjust her thinking. The North Atlantic thermohaline circulation was powerful, all right, but also changeable. It had not flowed steadily for millions of years as she had thought. Ice core samples from Greenland, combined with other findings around the North Atlantic Ocean, revealed a different history. The North Atlantic thermohaline circulation had ceased, or at least greatly decreased, a number of times in just the last one hundred thousand years. When that had occurred, the climate of Europe had become much colder than the climate experienced during the rise of human civilizations in the last five thousand years.

Morin had read enough. She closed the secret report and returned it to the ministry's secret safe. She now viewed Pelletier's upcoming visit with some trepidation.

The next day, Pelletier took the early morning TGV train from Nantes to Paris. By 11:00 a.m. he was already in Morin's office.

"Welcome, Richard," greeted Morin in her usual friendly but formal style as she extended her hand to Pelletier.

"Thanks for seeing me so quickly," responded Pelletier as he extended his hand toward hers for a formal handshake.

Pleasantries were brief.

"So what 'interesting information' do you have for me?" asked Morin.

"Marie Leclerc's team discovered a major pool of fresh water in the ocean south of Greenland," answered Pelletier. "It undoubtedly came from Greenland. We think that it will flow southward. The North Atlantic Drift could be affected as early as November or December. If fresh water discharges from Greenland continue or even increase, significant cooling could occur in France next year. Impacts on rain and snow patterns are also possible and basically unknown."

Morin's study of the secret report yesterday now paid off. She quickly grasped Pelletier's explanation and the dangers evident to French agriculture. If the fresh water incursion reflected a new regime of melting at the Greenland Ice Sheet, the cooling could be long term and basically irreversible from 2033 forward. She decided that President Alain Bouchard had to know about this new and unwelcome development.

Morin was no shy bureaucrat. Immediately she placed a call to President Bouchard. A few well spoken words, and she was speaking directly with him.

"President Bouchard, we have discovered something in the North Atlantic Ocean that could seriously affect France's national security," said Morin bluntly.

"Oh? This line is secure; what is it?" asked President Bouchard.

"I dare not tell you even on this line," answered Morin. "It's also somewhat bizarre. I have in my office the person who can best describe it. Can we see you in person in the next day or so?"

President Bouchard paused just long enough to contact his scheduling assistant.

"I can open an hour for you today at 14:30. Come here then," said President Bouchard, trusting Morin's judgment.

"Excellent. Thank you," responded Morin.

As President Bouchard disconnected his call with Morin, he smiled. He had not been entirely candid. The hour he had set aside for them was in reality the last part of his meeting with France's prime minister on their strategy to rescind France's recently announced plan to decommission all of its nuclear power plants. But any time national security was at issue, both President Bouchard and Prime Minister Pierre Rousseau had to be involved. He wanted Rousseau to hear first hand what Morin and her mystery expert had to say.

Morin was as savvy as she was aggressive. In the two hours preceding their audience with President Bouchard, she made sure that Pelletier understood the formal decorum they would encounter. She also helped Pelletier anticipate questions, skepticism, and maybe even hostility. She even guessed that President Bouchard might include a trusted staff member in their meeting.

Morin and Pelletier used every available minute to prepare a succinct report for President Bouchard. Morin's alarm chirped as Pelletier was noting their last idea. The time to leave had arrived. They left Morin's office, just a thin folder of materials in hand. The new French governmental office building was just a short walk away.

Morin and Pelletier had to pass slowly though the tight security screening required even of ministers in this age of miniature killing devices. One of President Bouchard's aides met them after the screening. He led them down a wide corridor to the presidential conference room. As they entered the room, they saw President Bouchard and Prime Minister Rousseau already standing, ready to greet them formally. Although Pelletier and Morin expected President Bouchard to have someone else present, they did not expect the prime minister to be that person.

After introducing Pelletier as SMER's director, Morin first gave a brief sketch of SMER's role with the Ministry of Agriculture.

"Dr. Pelletier called me yesterday," she said. "He told me that he had some 'interesting information' to reveal to me in person. I know him as a serious scientist who would not ask for a personal meeting without a good reason, so I asked him to come to Paris to see me today. As I told you on our call, that interesting information is a discovery that could be very dangerous to France. He can describe it better than I can."

Somewhat nervous, but not intimidated by the formal surroundings and presence of the two most powerful politicians in France, Pelletier then described what Marie Leclerc's team had discovered south of Greenland in the last two weeks. He also tried his best to summarize what that discovery could mean to French agriculture, especially the risk of crop failures due to much colder weather.

As Pelletier was speaking, President Bouchard struggled to see why this information was so important, especially to France's national security. He was thinking that variable weather is just a natural condition that French farmers had dealt with for centuries.

Pierre Rousseau was not similarly perplexed. He immediately understood the significance of SMER's discovery. As a junior diplomat twenty years ago, he had been required to study various international protocols on global warming in order to describe them to more senior officials at that time. He could see President Bouchard's puzzled expression, so he intervened.

"President Bouchard, the real danger here is whether the fresh water incursion will continue, and that depends upon what is causing ice to melt more than normal at Greenland," said Rousseau. "If new atmospheric temperatures are the cause, we could have a serious long-term problem."

"Remember the Kyoto Protocol?" he continued. "Back in 1997, signatory nations committed to reducing their discharges of greenhouse gases into the earth's atmosphere. The protocol was based on the premise that increasing concentrations of greenhouse gases such as carbon dioxide were increasing the temperature of the earth's lower atmosphere. This increase in turn could change world climate patterns in unexpected and unpredictable ways.

"We and our European neighbors worried about the prospect of global warming for the very reason that it could set in motion forces that could change the ocean currents that warm Western Europe. Severe disruption of the North Atlantic Drift could create much colder weather here."

"Do you really think that if this fresh water incursion continues we could have crop failures here?" asked President Bouchard.

"Unfortunately, yes," answered Rousseau.

Eloquent and forceful, Rousseau then recast SMER's discovery in national security terms. He even used the example of the colder weather from the Tambora volcanic eruption in the early nineteenth century. That event showed how colder weather could affect France's internal security by disrupting food supplies and thereby creating social unrest.

President Bouchard did not understand all of the details, but even the possibility that the SMER's discovery could lead to crop failures was enough. He was appalled at the mere prospect that France might not be self-sufficient for food. French agriculture was the envy of Europe. Its surpluses helped to supply European and other nations with badly needed food. For France to have to depend upon others was unthinkable.

"Pierre, we cannot allow this to happen," said President Bouchard. "But I am no scientist. How do we prevent it?"

"I don't know," responded Rousseau. "But I know one thing for sure. Public knowledge of SMER's discovery, especially its implications, could cause a huge stir, even a panic. SMER's discovery has to be kept secret."

"I agree," said President Bouchard.

"I assume you need time to evaluate fully SMER's discovery, right?" he added, turning his eyes toward Morin and Pelletier.

"Yes, we do," answered Morin quickly.

"OK, we have no choice but to order that your evaluation be kept top secret—you know the protocol."

Morin nodded.

"As for SMER, tell your team working in the detection program not to tell anyone what they found," said President Bouchard, now looking directly at Pelletier. "They need to understand that what they had previously considered proprietary data of the French government is now secret national security data."

Pelletier readily agreed as well. He was confident that Marie Leclerc and her staff would recognize the importance and danger of their discovery and would keep it secret.

Unknown to any of them, President Bouchard's secrecy orders came one day too late. On the other side of the globe, other scientists were making their own discoveries, and a bizarre coincidence would bring those discoveries and the United States to France's doorstep.

CHAPTER 6

ETOP

Secretary Rand's office sent to Karen Lewis all of the USDA questionnaires as soon as they were received. Karen had already assigned five young staff members to start assembling data when the first questionnaires arrived. Karen had ignored President Clark's priority about farmers' use of fertilizer. Instead, she had told her staff members to assemble information first from just two questions on the third page.

(1) What are the projected crop yields in your district for 2032?
(2) If projected crop yields are below normal, what are the causes?

By Friday, August 27th, Karen had received all but a few of the questionnaires that had been sent around the country. Karen's staffers worked through the weekend to compile information in the answers to her two priority questions. On Monday, they gave Karen three printouts that summarized those answers.

The first printout confirmed Karen's preliminary data from July. Crop yields for every kind of crop, whether corn or wheat or something else, were down universally across the United States.

The second printout collected the numerous causes for these declines that had been identified by extension office directors. *Not much help here*, Karen thought to herself at first. But as she looked over the summaries of the causes, a simple fact became apparent. Nearly every one of the causes was weather related. Some answers said too little rain, some said too much rain, still others said searing heat from cloudless skies, and yet others said reduced sunlight from perpetually gray skies. Just two answers identified insects or blights or molds as primary causes. None identified reduced use of fertilizer or insufficient fuel to farm properly.

The third printout arranged all of the answers according to regional zip codes. Karen could see from this printout that the odd weather reported was not random, but regionalized. The Midwest was hotter and drier than normal. The West Coast was wetter than normal. Other regions showed other abnormalities.

Karen began making notes as a prelude to figuring out what to do with this information. Just then, her secretary carefully opened the door of her office and peeked in.

"No interruptions," Karen snapped.

"I'm sorry, but it's a call from France," said Karen's secretary. "He is quite insistent, but hard to understand. Something about a vacation. I think his first name is Claude. I couldn't understand his last name."

"Claude?" said Karen. She knew immediately that it must be Claude Leclerc, Marie Leclerc's husband.

"I'll take it."

Karen had met Marie through their daughters. At the beginning of 2027, Karen's daughter Nicole had gone to the École des Beaux Arts at Tours, France, for a six-month series of courses on French painters. Karen herself had spend six months in Paris in an education abroad program while she had been an undergraduate at CSU, so she had been thrilled when Nicole had chosen France for her foreign experience.

Nicole had met Annette Leclerc in one of her courses just two days after lectures had begun. They had instantly liked each other. Annette had quickly included Nicole in her circle of friends. When Karen had traveled to Tours to visit Nicole, Annette had made sure that Karen met her mother and father, Marie and Claude.

Karen's fluent French and science background had cemented a personal and professional bond with Marie. Every September afterward, Karen and Marie had visited each other for a few days, alternating between France and the United States for their rendezvous. This year, it was Karen's turn to travel to Nantes to see Marie. Karen's trip was scheduled to begin on September 12th.

Karen had already almost decided to postpone her trip because of her new responsibilities with the USDA questionnaire. Claude's call would force her to make up her mind. Or so she thought.

"Marie wanted me to call you right away," said Claude, now comfortably speaking in French with Karen.

"Isn't she still on SMER's ship?" asked Karen.

"Yes, and she has to stay out there another week," answered Claude. "Something about more samples to find fresh water. Anyway, she wants you to postpone your visit a week. Can you do it?"

"Of course," said Karen. "In fact, that works better for me also. I will figure out an itinerary and text it to you."

"A call works too," said Claude.

Karen had forgotten how much Claude disliked texting and e-mails.

"I will call you as soon as I have made new plane reservations," said Karen, acceding to Claude's idiosyncrasy.

After a few exchanges updating each other about Nicole and Annette, Karen's call with Claude ended.

She was relieved. Now she could give uninterrupted attention to the many issues raised by her questionnaire and the 2032 crop declines in the United States. The most pressing questions were now obvious. Did abnormal weather really occur in every region of the country? If so, why?

The National Weather Service should know the answers, Karen thought as she looked in her Federal agency guide for the best person to contact there. A few calls later, Karen was speaking to the director of the research section of the National Weather Service. She was disappointed by what she learned.

He said that the National Weather Service had the underlying data that could be used to answer her questions, but it had no program to analyze that data in the comparative way she wanted. She then asked if he knew anyone who would have what she wanted. He knew of no one for sure, but he did suggest that she contact Paul Anderson, the director of ETOP. He knew Anderson, so he offered to call him to let him know that she would be contacting him. Karen readily accepted this help.

ETOP? Karen thought to herself. She remembered from her days at Colorado State University in Fort Collins that ETOP was located somewhere around Boulder, just thirty miles away from the CSU campus. But she had never had any contact with it. What exactly was ETOP? Karen went on the Internet to find out.

ETOP's web site showed that ETOP was the acronym for the Earth Temperature Observation Project. It was a national research laboratory formed by legislation passed by Congress in 2018. Its stated missions were:

- To measure changes in the earth's average atmospheric temperatures over time using scientifically reliable instruments and methodologies and
- To use that information to predict future earth atmospheric temperatures and weather patterns.

Karen did not understand why Congress felt a need to create ETOP with these purposes. She thought that global temperature measurements and modeling had been done for many years before 2018. Why this duplication?

Karen clicked on ETOP's historical summary. As she already knew, ETOP's headquarters were located outside Boulder, Colorado. Reading further, Karen found that Paul Anderson had been ETOP's director since its inception. She also found that ETOP used a variety of methods to collect data about the earth's atmosphere and oceans. ETOP used measuring instruments at land stations, on buoys or ships at sea, on satellites, and on balloons launched daily. The summary said that ETOP's network had been in place collecting data by the middle of 2020.

When Karen clicked on "reports," she found ETOP's 2032 report to Congress. Karen had no desire to try to become a global weather expert. Still, she felt that she needed to know something about what ETOP was measuring and doing, so she downloaded that report for possible future reference.

A day later, Karen received a message from the research director at the National Weather Service who had recommended that she contact Paul Anderson. He said that Anderson was now expecting her to contact him.

Karen wasted no time.

She called Anderson immediately. Karen was typically blunt. She asked him if ETOP had comparisons of 2031 and 2032 weather data for all measurement stations across the United States.

Paul was shocked. That was exactly what he and Marilyn Sawyer, his deputy director, had decided to compile just one month ago. Why would an Assistant Secretary of the United States Department of Agriculture be interested in the same comparison?

Paul did not reveal his surprise, nor the fact that ETOP was already compiling the kind of comparison that Karen said she wanted. What he told Karen was true, but not the whole truth. He told her that ETOP did not already have any comparisons prepared the way she described. He said that ETOP's comparisons were all oriented toward longer-term global or continental differences, not local differences year by year. However, he thought that ETOP could create the kind of weather summaries that Karen was seeking.

To learn more about why Karen wanted her comparisons, Paul suggested that she visit ETOP's headquarters to speak with some of ETOP's scientists. In that way, she could understand fully the strengths, but also limitations, of the summaries that ETOP could create.

Karen readily agreed. They set a time for Karen to come just two days away.

After she ended her call with Paul, Karen paused. She had to be very careful now. The crop production declines that she had spotted in July remained secret. She had to concoct a different story to tell Paul as her reason for visiting ETOP.

Back in Boulder, Paul also paused after his call with Karen had ended. A month ago he had discovered something very odd in ETOP's monthly data tables for July. These long tables summarized measurements of temperature and precipitation recorded by each ETOP station around the world. Column four of these long tables showed the difference between the precipitation at a station for the year to date and the historic precipitation at the same station for the year to date. The historic data were based on ETOP's observations during the last twelve years. ETOP had begun to create this and several other comparative calculations just two years ago. He had wanted to start tracking systematically the differences between current and historic weather conditions at each station.

When Paul had seen these figures, somehow he had thought that they looked too large. So he had done a quick check by treating them all as positive numbers, then adding them together. He had done the same thing with column four for July of last year. He had discovered that this year's total was twice as large as last year's.

When he had told Marilyn Sawyer this oddity, she also had been startled by such a large difference.

They had both realized that unless ETOP's computer program contained a glitch, a lot more places around the world had seen odd weather in July this year than in July last year.

Paul and Marilyn had looked at each other silently. The possibility that they both feared could now be occurring. Yet, at this point, it was still only a possibility. A single month of troubling data could just as well be a rare statistical occurrence. They needed more information to reach any real conclusion. They then had decided as a first step to compile comparisons between 2031 and 2032 measurements from all of ETOP's world-wide stations.

They also had decided that they should test MegaComp. This was a data comparison plan that Paul and Marilyn had created in concept two years earlier when they had modified ETOP's surface data tables to include systematic comparisons of ETOP's historic data. Creating these comparisons had been a simple computer programming task. After all, ETOP's database already contained ETOP's surface data and these were known to be very accurate. The problem was that ETOP's benchmarks were based on only twelve years of measurements. Everyone at ETOP agreed that twelve years was not long enough to represent true climatic averages or historic conditions.

In contrast, MegaComp would take data from thousands of meteorological stations around the world that were not part of ETOP's surface measurement system, but that had data going back many decades. Extreme care would have to be exercised in choosing the stations whose data would be included. Someone would have to identify and exclude all of the stations with data linkage and other problems that ETOP's network of stations had been created to avoid. Once the stations were chosen, huge amounts of data would have to be collected in one program. Only then could confident comparisons to historic conditions be made. Until now, the cost and complexity of MegaComp made the full plan only an idea, not a reality.

Marilyn had recommended that they test the MegaComp concept with stations in the United States. ETOP already had their historic data in a separate system. In that way they could identify most of the problem stations fairly quickly. Paul had readily agreed. Their new project had been launched with Marilyn as its leader. By now, MegaComp was fully in place for the United States.

Paul had hired Marilyn as one of the original young scientists who formed the core of ETOP'S research staff after ETOP had been created in 2018. Within a year, Paul had recognized Marilyn's strong potential not only as a careful scientist, but also as a person who could see beyond her specific work to understand the world-wide meaning of what she and others were observing. As she had progressed in her career at ETOP, Paul had come to see her as his preferred successor.

Although already in his mid-sixties, Paul had not seriously considered retirement until this year. His health was excellent and he remained committed to and excited about ETOP's mission. Still, he had begun to think that maybe ETOP would be better off if Marilyn took over now and gave ETOP renewed energy.

What Paul thought that he had spotted in ETOP's July data erased any thought of retirement for the near future.

Although he hoped that July 2032 was just an anomaly, forty years of experience in studying climate and weather, first as a graduate student, then as a scientist with the National Center for Atmospheric Research, and finally as ETOP's director, told him otherwise. He knew that increased vigilance to spot other signs of serious change was now necessary.

The call from Karen Lewis added a new dimension to his concern.

Karen flew to Denver International Airport on the morning of September 4th. A young intern from ETOP met her at the baggage carousel. They drove from the airport straight west along Interstate 70 toward the Rocky Mountains, then north on Interstate 25, then northwest along Highway 36 to Boulder. In the bright sunlight of a cloudless sky, Karen could see clearly the granite faces of the Front Range mountains overlooking Boulder known as the Flatirons. They were aptly named. They looked just like the bottoms of huge clothes irons resting upright.

Closer to Boulder, Karen could see the distinctive tan, modernist buildings of the National Center for Atmospheric Research perched on a rock outcrop outlined against the Flatirons south of Boulder. Half expecting to see ETOP's facility there, Karen was disappointed that she would not travel that far.

Instead, the intern headed toward the smooth top of a prairie mesa lying to the east of the Flatirons using a narrow and long paved entrance road that was marked only by a small sign. The intern turned into a parking lot fifty feet in front of a low gray concrete building. Because of heightened security after 9/11, a high chain link fence with a manned gate blocked the walkway that led to the building. The fence extended north and south several hundred yards from the gate and then east to surround three other buildings and many acres of prairie.

So this is ETOP's headquarters. Pretty basic, Karen thought to herself.

Paul Anderson was as curious about Karen's upcoming visit as Karen was about ETOP. He remembered no other time when someone from the USDA had contacted ETOP about a project or even had come to ETOP for a visit. Paul's intern had used his cell phone to call Paul as he and Karen had come near the parking lot, so Paul was ready to meet Karen after she passed security clearance at the gate.

"Dr. Lewis, welcome to ETOP," smiled Paul, extending his hand cordially to Karen.

"Pleased to be here, Dr. Anderson," replied Karen, shaking his hand.

These simple greetings revealed that each had done homework about the other. At no time during their call two days ago had either revealed anything personal. Now, they both knew that the other had received a PhD degree, and probably knew other details about each other's background.

"I expect you will want a few minutes to regroup from your day's travel," said Paul.

"You are right about that," said Karen with a relieved smile.

Paul then ushered Karen through the building entrance to a small conference room where a variety of breakfast munchies and drinks awaited. Karen was grateful for this spread of food. She had skipped breakfast to make her early morning flight and airline food was basically nonexistent. Small talk about her flight to Denver and drive to ETOP lasted only a few minutes.

Paul initiated discussion about Karen's proposed project for ETOP.

"If I understood you correctly, you said in your telephone call that you want comparisons of weather data from ETOP's stations in the United States," said Paul.

"That's right," responded Karen.

"I have arranged for you to discuss this type of project with Marilyn Sawyer," said Paul. "She is our deputy director and primary expert for data analysis. If we knew what you are trying to find out from this comparison, maybe we could also help you in other ways."

Karen was cautious in replying. By now, she had rehearsed her cover story.

"The USDA is compiling information about all factors that might enhance crop production in the United States," said Karen. "New fertilizers and genetically modified seeds are examples. The USDA is also seeking information about temporary weather trends. That is my bailiwick. For example, we know that El Niño events in the Pacific Ocean can have a big impact on growing conditions here. If we can identify these and other changes far enough in advance, our farmers can adjust their crops to maximize yields. The comparisons that I asked for may allow us to spot any current weather trends."

Paul readily understood the importance of this kind of information. Certainly, advance knowledge of likely upcoming weather could help farmers plan their crops. But something was amiss in Karen's description. He thought that the USDA had already started predicting temporary local weather trends after the major El Niño event of the late twentieth century.

This El Niño had begun developing rapidly in May 1997. Scientists had correctly predicted its weather effects in 1997 and 1998. California and the southern United States had experienced wet and stormy weather as predicted. The northern two-thirds of the United States had experienced warm and dry conditions, also as predicted. Those who had believed and relied on the predictions had altered plans accordingly. They had coped well with adverse conditions such as flooding and had benefited from improved conditions such as extra rainfall in normally dry regions. Those who had ignored or scoffed at the predictions did not fare as well. Agribusiness had been a sector that did not respond promptly to the predictions made at that time.

Paul thought that the USDA had used this El Niño as an example to farmers of the benefits of being flexible and relying at least somewhat on annual forecasts of major weather changing events. He did not understand why Karen would be doing a new project that he thought the USDA had been doing for many years.

As for how ETOP could help Karen, Paul knew that ETOP's mission focused on predicting long-term weather patterns that could result in new climates. Long-term changes would obviously have huge effects on agriculture. ETOP had computer driven models that they used to try to predict long-term changes that would be caused by conditions that they had already observed and by a range of possible future underlying conditions. But ETOP's role did not encompass trying to predict local weather from day to day, or month to month, or even year to year. The National Weather Service had that job, and did it very well. Maybe Karen had come to the wrong place to get what she really wanted, despite the way that she had described her project.

"Karen, ETOP does not try to predict local weather," said Paul. "Our data collection and analyses are oriented toward finding global changes. We have created computer-based models to try to predict what will occur under probable future conditions. We even have some models that try to predict regional changes. None of these models is designed to predict even annual local weather conditions. You need to see the experts at the National Weather Service."

Karen realized now that her cover story was flawed. Her effort to mask the truth went too far. As she had told Paul her story, even then she had suspected that the project she had described for him was, at best, only peripheral to the USDA purpose she had revealed in her story. She now risked losing a chance to learn the information she needed to assess the odd weather conditions her USDA questionnaire had revealed. She had to retrieve Paul's interest in her project.

"Dr. Anderson, my project for ETOP is designed to look at 2031 and 2032 as sample years," said Karen, making up a new cover story as she spoke. "They will be our baseline. Our department is also interested in longer-term trends from that baseline such as those ETOP is investigating."

Karen paused. She was not connecting with Paul. What to say now? Her preparation while on the airplane this morning would now be her savior. She had read ETOP's latest report to Congress.

"I saw in ETOP's report to Congress that ETOP has made projections about future atmospheric temperatures," said Karen.

"That's right," said Paul.

"Was that done using a computer model such as the ones you just mentioned?" asked Karen, stumbling to reengage Paul.

"Actually, several models. We averaged their projections," answered Paul.

"Several?"

"Yes, several. Models are difficult to construct. We cannot match all of nature's inputs, so each model contains simplifying conditions. That's one reason why different models can give somewhat different results. Our models have been consistent in one way. They all predict overall atmospheric temperature increases over time. They do differ somewhat on the amount of those increases even with the same assumed future conditions."

Karen still felt ill at ease, as she groped to reconnect her latest comments to what she urgently needed to know about odd weather across the United States this year.

"What about ETOP's models for regional changes?" she asked. "I did not see anything about them in ETOP's report to Congress."

Paul smiled inwardly, but otherwise remained stoic. He could see that Karen was very observant. Paul had decided long ago not to publish ETOP's regional projections. Clearly, they could be useful to the USDA in this new evaluation that Karen had just described.

"Karen, we have never published ETOP's regional projections," revealed Paul. "At this point, we just do not think that they are good enough to do so."

Paul, like Karen, was not being fully candid. Although ETOP's regional models were not as accurate as ETOP's global models, that did not render them useless. Paul had other reasons for not making them public, reasons that he was not about ready to reveal to anyone outside ETOP.

"Even the global projections that we have published have many qualifications," continued Paul. "We are working with very complex natural systems."

To Paul, Karen seemed disappointed with his answer.

In truth, Paul's answer only intrigued Karen more. She had come to ETOP just to get her project under way as soon as possible. She urgently needed to know whether the answers in her USDA questionnaire were correct in that US agricultural regions had experienced universally odd weather this year. If they were correct, what then? While reading ETOP's report to Congress, Karen began to suspect that ETOP somehow held a key to understanding why universally odd weather could have happened. Paul's qualifying statements did not shake that suspicion.

Besides, something about ETOP's report did not seem quite right. Karen felt that it had been carefully crafted to be accurate, but bland, just a little too much so. Karen's experience as a research scientist had taught her that measurements of natural systems, whether plants, or local ecosystems, or something else, were always difficult. Compiling those measurements to create an accurate picture of reality was never simple. The limited accuracy of many kinds of measurements, the need to select representative samples, and the sheer volume of total data conspired to make the truth elusive to discern. And the pictures that ultimately emerged from this process often contained surprises. ETOP's report did not even hint at possible surprises in future global conditions.

Karen suspected that ETOP experts such as Paul Anderson and Marilyn Sawyer knew a lot more than ETOP's report revealed. But she could not begin to find out what that was without learning more about how, and why, ETOP collected and evaluated the kinds of information it did. She would again use ETOP's report as her entrée.

"I saw in ETOP's report that ETOP has quite an array of ways to collect data," she said.

"We sure do," responded Paul.

"I think I remember instruments being on balloons, satellites, buoys, and land stations," said Karen.

"Also ships stationed at sea," added Paul.

"I missed that one," said Karen. She paused.

"Why so many different ways to collect information?" she asked.

"Each method has unique strengths, but also limitations," answered Paul. "Some of the methods overlap by measuring exactly the same thing. We do that on purpose to allow us to cross-check one method against another."

Paul was encouraged by Karen's question. Her initial description of the USDA's purpose for her project for ETOP had been disappointing. ETOP could not help her meet that purpose. But if the USDA wanted baseline conditions, then they must be interested in future changes as well. Paul saw advantages to teaching Karen a lot more about ETOP's work. Her knowledge could help the USDA avoid poor policies based upon broad, incorrect assumptions about future weather patterns.

"Karen, would you like to see what we do here?" asked Paul.

"Absolutely!" replied Karen, relieved that she finally had recaptured Paul's interest. She had also learned an important lesson. She was not very good at fabricating false stories. She had better be very careful when she discussed her project with Marilyn Sawyer. In the meantime, she had an opportunity at ETOP that she would not waste. She was ready to learn as much as she could in the next several hours.

Chapter 7

HISTORY

Paul had planned all along to give Karen a tour of ETOP, although her initial story made him temporarily question that plan. Luckily, the timing was perfect when Karen began asking questions about ETOP's instrument programs. ETOP would be launching a high altitude weather balloon at noon, just twenty minutes from then.

The large steel building that stored ETOP's weather balloons and instruments at this site was located two hundred yards east of ETOP's main building. A hundred yards beyond, and hidden by the storage building, was the launch site. It would take at least ten minutes to walk there.

Paul and Karen exited ETOP's headquarters building through a small back door. They stepped onto a five foot wide paved pathway. In the bright warm sunlight, Karen saw that it led toward a large storage building, but split before reaching it. One part of the path led to an entrance to that building. The other part went around its south side. She could not see where it led from there. Paul began to describe ETOP's operations as they started walking along the pathway through the natural prairie of this mesa.

"Karen, ETOP's work ultimately depends upon the accuracy of the measurements that we make every day," he said. "Those measurements allow us to identify the physical state of the earth's atmosphere from year to year. By physical state I mean the variety of conditions that describe the atmosphere. That would include concentrations of various gases, average temperatures in many places, and global average temperatures.

"The annual physical states are the foundations of our computer models. We create models to try to match the all of the conditions in the annual physical states that we have measured. If a model does that, then we have some confidence that its predictions for future physical states under some changed conditions will be valid as well. If our measurements are wrong, our models will be wrong. It's as simple as that. That's why we are so exacting with our measurements. ETOP has been doing this for twelve years now."

Twelve years, Karen thought. That is not very long to identify trends. The questions she had asked herself when she saw ETOP's website now returned. What about measurements before ETOP? Why have ETOP at all?

"Dr. Anderson …"

"Please, call me Paul," said Paul before Karen could continue. "You are back in the West. You know we are informal out here."

Paul again relied on his advance knowledge about Karen. He knew that Karen had been at Colorado State University for many years before taking a position with the USDA in Washington, D.C.

"With due respect, I don't understand why ETOP was created," said Karen. "Weren't global measurements being made and models being created long before ETOP was formed? Why the duplication?"

Good questions, Paul thought. Few people were so perceptive. In response, Paul began his story about how ETOP came to be.

"ETOP arose out of two sets of Congressional hearings that ended back in 2018," said Paul. "The first set of hearings was held in 2017. Those hearings dealt with the Kyoto Protocol and Paris Agreement. You are familiar with those agreements, aren't you?"

"I think so," said Karen. "If I remember correctly, the Kyoto Protocol dates back to 1997. It was an international agreement to voluntarily reduce greenhouse gas emissions. But it applied only to industrialized nations. The Paris Agreement expanded on the Kyoto Protocol with more ambitious reductions. I think that these were voluntary also and not very specific. Paris included many more nations than Kyoto. I remember that it was a big deal when China joined the agreement. Seems to me that Paris occurred around 2015 or 2016."

"Good memory," said Paul. "The Paris Agreement was reached at the end of 2015. You probably also remember that Kyoto and Paris were responses to concerns about increasing concentrations of greenhouse gases in the atmosphere. Even back then, there was no doubt that the increasing concentrations were caused by human activities.

"The big question initially in the early 1990s was whether this mattered to us humans. Research and data analyses were done by many scientists even before Kyoto. Much more research and data analyses were done after Kyoto and before Paris. That work convinced the scientists who were doing it that increasing concentrations of greenhouse gases were causing the earth's atmosphere to warm up in a significant way. That warming could then cause changes in regional climates. It's those changes that could harm many people."

"Didn't Kyoto and Paris run into a lot of objections for economic reasons?" said Karen.

"They sure did," said Paul. "The US government officially rejected the Kyoto Protocol in 2001. The expressed reason was that the US economy would be harmed by US compliance with Kyoto's requirements.

"The set of hearings in 2017 focused mostly on the Paris Agreement rather than the Kyoto Protocol. Of course, Kyoto was discussed somewhat as well because it was seen as a failure. Greenhouse gas concentrations had continued to increase just as much after Kyoto as before Kyoto. Despite those increases, most of the testimony at the hearings objected to the Paris Agreement. Again, objections were based on claims that the US economy would be harmed if the US made commitments to reduce its greenhouse gas emissions.

"Maybe surprisingly, many scientists also objected to the Paris Agreement, but for very different reasons. They said that the non-specific promises in Paris were not nearly enough to stop significant atmospheric warming.

"So we had objections that the Paris Agreement went too far and objections that it did not go far enough.

"Unfortunately, the rhetoric on both sides hid the most important purpose of both Kyoto and Paris. The modest goals for greenhouse gas reductions were just a tool. They were designed to accelerate the development of technologies that could replace the historic activities that created greenhouse gases in the first place. The technologies would have to be available on a huge scale. They would also have to be priced less than the prices of the historic activities they were to replace. Otherwise, they would not be used enough to make any real difference. The right set of technologies could achieve both continued economic success and diminished risk from increased greenhouse gas concentrations.

"Sadly, the 2017 hearings ended with no real commitment by the US to reduce its greenhouse gas emissions.

"Then, in 2018, a new set of hearings came about unexpectedly. The global terrorism that was so dangerous at that time seemed to be continuing without end. Some members of Congress and the Administration began looking more closely at conditions that led people to join terrorist groups in the first place. They also looked at other conditions that could affect national security. They identified regional climate change as a condition that could affect national security in a variety of ways. For example, a regional change could disrupt regional economies and economic opportunities for youth in those regions. And those youth were more likely to be swayed by terrorist dogma. Surprisingly few people realized that one of the purposes of the Paris Agreement was to reduce this kind of threat by minimizing the risk of regional climate changes.

"Senator Dean Wilson of Oregon arranged a series of informational hearings in the United States Senate on these underlying conditions and threats. His hearings eventually led to the formation of ETOP."

Paul and Karen had just walked past the ETOP storage building. Karen stopped walking, a quizzical frown on her face. Paul stopped as well to face her, wondering why she had stopped.

"You are losing me here," said Karen. "I still don't understand how Wilson's hearings led to ETOP. As I said before, weren't there already people who were compiling measurements that showed global warming and correlations to changes in the earth's atmosphere?"

"Sorry, Karen, you are right—it's not obvious," said Paul. "Wilson's hearings included a segment about regional climate changes and climate change generally. He asked me to testify one day because I had published some papers on the subject that were directed to the general public. At the time, I was a deputy director at NCAR."

Paul paused. His face became stern, with a tinge of anger.

"I was the last person to speak on the day that I testified. The hearing was supposed to be informational, but it quickly became confrontational. A few senators regularly cut me off with negative comments or loaded questions that were really only statements. They accused me of promoting 'junk science' when I tried to describe what we knew about changes in the physical state of the earth's atmosphere and human contributions to those changes. They dismissed the facts contained in the written summary of my testimony by claiming that the facts were biased in order to get more funding for research. They demanded absolute certainty for my conclusions and projections. They asserted that whatever climate changes had occurred or were occurring came solely from natural causes.

"I could have responded to those statements at the hearing, but I didn't have an opportunity to do so. The hearing ended abruptly at the scheduled time. Their 'natural causes' claim was particularly irritating. In my experience, so-called 'natural causes' are almost never identified. The senators certainly did not do so at the hearing. The very few 'natural causes' that I have seen identified consistently fail to match actual observations and measurements."

"Sounds to me like a belief only in natural causes is just a modern version of a belief only in 'God's will,'" said Karen. "That belief centuries ago discounted observations by people who were trying to figure out actual causes for human diseases. It surely delayed recognition and use of discoveries that could have saved lives."

"I have never thought of it that way before now," said Paul. "I like your analogy to 'God's will.' Your comparison to early efforts to figure out the causes for diseases fits here also. The human body is a complex natural system. Predicting its response to new viruses or chemicals will never be 'absolutely certain.' The earth's climates comprise another complex natural system. Predicting their reactions to changes in the composition of the earth's atmosphere will also never be 'absolutely certain.' To require absolute certainty about these effects before trying to eliminate underlying causes is just a prescription for inaction and acceptance of risk.

"As I said before, Wilson's hearing ended abruptly. I also did not have an opportunity to emphasize the most important aspect of the climate threat. We humans are causing changes in the composition of the earth's atmosphere that are exposing every person the earth to a huge, uncontrolled, world-wide experiment."

Paul stopped speaking in order to control the anger that had risen within him.

His outburst surprised Karen, especially where it occurred—the middle of an outside walkway on their way to watch the launch of a weather balloon. She still did not understand how the Wilson hearing led to ETOP, but she did understand a lot more about Paul Anderson. He was not a cold scientist, but a person genuinely concerned about people around the world.

Paul regrouped.

"Senator Wilson knew that his hearing about threats from climate change was a fiasco," said Paul. "He apologized to me afterward.

"Rather than slink back to NCAR, I decided to respond to the political rhetoric head-on. Of course, absolute certainty is impossible. But I thought that we could set up a system where the quality and genuineness of our measurements would be much harder to criticize. That's when I came up with the idea for a new research laboratory. I named it the Earth Temperature Observation Project.

"The director of NCAR at the time wholeheartedly supported my idea even though a new laboratory might compete with NCAR. Together, we approached Senator Wilson. We asked him to introduce legislation to establish ETOP based on a synopsis that I had prepared. Wilson was anxious to resurrect some good out of his contentious hearings so he was receptive to my ideas. His staff prepared a bill in record time.

"We were all surprised to find that the lapse of just three months had tempered acrimony from the hearings. Before the end of 2018, both the Senate and House passed his bill. Leaders from both parties pushed its passage. The president signed it within a week, despite lobbying for a veto by a few remaining opponents.

"ETOP's board of directors is comprised equally of people from both major political parties and the public. ETOP's neutrality has never been questioned. Synchtor Corporation won the initial bid to manage ETOP. They asked me to leave NCAR to become ETOP's director. Of course, I accepted their offer. We have continued in these roles ever since."

"Surprising story," said Karen. "The history of ETOP on its website doesn't even hint at the contentious background you described. I'll bet there's even more that you have not mentioned."

Paul hesitated to respond to Karen's invitation to add more. Yet somehow he felt that he could trust her even though they had just met. It would take a few minutes to walk the remaining distance to the launch site, just enough time to tell Karen about two problems that remained even today.

"We should start walking again so that I can show you our set-up before the balloon is launched," said Paul, turning toward the launch site. He and Karen set out again along the pathway.

"After Wilson's hearing, I also tried to figure out why the senators had completely discounted all of the work that competent scientists had done around the world," said Paul. "It was then that I recognized two major but subtle problems that still exist today.

"One problem is psychological. It's very difficult for some people to separate two underlying questions raised by the atmospheric changes that we are measuring. The first question is causal. Are disruptive climate consequences possible or even likely from the changed chemical composition of the atmosphere? If the answer is yes, the second question is remedial. How would we have to alter human activity if a decision were made to eliminate the underlying causes of these atmospheric changes?

"By not separating these questions, these people typically focus solely on the remedial question. That's a hugely difficult question to answer. Because it's so difficult, it's psychologically easier to deny that the question even exists. In other words, it's easier to deny that anything is happening that requires a remedy.

"The second major problem is ideological. American economic policy has long relied primarily on market forces to provide the best and least expensive goods and services to our citizens. And this policy has been exported to many other nations through multilateral trade agreements. This policy has led people to rely heavily on energy sources that create greenhouse gases because the purchase prices of those sources and the technologies to use these sources has been less than the purchase prices of alternatives. Yet that very reliance is what has caused changes in the composition of the earth's atmosphere. It's very difficult to admit that these changes can create climate dislocations that could adversely affect people around the world. That admission could then admit that this economic policy has been a short-term success but is a long-term failure for future generations."

Karen had no chance to follow-up on Paul's statements because they then reached the launch site.

CHAPTER 8

TECHNOLOGY

At the launch site Karen and Paul saw a partially inflated balloon stretched across an asphalt pad covered with carpet. At six feet in diameter, it was smaller than Karen had expected. Twelve feet of thin nylon rope led from the bottom of the balloon to a small gray box with an antenna. A technician crouched by the box with some kind of instrument. She appeared to be testing or setting something in the box.

"That little box there is pretty sophisticated," said Paul, relieved now to be showing Karen what ETOP did. "Inside is a device we call a radiosonde. The radiosonde takes temperature readings throughout the balloon's flight. Its electronics also link to global positioning satellites to give its location for each reading. It transmits all of that information by radio to our receiver over there next to headquarters."

Beyond the balloon storage building, and north of ETOP's headquarters building, she could see most of an antenna rising at least a hundred feet into the air. About ten feet from its top, two metal dishes pointed skyward. She was embarrassed that she had not previously noticed this imposing structure. Then she looked back at the little gray box in front of her.

"When we started ETOP, we standardized the radiosondes that we sent up with the balloons," said Paul as he saw Karen's quizzical expression. "That way we would know that our measurements were truly comparable from place to place. Standardizing also greatly reduced the costs of these instruments. You know, ETOP launches five thousand balloons daily around the world."

Karen did a quick mental calculation. *That was nearly two million balloons every year!* she thought.

"That five thousand compares to fourteen hundred daily launches by everyone around the world before ETOP," said Paul. "We use over two thousand different locations for our launches. We also standardized the balloon design to the tough versions developed in the 1980s. Before that, quite a few balloons failed in high altitudes. These failures prevented scientists from getting some real atmospheric conditions into the averages. Those averages did not show real conditions as accurately as we do today. We also standardized operating procedures around the world. The international cooperation to get ETOP's program under way was just amazing."

Karen had no idea that measurements using balloons could be so complicated. She was about to ask Paul a question, but ETOP's weather balloon diverted her attention.

The balloon began to rise off the ground and rose straight up into the air, lifting the gray instrument box a few feet above the ground and stopping. Karen noticed for the first time that the box itself was linked by a sturdy chain to a concrete block. Paul explained that they used a concrete block rather than a person to hold the balloon because ETOP's weather balloons were surprisingly difficult to hold onto, especially if any breeze came up.

At precisely noon, an ETOP researcher released the chain from the gray box. The balloon floated rapidly straight up in the calm air near the ground. After it reached a thousand feet above the ground, western breezes coming over the Rocky Mountains pushed it noticeably eastward. Karen and Paul watched the balloon until it was just a speck in the blue, cloudless sky.

The speck reminded Karen about the ETOP satellites that were described in ETOP's report to Congress. As she and Paul turned around and began walking back to ETOP's headquarters building, she began asking questions.

"ETOP's report mentioned satellites as well as balloons," she said. "What are satellites used for?"

"We use them only to measure air temperatures," said Paul.

"Air temperatures?" Karen asked. "How can they do that? The satellites must be moving around far above the atmosphere."

"They are carrying an interesting device," said Paul. "We call it a microwave sounding unit. MSU for short.

"They're used to measure average atmospheric temperatures over large geographic regions as the satellite travels around the earth."

Paul walked a few steps ahead of Karen before he realized that she had stopped. He turned back to her. She was looking up at the air space where the balloon had disappeared.

"You've got me on this one," she said. "How can a device up on a satellite measure atmospheric temperatures? Sounds like voodoo to me."

Paul laughed.

"It's scientific voodoo," he said.

Karen smiled.

"Scientific voodoo. Is that a new ETOP term of art?" she said.

"Sure, I just made it up. I can do that as ETOP's director, you know."

"OK," laughed Karen. "Tell me how your voodoo MSU works."

Paul reappraised Karen as he organized his thoughts to describe microwave sounding units in an understandable way. He had never before met a USDA researcher, but surely Karen must be one of the USDA's stars. She was intelligent, curious, and perceptive. She deserved his best effort to describe the most challenging, and controversial, method used by ETOP and the scientists who had preceded ETOP to measure atmospheric temperatures. Now, in the bright Colorado sunlight, Paul became a professor to his student Karen Lewis as they resumed walking on the pathway back toward ETOP's main building.

Paul knew that microwave sounding units were straightforward in theory, but very complex in actual use on a satellite. He decided to start with their theory, which was based on the presence of oxygen in the earth's atmosphere. Four steps should do it. After that, maybe he could avoid describing their limits as used on satellites. That description would be much longer and would get very technical.

For the first step, Paul simply reiterated what Karen undoubtedly already knew about oxygen in the earth's atmosphere. Oxygen comprised nearly twenty-one percent of all atmospheric gases. Its concentration was uniform around the globe, whether measured in the dense atmosphere at sea level or in the thin atmosphere tens of thousands of feet above sea level. Its concentration was also uniform from day to day and year to year. This dual uniformity meant that measurements that depended in part upon oxygen's concentration in the atmosphere could be compared from place to place around the earth and from time to time over many years.

As his second step, Paul described the way that oxygen molecules behave when exposed to infrared radiation. He said that oxygen molecules absorb infrared radiation and then re-emit that radiation at unique wavelengths in the microwave portion of the radiation spectrum. Microwave sounding units had detectors that measured the total amount of radiation received at the detector at several of oxygen's emission wavelengths. This amount of radiation was known as the brightness of the oxygen at each unique wavelength.

Paul's third step was more complex. He said that oxygen molecules emitted much more radiation at each emission wavelength when the oxygen was at certain pressures. It turns out that two of those pressures were found in two altitude zones in the earth's atmosphere. Those altitude zones existed because air pressures gradually decrease as altitude increases from the bottom of the atmosphere at sea level. One of those two pressure zones was the mid-troposphere. This was a zone roughly from 13,000 feet to 23,000 feet above sea level. When a microwave sounding unit measured oxygen brightness at the emission wavelength that corresponded to the mid-troposphere, it was measuring oxygen brightness within the range of the MSU and located mostly at that altitude zone.

Paul's fourth step finally tied the theory of microwave sounding units to atmospheric temperatures. He said that luckily oxygen's brightness at a specific emission wavelength also revealed oxygen's relative temperature. Because oxygen was commingled with all atmospheric gases, its temperature would always be the same temperature as the atmosphere at the same place.

Thus, when a microwave sounding unit was pointed in a specific direction and measured atmospheric oxygen's brightness at the appropriate wavelength, scientists could determine the relative temperature of the corresponding zone of the earth's atmosphere at that time.

There, I did it, he thought. Karen seemed to have followed his description. He then related the theory of microwave sounding units to the MSUs used on ETOP's satellites.

"The MSUs on our satellites have two major advantages over other methods of measuring atmospheric temperatures," said Paul. "They can measure oxygen's brightness in the atmosphere above a very large surface area of the earth for each reading. Localized anomalies are absent from these measurements. Satellite orbits also are flexible. We can choose them so that measurements are made over nearly the entire earth each day. Few gaps in coverage exist."

Paul paused, believing that he had fully answered Karen's question about ETOP's satellites. He had not.

"I'll bet it's not as simple in practice as you described," said Karen.

"Not even close," answered Paul.

"What are the problems?" she asked.

Paul was not sure that he wanted to get into this contentious subject.

Before ETOP, data from MSUs on satellites had been used in early calculations to discern trends in the temperature of the earth's mid-troposphere. Those early calculations had shown no changes in average temperature over the two decades when satellite data had been available. They did not agree with the warming trends shown during the same time period by compilations of temperature records derived from measurements by thermometers at surface stations. These early MSU calculations had convinced many non-scientists, and some scientists as well, that the compilations of atmospheric temperatures at the earth's surface were wrong. Thus, from their point of view, global atmospheric warming was a myth that humanity could ignore.

This attitude had been difficult to dislodge, even though the early calculations had been challenged by published accounts of later calculations that had used the same MSU data. These later calculations highlighted the uncertainty of MSU temperature data by finding that the earth's mid-tropospheric temperature had increased, rather than remained the same. Later calculations from measurements with more advanced instruments had confirmed the continuation of a slight warming trend in the mid-troposphere, but these also contained uncertainties.

ETOP's microwave sounding units were far better than early instruments, but calculations of atmospheric temperatures from the raw data still involved uncertainties that were extremely difficult to eliminate. Many other precise data, often difficult to obtain, were needed to make the calculations that would give true temperatures n the mid-troposphere.

Paul hesitated.

"What are the problems?" Karen repeated.

Paul again hesitated.

His hesitation only increased Karen's curiosity. She stopped walking and stared at him, expecting a response this time. They were only forty feet from the back door of ETOP's main building.

Before Paul could respond, the back door opened. Paul's secretary came out into the sunlight, waving at them cheerfully, oblivious to Paul and Karen's temporary stand-off.

"Your lunches are ready in the conference room," she announced loudly. "Marilyn is there, too."

Paul waved at his secretary, thankful for her interruption.

Paul did not want to get into a long recitation of the difficulties, and limitations, in using MSUs on satellites to calculate atmospheric temperatures. Data from these MSUs had many inherent problems when trying to discover trends in atmospheric temperatures over time. Solving those problems was one of the most difficult tasks ETOP had faced when Paul originally had devised its measurement network.

For her part, Karen realized that this discussion was getting far away from the information she needed most from ETOP. Her project for ETOP sought detailed information about odd weather affecting agricultural regions in the United States. Records of odd weather would be from surface measurements. Despite her initial expressed curiosity, she did not really need to understand how MSUs were used to calculate atmospheric temperatures. She had not yet learned anything at all about ETOP's surface stations in the United States. It was time to do so.

Paul and Karen resumed walking toward the back door of the main building, both looking at Paul's secretary as they quickly covered the remaining distance. When they reached her, Paul introduced her to Karen, then commented light-heartedly as they went through the doorway that a gastronomic delight awaited them in the conference room. He knew, and Karen suspected, that only box lunches would be there.

Neither Paul nor Karen spoke as they walked toward the conference room. Both were absorbed in their own thoughts.

Paul remained silent because he was hoping that Karen would not pursue the subject of microwave sounding units.

Karen remained silent because she was thinking about her project for ETOP. She wanted to know if the weather across the United States had really been as odd as reported by USDA district directors in answers to her questionnaire. Was odd weather really causing US crop production to decline in 2032? After all, agricultural patterns in the United States had developed over a century. The variety of weather that had affected each region during that century must have been huge. How would ETOP's data from its measurement stations across the United States provide an answer to this question?

What was "odd weather" anyway? How would she know if a real change had occurred in precipitation or temperatures?

Karen was well aware that record-setting events would be classified as odd weather. The years-long drought in California in the early 2010s was clearly odd weather under this standard. Huge rainfall in the winter that caused major flooding when there should have been snow was odd weather as well. Beyond record-setting weather, however, how extreme and how long did temperature and precipitation patterns have to exist to be considered odd weather when compared to hundred or even fifty-year records?

Paul had identified difficulties in using radiosondes and MSUs to measure real changes in just the temperatures of the mid-troposphere, especially before ETOP was created. What foibles lay within the surface measurements? And what about ETOP's projections, especially regional projections covering part or all of the United States? She did not quite believe that Paul had no confidence in those projections. What was he afraid of?

Karen's questions raced in her mind as they reached the conference room.

CHAPTER 9

MEASUREMENTS

The conference room was brightly lit. Three white boxes tied with purple ribbon were placed neatly at the far end of the conference table. An array of bottled waters, canned juices, and canned sodas sat on a small credenza. Standing to the left of the credenza was a powerfully built woman in her early forties.

"I'm Marilyn Sawyer," the woman said, not giving Paul time to introduce her. "Thanks for coming all this way to visit us."

"My pleasure," responded Karen. "Dr. Anders ..., that is, Paul, has been showing me around and telling me about ETOP."

"All business, as usual," quipped Marilyn. "Come on, let's relax with lunch before we get back to your purpose for being here."

Marilyn motioned for Karen to sit in the seat at the left side of the table so that Karen would not feel trapped between Paul and her.

The next twenty minutes were occupied with light conversation, although at one point Paul did ask Marilyn to describe her role at ETOP.

Karen was the last to finish her dessert. Hyper-energetic by nature, she had consumed every morsel of her lunch. She was now ready to get her project underway and to try to glean as much other useful information as she could from Paul and Marilyn. But she also knew that she had to be extra cautious.

Within minutes after meeting Marilyn, Karen felt like she was looking into a mirror—not physically, but mentally and psychologically.

Marilyn was four inches taller and much sturdier than Karen. She was also Asian by descent, having been adopted as a one-year old from a Korean orphanage by a couple living outside Modesto, California.

As an only child of parents who strongly supported her in every way, Marilyn proudly bore the name that they had given her.

Physical differences aside, Marilyn, like Karen, was smart, conscientious, and strong-willed. When Paul had asked Marilyn to describe her role as ETOP's deputy director for data analysis, Karen had sensed through Marilyn's description that Marilyn was also very good with data.

Although this sense gave Karen confidence that Marilyn could pull together the information she wanted, it also created a problem. Karen did not want Marilyn to know the real purpose behind her project for ETOP. Before coming to ETOP, she was confident that she had figured out directions for her project that would hide that purpose. The failure of her initial story with Paul had shaken that confidence.

Karen needed a new strategy.

She decided to postpone the details about her project until the last part of her visit. In that way, Marilyn, or Paul, would not have time to suggest alternatives that might lead them to see the odd weather patterns in the United States that Karen's questionnaire had revealed. Somehow, she had to create a delay.

Expressed curiosity became her tool.

"Paul told me that accurate measurements are the foundation of ETOP's projections," Karen said, looking at Marilyn.

"That's right," said Marilyn.

"Paul also told me about ETOP's radiosondes and voodoo MSUs," said Karen, glancing back at Paul.

"Voodoo MSUs?" asked Marilyn.

"A new term we invented," said Paul, shaking his head and rolling his eyes with some embarrassment.

"Sounds right to me," said Marilyn, recalling the challenges that ETOP had overcome to translate MSU measurements of oxygen's brightness into comparative atmospheric temperatures over time.

"Paul began to tell me about some of the problems you had to solve to get meaningful data from radiosondes and MSUs, but I couldn't convince him to explain your extra difficulties with MSU calculations," said Karen.

"Good thing," said Marilyn. "The process is very messy."

"Anyway, we have not talked at all about ETOP's surface measurements," continued Karen. "Did you have problems to solve there too?"

Karen expected a simple negative answer and was already trying to think of more questions to ask to continue her delay.

"Yes, quite a few," answered Marilyn.

"Really?" questioned Karen, genuinely surprised.

Her earlier discussion with Paul had taught her that basic comparative measurements were much more difficult than she had thought before coming to ETOP. Still, the difficulties Paul had talked about came from the devices used, whether balloons, radiosondes, or MSUs. Surface stations probably used simple thermometers. What could go wrong with them? Karen was perplexed and showed it.

Marilyn correctly guessed Karen's dilemma.

"It's not the thermometers, Karen, it's the sampling," said Marilyn.

"Sampling?" asked Karen.

"Yes, in a broad sense," replied Marilyn.

"I don't understand," said Karen truthfully.

"Remember, Karen, ETOP's missions are first to identify any global changes, then to figure out what those mean," said Marilyn. "We have to compile measurements from around the world and from different time periods. Since 2020, these measurements have all come from ETOP's facilities. Our stations and methods have eliminated all of the problems we saw with earlier compilations. Come on, I'll show you what I mean."

Marilyn stood up and began walking to the conference room entrance. Karen had little choice but to follow. Paul joined them as well. Karen thought that at least he knew where they were going.

Upon exiting the conference room, Marilyn strode briskly down a hall, with Karen by her side, Paul following behind. Marilyn spoke rapidly. She began explaining the problems that ETOP's surface system had solved.

Marilyn said that, before ETOP, all attempts to compile the average atmospheric temperatures at the earth's surface over time had used temperature measurements from existing national meteorological programs. Obtaining these measurements had been a monumental achievement.

The many weather stations that contributed most of this information had been manned by the total spectrum of humanity speaking numerous languages and representing all nationalities. That such an effort had even been possible was largely due to the World Meteorological Organization. The WMO had set standards for instruments and methods to be used in measuring temperature and other weather conditions so that real comparisons could be made from place to place. Many governments also had cooperated by making their data available to the scientists who had compiled these weather data to give a picture of the average atmospheric temperature over time. That picture was as accurate as could have been created before ETOP.

Marilyn, Karen, and Paul reached a door at the end of the hallway. Through a small glass window in the door, Karen saw that a downward flight of stairs lay beyond. How far down, Karen could not yet discern. She had not suspected that ETOP's unimposing low building also extended underground. Marilyn opened the door, still talking rapidly as they all passed through the doorway and began descending the stairs.

Marilyn said that, despite these achievements, compilations before ETOP had three important uncertainties for assessing true changes in the average atmospheric temperature at the earth's surface.

The most important uncertainty had come from the skewed distribution of locations where measurements had been made. Before ETOP, large areas of the earth had only a few weather stations and therefore relatively few measurements. The biggest gaps had been found in the oceans in the Southern Hemisphere. Those oceans had only scattered inhabited islands where weather stations had been established. Weather buoys had rarely been placed there as well. Supplemental measurements from ships traversing southern oceans also had been limited by the small amount of commercial ship traffic that had occurred there. Conversely, many weather stations had been well distributed for more than a century over some land masses such as the United States and Europe.

This uneven distribution meant that some areas of the earth had been under-represented and others had been over-represented in the compilations of average atmospheric temperatures. If the temperatures in the United States and Europe had been changing differently than the rest of the world, their contribution to the average could have been magnified.

Marilyn, Karen, and Paul reached a landing between floors. Marilyn did not slow down. She continued taking rapidly as they descended another set of stairs.

Marilyn said that a second uncertainty had come from the exposure of some weather stations to what was known as the urban heating effect. Marilyn explained that in most countries, urbanization meant that buildings and pavement replaced plants and exposed soil. These new conditions absorbed and retained sunlight differently. Often the effect was to warm the local atmosphere close to the ground, especially at night, compared to what had occurred before urbanization. Localized urban heating would have been recorded in urban weather stations. Because urbanization had increased around many weather stations after 1950, some people had thought that these weather station measurements erroneously recorded higher temperatures than would have existed without the new urbanization. And these purely local urban heating effects would have been included in the world-wide averages, giving an appearance of higher average atmospheric temperatures each year than actually existed.

Marilyn emphasized that the scientists who made average temperature compilations had been well aware of the urban heating effect. They had a choice. Either ignore the urban heating effect and compile average atmospheric temperatures from the data untouched or try to adjust some data to remove the urban heating effect.

Using the data untouched would create apparently greater warming, but would present a known false picture of what was occurring in the earth's atmosphere. Adjusting some data would require methodologies and judgments that could be criticized as inadequate or too aggressive. Universally, scientists had avoided falsity. Some had made adjustments to specific data to try to account for urbanization effects; others had omitted suspect weather stations in their compilations.

When scientists had compared rural land compilations against all-encompassing land compilations, they had found that urban heating had only a small effect on the compilations of average atmospheric temperature. At most, these unaccounted for effects had raised the estimated land temperature trends by ten percent of the measured trend. Still, for some people, the urban heating effect had remained an uncertainty. They had asserted that different adjustments should have been made or more weather stations should have been considered suspect and removed from the compilations.

Marilyn, Karen, and Paul reached the bottom of the stairs. Marilyn opened another door, leading to a hallway just like the one above, but shorter.

Surely, Marilyn is finished, thought Karen to herself as they exited the stairwell. Wrong. Marilyn continued talking rapidly until they reached a door at the other end of this hallway.

Marilyn said that a third uncertainty in comparing average atmospheric temperature calculations from one year to another had come from modernization. That is, some old weather stations had been replaced with new stations in different locations. Even small changes of location, such as moving the standard thermometer from one porch of a building to another porch several stories above, had been shown in some cases to cause different temperature readings for exactly the same weather conditions. These differences, however, had been more random than the urban heating effect. They had not necessarily been skewed toward calculating higher average atmospheric temperatures. Again, scientists had been aware of these problems and had adopted techniques to minimize them.

Marilyn stopped talking just two steps before the door at the end of the hallway. Karen saw a small sign above it, reading simply "Analysis Center."

Marilyn, Karen, and Paul entered the Analysis Center from the rear. The room was shaped like a small lecture hall. Its layout was similar to, but much smaller than, NASA's flight control center used for space vehicle launches. Two large screens dominated the wall at front center. The left screen showed a huge map of the world with many bright dots scattered around the map. The right screen showed columns of data. Three rows of desk-like surfaces faced these screens, each row being higher than the one in front of it. The surfaces were divided into several stations, each with a dedicated computer screen and a movable chair.

Karen quickly counted twelve screens and eight people, the back row being empty. While counting, she noticed that the display shown on the right screen changed to a graph. Impressive technology, she thought, but what was it really used for?

As Marilyn, Karen, and Paul stood in the back of the Center, Marilyn began talking again, this time less rapidly and more quietly, almost in a whisper. Despite her apparently impromptu decision to come to the Analysis Center, no one here seemed surprised to see them.

"ETOP's surface measurement program is designed to eliminate all of the uncertainties we just told you about," said Marilyn. "We have nearly four thousand stations carefully placed throughout the world. Each station measures temperature, humidity, precipitation, and atmospheric gas concentrations. Data are transmitted upward to satellites. The satellites then re-transmit the data ultimately to ETOP's headquarters. These stations are spread much more uniformly across the earth than the weather stations that were used for previous data compilations."

"See there, our stations are shown by lighted dots," she added, pointing toward the screen with the map.

Karen saw three different colors of dots—red, yellow, and green.

"Red dots show the locations of stations that were the same as weather stations that had provided temperature records before ETOP," said Marilyn.

Marilyn pointed out many red dots in North America, Europe, and Asia. Fewer red dots were located in South America, Africa, and Australia. Still fewer were located in the oceans, especially the oceans in the Southern Hemisphere.

"We still use pre-existing weather stations in fully urbanized areas or fully rural areas," said Marilyn. "No land-use changes are affecting those measurements. We also use all of the pre-existing weather stations in Antarctica and the Arctic."

"Yellow dots show the locations of new stations on land. We created new stations in different locations to replace some weather stations that had existed in 2018 in areas that were just then urbanizing. That was done to avoid an urban heating effect. We added other new land stations in regions that previously had too few weather stations contributing data to previous temperature compilations."

Marilyn pointed to the yellow dots in Africa and South America as examples.

"The green dots show the locations of new stations in the oceans," continued Marilyn. "Mostly, these are manned ships and unmanned buoys that remain stationary at a particular longitude and latitude. A few new stations are located on small islands."

Karen could see that most of the green dots were found in the South Pacific Ocean, South Atlantic Ocean, and Indian Ocean.

"Land-based stations are still more densely located than oceanic stations," said Marilyn. "We need more land stations because temperatures and weather systems are much less uniform over land than over the oceans."

Karen started to ask about the screen on the right side, but again Marilyn preempted her question.

"This screen on the right can display any data summary or compilation that the ETOP computers can make," said Marilyn with obvious pride. "We use it when someone finds a trend, or an odd datum, or a comparison, that we should discuss as a group. This is how we first identified the full cooling effects of the Soufrière eruption at the end of 2021."

Karen was impressed again with how ETOP was gathering data, but now she was also a little confused. If ETOP relied solely on data from its network, how could it do the compilation Karen wanted? She could see by the dots on the map that the number of ETOP stations in the United States was clearly less than the number of National Weather Service locations. She became concerned that ETOP's data would be too widely dispersed for her to be able to match ETOP's weather data to the information she got from her questionnaire to USDA extension offices.

In her zeal to describe what ETOP was doing, Marilyn did not notice Karen's developing confusion and concern. Neither did Paul, absorbed as he was in the right screen as Marilyn described its purpose.

This time, Karen stopped Marilyn with a question.

"I'm troubled," she began. "How can you do the comparison I asked for? You don't have enough ETOP stations in the United States to cover all the places I want."

Startled by Karen's question, Paul and Marilyn first looked at each other. Of course, Karen was right, they communicated without speaking. They had both gone astray prattling on about ETOP's work when they should have been focusing more on Karen's project. Paul spoke first.

"You are right," he said.

Karen smiled and nodded as she asked herself why she bothered to come to ETOP if they could not do what she asked for in the first place.

"We are not just going to use data from ETOP's stations," Paul quickly added.

"You're not?" responded Karen.

"We have a lot more data than that," said Paul.

"Oh?" said Karen cautiously.

"Here, sit down," said Paul to Karen, as he pulled up one of the chairs from the back row for her to use. Then he and Marilyn moved two other chairs to face her. They all sat down, forming a triangle.

"We decided long ago to use complete data from all US weather stations as a check on the weather data collected by ETOP's stations in the United States," began Paul. "We also collected the historic data from those stations. Those data cover more than one hundred years of measurements. Just two years ago we decided to create a program that can compare current data to those historic data. We now have plenty of data and a program to do the comparisons you described."

"We also have been collecting temperature data from the sources used by the old methods to calculate average atmospheric temperatures," added Marilyn. "And we have been calculating temperature changes using the old methods as well."

"This is one of the best decisions I made back in the beginning of ETOP," said Paul. "We can compare ETOP's global numbers to the compilations from the old methods for the same time periods. We have learned that the old methods are a lot more accurate than we had expected. During the last twelve years, we have strongly confirmed the accuracy of one of the previous methods and have generally confirmed the accuracy of all of the old methods, at least as they had been refined as of 2018. We can now make valid comparisons to average atmospheric temperatures back much further than just 2020 when our network began collecting data.

"We think that we can make the most valid comparisons back to about 1950. Before 1950, records of weather station measurements were affected by World War I and the mess preceding and during World War II. Many gaps in consistent measurements exist from the regions that were directly affected by conflict. Also, records from other parts of the world were fewer and fewer as we traced data back further and further from 1950. We have less confidence in the accuracy of annual averages calculated for periods earlier than 1950 simply because the sampling is not as good."

Marilyn got up, moved her chair in front of one of the computer screens and motioned for Karen to come watch. Marilyn sat down and clicked a few icons. A graph appeared on the screen that somehow looked familiar to Karen.

Of course, thought Karen, it was a graph she had seen in ETOP's report to Congress. This was the one that depicted changes in the average atmospheric temperature at the earth's surface. Now Karen understood why three temperature graphs were in that report. ETOP was measuring atmospheric temperatures in three different ways, and at different parts of the atmosphere. She now knew that ETOP used thermometers to measure surface air temperatures, radiosondes to measure air temperatures at many altitudes, and MSUs to measure air temperatures at two altitude ranges. Karen realized that comparisons among the graphs had to be tempered by knowledge about what was being measured, and how. She had only begun to get that knowledge herself.

Marilyn broke into Karen's train of thought.

"These are ETOP's data only, so they start in 2020," said Marilyn. "See that the average atmospheric temperature for 2031 is about 0.2 degrees Celsius higher than the average for 2020. That's a big increase for just twelve years. However, you can see that annual average temperatures bounce around some. The overall trend is upward, but even that trend is not uniform."

Karen leaned forward to see the screen more clearly.

"Look here in 2021," said Marilyn, pointing to the left side of the graph. "Average temperatures dropped in 2021 and did not rebound for three years. Soufrière caused that."

Soufrière? thought Karen. Marilyn had mentioned that name earlier. Before Karen could ask about it, Marilyn had switched to another graph.

"Here's the average temperature curve going back to 1950 using the earlier compilation method that Paul mentioned," continued Marilyn. "Look at the last twelve years. That curve is almost identical to ETOP's. Now go back to 1950 on the left. See that the average temperatures rose overall to 2020, but not uniformly. There's even a decline in 1991 which did not rebound for two years. That was caused by Pinatubo."

"What's Pinatubo," Karen asked.

"Oops, I'm sorry. We are so used to these names that we forget most people do not know what they are," said Marilyn. "Pinatubo is Mount Pinatubo in the Philippine Islands. It's a volcano on the Island of Luzon. In June 1991, Mount Pinatubo erupted with huge explosions over several weeks. Pinatubo sent an enormous amount of volcanic ash and sulfur dioxide into the earth's stratosphere. The sulfur dioxide remained in the stratosphere for many months. While there, it reflected a lot of sunlight back to space. The earth's atmosphere actually cooled until the sulfur dioxide gradually dropped out of the stratosphere."

"And Soufrière was another volcano?" asked Karen.

"That's right," answered Marilyn. "Soufrière is found at the eastern end of the Caribbean Sea. It's on Saint Vincent Island. Its eruptions at the end of 2021 were even larger than Pinatubo's. In fact, its tephra load was four times as large."

"There you go again," interjected Karen. "What's tephra?"

"Just a vulcanologist's term for all the material ejected by an … explosive volcano," said Marilyn. She had almost said stratovolcano, but caught herself before using yet another technical term.

"You see, Karen, Pinatubo and Soufrière masked for a few years what was really happening with atmospheric temperatures," continued Marilyn. "But they also had some benefits from a scientific perspective, especially Pinatubo. The first computer models had predicted increases in average atmospheric temperatures that were much greater than later observed. Scientists were just beginning to appreciate the cooling effects of sulfur dioxide particles and other aerosols when Pinatubo erupted. Pinatubo was a huge natural test of revised models. The models were refined again based on Pinatubo's effects. By 2021, most models had been refined so well that they had correctly predicted the observed effects of the sulfur dioxide from Soufrière."

"Careful, Marilyn," interjected Paul. "Don't give Karen the idea that those atmospheric temperature models are perfect. I've already told her that they have some serious qualifications."

"Right. I didn't mean to mislead," said Marilyn. "But a few models are pretty good."

Karen watched Paul and Marilyn spar for a few minutes about the merits of several different computer models.

While listening to them, Karen tried to figure out whether any of this debate could help her understand the uniformly decreased crop yields that were reported in her USDA data. She could not see how an average temperature increase of less than one degree would make any difference at all. Variations far greater than that occurred every year at every farm.

Paul and Marilyn finished their mini-debate with a draw. They agreed only that the increases in average atmospheric temperature that ETOP had measured were closer to the models that had predicted relatively large increases than the models that had predicted relatively small increases.

As he looked back toward Karen, Paul could see what had by now become a familiar expression on her face. She was trying to think of an answer to an unexpressed question. Paul would make sure that he found out what that question was and would try to answer it.

CHAPTER 10

CONSEQUENCES

"We went astray again, didn't we?" asked Paul.

"Pretty much," said Karen politely. "I just don't see how such small temperature increases will make any difference for people like the farmers I deal with."

"You'd be right if these little temperature changes were uniform everywhere and nothing else changed," said Paul. "But that is not what we are dealing with here. The changes in average atmospheric temperatures that we have measured are not uniform everywhere. They reflect some greatly increased annual temperatures in some regions and even decreased annual temperatures in a few other regions. You have to understand what changes in average temperatures really mean.

"Temperature is just one way to measure heat. When the average atmospheric temperature increases, atmospheric heat has increased. Heat exchange equilibriums between the atmosphere and oceans or land will change. It's those equilibriums that create our weather. The amount of rain and wind and storms and other weather phenomena are all derived largely from those equilibriums.

"As you know, the average weather over time is what we all call 'climate.' So these little world-wide temperature changes can ultimately alter heat exchange equilibriums, which in turn can change local climates. Those local changes could be significant. I think that these changes would affect your farmers."

"Probably so, but climate change sounds so gradual," said Karen. "Even if temperatures continue to rise, climate changes must take a long time."

"Maybe yes, … maybe no," said Paul, hesitating. He paused. Should he share with Karen the phenomenon that he and Marilyn really feared? Paul had described it years ago in conferences with climatologists, but he had avoided its reference in official ETOP publications. No ETOP report even hinted at it. He could not afford accusations of alarmist science and consequent decreased support for ETOP's mission.

He glanced at Marilyn. She made a slight, almost imperceptible gesture conveying "no."

Paul tempered his comments.

"We are just not sure how fast local climate changes will occur under changing conditions," said Paul. "As I said before, temperature changes are not uniform around the world when the average atmospheric temperature increases. You heard Marilyn and me discuss some of the computer models that try to predict changes in the earth's average atmospheric temperature. Imagine trying to predict climate changes.

"The climate of a region includes not only temperature patterns, but also precipitation and wind patterns. That's what people want and need to know. That's why many people have tried to create computer models just for this purpose. As I said earlier, we even have some here at ETOP. These models are unbelievably complicated. They require huge computers to do all their computations.

ETOP has models for nine different regions in the United States, including overlaps into Canada and northern Mexico. We also have models for four regions of Europe and for the central Mideast. The past predictions from these models have, at best, only crudely matched what actually has occurred in the regions modeled. That's why we have not published their predictions. Even the latest of these models have only confirmed what we already knew in 2018."

"What was that?" asked Karen.

"That what we know is that we do not know," said Paul.

"What we know is that we do not know?" asked Karen.

"That's right. What we know is that we do not know," repeated Paul. "Remember when I told you about the 2018 Senate hearings? Remember that 'absolute certainty' came to rule the questions?"

"I think so," stammered Karen, not sure that she remembered this point. Obviously it was very important to Paul.

Paul continued. "Climate change models simply cannot predict with certainty what will occur in a specific region when the earth's average atmospheric temperature reaches a certain level. That was true in 2018 and it is still true today. In the Senate hearings, some of us tried to get the politicians to look at risks rather than certainties. We might just as well have barked at the moon. They dismissed all of the possibilities or probabilities as doom and gloom prophesies with no proof. They just refused to see that when atmospheric temperatures continue to rise, the least likely occurrence is no climate changes at all."

"But you got ETOP from those hearings," said Karen, trying to be optimistic.

"ETOP was needed politically, not scientifically," said Paul. "Look at the comparisons on the screen there," he added, pointing to the graphs that remained on the computer screen in front of Marilyn. "There are no real differences between the averages measured by ETOP and the old methods. We've spent twelve years measuring the problem and no significant resources trying to prevent it.

"Too many people put on blinders that kept them from the hard work of looking seriously at real risks. Those people believed that climate changes were mere speculation. They did not see that a 'do nothing' attitude was based on the greatest speculation of all. That speculation assumed that the largest changes in the chemistry of the earth's atmosphere in hundreds of thousands of years would not affect local climates at all.

"Other people expressed an attitude that climate changes were inevitable anyway so everyone would simply have to adjust to them. They often assumed that adaptation would be technologically possible and economically easy. The temperature changes that ETOP has measured were inevitable only because people chose to make them so. We may have missed opportunities to change at a critical time."

Karen had not expected this second outburst from ETOP's director. Before coming to ETOP, she had thought that he would simply introduce her to one or more ETOP scientists who would do the actual work to make the comparisons she wanted for her USDA project. On the airplane she had developed a hunch that ETOP held a key to understanding why the United States had universally odd weather in 2032, if in fact her project would show that this was true. Her bungled story and strategy of delay had exposed her to much more information than she had expected. Now Paul Anderson revealed great frustration about inaction to avoid possible climate changes. *Why was he so perturbed? Were major climate changes closer than ETOP's reported graphs indicated? How would they know?*

Karen kept her questions to herself. She tried to return to why she had come to ETOP in the first place. Her USDA questionnaires consistently identified odd weather as the cause of reduced crop yields in each extension office district. Perhaps universally odd weather was more than an anomaly. Maybe it was a harbinger of climate changes in the United States. She could not dismiss this possibility. She decided to find out more, without revealing what she knew already.

"If climate change is happening in a region, how will you know?" asked Karen.

Paul and Marilyn looked at each other as Karen finished her question. They both knew that Karen had asked exactly the question that had been vexing them for a decade.

Paul began to wonder whether Karen's project was something more than she was telling them. She had not talked much about it since she first came to ETOP this morning. She had been uncommonly inquisitive about everything else. Still, her question was legitimate and related to the topics they had been discussing. Paul had a ready response.

"Secondary indications," said Paul.

"Secondary indications? What's that?" asked Karen.

"Let's give her some examples," interjected Marilyn.

"Go ahead," said Paul, knowing that Marilyn knew as much about this subject as any scientist on the planet.

"Let's look at glaciers," said Marilyn. "Starting before the 1990s, naturalists began noticing that high altitude glaciers throughout the Northern Hemisphere were shrinking. Many have since melted away."

"And then around 2000, scientists identified a trend that ice in the Arctic Ocean was melting more in the summer than had been observed thirty years earlier," added Paul. "Of course, summer sea ice did not decrease in every year measured then or since. Variable weather dynamics can still affect that amount. But the trend to less and less Arctic sea ice is unmistakable. Northern permafrost has also gotten warmer in those places where it has been monitored."

"Many non-scientists saw these Arctic changes as an indication that the earth was warming somewhat," said Marilyn. "Then, when hearing of instances where a few glaciers were expanding, such as in western Norway, or when hearing that sea ice around Antarctica had been modestly increasing, they changed their minds. The public perception did not understand that all of these changes reflect a lot more than local warming or cooling.

"Precipitation and wind patterns were changing also. In other words, some local climates were changing, and changing very fast. The flora and fauna of these regions have been hugely affected.

"The death of many polar bears is the most noticeable and publicized example from the widespread warming in northern Canada. Many bears have starved because they have not had their customary ice flows from which to ambush seals and other sea going prey. It's now doubtful that polar bears will survive as a wild species. Their demise means that seal populations have exploded. Seals are now so numerous that some people consider them to be a threat to many northern fisheries."

"The polar bear story is just one example of a native species changing its survival range," said Paul. "Polar bears individually cover such a large range that their demise shows climate changes over a large area. Probably more significant, but much harder to spot, are changes in the survival ranges of insects, other invertebrates, and small plants. These will clearly signal local climate changes if they are found."

"Changes in forests can be a secondary indication also, but they will be hard to identify at first," added Marilyn. "What appears to be a healthy forest may actually be dying if replacement seedlings are unable to grow or mature trees are stressed because climatic conditions have changed."

"Some secondary indications will be problems as well as indications," said Paul. "If insect pests such as European corn borers expand their survival ranges, many farmers will have to contend with them for the first time."

"Secondary indications are not restricted to changes in natural plants and animals," said Marilyn. "Increased insurance claims for weather related damages to structures could show climate changes. Of course, increased claims would have to be adjusted for increased numbers of structures in the stricken areas. Even declining crop yields could show climate changes, especially if the same crops have been planted over many years with the same methods."

Karen cringed. Had ETOP already discovered the declines in US crop production that she had observed in 2031? Maybe ETOP had already identified those declines as a potential secondary indication. If so, of what was it an indication? Karen remained silent. Her projection that US crop production would decline further in 2032 was still top secret. Secretary Rand was very clear about that. This whole discussion with Paul and Marilyn was getting uncomfortably close to that secret. She had to change subjects without revealing her concerns. That meant waiting until any reference to crops ended.

Paul and Marilyn continued speaking, unaware of Karen's dilemma.

"You know, Karen, we have a small group at ETOP whose mission is to read widely to see whether any secondary indications have been discovered," said Paul. "It's difficult work. People who write articles about discoveries may not suspect that their discoveries could be secondary indications of climate change. Our people have to imagine at first how some new finding could be a secondary indication. Then they need to consult with other scientists here and elsewhere to see if their imaginations have any basis in good science."

"Something may happen that we did not at first recognize as climate related," said Marilyn.

"Undoubtedly there will be some surprises, too," added Paul.

Karen saw her opening.

"Is absolute certainty about these changes still politically required today?" she asked.

"Generally so in the United States, with a few exceptions in the Senate," answered Paul.

"The Europeans and most of the rest of the world discarded that notion long ago," added Marilyn.

Karen glanced at her watch. She had only a half hour remaining at ETOP. Her delay strategy had worked.

"At least my project doesn't get into this quagmire," said Karen, refocusing discussion on her primary mission at ETOP. "I think that my project will be far less daunting than the many complicated analyses you do here at ETOP every day."

Paul and Marilyn nodded agreement. Like Karen, they also noticed that Karen had little time left on her visit. They all quickly left ETOP's Analysis Center and returned to the main conference room on the first floor.

Karen succinctly described what she wanted. She gave Paul and Marilyn each a single sheet outline of her project with six bullet points.

Karen's preparation paid off. Only one of the points created real discussion. That point covered only temperature comparisons.

Karen wanted ETOP to compare for each location the annual temperature averages in 2031 and 2032 to the annual temperature averages from 2030 back over a hundred years to 1920.

Marilyn said that ETOP could do this comparison, but that Karen had to be cautious about some of the numbers. She said that ETOP had the data, but the annual temperature averages so far back into the twentieth century may not be correct for each location. One or more of the uncertainties she had described for Karen earlier could apply. Except for this qualification, neither Paul nor Marilyn suggested alternative approaches in the short time remaining. Marilyn promised that Karen's comparisons would be done by September 24th.

Karen was pleasantly surprised at how quickly Marilyn thought she could compile Karen's comparisons. Even if she questioned in her own mind why this was possible, no time remained to ask. It was time to go.

Paul and Marilyn walked with Karen past ETOP's security gate to the car then awaiting Karen in ETOP's parking lot at the entrance walkway. They shook hands and bid her a safe return flight to Washington. Paul and Marilyn waved to Karen as she and ETOP's intern sped out of the parking lot and entrance road to retrace their path to Denver International Airport.

"Interesting lady," said Paul, as he and Marilyn turned back toward the headquarters building.

"We gave her an earful," said Marilyn.

"Indeed. Do you think she suspected?" asked Paul.

"Doubtful," answered Marilyn. "You had a close call at one point, but you recovered nicely. There was too much for her to absorb to figure it out herself."

"Good," said Paul.

Karen returned to Washington late that evening, exhausted from a long and intense day. She felt that her trip to ETOP had been a success. Her trip had been prompted by the data summaries her staff had prepared from just two questions in Karen's USDA questionnaire. During the next two weeks, her staff assembled and summarized the answers to the remaining questions. These summaries created other revelations. Most important, President Clark had been wrong. The new petroleum reality was not causing US crop declines. Not a single extension office director had identified high fertilizer prices as a cause of the declining crop yields reported from his or her district.

Karen told Secretary Rand this result the day before she left for France for her postponed visit to see Marie Leclerc. She expected him to convey it promptly to President Clark. No doubt the president would not like it.

Karen did not tell Rand about the odd weather that her questionnaires had revealed. She wanted first to have ETOP's compilation to be sure that hard data supported odd weather as the most likely cause of poor crop yields. She was confident that she would get ETOP's comparisons before September 25th, the day after she would be coming back from France.

CHAPTER 11

STORY

Karen arrived on schedule at Charles de Gaulle Airport near Paris after an all night flight across the North Atlantic Ocean. Although she could have rented a car at de Gaulle and driven to Nantes, she always preferred to take the Metro subway into Paris to spend a few hours in that magical city before leaving for Nantes. Besides, riding the TGV from Paris to Nantes was far easier than driving.

Karen checked her suitcase at a Metro station in central Paris and rode an escalator to the ground surface. As she exited the Metro, the distinctive buildings of central Paris captivated her again. She walked from block to block for two hours under a sunny sky to re-immerse herself in the city. Aromas of freshly baked bread, storefronts with artistically displayed food and goods, people enjoying their coffee at outside café tables, and even background sounds from cars and buses brought back warm memories on this cool September morning. She passed a number of historic landmarks, but paid more attention to the people and kiosks on the sidewalks. Everyone seemed to be in good spirits, chattering with friends on the sidewalks and shopkeepers nearby.

At noon, Karen returned to the Metro station to pick up her suitcase. She then took the Metro to the Montparnasse train station. When she arrived there, she noticed immediately that the station was much more crowded than she remembered from two years ago. Evidently, high gasoline prices from the new petroleum reality had caused even more people to use France's excellent trains over automobiles.

The TGV ride from Paris to Nantes was rapid and smooth. The French countryside glowed under a bright afternoon sun. Despite the beauty, Karen watched for any signs of problems in the many wheat fields she passed. Perhaps France had experienced production declines like the United States. But most fields had already been harvested, so she could tell nothing about their yields. In less than two hours, the TGV pulled into the Nantes train station.

Karen stepped from the TGV onto the station platform, looking for Marie Leclerc. Finding her would not be easy. Although a very pretty lady, Marie's average height and weight and dark brown hair made her blend in with a typical French crowd. Marie saw Karen first. Marie's hand shot into the air, waving wildly to draw Karen's attention. In moments, Marie greeted Karen with her usual Gaulic enthusiasm.

Marie was by far the most talkative scientist Karen had ever known. Even before they got into Marie's Renault, Karen had learned that Annette had just gone to Paris on a post-graduate art scholarship, that Claude was expanding his bakery, and that their toy poodle had injured its foot chasing the neighbor's cat from their small yard.

Despite Marie's rambunctious driving, they arrived safely at the Leclerc home in the northern part of Nantes. That afternoon and the next three days were filled with endless chatter, mostly from Marie. Sumptuous eating abounded as well. Claude's bakery had made special pastries that Marie and Karen consumed in such great numbers that daily resupplies were needed. The pastries were great, but the gastronomic prize belonged to Claude's famous escargots. He fixed them as an appetizer on the second night that Karen was there. Claude had made his escargots each time that Karen had visited, and each time they seemed to be even better than the time before.

In what seemed like a wink of an eye, September 23 arrived. Karen had to leave to go home to the United States. The nail-biting car ride with Marie to the Nantes train station, the TGV's speedy passage through the French countryside, and the crowded Metro ride to de Gaulle Airport had Karen in the terminal awaiting her flight well before its scheduled departure. She boarded her plane before dark.

The now aged Boeing 777 jet sped down the de Gaulle runway and swiftly climbed into the air to cruising altitude. Karen leaned back, closing her eyes to recount and savor her time with Marie.

Nearing sleep, suddenly Karen became wide awake and sat up, as if startled by a noise. She had just realized something very odd about her visit with Marie. Unnoticed in the frenetic activity of her visit,

Karen now recognized that Marie had never spoken a word about her experiences in the North Atlantic Ocean this year. Nor did she take Karen to the port to see SMER's ship. Although Karen had asked a few general questions about Marie's latest voyage, Marie had never answered any of them. Instead, Karen now saw that Marie had skillfully avoided any answers by banter that led away from the question. How odd, Karen thought, remembering that in past years Marie always had some tales of adventure about her summer voyage. Why would Marie, of all people, be silent?

Karen puzzled over this question for several minutes. What was different about this year? Of course, Karen's trip had to be postponed because Marie had to spend an extra week at sea. That was certainly one difference. What else? Karen could think of nothing else.

She reflected on that postponement. How did this come about? Claude had called Karen. What did he say? That Marie had to spend an extra week at sea. Did he say anything else? Karen thought hard. All that she could remember was his saying something about fresh water samples.

Fresh water samples? In the ocean? That made no sense.

Or did it? Karen remembered that Paul Anderson and Marilyn Sawyer at ETOP talked about secondary indications of climate change, and that there would be surprises. Fresh water in the ocean would surely be a surprise. Could fresh water also be a secondary indication? Karen stopped herself. She was probably reading too much into what she remembered that Claude had told her.

When Karen returned to her USDA office the next day, a package from ETOP was at her desk. She knew that it had to be the comparisons she had asked ETOP to make. Somehow, she was not surprised that Marilyn Sawyer had finished her project ahead of time.

As summarized in Karen's outline, ETOP's project was to compare surface air temperatures and precipitation recorded at all active weather stations in the United States in 2031 and 2032 to historic air temperatures and precipitation. Although the basic idea was simple, its execution was not.

Karen recognized that almost no annual temperature or precipitation figures would match precisely the averaged figures for any location. She had created a scheme to determine if differences between 2031 or 2032 figures and historic averages were significant. She had asked

ETOP to compare 2031 and 2032 figures not only to historic averages, but also to bands of values around those averages. Two bands were chosen. One would encompass fifty percent of all values recorded in the historic time period. The other would encompass ninety percent of all values recorded. These kinds of comparisons required huge numbers of calculations.

Karen purposely did not ask ETOP to make any summary analyses of the data comparisons she asked ETOP to make. She even asked that the weather stations be arranged alphabetically rather than by state or region. That arrangement would mask the regional trends that Karen's USDA questionnaires had uncovered.

Despite her fatigue and jet lag, Karen could see by scanning the data in ETOP's package that Marilyn's compilations did exactly what Karen wanted. Then, using pre-selected weather stations as samples, she looked through the mound of comparisons. These samples confirmed the qualitative information she had obtained in her USDA questionnaires. Most air temperature and precipitation figures for 2032 fell outside the ninety percent band. The weather at these stations was clearly different than average, but generally not so different as to be record-setting. Now Karen needed to see if the differences were consistently the same by geographic region. She asked one of her staff members who had compiled information from her questionnaire to reorder the data from ETOP.

Less than a week later, on September 30, Karen's staff member gave Karen a neatly printed volume of ETOP's data that had been reorganized by geographic location. The data revealed an unmistakable story. In 2032 every region of the United States had experienced significantly different temperatures and precipitation from historic averages. And the differences matched the oddities that had been reported in the answers to Karen's USDA questionnaire. The data for 2031 were similar but not as extreme.

What should she do now? She could not very well call the president to tell him what she had found. She did not feel comfortable yet in talking to Secretary Rand, either. This year and last year could just be statistical flukes. Paul Anderson told her clearly that odd weather for just one or two years does not show climate change. Longer periods of oddities were needed. How could she know if these odd weather data meant anything?

Secondary indications, she thought to herself. What about the fresh water near Greenland that Claude Leclerc had mentioned?

Karen did not dare to contact Marie about her recollection of a few words from Marie's husband. That contact could lead to Marie's asking why she was so interested in a fresh water possibility. These inquires in turn could create an awkward discussion with Karen having to be vague. The US crop production problem was still top secret. Instead, Karen decided to tell ETOP about Marie Leclerc and SMER.

Karen found Marilyn's card in the upper drawer of her desk, reached for her telephone, and punched in Marilyn's direct dial number.

"Hi Marilyn, this is Karen Lewis."

"Karen. Good to hear from you."

"Thanks for the compilation. It's exactly what I wanted."

"Good. The data bands were tricky. We finally adjusted our program. Then our Cray computers went to work. We did your compilation in just three hours. That's why I sent it to you early."

Karen paused, thinking about how best to phrase what she really needed to say.

"That's not the main reason for my call," said Karen.

"Oh?" said Marilyn.

"Remember when you and Paul told me about secondary indications of climate change?" said Karen.

"Sure."

"What about fresh water in the ocean?"

"Fresh water? Where?"

"In the North Atlantic Ocean."

"Near Greenland?"

"Probably."

The telephone line was then silent so long that Karen began to think that Marilyn had been disconnected.

"Marilyn?" said Karen.

"I'm here," answered Marilyn. She then spoke slowly and deliberately. "That could be very significant," said Marilyn. "It depends upon how much water, how fresh it is, and where it is relative to Greenland. A lot of fresh water could impact the North Atlantic Drift."

"I see," said Karen slowly.

"Is this just a hypothetical question?" asked Marilyn.

"I'm not sure," answered Karen. "I'll tell you a story and let you decide."

Karen then told Marilyn about her friendship with Marie Leclerc. She described Marie's role with SMER and the summer voyages Marie took annually in the northern North Atlantic Ocean. Karen recounted how Marie had been uncharacteristically silent about her voyage this past summer. Then she told Marilyn about Claude Leclerc's telephone call when he postponed Karen's trip to France. She told Marilyn that Claude had said that Marie had to stay at sea for another week because she had to take more "fresh water" samples.

As Karen had hoped, Marilyn expressed interest in her tale. Karen gave Marilyn enough information about SMER to allow Marilyn, or someone else at ETOP, to find data that SMER had published about salinity measurements made during Marie's voyages. She felt that someone at ETOP would understand those measurements much better than she could. Maybe this past summer's data would even be available already on a SMER website.

Marilyn said that she would look for data reported by SMER. On that positive note to Karen, their call ended.

After their call, Karen began to think of ways that United States crop data could be integrated with the weather comparisons done for her by ETOP. Karen expected to receive the largest group of solid numbers on US crop production and yields on October 7th, now just a week away. As soon as she got those data, she could juxtapose them against the regional breakdowns of ETOP's temperature and precipitation comparisons. Then she could tell Secretary Rand what she had found. Perhaps by then Marilyn would have found and evaluated SMER's data to see whether they had any bearing on the odd weather revealed by ETOP'S comparisons.

Back at ETOP, Marilyn walked immediately to Paul's office after Karen's call to tell him what Karen had told her. Paul was skeptical.

"Marilyn, I think that Karen is reading far too much into her visit with Marie Leclerc," said Paul. "Plus, she is reconstructing a short telephone call that she had several weeks ago with Claude Leclerc."

"I understand all of that," said Marilyn. "I still think that Karen is on to something important. I don't know what that is exactly. Her comparisons project was unusual in the way that it was constructed. Now she has a fresh water caper that she wants us to investigate.

Something is troubling Karen. Otherwise, she would not be telling me about Marie Leclerc based on such thin information."

"Why do you think that Karen's project was so unusual?" asked Paul, testing Marilyn's hunch.

"Paul, Karen's comparison's project was very odd. She did not want any summaries prepared, although we easily could have done those after the main comparisons were completed. She also asked for the data to be arranged alphabetically by weather station name rather than by state or region. It was as if she did not want to know, or, more likely, did not want us to know, whether her data show regional patterns. The data themselves also are odd. The conditions reported at US weather stations this year were nearly all outside the ninety percent band of historic conditions, even though few were record-setting."

Marilyn's description of Karen's comparisons project convinced Paul that her hunch could be correct. Karen may very well have known more than she was revealing. If Karen was troubled enough to tell them about Marie Leclerc, then they should at least see if SMER had found anything interesting. Paul agreed with Marilyn that Karen's story deserved follow-up.

Marilyn promptly assigned one of ETOP's "secondary indications" personnel to find all data published by SMER on North Atlantic Ocean weather, currents, and water, especially anything pertaining to 2032.

CHAPTER 12

DECLINES

Karen Lewis was among the first people to receive monthly USDA compilations on US crop production and yields. These compilations were now fully automated. Statistics were available within a few days after field data had been entered locally at the end of each month. Karen received her copy for September 2032 as expected on October 6. She examined it immediately.

Karen's summertime projections had been accurate. Production for every crop in every region had declined from 2031. Food shortages in the United States were not imminent, but low production surely would push food prices up in the next few months. Exports probably would fall to a historic low in the twenty-first century.

Karen was no politician, but even she could see that this revelation could become a major issue in President Clark's reelection campaign. She did not have to wait long to have this possibility confirmed.

Shortly after he was elected in 2028, President Clark had created a small personal staff to identify and follow issues that might become important later during his presidency. After Secretary Rand told him in August 2032 about a food shortage possibility in the United States, he directed one member of that staff to collect and assess USDA data on crop production as soon as they were published. That member received September's statistics as quickly as Karen. He wasted no time in studying them. Within a day, he told President Clark about the crop production declines evident in the USDA statistics. President Clark, in turn, demanded to see Rand in his office the next day. He said that he wanted to see Karen Lewis as well.

When Rand called her to come to his office on the afternoon of October 7, Karen naturally assumed that he wanted to discuss the September crop production reports. She did not expect to be told to get ready for a meeting with President Clark the next morning. She also did not expect to be told that Rand had never told the president the results of Karen's USDA questionnaires. At this point, President Clark did not know that the new petroleum reality played no role at all in the reduced crop yields occurring in 2032. Now, Karen had to help Rand get ready to tell the president not just one, but two, unpleasant facts. Reduced US crop production was now a genuine problem and the president was wrong in his strong belief that the new petroleum reality was the culprit causing this problem.

Karen returned quickly to her office to organize her thoughts, the new crop production data, and the results from her questionnaire. She also performed quick comparisons against the odd weather data that ETOP had compiled for her. Karen knew that she would have only a half hour with Secretary Rand the next morning before they had to leave for the White House. She needed a simple but accurate summary that Rand could assimilate and use to augment his own ideas about the causes of declining crop production.

While immersed in her work, and despite another dictate that she wanted to be left alone, Karen sensed that her office door was being opened gently. Karen looked up. Soon her secretary stood in full view in the doorway.

With understandable trepidation, her secretary said that Karen had received what she thought was another important telephone call. Karen agreed when she heard the two names. The call was from Marilyn Sawyer and Paul Anderson.

Marilyn did most of the talking. She said that ETOP's researcher had found numerous SMER publications on North Atlantic fisheries, but none on physical aspects of the North Atlantic Ocean. One SMER article showed a photograph of a SMER ship that matched what Karen had described, but no article mentioned summertime voyages in the North Atlantic near Greenland. It was as if these voyages had never occurred. Marilyn emphasized that this was very unusual for a nonprofit group like SMER. Normally, these groups tried to get their research out to the public as quickly as possible.

Marilyn ended their call by saying that she and Paul could not speculate about what SMER may have found based on a cryptic statement about fresh water by someone who was not even there. They needed hard, reliable data, if any existed. She suggested that Karen might be able to use her friendship with Marie to get whatever data SMER had collected.

Karen could sense that Marilyn and Paul doubted that SMER was actually collecting data, or that if it were, the data were comprehensive enough to be useful.

Karen was now perplexed. Karen had seen SMER's ship during other visits with Marie at Nantes. Marie could not have been making up stories about her summertime voyages. Did SMER have some reason not to publish Marie's measurements? Were they just too repetitive to have scientific value? Did they reveal nothing new? If so, why did they continue voyages for fourteen years? Karen knew that she could not answer these questions now and certainly not on her own. Her search for the answers would have to wait. She had more pressing concerns to get ready for tomorrow's meeting with President Clark.

Karen's half hour with Bill Rand was just enough for him to understand the essence of Karen's summary. During their limousine ride to the White House, he told Karen in almost a whisper what he was prepared to tell the president. Even though White House limousine drivers had full security clearance, he did not want anyone other than Karen to hear his opinions.

Just like government offices in France, in this era of tight security, even US Cabinet members had to pass through weapons detection devices when entering the White House. Secretary Rand had reminded Karen of this fact before leaving the USDA building. Neither he nor she carried anything that might require extra scanning. Within moments, they had passed through security and were escorted to the Oval Office.

To their surprise, both President Clark and Vice President Lois Van Waters greeted them. Rand knew that national security concerns were just about the only reason the president and vice president would be together at a briefing. Karen could tell from Rand's subtle reactions that he believed the president was very troubled.

President Clark was forthright.

"Bill, I've seen a summary of the September crop production reports. They confirm what Dr. Lewis projected back in July. You told me then that this kind of result could be a trend leading to actual food shortages in the United States, maybe even next year. I asked you and Dr. Lewis to come here promptly to tell us what you think now. Do we have a problem or not?"

Rand braced himself to answer slowly and clearly.

"We have a problem, Mr. President."

"Are you sure?" asked President Clark, staring intently at him.

"Yes."

President Clark grimaced slightly and looked at Vice President Van Waters as if to say "I told you so."

"This new petroleum reality is even worse than we have thought," said the president. "We have to get prices down so our farmers can afford to buy the fertilizers they need. We have failed in our efforts to find enough new sources of oil to force lower prices. We've got to have other sources. I really did not want to suggest this before the election, but now maybe I have no choice. I think we need to make synthetic petroleum from coal, just like they talked about in the 1970s. That will get the prices down."

"Mr. President," boldly interjected Rand, believing that he was interrupting the president's extemporaneous thinking.

"Yes, Bill," said President Clark, only mildly peeved. He had finished his initial thought.

"Reduced petroleum prices will not make any difference," said Rand.

"What makes you say that?" asked the president. Merely stating this question reminded President Clark about his request to Rand almost two months ago to find proof that high petroleum prices were having a bad effect on US crop production. Despite his urgency at that time, he had been so focused on other petroleum issues and reelection that his request dropped low on his list of priorities. He had ignored Rand's request for a meeting three weeks ago. He had been so busy traveling on his reelection campaign that only urgent issues got his attention. That did not include crop production, at least until now. He directed his attention squarely at Rand.

"Karen sent a questionnaire to all of our USDA extension offices in mid-August," began Rand. "Many questions asked in one way or another whether farmers in the district had used less fertilizer than normal. If so, had this occurred because fertilizer prices were so high?

The answers she got were uniformly negative. Apparently, American farmers believe that proper amounts of fertilizers are too important to crop yields to reduce their usage despite their increased cost. Karen's questions about the use of diesel fuel or gasoline in farm equipment got similar answers. Planting, irrigation, and harvesting techniques had not changed. These answers convince us that the new petroleum reality is not a factor in the crop production declines this year."

In an odd way, Karen was proud of Rand for saying what he did and so forcefully. She knew that this is what Rand had believed all along from his years of practical experience with farmers. His intuition had already told him what the answers to her questionnaire confirmed. Now President Clark had to deal with facts that did not fit his assumptions. From the frown on his face, Karen could see that the president was struggling to adjust. Fortunately, Vice President Van Waters helped him along.

"Mr. President," Vice President Van Waters began formally. "This new petroleum reality has been vexing to everyone, certainly the way it sprang up so quickly. Dislocations are nearly everywhere. We know its adverse effects on our transportation, chemical, tourism, and other industries. It's only natural to think that it could adversely affect our crop production as well. Certainly your logic of how it could affect agriculture made sense. It just so happens that in this case your good logic does not match the facts that Dr. Lewis has uncovered."

President Clark was again thankful that Lois Van Waters was his vice president as he struggled to adjust his thinking on this problem.

From outside appearances, the president and vice president had been an odd pairing during President Clark's election campaign and successful election in 2028. Their political experience had been vastly different—Clark had held elective office for twenty years as a governor and then US senator; Van Waters had served less than three full terms in the US House of Representatives. Even their physical appearances were vastly different. Clark had towered over Van Waters' five foot six inch frame whenever they appeared together. He had looked and acted authoritative. In contrast, Van Waters had been and still was a natural blonde with crystal blue eyes who had looked more like a former competitive skier than a political force.

But natural strengths of the president and vice president had proven to be complementary rather than conflicting. Their excellent rapport had also benefited the country in many subtle ways and would do so again here.

President Clark soon accepted the fact that his original assumptions had been incorrect. His biggest concern now was how to solve the crop production problem. That would take hard work and time. But he was also concerned how this problem might work its way into the last month of his reelection campaign. That possibility required some urgent answers.

"So what is going on here, Bill?" asked President Clark. "Do you know?"

"We think we are beginning to know, but just beginning," answered Rand.

"Elaborate," said the president before Rand could continue.

"Karen's USDA questionnaire included some other questions," said Rand. "Karen can describe them better than I."

Karen responded to her cue. She described briefly the questions that she had included on the last page of her questionnaire. She pointed out that the answers to those questions clearly showed that the directors of USDA extension offices thought that crop yields would fall in nearly every district. The recent crop production statistics confirmed the accuracy of those beliefs. Those directors also universally thought that abnormal weather was the culprit.

Karen then briefly described her visit to ETOP, focusing on the weather comparisons project that she had given to ETOP while there. Finally, she summarized the information that she had gleaned from ETOP's project for her. That information left no doubt that every geographic region had experienced odd weather in 2032 and also to a lesser degree in 2031. Nearly all average annual temperatures in 2032 were outside ninety percent of previous recorded annual weather conditions. Precipitation data also were strange.

Rand then took over as he and Karen had planned. He described conditions in the western part of the Midwest, including Kansas, Nebraska, Iowa, Minnesota, and South Dakota, as an example of the odd weather that had occurred in just one agricultural region. In that region, little rain fell after June, preventing corn, wheat, and other crops from reaching robust maturity in August and September. Rand said that the answers to one of Karen's questionnaires had tipped her off to an oddity about this lack of rainfall. An extension office director in Nebraska named Wyzanski had said to be cautious about annual precipitation records in his region. Evidently lots of rain had fallen in March and April, but little had come in July and August when needed. Karen followed up on this idea with her ETOP data. Sure enough, total precipitation for the year was above normal in the western Midwest states, but much of this precipitation had come as early spring rain rather than snow. The water had simply flowed away in the Missouri and Mississippi Rivers rather than remaining as a base from which summer rains would evolve.

Rand then described why odd weather in all regions, not just the western Midwest, was so unusual and important. Drawing on his thirty years of experience in United States agriculture, he said that droughts or floods that would adversely affect crops nearly always were restricted to one or two regions of the country. Other regions were not affected or even enjoyed exceptionally good conditions to create bumper crops.

A good example was the El Niño weather system of 1997 and 1998. Although floods and heavy rains had destroyed crops in some regions, a warm winter and normal precipitation in other regions had allowed normal or even increased crops. Overall, there had been a lot less decline in total US agricultural production than appeared likely from some regional results.

Rand said that very rarely, most, although not all, of the United States was affected by unusual weather conditions. The drought of 2008, which was similar to the 1988 drought twenty years earlier, was one of those rare events. Even then, lost production from crops as far apart as California and Georgia, North Dakota and Texas, was temporary and had been partly counterbalanced by increased production from crops in remaining regions. Severe declines in a few regions could certainly be catastrophic to farmers in those regions, but they were not historically a major problem for the food supply of the United States as a whole.

Rand emphasized that these balancing patterns of agricultural production occurred because the United States spanned a whole continent. Many other nations had not been so fortunate when regional anomalies had occurred. Droughts, such as those in Argentina at the beginning of the twenty-first century, or floods, such as those in eastern Africa nations just five years ago, destroyed most of those nation's crops. Food imports, especially grains, became essential for human survival in those nations. The United States had never had a situation like that, even during the Dust Bowl era of the 1930s.

"When you said we have a problem, you certainly don't mean to say that we have a shortage problem already, do you?" President Clark asked bluntly.

"No, not yet anyway," said Rand.

"What do you mean, 'not yet'?" asked President Clark.

"The problem we have today is odd weather this year," said Rand. "I want Karen to tell you what she has learned about its being maybe more than that."

Karen again was ready. Rand had warned her that their briefing with the president might lead to her having to describe what she had learned at ETOP.

"When I went to ETOP, I learned that the average temperature of the atmosphere at the earth's surface has risen a lot in the twelve years that ETOP has been measuring it," said Karen. "Or at least they think it is a lot. It's actually very small in absolute numbers. They said that these little increases could create significant local weather changes even though the overall temperature increases by themselves appear to be very small. They also said that abnormal weather at a location becomes the changed climate for that location if it occurs long enough. So they are watching for evidence of current climate changes. They are also looking for new dynamics that will cause regional climate changes, not just changes in the average atmospheric temperature. A new climate in a region can certainly affect the success of historically planted crops in that region."

"Dr. Lewis, are you saying that the United States is experiencing climate changes that are affecting our crops?" asked President Clark, trying to reach a conclusion from Karen's description.

"No, at least not now. As far as I can tell, no one knows for sure," answered Karen. "ETOP has some computer models that are designed to predict possible climate changes in all regions of the United States. They also have models for Mexico and Canada, and even models for Europe that include Great Britain, France, and Germany. But they don't have enough confidence in the predictions of these models to publish them."

"Continue," said President Clark, aware that he had interrupted Karen and curious to hear more about what she had learned.

"ETOP's people were very clear that just one year of odd weather does not mean a changed climate," resumed Karen. "But they also said that long-term weather records were not the only way to identify a climate change. What they called 'secondary indications' are equally important. These could show a climate change long before a string of weather records showed it. They are looking for these also."

"Have they found any of these … What were they?" interjected President Clark.

"Secondary indications," repeated Karen.

"Yes. Secondary indications. Have they found any of these?" he asked.

"The only ones I know about for sure in the United States are shrinking high altitude glaciers," answered Karen.

"Shrinking high altitude glaciers," repeated President Clark, satisfied with this comforting answer by believing that this did not amount to much. Vice President Van Waters was not similarly comforted. She sensed that Karen knew more than she had just said.

"What about anywhere else," she asked, looking at Karen.

"Maybe in the North Atlantic Ocean," said Karen cautiously. She did not want to tell her story about Marie Leclerc. She was not sure that it really meant anything, at least not yet.

"What secondary indication in the North Atlantic?" asked Van Waters, not letting Karen off the hook and curious about how something in the North Atlantic Ocean could be important.

"There's some indication that a French nonprofit organization has found fresh water in the northern North Atlantic Ocean," said Karen. "ETOP thinks that this could be important. I don't know why. They mentioned something about a North Atlantic Drift. ETOP has tried to get SMER's data, but they cannot find any that have been published. They said that this is very odd for a nonprofit organization. Usually nonprofits try to get their findings to the public as soon as possible. And these studies have been conducted for fourteen years."

"What's SMER?" asked Vice President Van Waters.

"SMER?" asked Karen, unaware that she had used this term.

"Yes, SMER," said Vice President Van Waters. "You said that ETOP has tried to get SMER's data."

Karen became embarrassed, realizing her mistake. Although chagrined that she had identified SMER, she did not try to avoid the question.

"La Société de la Mer," answered Karen, revealing by her perfect pronunciation that she spoke French fluently.

Again, Vice President Van Waters sensed that Karen was not telling the whole story about her knowledge of SMER. Before she could follow up with another question, President Clark intervened.

The president had heard enough for now. Real solutions would take time to develop. As for how the decline in crop production would play into his campaign for reelection, he now knew that the crop production problem was more complex than he had thought. He was confident that his opponents would not have any analysis such as done by Karen. He believed that they would not understand the significance of the crop production reports that had just been compiled, especially as compared to 2031 and earlier years. His strategy, at least as expressed to Rand and Lewis, was now to postpone serious consideration of what to do about this problem until after Election Day on November 2nd.

President Clark thanked Rand and Lewis for their clear and thorough briefing. He said that it was a lot of information to absorb. He would ask their advice after he and Vice President Van Waters had thought further about that information. He also cautioned them to keep their investigation and conclusions secret.

As a formal ending to a difficult meeting, Bill Rand and Karen Lewis shook hands with the president and vice president, then were escorted out of the Oval Office, down the hall, past security, and into their waiting limousine. They would soon return to USDA headquarters.

Vice President Van Waters had remained with President Clark.

"Did you understand all of that, Lois?" asked President Clark. Although they maintained strict titles protocol when meeting with people other than Cabinet members, informality ruled when just the two of them were together. Four years of working together had created great mutual respect and friendship.

"Not all of it. How about you?" she answered.

"Me either," said President Clark. "Other than we may have a real problem brewing here."

"I agree."

"I want you to handle it," said the president. "This new petroleum reality is enough for me. I think I understand it better anyway."

"You know, I think what Dr. Lewis was talking about at the end might be very important," said Vice President Van Waters.

"Which part?"

"Those secondary indications."

"How so?"

"As unlikely as it seems, if we really are having regional climate changes, we need to know right away. That outfit SMER intrigues me. Why wouldn't a nonprofit organization publish their discoveries? It just does not make sense. Maybe SMER is doing work for someone else. Dr. Lewis said that SMER is a French nonprofit organization. I wonder if SMER's work is really for the French government. They are always secretive."

"Hmm. What are you suggesting?"

"I'm suggesting we ask Melissa to find out what she can."

"She'd be the best person, all right," said President Clark. "I think we should talk to her together. I'm not sure that I would get the concepts right. Besides, it will take both of us to convince her that this is important enough to add to her agenda with Rousseau. Her trip to France is already going to be plenty difficult."

Chapter 13

SECURITY

Melissa Straus was the fourth woman to hold the position of United States Secretary of State. Like Madeleine Albright more than thirty years before her, Secretary Straus had been the United States Ambassador to the United Nations just before her appointment at the end of 2028. President Clark had selected her in part because of her strong background in economics. Before becoming the UN Ambassador, she had been a professor of economics at the University of Chicago. At the time she became secretary of state, the world had been relatively peaceful and economic issues among nations had dominated international relations. She had been a logical and popular choice.

Just four months later, economic issues had been pushed aside as a new international security threat had appeared from nowhere. This bizarre and frightening event had forged a friendship between Melissa Straus and France's Prime Minister Pierre Rousseau. President Clark and Vice President Van Waters now hoped to exploit that friendship in her new assignment to find out about SMER.

The bizarre event had occurred on Easter Sunday 2029. A small group that later had become known as the "Anti-Cult" had executed the first visible part of their plan to create chaos and hatred among religious populations of the world.

Their plan had begun two years earlier. The group had learned from public reports that expansion and new construction at the Epinal Nuclear Power Plant in eastern France had been scheduled for sometime in late 2028 or early 2029. Someone in the group also had figured out that refueling at the plant would occur in April 2029. One by one, members of the group had obtained employment at the plant before that date.

The construction project had actually begun in January 2029. The first step had been to dig a large hole to accommodate the expansion near the existing plant. By April, long bed dump trucks had been regularly hauling dirt from Epinol to a fill site twenty-seven kilometers away. As predicted by the Anti-Cult, half of the reactor's fuel rods had been replaced in early April. The spent fuel rods had been put into temporary canisters awaiting transport to France's recycling plant. The stage had been set for the Anti-Cult's plan.

All of the group members had volunteered to work on Easter Sunday. They had been alone at Epinol except for guards on the perimeter.

The group had tagged two dump trucks that had been loaded with dirt just before quitting time on Good Friday. While the trucks had been idle on Easter Sunday, the group had quietly used hand shovels to unload most of the dirt from each truck. Then they had used the plant's quiet electric forklift to place in the trucks fourteen canisters that had contained spent fuel rods. The group again had used hand shovels to cover the canisters with the dirt that they had just unloaded. They had then spread the excess dirt by hand back into the pit from which it had come. They had set up phony cardboard canisters to replace the real ones that had been taken. The dump trucks had been critical to their plan because they were among the few ordinary vehicles that could carry the heavy fuel rods. The group's quiet stealth had succeeded. No guard or anyone else had seen any of this activity.

On Monday morning, normal construction work had resumed. Regular drivers had driven the two dump trucks out of Epinol's secure area. Along the road to the fill site, both dump trucks had been hijacked. The two trucks had been found abandoned sixteen kilometers away next to a front loader that evidently had been used to transfer the canisters quickly to some other kind of sturdy vehicle. The entire operation had obviously been very carefully and cleverly coordinated.

A huge manhunt had ensued, not only in France, but throughout Western Europe. The identity of the group responsible for stealing the fuel rods had remained a mystery for many weeks. The personnel who had been employed at the nuclear power plant had been the sole link to the group. All of them had vanished after leaving work at the end of their shifts early Monday morning before the dump trucks had been hijacked. Additional extensive research into their backgrounds had turned up nothing.

The mystery surrounding the responsible group had made the whole episode more and more frightening. Most national leaders had begun to believe that silence meant only one thing—the group had intended to use the radioactive fuel rods rather than to seek ransom or some other political gain in exchange for the rods.

The greatest fear had been that the group would surround an ordinary bomb with the highly radioactive rods and then explode the bomb in a crowded place. The released radiation could then cause sickness and death among many more people than an explosion of the bomb by itself could achieve.

No one had imagined that the hijackers could even begin to make a real nuclear bomb. Everyone had known that rare expertise and sophisticated facilities were needed to extract Plutonium 239 from spent fuel rods in order to make weapons grade material needed for such a sinister purpose.

France had asked and received help from the United States and Russia to find the perpetrators. That help had been given primarily in the form of satellite surveillance to try to find any suspicious place where the radioactive fuel rods could be stored.

On June 25, 2029, a United States reconnaissance satellite had taken an image of an object that could have been one of the temporary canisters. It had been located on a farm in southeast France in an open space between a barn, silo, and construction crane. Secretary of State Straus had promptly conveyed this information to Prime Minister Pierre Rousseau. By that time, the two had been in frequent contact as the details of the nuclear heist had unfolded. Personal contact had continued throughout this crisis.

Armed with the image, French commandos had quietly surrounded the farm. They then had quickly overrun it, finding no real physical resistance. The group's members had relied on secrecy, not force, to protect their operation. The real purpose of the crane to move fuel rod canisters around had been disguised by its apparent use in erecting a new silo.

Shockingly, the raid had uncovered much more than the fuel rods. It also had uncovered a sophisticated Plutonium extraction plant hidden in a large underground complex that had been accessed from the farm's barn.

A firestorm of criticism had erupted against the French government throughout Europe and the world. Critics complained that the French government had not only allowed the nuclear fuel rods to be stolen, but also had failed to detect the creation of the Plutonium processing plant at a provincial farm long before then. The criticism had been especially harsh because the French government had initially loudly surmised that the fuel rods must have been moved out of France. After all, moving large objects between Western European countries had been relatively easy at that time because national borders had been relaxed after a unified commercial Europe had been created in the early twenty-first century.

French nuclear experts had at first believed that the Plutonium extracted by the underground plant could not be used to make a nuclear bomb. High grade Plutonium 239 would be needed for this purpose. Nuclear experts had thought that the Plutonium extracted by the methods employed in the underground plant would not be pure enough because it would contain too much Plutonium 240 that had been created as a by-product of the nuclear reactions in the power plant's reactor.

Then, a week after the commando raid, a new weapons design had been discovered in the computers found at the underground plant. There was no doubt that the group had intended to make a nuclear bomb, and, surprisingly, the new design had been perilously close to a workable device.

Eventually, more than ninety people had been arrested and convicted of treason. Among them were four physicists who clearly had possessed the knowledge necessary to design a nuclear bomb using Plutonium 239. The sophistication of the Plutonium extraction plant and the new design had shown that they had used their expertise for that very purpose.

The computers found in the raid at the farm also had contained detailed plans to steal more fuel rods from another nuclear power plant in France and sketchy plans to obtain fuel rods from a nuclear power plant in Russia. French espionage experts had believed that the plans drawn up for this second French nuclear power plant could very well have succeeded. Although the sketchy plans for the Russian power plant had been given to Russia, the Russians had remained quiet about the plan's potential for success. Collectively, the amount of Plutonium 239 that might have been stolen from these two plants would have been enough for three nuclear bombs if successfully separated from the other material.

In order to maintain secrecy, the responsible group purposely had not used any consistent name for itself. The French military had initially named the group the Anti-Religion Cult, based on the contents of the computers discovered in the raid. Those computers had shown that the group's goal had been to attack the major religions of the world by destroying their most holy places. The group also had planned to kill millions of followers at the same time by exploding their nuclear bombs when huge religious celebrations were being held. Documents had contained specific plans for moving a bomb to the Vatican in Rome and also to Mecca in Saudi Arabia.

The Anti-Religion Cult, which quickly had been dubbed the "Anti-Cult" by the French news media, had remained a mystery even to that day. The actual motives for the plans uncovered at the raid had never been wrested from the Anti-Cult's members. Based on the nature of these diabolical plans, most people believed that the Anti-Cult's purpose had been to create chaos and hatred among religious populations of the world. Or maybe the Anti-Cult just hated all religions. No one knew for sure.

Whatever the Anti-Cult's ultimate motives had been, its near success had created a shockwave in international thinking. Before the Anti-Cult, security analysts in all nations had assumed that the primary danger from newly created nuclear bombs had been from rogue nations. Clearly some nations beyond the historic nuclear club possessed the capability to organize an infrastructure of people and equipment that could be sophisticated enough to make fissionable material. Those nations could potentially make Plutonium 239 in a nuclear breeder reactor or could even concentrate natural Uranium into high grade Uranium 235. That sophistication might also be used to build nuclear bombs.

No one had previously suspected that a small unknown group could possess the knowledge, skills, and resources to create a nuclear bomb from Plutonium 239 found in spent fuel rods of a nuclear reactor. The Anti-Cult had shown that this danger also was very real.

The Anti-Cult incident had caused reevaluation of all nuclear power plants across the world. This reevaluation had extended far beyond tightening security at the plants. For a decade, the international community had already been wrestling with the issue whether nuclear reactors should be used on a world-wide basis as a major way to produce electricity. Politically stable nations such as the United States, France, and Japan had been using them, but, following that example, other less stable or autocratic nations had wanted them as well. Even though nuclear weapons programs were very different from nuclear power plant programs, many nations, including the United States, had not trusted fringe nations with any kind of nuclear program. They had been concerned that the expertise gained from using any nuclear process could be too easily transferable to nuclear weapons development.

The international community had also long recognized that sophistication was needed in operating a nuclear power plant in order to avoid meltdown or other potential hazards. The Chernobyl incident in the Soviet Union in 1986 had shown that even an advanced nuclear nation could have a catastrophe. With the added risks shown by the Anti-Cult incident, many nations, including France, the United States, and Russia, had begun to question whether nuclear power plants should be used at all.

By early 2030, France had reached a startling conclusion. France had decided that its nuclear power plants did not provide enough value to France to overcome the risk of another danger such as the Anti-Cult incident. France had then decided to stop using nuclear power plants altogether, even though almost eighty percent of the electric power used in France at that time had come from these plants. France had hoped that its example would dissuade other nations of the world from adopting a nuclear option for producing electric power. France had particularly wanted to dissuade those nations where tight security might be more difficult to achieve than in France.

President Clark and the United States Congress had come to the same conclusion three months later. This new policy had been less significant in the United States because a far smaller proportion of the electric power used in the United States had come at that time from nuclear power plants. In addition, this new policy had helped to diffuse the contentious problem of nuclear waste disposal.

Now, in early October 2032, France was scheduled to decommission the first of its many nuclear power plants. In September, however, Secretary Straus had received a formal letter from her friend Prime Minister Rousseau. He had said that France had decided not to decommission this first nuclear power plant in October, or at any other time. He had revealed that the French Council of Ministers had secretly rescinded France's decommissioning policy several months earlier. France had instead decided to continue using all of its nuclear power plants, but under new security systems. Rousseau's letter had revealed no reason for this decision.

President Clark had become angry when he got this news. He could not believe that France would renege on its plan to reject nuclear power. Hadn't France learned enough from the Anti-Cult incident? Or was this decision driven by economics? Had France planned to use petroleum for its replacement power plants? The new petroleum reality would certainly make that plan untenable.

President Clark had ordered Straus to go to France to see Rousseau personally to find out the truth. He also wanted her to persuade Rousseau to get France to revert to the decommissioning policy that France had adopted in 2030.

Straus had immediately contacted Rousseau and scheduled a meeting to see him in Paris on October 14, 2032. It was in this context that President Clark and Vice President Van Waters told Straus about SMER and ETOP and asked her to find out what she could about SMER when she saw Rousseau.

Straus was well prepared to talk to Rousseau about nuclear power plants. But how could she subtly ask about SMER and expect to get any meaningful answer? After all, it was not related to nuclear power plants, nor to Plutonium or Uranium, nor even to electricity.

And why ask? Despite efforts by President Clark and Vice President Van Waters to convince her why SMER could be important and connected to the French government, they gave her few details to work with. About all she knew was that she could offer some unpublished ETOP projections about climate changes as an exchange for SMER data if the French government had them. What was going on here? She just did not understand why some fresh water floating around in the northern North Atlantic Ocean would matter to anyone but a few scientists.

Straus arrived on schedule at Charles de Gaulle Airport outside Paris in the evening of October 13. She was taken promptly by limousine to the exclusive hotel in Paris that the French government used for visiting foreign dignitaries. When she arrived there, she was given a sealed envelope from Rousseau. His handwritten note was inside. It read simply "Wear good walking shoes. We will have a long day tomorrow."

Rousseau was well known to the French public as a dashing and charming politician. Only close associates knew that in private he was brutally frank. Through her regular contacts with Rousseau relating to the Anti-Cult incident, Secretary Straus had become part of that small group of associates. She knew Rousseau well enough to believe his simple admonition. Obviously tomorrow they were not going to have just a meeting in a conference room. But, what had Rousseau planned?

Straus's day with Rousseau began as originally expected. Her French foreign ministry escort took her from her hotel room to a waiting ministry limousine, which then took her directly to the foreign ministry building. Rousseau met her personally as she exited the limousine there. An embrace between friends preceded their walk along a traditional red carpet that had been spread from the curb to the building's entrance.

On this sunny, dry, and warmer than usual day for mid-October, Rousseau and Straus were contrasting figures on the red carpet as they exchanged pleasantries along its course. Rousseau was tall, thin, and impeccably dressed in a dark custom-tailored suit with a sky-blue silk tie. Straus, on the other hand, was of medium height, a bit chunky from too much foreign travel, and dressed in her signature gray pants suit that matched her gray hair.

Just a few minutes after entering the building and passing through security, Straus and Rousseau arrived at a small conference room. Straus' Secret Service guard and Rousseau's guard remained outside. Straus and Rousseau each had an interpreter in the conference room. Rousseau introduced a fifth mystery person to Straus, but did not at first explain that person's role in the meeting. A large map of France and some sort of facility diagram were clipped to two wall boards.

The interpreters were a formality. Rousseau spoke English fluently. At least with his friend Melissa Straus, he was happy to use that skill. Rousseau first explained that the map of France was there to show Straus the locations of all electric power producing facilities in France. The nuclear power plants were distinguished by a stylized symbol of an atom. Straus could easily see that the nuclear power plants far outnumbered all the other facilities. Rousseau told her that almost eighty percent of France's electric power still came from these nuclear power plants.

Rousseau then turned to the facility diagram. Without his saying so, Straus guessed that this was the nuclear power plant that had been scheduled for decommissioning this month. She was only partly correct. It was indeed a nuclear power plant, but not the one scheduled for decommissioning. Instead, the plant was an example of the new security designs that France had created.

Rousseau finally identified the role of the mystery person in their meeting. She was an engineer who knew the details of France's newly designed security systems for all of its nuclear power plants. This engineer then summarized the main features of these designs, pointing from time to time to the example facility diagram. Straus found her summaries to be very technical and difficult to follow. She asked a number of questions to try to understand what France had created.

Rousseau had anticipated this very problem. He had correctly thought that Straus would not easily be convinced that the new security systems would be effective. That is why he planned to take Straus to the very facility shown in the diagram. It was the Chirot Power Plant located eighty kilometers west of Paris. Rousseau explained that the diagram was only meant to introduce Straus to France's new security designs. He said that she would now see the systems for herself. Then she would appreciate how effective France's new security methods really were.

In the ride of less than an hour from the foreign ministry building to the Chirot Power Plant, Rousseau explained to Straus, as best he could, the extreme steps that France had now taken to keep its Uranium and Plutonium secure.

Guards were now being used in all areas of each plant, not just its perimeter. Spent fuel rods that had come from the reactor were now either encased on site for permanent disposal or transported immediately to France's recycling facility. Daily personnel assignments were now being made by two plant managers, rather than being based on requests by personnel for specific days. Other new security steps were more technical and would have to be explained at the power plant by the engineer Straus had met.

The Chirot Power Plant came into view four kilometers before the ministry's limousine pulled up to its entrance gate. Straus was surprised at how small it was, at least that portion visible above ground. The two nuclear power plants she had toured in the United States after the Anti-Cult incident were much larger. She had to remind herself that the nuclear path taken by France many decades earlier was much different than that taken by the United States. France had employed common designs for its numerous small nuclear power plants, thus gaining experience with each plant that could be translated into improvements for the other plants. In contrast, most nuclear power plants in the United States were very large and had been custom designed. Their failure rate was much higher than that in France, at least in the sense that the power plants proved far too costly to keep operational. Many engineers believed that France's success had occurred because experience gained with one plant usually applied to another.

As they arrived at the entrance gate, Straus began to see first hand the new comprehensive security system now in place. Their limousine stopped at an exiting station fifty meters from the entrance. No ordinary vehicles were allowed entry into the plant's area. Rousseau, Straus, and their entire entourage had to leave their limousines, pass individually through two detectors manned by guards, and then walk along an enclosed pathway to the entry itself. From there, they boarded a small bus that never left the facility except for major repairs. The bus took them to the control center only two hundred meters away. Their tour would begin formally there and would be on foot.

Over the next two and a half hours, Straus saw and learned about eight new security features at the Chirot Power Plant. Most of these were technological, such as a new low frequency scanner for boxes of supplies that had to enter the grounds. Two of the new features related to personnel, such as the omnipresence of security guards. Obviously, none of the new features was cheap. Rousseau explained that France believed that the extra cost was well justified to prevent any more fuel rods from being stolen. He also emphasized that the cost was less than first appeared because the commonality of France's nuclear power plants allowed the same new systems to be installed at each plant.

Despite her skepticism, Straus admitted to herself that France had done a thorough job in creating security for its fuel rods. They seemed to have thought of everything. But was that enough? That's also what everyone had thought before the Anti-Cult incident had proved them wrong. What flaw existed here that a smart, motivated, patient, and organized group could find?

Whatever that flaw might or might not be, she knew that the US position on nuclear power plants had remained firm after the Anti-Cult incident. Every nuclear power plant posed too great a threat to national security and must be decommissioned. Until recently, France had been firm on the same policy. It was now Straus's turn to try to convince Rousseau that France's new shift away from that policy was a mistake.

Somehow, in that process she also had to try to find out something about a wholly different subject, an ocean research project being done by an obscure nonprofit organization known as SMER.

Chapter 14

EXCHANGE

Straus had to pick the right timing to achieve her goals. The tour itself, the sumptuous luncheon at the Chirot Power Plant, and even the limousine ride back to Paris offered no sensible opportunity for proper dialogue. Back at the ministry building, Rousseau and Straus returned to the conference room. The interpreters were dismissed temporarily as unnecessary. Two security men remained outside in the hall guarding the door. Rousseau and Straus found themselves alone.

"You see, Melissa, we have made our fuel rods entirely secure," said Rousseau confidently as he finished his third summary of what they had seen at the Chirot Power Plant. If nothing else, Rousseau was persistent.

"Very impressive," said Straus. "It looks like you've tried to think of everything."

"We believe we have thought of everything," said Rousseau firmly.

"Maybe," said Straus. "But you know the American policy on nuclear power plants."

"Of course, that was our policy also in 2030," said Rousseau.

"President Clark wanted me to remind you that no matter how careful we think we are, nuclear power plant risks are inevitably there," said Straus. "The Anti-Cult incident proved that."

"I expect him to say that, but he has not seen what we have done now," said Rousseau.

"Of course, he hasn't seen your new systems, but just the nature of these plants makes Plutonium too accessible," said Straus. "Besides, if France backs off its decommissioning policy, Russia might do the same thing. Other countries may also follow your reversal. Their security methods may not be anywhere near as good as yours. That puts all of us at risk. France will be in danger as well."

"We have decided to advise Russia or anyone else on their security plans if they want help," said Rousseau. "So I don't think you should assume that their security will not be very good. Besides, they are just as concerned as we or you to keep Plutonium away from anyone dangerous."

Straus could see that her approach was not working. She changed tactics.

"After the Anti-Cult incident, the United States promised to help any nation decommission its nuclear power plants," she said. "Of course, that promise included France. We offered expertise and money to dilute all the Plutonium and Uranium 235 and to put them into permanent storage. That offer still stands. It's the only sensible way to go."

"Melissa, please, your government is still blinded to the real problem here," said Rousseau. "We are not keeping our nuclear power plants because we think they are so wonderful. We have no other choice, at least not yet."

"Why not? The United States doesn't need nuclear power plants. Why should France?" asked Straus.

"We do not want what you have, and you should not want them either," said Rousseau sharply.

Rousseau's brisk response startled Straus, being far different from his cordial attitude throughout the day. She also did not understand what he was talking about.

"I'm not sure what you mean," said Straus cautiously.

"It's simple," responded Rousseau. "Most of your old power plants use coal and most of your newer plants use natural gas. We do not want to use either fuel."

Straus expected Rousseau to be well prepared to defend France's decision to retain its nuclear power plants, but this was a new rationale. She recognized that she was beginning to get outflanked by his preparation.

As an economist, Straus could understand why France would not want to use petroleum for its electric power plants. The new petroleum reality made that reliance far too risky and expensive. But she thought that coal and natural gas were readily available in Europe as well at the United States, so supply should be adequate and prices should remain reasonable for many years. Why didn't France want to use coal or natural gas? What was France looking for? Her eyes alone asked these questions.

"We want to use sustainable energy, pure and simple," Rousseau said.

Sustainable energy? thought Straus. That must be what Americans usually called "renewable energy." She knew that wind and sunlight were in this category and that some American utilities used many large wind turbines and broad fields of solar panels to make electricity. But the proportion of total electricity produced this way was still small. She was not sure what else would be in the "renewable" category. No matter. Her mission here was to get France to decommission its nuclear power plants just as the United States was doing. If France wanted to use sustainable energy for its electric power production, that was fine with her.

"Go ahead," she said.

"It is not that simple," responded Rousseau. "After the Anti-Cult incident, we began examining all of the sustainable energy sources we thought would be most promising. We looked at the water cycle, at wind, at the sun, even at tides and waves. None of the technologies that we found to use these energy sources could be combined in the massive amounts needed to meet all of France's demands for electricity."

Straus was tempted to ask for more specifics, but France's conclusion is all that mattered now. Rousseau had left no doubt about what that was.

For his part, Rousseau wanted to explain why putting dams on France's rivers to create water heads for electric turbines would ruin far too much land that France needed for agriculture. He wanted to demonstrate that big dams and reservoirs would also create ecological messes. He wanted to tell her that river run electric turbines were not yet reliable enough to use on a large scale. He also wanted to tell her that France already used large wind turbines, but had not figured out how to make wind a primary electricity source because it came and went, not always predictably. He wanted to express all of France's frustration in finding sustainable energy alternatives so that Straus could report France's frustration in detail back to President Clark.

"Pierre," Straus said, "I think France is making this far too difficult. Just use coal or natural gas like we do in the United States. We have lots of both. If you think France or Europe does not have enough, I'm sure good sources could be found at sensible prices, whether in the United States or on the world market."

Straus's response was disappointing, but just about what Rousseau had predicted. She was mired in the past, just like the American government, still only able to think seriously about traditional fuel supplies and prices. He was chagrined that the American government still refused to see the risks that Europe faced because energy usage patterns of the twentieth century had continued far too long into the twenty-first century. Despite his personal friendship with and respect for Straus, he could not avoid getting perturbed.

"Melissa, you Americans may have thought that the ideas in the 1997 Kyoto Protocol were radical, but I assure you that we in Europe did not think so," said Rousseau. "In fact, the emission limitations in Kyoto were woefully inadequate to prevent greenhouse gases from continually increasing in our atmosphere. We already had too much at the time of Kyoto. We have much more today despite the 2015 Paris Agreement."

Straus kept quiet. She could see that Rousseau was launching into a lecture he wanted her to hear.

"Everyone knew that the Kyoto limitations would not accomplish long-term stability in atmospheric greenhouse gases. Those limitations were designed primarily to force industrialized nations to develop replacement technologies that would provide the same benefits as fossil fuel combustion at comparable costs. These replacement technologies would be the real saviors when they were adopted world-wide by everyone.

"Yet the United States opted out of the Kyoto Protocol in 2001. France signed on to the Protocol, but we relied a lot upon nuclear power in our electric industry to meet our Kyoto commitments. Germany and Denmark used wind turbines to reduce their greenhouse gas emissions to Kyoto levels, but not beyond."

"I think that the United States, France, and a lot of other countries have made a big mistake in the last four decades," Rousseau continued. "All of us decided that new energy development should be almost entirely a private industry enterprise. Even technologies that use nontraditional and sustainable energy sources were treated this way.

"Sure, the US and French governments did some basic research, but not nearly as much as needed. I know that for many years the United States spent more money for research on traditional energy sources such as coal-fired power plants than on potential new sources. We should not be surprised that neither the United States nor France has any sustainable energy technology that we can now use on a truly massive scale. Even combinations of those technologies are inadequate to cover all of our electricity needs, much less to replace the gasoline, kerosene, and diesel fuel used in transportation. We should have treated energy development as a national security issue just like we have done for weapons development. Can you imagine where our military technology would be if we had let market prices determine its development rather than strategic needs?

"We here in France are frustrated now that we cannot use sustainable energy methods to meet all of our needs. We want to play our part in avoiding whatever problems increased amounts of atmospheric carbon dioxide and other gases might bring. At least our nuclear power plants do not aggravate the situation by pumping even more carbon dioxide into the atmosphere. We will stay with them."

Straus knew now that she could not budge Rousseau from his or France's adamance. He was clearly convinced that France must keep its nuclear power plants. She also felt unprepared to respond to his stated reasons for rejecting the fossil fuel alternatives being used in the United States. She did not like her disadvantage.

Rousseau had mentioned "greenhouse gases." *Why would he be talking about greenhouse gases at all, and why would he say "We already have too much"? How would he know? He was a politician, not a scientist. What was going on here?*

"I didn't know you felt so strongly about all of this," said Straus, as a way to cool Rousseau and encourage a return to a more open dialogue.

"It's not just me, Melissa," said Rousseau. "France is going to have a terrible time if the North Atlantic Drift changes. We cannot do anything that might make the situation worse." Rousseau leaned forward to make his point.

North Atlantic Drift? thought Straus. She had heard that name before.

Of course, President Clark and Vice President Van Waters had used that name in their description of SMER. She reflected on what they had said. She paused before speaking again.

"So, Pierre, you think there is too much fresh water in the northern North Atlantic Ocean already?" asked Straus.

Rousseau was stunned. *How did Straus know about that? She could not possibly have guessed it. Did the Americans have a research ship out there this summer? Or did somebody tell them about SMER's discovery? But who and why?* SMER's discovery was supposed to remain secret as classified national security information.

Rousseau was a skilled negotiator. He did not outwardly reveal his surprise. But his silence, just a little too long, told Straus that she had struck a nerve. Maybe SMER really had found something important. And maybe SMER's silence in the world of published scientific research was no accident. Could SMER be a covert agency of the French government? And what exactly had SMER discovered that summer? Straus was now determined to find out. She knew that direct questions would fail, so she began a spiral ride toward the information she really wanted.

"Are you familiar with the Earth Temperature Observation Project?" she asked.

"The name sounds familiar," said Rousseau slowly. He knew very well what ETOP was. He even knew where each of its observation stations was located in France.

"What is it?" he added disingenuously.

"It's one of our national research laboratories," said Straus. "It was created to improve monitoring of the earth's atmosphere around the globe," she added. "ETOP's data show that the average temperature of the atmosphere at the earth's surface has risen a lot in the last twelve years. At least they think it's a lot. They have made projections about what that means for climates in some regions. The regional projections are not public. Given your concern about the North Atlantic Drift, would you be interested in getting ETOP's projections for France?"

Rousseau hesitated before answering. What was Straus really offering here? He recalled that French scientists were also working on the potential effects on France from rising atmospheric temperatures. But he also knew that France did not have a global monitoring program anywhere near as extensive as ETOP's.

"Maybe," he responded slowly.

"Well, we need something from you as well," said Straus bluntly, as Rousseau had expected.

"What?" he said.

"Information on the fresh water in the northern North Atlantic Ocean," said Straus.

"What makes you think we have anything like that?" asked Rousseau.

"Circumstances," answered Straus. "Circumstances that point to France."

Silence ensued as the two debated internally whether to continue this game. Straus made one more move.

"We know about a nonprofit group called La Societé de la Mer," she said. "We know that it is based in Nantes. We know that it has been making salinity measurements in the northern North Atlantic Ocean for fourteen years. We also believe that it found lots of fresh water there late this summer. Yet nothing at all about any of its measurements can be found in published literature. Rather odd, don't you think?"

Rousseau had heard enough. To him, it appeared that the US government clearly knew about SMER's discovery. If he did not give SMER's data to the United States to evaluate, the United States would create a program for next summer to collect the same information that SMER would be collecting. The Americans might not keep their findings secret. Besides, if ETOP had SMER's data now, maybe it could create projections that would help France evaluate its own projections. Ultimately, making the best decisions on whether or how to change France's agriculture for 2033 was most important. Exchanging information now made the best sense for France.

"Melissa, what I am about to tell you must be kept secret between our governments," said Rousseau. "You said that ETOP has regional climate projections that are not public. You said that it has projections that include France. Am I correct?"

"Yes."

"We need access to that information to assess along with what SMER has learned. Can we get it if I tell you about SMER and give you SMER's findings?"

"Agreed," said Straus simply and quickly, knowing that President Clark had hoped for this very exchange.

"SMER does have a measurement project in the North Atlantic Ocean," said Rousseau. "It is really my government's project. It began in 2018. We wanted to learn as soon as possible if the Greenland Ice Sheet began to melt very fast. If it did, lots of fresh water could flow into the northern North Atlantic Ocean. That could diminish the North

Atlantic Drift. Weather patterns in France could change. We figured that early knowledge of this effect would allow us to encourage our farmers to plant seeds better suited to those new patterns, without necessarily telling them exactly why. We would need the information, but not a panic it might cause. SMER was chosen because our measurements program was consistent with SMER's other operations. We believed that no one would suspect that this program was really being done for the French government. That's why the data have never been published."

"We suspected as much," said Straus, pleased that she had been able to confirm Vice President Van Waters' suspicion.

"Just two months ago, SMER discovered a lot of fresh water southeast of Greenland," continued Rousseau. "We are now evaluating what SMER's discovery means to France and Western Europe."

"We would like to evaluate SMER's discovery as well," said Straus.

"Undoubtedly," said Rousseau. "We'll provide SMER's data to you."

Straus sat back in her chair. Her mini-game with Rousseau had ended with victory. But she thought it was insignificant. Her mission to France was to get France again to agree to close and dismantle all of its nuclear power plants. That mission had been a failure. A question from Rousseau interrupted her dejection.

"How did you find out about SMER's discovery?" he asked.

"Blind luck," answered Straus crisply.

Rousseau made no further inquiries. He knew that Straus was just as tough and clever a negotiator as he was.

During the next hour, Rousseau made sure that France would get the climate projections it needed from ETOP and that the SMER data France would give to the United States would remain secret. He insisted that the SMER data be delivered by diplomatic pouch directly to Straus. He said that he expected that anyone in the United States who would see it would have national security clearance. Rousseau promised that the ETOP projections that Straus would deliver to him would be handled the same way.

Straus agreed.

Rousseau then promised to deliver the SMER data on November 5th, just three days after the US presidential election. By setting that date, he thought that if President Clark were not reelected, he would have time to stop delivery of the SMER data until he could be assured that it would be protected by the new president and secretary of state.

CHAPTER 15

QUESTIONS

Melissa Straus was not looking forward to giving her report to President Clark. She had not been able to budge Prime Minister Rousseau at all. He had not agreed to close down even one nuclear power plant, much less to change France's policy back to closing down and dismantling all of its nuclear power plants. She had only one thing to show for her efforts. That was an agreement by Rousseau to send her some obscure data on water in the North Atlantic Ocean that was obtained for the French government by a small nonprofit group. Some success, she thought to herself.

President Clark was on a campaign trip when Straus returned to Washington, D.C. As she came to her office late on Friday afternoon, October 15, she learned that he had left a message for her to meet with him and Vice President Van Waters in the Oval Office at 2:00 p.m. on Monday. She took a few minutes to look at her e-mail, regular mail, and internal State Department mail before leaving for a weekend's rest. Only one item seemed out of the ordinary. Her internal State Department mail included a long report that purported to summarize the agricultural export policies of thirty-seven countries.

The report had been prepared by the newly formed creative group in the State Department. Straus did not know why she should be receiving a report like this at this time. She certainly did not request it. Its cover note simply said that she might want to know about the possibilities discussed in the report. She lifted the report and flipped a few pages. It looked like someone's research thesis. It was undoubtedly very dull reading. She was not going to waste her time with it, so she told one of her assistants to read the report, prepare a synopsis, and tell her whether it contained any useful information.

By the time of Monday's meeting with the president and vice president, Straus had regained her normal enthusiasm and energy even though she believed that she had only bad news to convey. At the meeting Straus told them about Rousseau's adamancy. She told them that France would continue to use its nuclear power plants no matter what the United States preferred. She summarized why Rousseau believed that this policy was necessary, although she spared them the details of Rousseau's tirade.

As Straus gave her report, President Clark nodded in a way that showed thoughtful understanding of France's decision, even though he did not agree with it. Straus could not quite understand why the president was so mellow about France's turnaround. She surmised that the president knew that nothing could be done about France's new policy before Election Day. Maybe his only interest now was to keep this new controversy out of the presidential election. At least for now, France's new policy remained secret, which suited him just fine.

Almost as an afterthought, Straus also told the president and vice president what she had learned about SMER and described her agreement with Rousseau to exchange information.

Both the president and vice president perked up with this news. They appeared to be very pleased with Straus' success. They asked her questions about why the French government created its North Atlantic research project, why it chose SMER to do it, what the research project really was, and why France treated the research as top secret.

Straus could only answer part of their questions. When she had met with Prime Minister Rousseau, she had focused primarily on how to get the SMER data, not on what it was. She had no inkling that the president and vice president would be so interested in the details surrounding SMER.

Why, indeed, would they have such a strong interest? Straus' puzzlement rose further when President Clark told her to give the SMER data from France directly to Vice President Van Waters. Nothing more was said except to thank Straus again for making a good deal with Rousseau.

Another month would go by before Straus would appreciate why the president and vice president acted the way they did.

Promptly after the meeting with Straus, Vice President Van Waters ordered expedited security checks on Paul Anderson and Marilyn Sawyer. Karen Lewis had already received this clearance. Bill Rand, of course, had received this clearance as well before being appointed the Secretary of the Department of Agriculture. Van Waters wanted all of them to be able to see the SMER data promptly after it arrived from France.

In just two weeks, on the day before the election, Van Waters received reports from the FBI stating that Paul Anderson and Marilyn Sawyer had qualified for top level security clearance. The report on Paul contained an unusual item. A clear plastic container held a DVD. Attached to the container was a hand-written note from Matthew Byrd, the director of the FBI. The note said simply:

"Vice President Van Waters: You may want to look at the enclosed DVD about Paul Anderson. It gives a good idea of who he is. Regards, Matthew Byrd."

Why would the security report on Anderson contain a DVD and why would Matthew Byrd write a personal note about it?

Campaigning was over. At this point, nothing else could be done to affect the outcome of the election.

Van Waters decided to look at the DVD, at least enough to test Byrd's recommendation. Besides, she was curious to see what Paul Anderson looked like and to gain some general impression of him. The DVD's title revealed little: "Lecture by Dr. Paul Anderson at Stanford University, May 10, 2019." This was hardly a normal find in a security report.

Van Waters inserted the DVD into the slot in her personal computer, clicked a few icons, and began watching a thirteen year old image of Paul Anderson at a lecture podium.

The first minute of images showed her that Anderson was lecturing on global atmospheric warming and climate change, hardly a surprise because he was introduced as the director of the new Earth Temperature Observation Project. She watched Anderson describe atmospheric heat exchanges, the roles of gases such as carbon dioxide and methane in those exchanges, and the prevailing weather patterns in the Northern Hemisphere, all while using graphs and photographs to illustrate points. She did not follow all of the technical descriptions. She was about to stop and exit the DVD when Anderson made an obvious transition. She soon became riveted to her video screen as he spoke.

"We have to step back from the details. Many people do not understand that we have to look at this problem differently from a routine scientific experiment where the variables are controlled. What we do know for sure is that greater concentrations of greenhouse gases initially add energy, that is, heat, to the earth's lower atmosphere. We call that part of the atmosphere the 'troposphere.' We can also estimate the amount of heat added by increased concentrations of specific gases such as carbon dioxide or methane. Then big difficulties begin.

"More heat means more water evaporation. That means more water vapor in the air. Because water vapor is a greenhouse gas, more water vapor will mean even more heat because it will absorb more infrared radiation coming from the earth's surface. On the other hand, if the extra water vapor forms more clouds, the additional clouds will reflect more sunlight, preventing some sunlight from reaching the earth's surface. This will mean less heat in the atmosphere. To make things even more complex, some kinds of additional clouds may not only reflect sunlight but also trap more infrared radiation from the earth's surface, thus adding heat to the atmosphere.

"How much any additional clouds will counteract or augment the warming effect from increased atmospheric water vapor is not fully known. We are doing the best we can to understand these dynamics.

"Unfortunately, we have no direct analogs in any climatic record that we have been able to construct from the past. We have to rely on computer models to try to match observations of actual changes over recent time. Then we use these models to project what will happen under future changed conditions. However, the earth's multiple climates are enormously complex. They are created by reactions among billions of physical, chemical, and biological forces.

"If greenhouse gases become more and more concentrated in the troposphere, predicting with certainty what will happen to each of earth's climates will be impossible. Even trying to predict average atmospheric temperatures on the earth's surface or at some altitude in the troposphere is proving to be very difficult. Predictions are complicated by the fact that detecting whether average temperatures have changed at all is difficult as well. Changes have to stand out over time against the noise of normal variations. And we are not even sure what normal variations are.

"The devices and methods that we need to collect enough accurate data to determine normal variations have been around only a few decades. The so-called natural system that they are measuring is not the natural system that existed in 1900. The frequency or duration of natural patterns of climate may already have been altered when we started using these measuring devices. And even today's climate system is changing as greenhouse gas concentrations in the atmosphere continue to increase. We are trying to understand statistically significant variations caused by changing forces we do not fully understand."

Here, Anderson paused for emphasis.

"What we know is that we do not know."

Van Waters stopped the DVD and reran the last passage.

What we know is that we do not know, she repeated to herself. *Was that true today as well, even with ETOP? If American farmers could not know the general range of weather they would have, how could they make adjustments in crops to cope with a new set of odd weather conditions? What did Anderson really mean here?*

She returned to Anderson's lecture.

"What I mean by this is we do not know and will not know with certainty what will happen climate-wise in a particular place until it actually happens.

"The attitude that we must be certain what will happen before acting to stop increasing the concentration of greenhouse gases is committing us to grand experiments on a global scale. That's why ignoring the problem is so dangerous. The problem has to be viewed from the perspective of risks, not certain proof. The least plausible result is no change at all.

"The risks are worse than one might at first think. Look at how greenhouse gas concentrations are increasing, especially carbon dioxide. We have no recent historic analogs to this pace of change. Air trapped in ice cores going back hundreds of thousands of years shows nothing like this. When carbon dioxide concentrations did begin to increase or decrease back then, the rates of change were much smaller than the rate of increase we are seeing now. Concentrations of carbon dioxide were also always much lower then than today.

"The converse is true also. The best evidence is that human activities are primarily responsible for the current increases in the concentrations of carbon dioxide, methane, nitrous oxides, and chlorofluorcarbons in the earth's atmosphere. Taking carbon dioxide again as an example, even if we

were to stop immediately all human activities that add large amounts of carbon dioxide to the atmosphere, we know of no way to reduce the carbon dioxide levels at anywhere near the same rate as the increases that have occurred in the last sixty years.

"Equally problematic, an insidious and subtle problem still exists. The impacts of current increased elevated levels of carbon dioxide are probably not yet known. The oceans are the great unknown. They act as a huge heat sink. When increased atmospheric concentrations of greenhouse gases add energy to the earth's troposphere, the oceans absorb a lot of that energy. They delay the changes in atmospheric temperatures caused by that extra energy. The extent of this delay has been estimated using different assumptions about the depth and movement of water actually involved in the heat exchange. Some scientists think that just four or five years are needed for equilibrium to be reached. Others believe that the time period is ten years or even much longer. No one really knows for sure.

"Carbon dioxide concentrations have been increasing during the entire time that models have been created, so we have not had a way to observe how long it takes for equilibrium to be reached at a particular concentration. It is a moving target. Whatever atmospheric heat impacts the current concentrations of greenhouse gases will bring, we have not experienced them yet. We do not even know whether we have yet experienced the full impacts of concentrations that existed ten or twenty years ago. This means that the full impacts of current increased concentrations could be ten or twenty or more years away.

"As I said before, many scientists have created global climate models to try to predict changes based on increased greenhouse gas concentrations. All of them share important limitations. They incorporate only the parameters that people think of. The models also have to assume gradual changes in those parameters over time because formulas require smooth mathematical relationships. They simplify complex relationships and are unable to predict precisely how all factors may operate together. In other words, models of natural systems are almost always conservative in predicting what could occur.

"Let me give you all an example. Remember the chlorofluorocarbons that were widely used in the middle of the twentieth century? In the 1970s, some scientists realized that if these gases migrated up to the earth's stratosphere, they could react with the ozone layer that is there. This ozone layer shields us from most of the sun's ultraviolet radiation. They showed in laboratory

experiments that CFCs act as a catalyst to break ozone down. Just one CFC molecule could destroy thousands of ozone molecules.

"They then created models to try to predict what would happen in the stratosphere if various concentrations of CFCs occurred there. The models predicted gradual decreases of stratospheric ozone world-wide. Everyone agreed that these decreases would be very serious. Many nations acted quickly to deal with this problem. That is why the Montreal Protocol was negotiated and signed in 1987. In the Protocol, the most important producing nations all agreed to reduce CFC production because of those predictions.

"What actually happened when higher CFC concentrations occurred in the stratosphere was far more dramatic—and dangerous— than models had predicted. A huge hole in the stratospheric ozone layer opened up over Antarctica in October and November. This annual phenomenon has now been explained, but only in retrospect. It's caused by a combination of conditions working together. The models did not and could not have predicted this combined result. Even if a model or a scientist had predicted the ozone hole, the prediction probably would have been dismissed by many people, especially non-scientists, as the improbable musings of a doom and gloom environmentalist. Yet the ozone hole undeniably did occur.

"Let's go back to the climate models. Just like the CFC models, the only way climate models can be constructed is to assume gradual changes in the given parameters over time. Climate models are vastly more complicated than the CFC models. Many more variables have to be included. Some of these are interrelated, such as heat exchanges from water evaporation and prevailing winds caused by the earth's rotation. Like the CFC models, the formulas in climate models also use smooth mathematical relationships that can predict only gradual changes over time. But gradual changes are not necessarily the way that weather and ultimately climate changes happen in the earth's systems.

"For example, our historic records from Greenland ice cores show that severe climate changes occurred there in just five to twenty years during and after the most recent Ice Ages. Apparently some thresholds exist where climate changes occur very rapidly. We believe from findings in other places around the world that these changes were global changes, not just local changes. But we really do not know for sure the details of those changes.

"For example, maybe an ocean current changed direction or stopped. We know that this is possible. The Somali Current off the East Coast of Africa changes directions each six months.

"The climate models probably can never predict thresholds and the details of extensive changes after a threshold is crossed. I call these changes 'global climate disruptions.'"

Vice President Van Waters watched the last few minutes of Anderson's lecture and sat back in her chair.

Her mind raced with questions. How much of this lecture was valid today? And what about climate disruptions? No one had even hinted at this kind of problem in looking at the recent US crop declines. If these declines were caused by odd weather patterns that were new and changing, how could they predict next year's odd weather? And how about the year after that? Were climate disruptions underway in the United States? She now realized that they did not know anywhere near enough to be able to make good decisions about US crop production next year, much less in later years.

Van Waters thought that the sooner she got ETOP's experts involved, the better. But first, she and President Clark had to be re-elected. Although polls had President Clark well ahead in the race for president, the electorate could be fickle. Van Waters would wait until after tomorrow's election to make her move.

Chapter 16

DATA

Election Day on November 2, 2032 vindicated President Clark's policies during the past four years. He received a large majority of the electoral votes and a popular vote margin of more than six percent.

Surprisingly, the one issue he feared most never became an issue in the presidential campaign. Only a few politicians recognized that US agricultural production had declined in 2032. None realized that the declines in 2032 were actually much greater than they appeared because so much land had been added to the farm base at the beginning of the growing season. The subject was simply absent from the political discussion. Almost all of the rhetoric on the economy centered on the new petroleum reality, both prices and supplies.

This absence of discussion did not deceive President Clark. He believed the small cadre of individuals in the USDA who had alerted him to a potential danger of food shortages. Events would soon accelerate his need to deal with this potential problem.

Just three days after President Clark's reelection, Secretary of State Straus received a visitor at the State Department headquarters. She was a diplomatic courier from Prime Minister Pierre Rousseau. She carried a brown leather pouch, clearly marked in the corner with "diplomatic exemption" and an official seal of the government of France. The pouch was the size of a large telephone book.

The courier insisted on seeing Straus alone in her office. Despite her staff's misgivings, Straus agreed to this procedure. What her staff did not initially know was that Rousseau had sent Straus a message that the courier would be coming when she did. The courier matched precisely

Rousseau's description of her, including her impeccable dark blue pants suit with a small emblem of the French flag on its left shoulder.

With great solemnity, the courier took a key from the right side pocket of her suit jacket, raised the diplomatic pouch in her left hand, then inserted the key into its lock. With a quick turn of her wrist, the lock popped open. The courier then opened the pouch and pulled out a box wrapped with dark blue paper. She handed it to Straus. Straus now had the SMER data from the North Atlantic Ocean, just as Rousseau had promised.

Straus nodded to the courier, acknowledging that she had received what she had expected. Immediately after the courier left her office, she called Vice President Van Waters to tell her that the SMER data had arrived.

Upon hearing from Straus, Van Waters smiled with satisfaction. But she now had a dilemma. She wanted ETOP to analyze the SMER data promptly, yet neither Paul Anderson nor Marilyn Sawyer knew anything about the tasks they would be asked to perform. They did not even know about their being considered for national security clearance. Someone had to inform them and get them to agree to analyze the SMER information and under condition of secrecy. Given the unusual status of the SMER data, Van Waters decided that she would be that someone.

Paul Anderson was just going out his office door for lunch when his secretary stopped him. She said loudly for the benefit of others nearby that Paul had a telephone call, but then she whispered privately to him that it was the vice president. Paul asked her quietly in return if she really meant *the* vice president. She nodded yes.

As he walked back inside his office to pick up his telephone, Paul was skeptical. He had an old college friend who was known for pulling pranks such as pretending to be someone else. Besides, why would the vice president want to talk to him?

"Dr. Anderson?" said Van Waters.

"Ye--es," answered Paul slowly.

"This is Vice President Van Waters," she said.

"What can I do for you?" asked Paul politely.

"I understand that you met with Karen Lewis from the USDA," said Van Waters. "ETOP has done some work for her. You compiled US weather information, correct?"

His college friend could not possibly have known this information. But how did ETOP's technical compilation for Karen Lewis come to the attention of the vice president? And why would the vice president care about it?

"That is correct," said Paul.

"Dr. Lewis also asked you to find some information published by an organization known as SMER, correct?" said Van Waters.

"That is correct also."

"I would like you and your colleague, Marilyn Sawyer, to come to Washington to discuss both of those subjects with us," said Van Waters. "Of course, Dr. Lewis will be included in our discussions as well."

Paul could not very well decline a direct request from the Vice President of the United States. He agreed to come to Washington to meet with whomever she chose and on the day and at the time she selected.

Paul and Marilyn were both perplexed about Vice President Van Water's request. They guessed that Marilyn's hunch about Karen Lewis was correct. Karen did not tell them her real purpose for the project on weather data that she had asked ETOP to do. But, what was her real purpose? And why would the vice president become involved? What about SMER, that obscure non-profit research group in France? How did that fit in? Paul and Marilyn had many questions, but no answers. They would not begin to get answers until they saw Van Waters at the Executive Office Building in Washington.

On the following Monday, Vice President Van Waters was all business. She was already in a small Executive Office conference room when each of her invited guests arrived. By plan, Karen Lewis and Bill Rand had arrived first. Van Waters had already told them what she wanted to accomplish with Paul Anderson and Marilyn Sawyer. When Paul and Marilyn arrived, Van Waters quickly introduced them to Bill Rand, knowing that they already had met Karen Lewis.

"What I will be asking you to do must remain secret, at least for now," began Vice President Van Waters. "These tasks are part of a very important project for the United States. We have given both of you national security clearance. I cannot tell you more unless you agree to keep secret everything that I tell you today."

Paul and Marilyn hesitated.

Failing to get a prompt response, Van Waters assured Paul and Marilyn that neither the tasks they would be asked to do nor their national security clearance would impede their work at ETOP.

Paul and Marilyn looked at each other, probing the other's eyes for an unexpressed concern. Paul nodded affirmatively ever so slightly, Marilyn returning the gesture. They turned back to Van Waters.

"I agree to treat everything that you say today as a national security secret," said Paul.

"I agree also," added Marilyn.

Van Waters then gave Paul and Marilyn an oath to affirm their allegiance to the United States and to keep secret all information that they received that was so designated. Paul and Marilyn did not suspect, but would soon learn, that the information Van Waters would reveal to them would change their lives.

"Our crop production dropped significantly last year and even more so this year almost everywhere," said Van Waters. "Production has fallen so much that we could have food shortages in the United States as early as next year if this trend continues. Karen's project for ETOP was designed to find out whether odd weather has been a factor, or even *the* factor, that caused these declines."

Paul and Marilyn could hardly believe what they had heard. Before they could fully comprehend what the vice president had said, Van Waters asked Karen Lewis to explain how she had used the ETOP report that she had received from Marilyn.

"We evaluated the data in your report by reorganizing it into agricultural regions," said Karen. "Our evaluation shows that statistically very odd weather has occurred in every region of the United States in 2032 and also occurred to a lesser degree in 2031. These data confirm what we have learned anecdotally from answers to a questionnaire that we prepared and sent to USDA extension offices around the country. Those answers universally report reduced crop yields. Nearly all answers attribute the declines to odd local weather. We need to know whether these odd weather patterns are statistical anomalies or real changes in the local climates."

"We want you to answer this question for each region, or at least to tell Dr. Lewis whether an answer is possible," added Van Waters.

This was familiar territory to Paul and Marilyn. In their work at ETOP, they were constantly trying to answer similar questions on global and continental scales. They also knew that regional and local questions were much harder to answer.

Based on this experience, Paul had a ready response, one that the vice president would not like.

"We already know that the data ETOP collects regularly will not answer this question by region," began Paul. "Regional weather has been extremely variable in the last hundred years. All of the recent annual anomalies we have seen fit within some prior measurements. Although I must say that the total pattern of odd weather throughout the United States this year appears to be unique. Still, one year standing alone cannot support conclusions about climate changes. We are searching for secondary indications that might provide additional guidance about what is happening. If we find some, maybe your question can be answered for some regions. Otherwise, it cannot be answered, at least not now."

Paul had said what Van Waters had thought that he would say. Karen had forewarned her about ETOP's interest in "secondary indications." Van Waters now planned to use this interest to get Paul and Marilyn involved in her project. She wanted them to agree to evaluate the SMER data that she had received from Secretary of State Straus. To accomplish her goal, she first had to reveal the truth about SMER, beginning with what Paul and Marilyn already knew.

"I know what Karen has told you about Marie Leclerc and SMER," said Van Waters. "Karen suspects that SMER may have discovered something new from its salinity measurements this past summer. I know that you told Karen that you have been unable to find any data on salinity measurements published by SMER. Karen's suspicions are not just a product of her imagination. They turn out to be correct.

"Secretary of State Straus met recently with Prime Minister Rousseau of France on other subjects. At our request she also probed Rousseau about SMER. By clever diplomacy, she learned that SMER does indeed have an ongoing project to measure ocean salinity. SMER's project was created and is still funded by the French government. The French want the data that SMER collects to be kept secret. That is why they never have been published. Only a few people know about SMER's project and its real purposes. Fewer still have access to the data SMER collects.

"Secretary Straus also learned from Rousseau that SMER discovered unusually low salinity water in the North Atlantic Ocean near Greenland this summer. I don't know whether the salinity is so low that you will consider it to be a secondary indication. But maybe it could be that low."

Awaiting their reaction, Van Waters thought that she was getting close to reaching her goal. Marilyn's facial expression revealed real interest in SMER's discovery. Paul was more circumspect.

"I agree generally with your suggestion, but only if the actual measurements show a significant discovery," said Paul.

Van Waters was ready for this kind of response.

"Secretary Straus negotiated a deal with Rousseau," she said. "France has agreed to share all of the SMER data with the United States. Straus received a package with the SMER data last Friday as promised. We can now analyze those data when we meet our part of the deal. You see, in return for the SMER data, Secretary Straus agreed to give France ETOP's unpublished climate projections for the region of Europe that encompasses France."

Van Waters paused, giving Paul and Marilyn a chance to absorb what she had just said. She was also not sure how they would react to the commitment made by Straus without even consulting ETOP.

Paul immediately understood what had happened. The president, vice president, and secretary of state had seized upon a rare set of coincidences that gave an opportunity to get information that they thought might help someone understand US crop declines. They were acting just as he hoped leaders would act. The US crop decline could become a huge problem, not only for the United States, but for the world at large. No lead to solving that problem, however tenuous, should be left hanging. Paul was not going to have ETOP stand in the way of these efforts.

"We can give you ETOP's regional projections very quickly," said Paul. "How do you want them delivered?"

Van Waters was relieved. She had not wanted the hassle, and delay, of having to get ETOP's projections through some national security process.

"We need both printed and electronic versions of the projections, along with back-up data," answered Van Waters. "Send three copy sets directly to Secretary Straus. Straus will give a set formally to France, just as France has provided the SMER data to us."

Van Waters then specifically asked Paul and Marilyn to analyze the SMER data. She got the commitment she wanted.

"The SMER data will be delivered personally to Paul at ETOP," said Van Waters. "We have strict security agreements with France for everything from SMER. I have arranged for you to see a CIA security expert after this meeting to learn those security requirements. Contact Karen when you have reached your conclusions. Contact her in any event by December 1st, even if you cannot reach conclusions by then. Here is a list of codes to use for various conclusions or lack of conclusions. That way you do not have to use a private secure line."

As she ended the meeting, Van Waters was grateful that Karen Lewis had not only followed her intuition about SMER, but had contacted ETOP in the first place. President Clark would be pleased with how quickly progress would now be made on trying to understand the future of US agriculture.

Paul and Marilyn met with the CIA agent immediately after their meeting with Van Waters had ended. He told them how to set up secure document storage and use within ETOP. After this had been done, a package with the SMER data would be delivered to Paul. He also warned them that the materials were written in French and asked whether they would need an interpreter from the CIA. Paul and Marilyn declined, preferring to rely on Paul's previous experience with that language.

The security instructions were straight-forward and easy to implement. Paul bought a small safe that fit beneath the work table in his office at ETOP in such a way that it could be seen only from an odd angle. Only he and Marilyn knew its combination and few people even knew about its existence. They created simple check-out procedures for all SMER documents. Everything had to be returned to the safe each afternoon. Only one standalone computer with a complex access code would be used for analyzing the data. Storage drives would also have to be placed in the safe every afternoon.

When the security measures were in place, Paul called the CIA agent and gave him the prearranged coded message. The agent told Paul exactly how, when, and by whom the top-secret package would be delivered to him at ETOP.

On Friday afternoon, November 12, 2032, at precisely 2:20 p.m. as promised, a US State Department courier walked up to ETOP's security gate. He asked to see both Paul Anderson and Marilyn Sawyer. Having been expected, he passed quickly through ETOP's security. Paul and Marilyn met him at ETOP's headquarters entrance and promptly took him to ETOP's main conference room. Paul closed the conference room's door for privacy. At Paul's request, the courier sat down in a chair on the left side of the conference table. Then Paul and Marilyn sat down across from him.

The courier said that he had their package, but that each of them first had to read and sign a short letter from Vice President Van Waters. The courier handed the letter to Paul. "United States Classified: Top Secret" was stamped at its top. The letter identified the contents of the package by coded numbers. It also contained an acknowledgment that Paul and Marilyn would keep the contents secret and would take specified steps to keep the information secure. The CIA agent in Washington had forewarned Paul and Marilyn that this letter would accompany the SMER data. It was exactly what they had expected. Paul and Marilyn signed the letter and gave it back to the courier.

The courier then opened his briefcase, removed a package wrapped in dark blue paper, and placed the package on the conference table. He said, "That's it; good luck," and stood up to leave. Paul took him to ETOP's lobby, thanking him along the way for bringing the package. Within seconds, the courier exited the front door, walked quickly past ETOP's security gate, and was gone. He seemed to disappear in the sunshine of the ETOP parking lot like a ghost that had arisen from some bright afterworld for a brief earthly visit.

Paul quickly returned to the conference room. Marilyn had not touched the package. It sat on the table like a surprise birthday present accompanied by high hopes but modest expectations. Paul deferred to Marilyn to open it. She carefully slit the tape that bound the cover paper and removed the paper without a single tear, revealing an ordinary brown cardboard box with a removable lid. It was just large and deep enough to hold a ream of standard photocopy paper. She lifted its lid. A letter from the vice president lay on top of a stack of papers. The letter was addressed to Paul Anderson and Marilyn Sawyer.

Marilyn removed the letter, beneath which she found a table of contents in English, then a table of contents in French, and finally numerous sheets of paper that were copies of data on salinity measurements taken in the North Atlantic Ocean. The headings and data descriptions were in French. On the side was a flashdrive labeled simply "SMER L'Atlantique du Nord."

Van Waters's letter confirmed that the data sheets were from SMER. Her letter also repeated what she had told Paul and Marilyn in Washington. It said that SMER's summertime voyages were done for the government of France and that France treated SMER's data as secret national security information. The letter also summarized why France treated them that way.

Just one paragraph described the task assigned to Paul and Marilyn. As stated at their meeting, the vice president wanted them to analyze whether or how the SMER data affected ETOP's ability to answer the question raised by Karen Lewis's research. Were US regional weather oddities just anomalies or were they part of long-term climate changes? The letter also directed Paul and Marilyn to report their findings only to Karen Lewis at the USDA. The vice president reiterated her December 1 deadline to report back, although she clearly understood that firm conclusions most likely would not be possible by then.

Paul and Marilyn each separately studied the vice president's letter while the other looked quickly through the many pages and thousands of entries of data provided. No doubt SMER had been taking salinity measurements for many years in the northern North Atlantic Ocean. The question now was whether these data, especially those from the summer of 2032, would provide new and important facts about the state of the world's climates. Paul asked Marilyn to assemble the data in ways that might answer this question. They both would then evaluate what those data showed.

That very afternoon, Marilyn began working diligently on her assigned task. It proved to be surprisingly simple because of the flashdrive and the way the data were organized. Whoever assembled the data obviously wanted ETOP to be able to assess them quickly. In less than a week, a clear picture emerged.

In the late summer of 2032, a huge pool of very low salinity water existed at the surface of the northern North Atlantic Ocean. It extended from the southeastern shores of Greenland southward at least two hundred miles. Salinity data for the same locations just one year earlier gave no hint of a similar pool.

The southern edge of this pool appeared to be expanding or moving southeasterly, at least according to just three weeks of data collected in August and September 2032. These limited data were not enough to draw firm conclusions about the pool's ultimate destiny. It could dissipate by mixing with deeper sea water. But it could also continue moving largely intact at the rate existing in September. If it did so, it would reach the North Atlantic Drift that very fall.

SMER's discovery was both unexpected and ominous. Paul and Marilyn knew that a large amount of cold and low salinity water could disrupt the warm North Atlantic Drift.

No wonder France wanted SMER's findings to remain hidden as top-secret information. Nothing could be done to change the pool of low salinity water or its movements. There was no need to have French and Western European citizens stirred up trying to guess what might happen in the next few months. It was better to wait to see what in fact did happen and then make decisions based on observations, not speculation.

CHAPTER 17

SOURCE

What caused the odd pool of fresh water that SMER had discovered south of Greenland?

Paul and Marilyn asked themselves this question on Wednesday, November 17th when Marilyn gave Paul her evaluation of the SMER data. The answer to this question could determine whether this odd pool of water signaled long-term climate changes that would significantly affect crop production in the United States.

Paul and Marilyn knew that the salinity of ocean water varied from place to place and time to time. Salinity variances even helped drive massive deep water ocean currents such as the thermohaline circulation. Despite their importance, these variances were relatively small except locally near land where major rivers poured fresh water into the sea.

The very low salinity pool of water that SMER had discovered was similar to the low salinity water found at the mouths of big rivers. The size of the pool was far too large to have been created by fresh water from any normal river, and no river was anywhere close to the pool anyway. The Greenland Ice Sheet was the only nearby source of large amounts of fresh water. It must have started melting or calving very rapidly in the summer of 2032. But why?

Paul and Marilyn thought that only two causes were plausible. One was new volcanic activity underneath the ice sheet. The other was significant atmospheric warming around the ice sheet.

Paul and Marilyn listed the different factual signatures of each cause. The list would tell them what recorded observations to look for in order to discern if one, or both, of these causes was at work.

New volcanic activity would be relatively local, almost certainly less than twenty miles square. The heat from this activity beneath the Greenland Ice Sheet could cause part of the bottom ice to melt. Fresh water beneath the ice sheet could then flow directly to the sea underneath the ice, just like an ordinary river. Or the water could act as a lubricant, making glacial ice move downhill faster than normal. As the ice reached the sea, ice would calve off to form icebergs. Given the amount of fresh water needed to create the pool that SMER had discovered, the physical appearance of the Greenland Ice Sheet should have changed noticeably where either mechanism had occurred.

Where melted water had vacated significant space beneath the ice, the ice sheet should have collapsed. Or, where base water had acted as a lubricant, the number and total volume of icebergs near Greenland should have increased in a geographically concentrated area. The SMER data did not contain any information about ice sheet changes or icebergs near Greenland. However, satellite photographs could identify significant localized changes in the Greenland Ice Sheet and could also show icebergs. Even if no one had seen and reported new volcanic activity, these photographs should provide a way to investigate new volcanic activity as a possible cause of the low salinity pool of water.

Without saying so, Paul and Marilyn both hoped that new volcanic activity had caused the fresh water incursion. Volcanic activity would most likely be only temporary, maybe a few months or at most a few years. As such, it would not create a lasting threat to the North Atlantic Drift and Western Europe.

Unlike volcanic activity, if significant atmospheric warming around Greenland was causing fresh water to be released from the Greenland Ice Sheet, melting or increased glacial ice movement would have occurred over large areas. This effect would be much less visible from satellite photographs than more localized effects from volcanic activity.

The only way to identify this possible cause was to examine temperature histories at numerous places around Greenland. Hopefully, ETOP's temperature measurements in or near Greenland would be enough to discern the existence or non-existence of this potential cause.

Like volcanic activity, significant local atmospheric warming could be a short-term anomaly. But it could also be long lasting, at least in human terms. Paul and Marilyn both knew that ice core records from Greenland had shown that long-term climatic changes, especially significant warming, had occurred historically in just a decade or two during the Ice Ages. This meant that the Greenland Ice Sheet could start unleashing more and more fresh water very quickly, whether as water or as icebergs.

Paul and Marilyn divided their investigation. Marilyn would examine the possibility of volcanic activity, which would require research off-site from ETOP. Paul would examine the possibility of local atmospheric changes, for which ETOP probably already had all the data he needed. Both began their tasks promptly. Marilyn left to go to meet with volcano experts at the National Oceanic and Atmospheric Administration a few miles away. Paul went to ETOP's analysis center just downstairs to access ETOP's detailed records.

Paul's initial task was simple. He quickly obtained temperature data from ETOP's six stations in and around Greenland. They showed that the average temperature there had increased three degrees Celsius from 2020 to 2032, with most of the increase having occurred in the last five years. The large size of this increase surprised him. He knew that the increase in the average atmospheric temperature at the earth's surface over the same period had been far smaller, only about 0.2 degrees Celsius.

Despite his initial surprise, the Greenland data did not at first concern Paul because he was well aware that regional atmospheric temperatures varied a lot more over short time periods than global atmospheric temperatures. Three decades ago, Greenland had shown almost no increase in temperatures during a period when other regions in far northern latitudes had seen the largest increases on the planet. Greenland could now just be catching up and moving ahead briefly in a back and forth dynamic with those other regions.

Paul thought that even the three degree temperature increase at Greenland might not have been enough to tip the balance to net annual melting in the Greenland Ice Sheet. The amount of melting in 2032 had to have been extraordinary. Maybe Marilyn's investigation would identify new volcanic activity that would augment the effects of local atmospheric warming.

But what if Marilyn did not find any volcanic activity? Then it would be important to know whether Greenland's change was temporary or long-term. Was a rapid decrease in local average temperatures just as likely in the next twelve years? What about a return to historic conditions existing two centuries ago? What atmospheric dynamics were at work here?

Paul knew that finding the answer to these questions was not an academic exercise. If the huge influx of fresh water into the North Atlantic Ocean continued from year to year, the North Atlantic Drift could be disrupted for a long time. Western Europe could then have much colder climatic conditions than any time in recorded history.

Poor growing conditions for crops, or at least very different growing conditions, were possible. Because all agricultural systems had been developed based on historic conditions, coping with these new and sudden conditions would be extremely difficult, even for the technologically advanced nations of Western Europe. Paul knew that crop planning in Western Europe now hinged on the temporary or long-term nature of the melting that had occurred in the Greenland Ice Sheet in 2032.

An even more insidious possibility loomed in Paul's mind. The anomaly at Greenland could be the first step in Paul's feared global climate disruptions. Increased energy exchanges in the earth's atmosphere, represented by the global atmospheric warming that ETOP had observed, could be creating new atmospheric energy patterns. Massive adjustments could be underway in climates around the world. Karen Lewis had discovered widespread odd weather from her examination of ETOP's data for the United States. This discovery was already consistent with the beginnings of global climate disruptions.

A sense of urgency now prevailed. Paul had to try to answer the questions posed by SMER's discovery. He knew of only one way to start.

CHAPTER 18

CHANGES

On Thursday morning, November 18, 2032, Paul sat down alone at his office desk. He treated his task like a final examination in college. He pretended that he was asked to answer two questions central to Vice President Van Waters' assignment to ETOP.

- Was the warmed atmospheric condition at Greenland in 2032 temporary or long-term?
- Did this warmed atmospheric condition signal a real change in the regional climates of the United States?

Paul looked straight ahead across his oak desk toward his outside window facing south. Its blinds were open. Bright sunlight pierced the left side of his window, shining directly onto a large free-standing globe of the earth that Paul had placed in front of his desk this morning.

Paul thought about what he saw on the globe and had seen from many photographs taken during space explorations in the twentieth and twenty-first centuries. The earth was unique. Oceans covered nearly three-fourths of its surface, giving the earth its distinctive look and nickname of the "Blue Planet."

Although oceans dominated the earth's surface, land masses were the most important to humans. People not only lived on them, they also derived most of their food from them. Even a cursory look at his globe showed that most of the earth's land masses were found in the Northern Hemisphere. Especially important were the land masses in the temperate zone, where most of the world's people lived and where most food for humans was produced.

Above the earth's surface, swirls of white clouds gave form and definition to what otherwise would have been an invisible atmosphere surrounding the earth. This atmosphere, thin and light, retained enough of the sun's radiation to provide the warmth needed to sustain life on the earth. Atmospheric dynamics had given each region a unique climate to which the people, animals, and plants living in that region had adapted.

Paul had neatly organized his desk for his task. Preferring techniques of an earlier day, he had placed a stack of lined paper and two pens on the right side, a glass of orange juice on the left side, and a single piece of paper in the upper middle. On that single piece he had written the two questions for his simulated examination. Nothing else was present. He would draw entirely upon his existing knowledge.

Paul picked up a few pieces of paper, placed them below his exam questions and picked up a pen. He again looked straight ahead, this time closing his eyes briefly. He was ready to start.

"CLIMATE," he wrote in capital letters. Just one word, but so important. His mind raced ahead, his pen lagging behind.

Paul knew that climate was the average weather affecting a place over time. Weather, in turn, was that combination of atmospheric features that affected a place at specific point in time, whether heat, moisture, wind, or sunlight. Paul reminded himself that changes in climate did not just happen, they were caused by something. What could cause continent-wide changes in United States weather from, say, seventy years ago?

Paul knew that in the distant past the earth's surface had experienced dramatically different climatic conditions than existed today. Millions of years ago, the earth's climates had been much warmer. They had allowed dinosaurs to flourish in rich vegetative environments around the globe. At the other end of the spectrum, climates as recently as 20,000 years ago had been much colder. They had created the last glacial maximum of the Ice Ages when ice sheets a mile or more thick had covered northern regions as far south as Minnesota and Maine.

These extreme variations had caused some people to believe that whatever changes in climates were occurring today were just part of another inevitable natural cycle. Paul knew otherwise. Even these historic climate variations had not appeared randomly. They had been generated by changes in the amount of energy in the earth's atmosphere. And the relative amounts of that energy were measured by the average atmospheric temperatures of those times.

To what extent had average atmospheric temperatures changed in the last seventy years?

ETOP had data that answered that question. As shown to Karen Lewis during her visit to ETOP just two months earlier, the data compiled by ETOP and earlier compilations showed that the average atmospheric temperature at the earth's surface had risen from seventy years ago, albeit not at a steady rate and not every year. The largest variations had occurred after the eruptions of Mount Pinatubo and Soufrière when the atmosphere cooled temporarily.

In the recent historic record, the high atmospheric temperature observed in 1998 had begun a fifteen-year period that had spawned considerable controversy. During that period, the temperature had risen far less than in previous decades. The 1998 high point had been a record that had been matched only a few times in the last years of that time period.

When that record high had first been observed, some non-scientists had claimed that it was just the first of many upcoming record high temperatures that would have catastrophic impacts. Later, when average atmospheric temperatures had been less than the 1998 record, other non-scientists had claimed that atmospheric temperatures had remained flat with no increases at all. That claim had expanded into assertions that global warming was a myth. Both groups of non-scientists had falsely represented the data by treating 1998 as a new norm. It was not.

The 1998 measurement was just one of many measurements of annual average atmospheric temperatures. There always had been and would be variations in these annual average temperatures. The multi-year trend of those annual temperatures, rather than a single year, revealed whether or not the average atmospheric temperature was changing. Despite the 1998 record, the multi-year trend during the fifteen-year period had been an increase, albeit an increase at a rate less than had been measured for the previous two decades.

The fifteen-year slowdown in the temperature increase had been attributed primarily to two factors.

The most important proposed factor had been internal climate variability resulting from increased ambient aerosols in the atmosphere.

The amount of upper atmospheric aerosols had increased because of a larger than normal series of volcanic eruptions, even though none of these eruptions had been major like the eruptions of Mount Pinatubo and Soufrière. These ambient aerosols had been augmented by a new and huge brown haze of low-altitude aerosols that had developed over much of Asia. This brown haze had reduced local temperatures, which in turn had affected the compilation of average atmospheric temperatures at the earth's surface.

The second proposed factor for a fifteen-year slowdown in the temperature increase had been a slight diminution in sunlight from 2001 to 2009 pursuant to the sun's historic eleven-year cycle. That diminution could tend to reduce atmospheric temperatures, however slightly.

Whether or not these factors had been correctly identified as responsible for the fifteen-year slowdown, at the end of this fifteen-year period the year 2014 had established a new undisputed atmospheric temperature record for modern times. Later years had shown important temperature increases as well.

So if the average atmospheric temperatures had increased after 2014, what could be causing this trend?

Since at least the 1990s, various scientists had warned that continually increasing concentrations of greenhouse gases in the earth's atmosphere would increase the temperature of the atmosphere. And those increases potentially could bring other changes that would adversely affect many people, other creatures, and whole ecosystems on the earth. Many books, reports, and media programs had presented this information, sometimes in summary fashion that incorrectly oversimplified what these scientists had actually been saying.

Skeptics had dismissed these warnings as biased or unsupported by later events, pointing out that some predictions by scientists about atmospheric warming did not occur. Skeptics also had pounced upon incorrect versions of what scientists were actually saying, claiming that the conclusions presented had flaws that in turn showed that the whole basis for the warnings also was flawed.

Even more than atmospheric warming, Paul knew that a food shortage in the United States was so unprecedented that few would believe its possibility. He also knew that any suggestion that global climate disruptions were the underlying cause of this remote possibility would be met with far greater skepticism than any skepticism experienced with predictions of atmospheric warming. So, to be sure he was not missing some important fact, Paul looked at all of the most important physical phenomena that affected the amount of energy in the earth's atmosphere. And he would go back to basics, questioning every part of the evidence that might provide answers to his two questions.

He then wrote four words to direct his thinking—gases, aerosols, sunlight, and surface.

Had any of these changed in the last seventy years?

One set of changes was obvious. The gaseous composition of the earth's lower atmosphere was definitely different now than then. ETOP's data, both those measured by ETOP and those collected from earlier reliable sources, showed this fact conclusively. Paul wrote down brief notes summarizing these changes.

In 1958, scientists had begun making daily and very accurate measurements of atmospheric gas concentrations at the observatory on the summit of Mauna Loa on the Big Island of Hawaii. They had focused initially on carbon dioxide. When they had started, the atmospheric concentration of carbon dioxide had been 315 parts per million. By 1998, its concentration had reached 365 parts per million and had crossed 400 parts per million in 2014. Now, in 2032, its concentration was 440 parts per million. Measurements of the concentrations of some other gases, such as methane, nitrous oxide, and chlorofluorcarbons showed that they also were higher than in 1958.

Paul was tempted to begin summarizing whether or how each of these changes in gaseous concentrations mattered for atmospheric temperatures. But the other physical phenomena that he wrote down could also affect those temperatures and in different ways. So instead, he went back to his short list. Aerosols were next.

As the eruptions of Mount Pinatubo and Soufrière had demonstrated, significant amounts of the right kinds of aerosols in the atmosphere reflected sunlight enough to measurably cool the earth's atmosphere. Ambient volcanic aerosols from lesser eruptions acted the same way but with less effect. Increases and decreases in volcanic aerosols clearly could impact average atmospheric temperatures, although these impacts from any particular volcanic eruption would be relatively short term.

Changes in ambient volcanic aerosols in the atmosphere from year to year also may have occurred in the last seventy years. Except for big eruptions, the ambient amounts of volcanic aerosols in the atmosphere had been very difficult to determine from year to year. Only in the twenty-first century had technology been developed that could measure these ambient aerosols. Thus, at this point in his mini-exam, Paul could not discern whether ambient volcanic aerosols had actually changed since seventy years ago.

Beyond volcanic aerosols, Paul knew that different kinds of aerosols from other sources also could affect atmospheric temperatures.

Especially since the middle of the twentieth century, scientists had observed steady increases in the amounts of low-altitude aerosols in the air above some land regions. These aerosols had been commonly seen as local brown hazes, especially in and near urban areas. Although individual low-altitude aerosols quickly dropped out of the air, aerosol levels had increased because their ongoing sources had increased. Very simply, more and more aerosols were being added daily to local atmospheres by increased ongoing combustion of coal and other fossil fuels. The large Asian brown haze that had affected atmospheric temperatures in the first decade of the twenty-first century had been attributed to these activities. Especially important had been the greatly increased combustion of coal by China as part of its rapid industrialization beginning in the last decade of the twentieth century.

Some of these low-altitude aerosols, especially sulfates, cooled the atmosphere by reflecting sunlight. Reflection occurred directly and also indirectly by the aerosols acting as nuclei to condense water, forming clouds. Increased amounts of other aerosols, such as black carbon or organic carbon, had also been observed, but their effects were not well understood.

Even increased airplane traffic had created more thin-cloud trails at high altitudes. These trails had increased reflection of sunlight back out to space but also had increased absorption of heat radiation from the earth's surface. Their net effect also was not fully understood.

The third physical phenomenon on Paul's list was sunlight. Had the amount of sunlight received by the earth through space changed in the last seventy years?

Both energy calculations and historic events had shown that small long-term changes in the amount of sunlight striking the earth could have huge effects. Maybe the sun was just now beginning one of those changes.

Paul first looked at possible variations in the sun's output, commonly known as brightness and scientifically labeled irradiance. Irradiance changes would cause the earth to receive more or less energy from sunlight. If the sun's irradiance had changed by just a small percentage, the heat content of the earth's surface and lower atmosphere would have changed by the same percentage over time. Many scientists used to think that the sun's irradiance was constant on a daily and annual basis, at least during periods of many decades or even centuries. Measurements that were possible only after satellites became available for research proved this idea to be wrong.

Measurements of total solar irradiance by satellite instruments since 1979 showed that the sun's irradiance changed by small measurable amounts every day. The same measurements showed that average irradiance also changed by small amounts over just a few years. A roughly eleven-year cycle of higher and lower irradiance had been identified. This cycle corresponded generally, but not precisely, to the approximate eleven-year cycle of sunspot activity that had been known for centuries.

To provide a baseline of irradiance for comparisons, scientists had calculated a twenty-four year average amount of energy radiated from the sun toward the earth as measured from the satellites. They called this irradiance the "solar constant."

Paul remembered that studies had been done to compare the solar constant to the average solar irradiance during the few full eleven-year solar cycles that had existed during the period of satellite observations. These studies had most recently included ETOP's observations. The solar constant and the average solar irradiance in each of the eleven year cycles was the same. These observations proved that no overall change in the sun's irradiance had occurred since satellite measurements had been available.

Paul even briefly considered whether any changes in the earth's orbit had occurred that would affect the amount of sunlight received by the earth. The earth's orbit around the sun changed from circular to elliptical and back again over time. Especially when combined with changes in the earth's axis tilt and orientation, these changes were thought to have been the driving forces behind the intermittent Ice Ages that the earth had experienced in the last one million years. Those changes would affect the total amount of sunlight received by the earth even if the sun was emitting light at a constant rate.

But orbital changes were gradual and slow. They would not be discernible over a period of seventy years or even several hundred years. Orbital changes could not have changed the amount of sunlight striking the earth in the last seventy years.

Paul concluded that possible changes in sunlight striking the earth could not be a cause of recent increases observed in average atmospheric temperatures.

Finally, Paul looked at the earth's surface as the fourth physical phenomenon on his list. Did it change in some way in the last seventy years that would have affected the amount of sunlight reflected back out to space? Scientists called this feature the earth's surface reflectivity. Increased reflectivity would promote cooling, whereas decreased reflectivity would promote warming as more sunlight would be absorbed and re-emitted as infrared radiation.

During the Ice Ages, ice had covered larger and larger areas, especially on the continental land masses of the Northern Hemisphere. These great increases in what was known as the earth's crysophere had reflected more and more sunlight back out to space. So these increases had enhanced the atmospheric cooling that orbital changes had initiated. The opposite effect could occur if the earth's cryosphere were now decreasing.

Paul knew that changes in sea ice had occurred during the last seventy years. Arctic sea ice had decreased, but Antarctic sea ice had increased. The most accurate measurements came from satellite images that began being recorded in 1978. On balance, probably less sea ice existed now to reflect sunlight than had existed seventy years ago, but not so much less that total surface reflectivity had changed in a significant way. The disappearance of high altitude glaciers also decreased reflectivity, but the combined reflective surface area lost was very small compared to the earth's total cryosphere. Although changes in the earth's cryosphere had significant local effects, especially in the Arctic, and eventually could have significant global effects, Paul concluded that those changes had not been a factor in whatever had occurred with average atmospheric temperatures during the last seventy years.

Paul finally considered one other set of changes on the earth's surface. This set of changes began some 11,000 years ago, when humans began cultivating land to create crops. Over the millennia, humans had made more and more changes to existing vegetation, replacing it with crops, orchards, and dwellings. By modern times, the list of human changes included cities, reservoirs, roads, and a multitude of other land uses. These changes had altered the way that the land and its vegetation absorbed sunlight and emitted energy back to the atmosphere.

One-by-one, each of these changes had been a tiny contributor to changed energy in the earth's atmosphere. But the number and magnitude of these changes had accelerated with a burgeoning human population in the twentieth and twenty-first centuries. Nevertheless, even considering the aggregate of these changes by 2032, few scientists believed that human land uses made an important difference in surface reflectivity.

Paul stopped jotting down notes. He had covered the four physical phenomena on his list. He put down his pen, stood up briefly to stretch and promptly sat down. He did not have time to waste.

Paul was now ready to assess how the atmospheric changes in the last seventy years that he had identified could potentially impact weather and ultimately climates in the United States. He began with the changed gaseous composition of the atmosphere.

A tapping on his office door interrupted his thoughts. It could only be his secretary, as he had told her to block anyone else from contacting him.

"Come in," he said loudly, somewhat perturbed.

The door opened quickly. His secretary charged in, obviously excited, and began talking rapidly as she raced toward his desk.

"We have a big problem," she blurted. "Our monitors detected a huge solar flare just three minutes ago. Charles said that lots of particles from the sun will start hitting our satellites very soon. They need you now."

"Damn," exclaimed Paul, using rare profanity. He immediately abandoned his task and got up from his chair. His mini-exam would have to wait. He rushed out of his office and down the hall toward ETOP's satellite control center.

It was 11:53 a.m.

CHAPTER 19

SATELLITES

Paul reached ETOP's satellite control center, took a deep breath, and opened its door. Before him was a brightly-lit rectangular room with four desks lined up against the right wall. A computer screen on each desk faced toward the center of the room. An ETOP engineer was seated in front of and looking intently at each screen. Charles Tate, ETOP's lead satellite engineer, was at the second desk from the door. He turned back as he heard Paul enter.

"The particles storm will begin in fourteen minutes," he said. It could be really bad. The solar flare was huge."

Paul had planned for this kind of problem when ETOP's satellites were designed fourteen years ago.

Well before ETOP, satellite designers had known that large solar flares in the late twentieth century had damaged the electronics of some satellites. Historically, much larger, but rarer, solar flares had also occurred from time to time. These very large solar flares would clearly do more damage and even make a satellite useless.

Although Paul had designed ETOP to have four satellites in orbit at the same time so that they would have redundant data in case one satellite failed, a strong solar flare was the one event that could make all satellites fail at the same time. Should this occur, many months would pass before other satellites could be placed in orbit. ETOP could then have a large data gap that would harm its ability to discern correctly whether climate changes were occurring.

To avoid this problem, Paul made sure that ETOP's satellites had the best technology known to withstand large pulses of ultraviolet radiation, x-rays, and particles that would come from a huge solar flare. On each satellite, two features protected both the microwave sounding unit and the solar irradiance monitor.

One feature was an electronic trip device designed to shut off most of the instrument's electronic circuitry if a designated threshold of ultraviolet radiation had been exceeded at the satellite's solar panels. This circuitry would later be reconnected automatically after a preset three-hour delay using power from a reserve battery on the satellite.

The second feature was an opaque cover of a unique material that would fully close automatically within six minutes after the ultraviolet radiation threshold had been detected. This cover would reduce the amount of particles that struck the two detectors.

Or at least that was the way these devices were supposed to work.

Unfortunately, no cover could protect the detector from a pulse of ultraviolet radiation or x-rays because these kinds of energy would reach the satellite at the same time as the light that permitted anyone, or any device, to see that a solar flare had occurred.

ETOP's satellites were now going to be tested for the first time by a monster solar flare.

Paul quietly fixed his eyes on Charles' computer screen. ETOP's special monitoring programs had turned on automatically when the ultraviolet radiation pulse had occurred at the first satellite. A timeline flashed on the top of the screen. When Paul first saw it, it read 5:31. That was the number of minutes and seconds from the time the solar flare's ultraviolet radiation hit the Donner satellite. In turn, that time was eight minutes after the solar flare had erupted from the sun, the time required for light to travel from the sun to the earth.

Charles brought Paul up to the second on what had happened.

"There, see—the MSUs and irradiance monitors disconnected almost immediately," he said, pointing to his computer screen. "This is Donner, but all of our satellites reacted like they were supposed to."

Paul could see on the screen that the other three satellites also reported back that their instrument covers had closed.

Paul was most concerned about ETOP's microwave sounding units. They were safe, at least for now. He knew that MSUs had to be kept continuously active and accurate. This unwelcome solar flare now threatened those features.

Paul reflected on his meeting with Karen Lewis just two months ago. He had told her about the problems with earlier radiosonde data collected by using weather balloons. He also had summarized the improvements that ETOP had made in its radiosondes and also the way that ETOP used its weather balloons to eliminate those problems. He never did have to tell her about the problems inherent in using MSUs on satellites, or the improvements that ETOP had made to avoid those problems. He did not want to revert back to the uncertainties that had vexed scientists before ETOP when calculating atmospheric temperatures using MSUs.

As he had told Karen, the scientific basis for using MSUs to measure atmospheric temperatures was sound. The problems did not lie in the scientific principles, but in the sampling limitations that were inherent in satellite operations.

The first use of a satellite microwave sounding unit had begun in 1978. The original purpose of MSUs on satellites had been to assist in making weather predictions. For this purpose great accuracy was not needed for atmospheric temperatures that were calculated from MSU brightness measurements.

The first MSUs and other early units had lasted only one or two years. Replacement units had been launched regularly so that satellite MSU data would be available every day for weather forecasting. Sometimes two functioning MSUs had been in orbit at the same time, sometimes only one. Scientists had found that consistent calibration of different MSUs had been a difficult challenge. Yet in order to determine atmospheric temperature changes over time, great accuracy and consistency in brightness measurements were needed to link the brightness data from MSUs on different satellites. Everyone had expected that average temperature changes would be small over periods even as long as several decades.

Consistent instrument calibration had been just one of many challenges that had affected the validity of analyses using MSU data. Converting oxygen brightness data to equivalent atmospheric temperatures was a straight-forward calculation. But what was the brightness actually measuring?

MSUs were designed to scan back and forth perpendicular to the path made by the satellite as it crossed the earth's surface. They operated like a camera, taking snapshots of oxygen's brightness at eleven different angles toward the earth. These angles varied from pointing straight down to pointing nearly toward the earth's horizon. The MSUs detected and recorded oxygen's brightness at each position.

Comparing atmospheric temperatures over time required adjustments based on a number of precise facts about the satellite's location over the earth's surface, the satellite's altitude, and the MSU's direction relative to the earth's surface when measurements were made. Even comparing measurements over time by the same MSU on one satellite was complicated by the fact that the satellite slowed down or speeded up relative to the earth's surface with each orbit around the earth. This meant that the satellite would cross the same place on the earth's surface at slightly different times of day. A satellite that had begun its orbit by crossing the equator at noon may have been crossing the equator in the same place at 2:00 p.m. two years later. This factor, known to scientists as diurnal drift, had to be taken into account when comparing atmospheric temperatures that were calculated from MSU measurements taken on different days from the same satellites.

ETOP's scientists had created a new third generation microwave sounding unit by 2020. This new MSU had a longer life and greater accuracy than earlier MSUs in order specifically to measure potential atmospheric temperature trends.

Since then, ETOP's new MSU had been on each of the four ETOP satellites in orbit simultaneously around the earth. The four satellites were also orbiting the earth in such a way that two MSUs would measure the same air space at the same time at least once each day. The five thousand balloons with radiosondes that ETOP launched daily included at least one thousand balloons that were coordinated with the movement of these satellites. The satellite MSUs and the radiosondes on these balloons measured the temperatures of the same air spaces at the same times. Comparing these measurements helped to assure that both sets of instruments remained calibrated accurately. These comparisons also established error ranges for both kinds of instruments. Unfortunately, MSU measurements still had to be adjusted for diurnal drift when doing temperature comparisons over time.

Despite uncertainties caused by diurnal drift, Paul was optimistic that data from ETOP's radiosonde and MSU measurements had been accurate enough to discern atmospheric temperature trends at the mid-troposphere, at least until this solar flare occurred. He was much less willing to rely on data that extended the time period for comparison back to the first satellite data obtained in 1978. He could only say that ETOP's observations were consistent with the mid-range of the various temperature trends calculated by different scientists from observations that had preceded ETOP.

Now, a huge solar flare threatened ETOP's microwave sounding units, irradiance monitors, and the overall electronic circuitry of all four ETOP satellites. Even if all remained functioning, many tests would be needed to assure that their accuracy remained. Fortunately, ETOP's radiosonde program provided a prompt tool to test whether all four MSUs were giving initially correct readings. The irradiance monitors, overall circuitry, and settings of each satellite would take much longer to test. If the accuracy of the MSU and irradiance monitors could not be assured …

An exclamation by Charles interrupted Paul's thoughts.

"They did it!" he said, pointing at his computer screen.

Paul saw on Charles' screen that the fourth satellite had closed its protective cover for its instruments. The time was exactly six minutes after the ultraviolet radiation pulse had been detected. The protective devices on all satellites had worked just as they were supposed to.

From here, each satellite was supposed to be dormant for three hours.

No communications with ETOP'S satellites would be possible until their batteries reactivated their circuitry at three hours from the ultraviolet radiation pulse. A waiting game began.

In the interim, all of the satellites orbiting the earth, not just ETOP's satellites, would be bombarded by enormous amounts of particles streaming from the sun. Paul hoped that most of these satellites also had effective protective designs. Otherwise normal communications around the world would be a mess.

He hoped that one satellite in particular would keep operating during the ion storm. Certainly it was designed to do so. The National Oceanic and Atmospheric Administration of the United States had launched a special satellite eleven years ago for the very purpose of measuring large pulses of ultraviolet radiation, x-rays, and particles from the sun. If it survived the current onslaught, its data should reveal a lot about the amounts and kinds of energy from a very large solar flare.

Paul was not about to stand around for three hours watching Charles' computer screen. He told Charles that he would return at 2:30, then left ETOP's satellite control center to return to his office.

He had walked only a few steps from the center when he heard a familiar voice behind him.

"Paul, what's going on?" the voice asked. It was Marilyn Sawyer.

Paul stopped and turned to face her as she walked rapidly toward him.

"A huge solar flare, the biggest since we started ETOP," Paul answered.

"How are the satellites doing?" Marilyn asked quickly.

"OK so far," Paul said.

Marilyn was visibly relieved. She knew as much as Paul about ETOP's need for functioning satellites.

"I was just finishing up at NOAA when I felt my cell phone activate," said Marilyn. "I received only three words from your secretary: 'problem, come now.' So I came back right away."

"We can't do anything now but wait," said Paul. "You said you were finishing up at NOAA. Do you have an answer yet?"

Paul was purposely vague in this open hallway. Marilyn needed no more clarity.

"I am getting there," she answered. "I need to check a few more things. How about you?"

"Same status," said Paul. "I was making pretty good progress when this problem hit us. I am coming back to the control room at 2:30, so I probably can't finish today. I still want to get together with you tomorrow morning."

"Agreed. Still at 9:30?"

"Yes."

CHAPTER 20

CAUSES

Paul was glad that Marilyn, like he, had not quite finished her investigation. Before the satellite crisis had occurred just twenty minutes ago, he had only been able to summarize the physical phenomena that could have changed and thereby affected the amount of energy in the earth's atmosphere in the last seventy years.

Two of those phenomena—sunlight and surface—had not changed enough to have contributed to the overall increase in the amount of that energy that had been observed as average atmospheric temperature increases. On the other hand, the other two phenomena—gases and aerosols—had changed enough to be considered potential factors in those increases.

Despite what he had told Marilyn, he hoped that he would have some conclusions by tomorrow morning, at least if he did not have to deal with some other ETOP crisis.

Paul returned to his office, picked up his sack lunch and bottled water from a side chair, and settled in at his desk. He had expected a long day with his simulated examination, and had wanted to retain his focus by staying in his office all day.

In an odd way, the satellite crisis had energized him. He felt at least as sharp as he had felt early that morning.

Paul recalled the many times over the last twenty years that he had given presentations that summarized the role of greenhouse gases in the earth's atmosphere. He even remembered being nervous at his first presentation thirteen years ago at Stanford University as the director of the newly-formed ETOP. But those summary presentations lacked the scientific detail that he now needed to apply to answer the question whether the warmed atmospheric condition at Greenland in 2032 was temporary or long-term.

As he was about to begin, his globe of the earth again drew his attention. This time, early afternoon sunlight, more intense and at a different angle than sunlight this morning, gave the globe a halo-like glow. He imagined that the glow was caused by that magical feature of the earth itself—its marvelous atmosphere.

Paul knew that the unique composition of the earth's atmosphere had allowed just the right balance of warmth to sustain the huge array of life that had developed over time. Paul made a few more notes, while drawing on his memory to remind himself how this worked.

The sun was the initial actor in this play, with certain gases in the atmosphere having critical roles. Radiation from the sun bathed the earth with energy every day. Part of this sunlight was reflected, mostly by aerosols found in the upper atmosphere, clouds in the lower and middle atmosphere, and snow and ice on the earth's surface. The ultraviolet portion of sunlight was largely absorbed by ozone in the upper atmosphere. The rest of the sunlight passed through the atmosphere and was absorbed by the earth's surface. This warmed the surface, which then emitted heat back to the earth's atmosphere as infrared radiation.

Based on the amount of sunlight that was absorbed and heat re-emitted, the average atmospheric temperature at the earth's surface would have been a chilly eighteen degrees Celsius below zero if the earth did not have an atmosphere. At that temperature, all water on the earth would be frozen. Nearly all life that was known could not survive.

Fortunately, the earth had an atmosphere, and one that contained beneficial gases that had been given the name "greenhouse gases."

When the earth's surface emitted infrared radiation back to the atmosphere, this infrared radiation directly warmed only the air close to the ground. However, throughout the atmosphere greenhouse gases absorbed some of this infrared radiation rather than allowing it to pass back through the atmosphere out into space. In chemical terms, the greenhouse gas molecules absorbed unique wavelengths of the infrared radiation emitted by the earth's surface. This absorption increased the vibrational and rotational energies of these molecules. In turn, these increased energies warmed the gases surrounding the greenhouse gases.

The combined effects of these atmospheric processes around the world made the actual average temperature of the atmosphere at the earth's surface about fifteen degrees Celsius above zero. This was thirty-three degrees warmer than the atmosphere would have been without the greenhouse gases.

The earth's atmosphere was strangely unique. Nitrogen and oxygen comprised more than ninety-nine percent of the earth's atmosphere, but did not act as greenhouse gases. The gases that did act as greenhouse gases were all found in very low concentrations, and so were known as trace gases. Non-scientists sometimes had a hard time understanding why they were so important. Some people even tried to denigrate their role, scoffing at the importance of any changes in their concentrations, by harping about their tiny amounts in the earth's atmosphere.

Paul knew better. He sometimes used fresh water as an analog to the importance of greenhouse gases in the earth's atmosphere. Compared to the total amount of water on the earth, which was predominantly salty ocean water, the amount of fresh water was minuscule. Yet humans could not survive without that relatively tiny amount. So it was for trace greenhouse gases. They alone kept the earth habitable.

Water vapor was by far the most important greenhouse gas. Its influence on the amount of heat in the earth's atmosphere was very complex because of the multiple roles that water vapor and water played in the atmosphere. In addition, the concentration of water vapor in the atmosphere varied tremendously from place to place. The public and weather reporters referred to these variances as the "relative humidity." That complexity and variance caused Paul first to focus on other greenhouse gases whose amounts and roles were much easier to discern.

Greenhouse gases such as carbon dioxide, methane, and nitrous oxides, had historically been products of the earth's biosphere and other natural forces. They had been in the earth's atmosphere back as far as detection had been possible. But by the time Congress had created ETOP in 2018, their concentrations had increased from base levels at the beginning of the twentieth century to levels not seen in the last eight hundred thousand years. Those concentrations had continued to increase and were even higher by 2032.

Another group of greenhouse gases called chlorofluorcarbons did not exist in nature. They had been created by humans in the twentieth century. From a base level of zero, atmospheric concentrations of chlororfluorcarbons had increased steadily until the last decade of the twentieth century.

The increased concentrations of these greenhouse gases meant that each gas had contributed increased energy to the earth's atmosphere. The amount of that contribution differed for each gas, depending upon its chemical character and its total concentration in the atmosphere. Molecule-for-molecule, methane was a much stronger greenhouse gas than carbon dioxide. But carbon dioxide's concentration in the atmosphere was much higher than methane's concentration. On balance, carbon dioxide contributed far more atmospheric heating through its absorption of infrared radiation than did methane.

The lowest region of the atmosphere, known as the troposphere, contained most of the total gases in the earth's atmosphere, including most of its greenhouse gases. As such, the troposphere was what primarily kept the earth's surface habitable.

Weather dynamics assured that trace greenhouse gases other than water vapor were uniformly distributed in the troposphere. Their concentrations were essentially the same in Antarctica as they were in Hawaii.

These uniform concentrations allowed scientists to calculate the total amounts of these trace greenhouse gases in the atmosphere. Those amounts in turn allowed fairly precise estimates of the total amount of infrared radiation that each of these gases absorbed to provide a heating effect. From these calculations the independent atmospheric heating effects of each gas could be estimated.

Scientists had made estimates of the independent heating effects of increased concentrations of carbon dioxide and the trace greenhouse gases other than water vapor. Those estimates revealed an initially puzzling fact. The total heating effect of all of these increased trace gases could not account for all of the increased annual average atmospheric temperatures that had been observed.

This fact had led some non-scientists to claim that increased concentrations of carbon dioxide and other trace greenhouse gases were really not very important and that whatever warming had occurred had come from natural causes.

Paul knew that this assertion ignored known secondary effects of these increased concentrations. The most important secondary effect was an increase in the average concentration of water vapor in the atmosphere. Simply stated, warmer air could contain more water vapor. More water vapor would absorb more infrared energy which in turn would further warm its surrounding air.

How this known physical fact played out in the earth's atmosphere, however, was anything but simple.

Paul then returned to water vapor's role as a greenhouse gas. The total amount of water vapor in the earth's atmosphere was determined by its equilibriums with water surfaces on the planet. Those water surfaces took many forms. By sheer size, the most important water surfaces were the oceans, but lakes, rivers, ice, snow, soil moisture, and even plant leaves also contributed to this equilibrium. Water evaporated from these surfaces and eventually condensed again as mist, rain, snow, or hail, all in a great hydrologic cycle. The total equilibriums in the hydrologic cycle depended upon the total amount of energy in the earth's troposphere. If that total energy increased, no doubt the average total amount of water vapor in the troposphere also would increase.

The observed increased concentrations of greenhouse gases other than water vapor clearly had increased the amount of energy in the earth's troposphere, but was there really a multiplier effect with increased total water vapor? Would other water-related phenomena reduce or even prevent a multiplier effect? These questions permeated all attempts to understand whether the changed gaseous composition of the earth's atmosphere significantly affected the average atmospheric temperature and eventually the earth's climates.

By itself, increased total atmospheric water vapor would add more heat to the earth's atmosphere as a typical greenhouse gas. But water vapor was not a typical greenhouse gas. Not only did its concentration vary greatly from place to place and from time to time around the world but also it transformed itself depending upon atmospheric conditions.

Water vapor's condensation into tiny droplets, forming clouds, was the most important transformation from the viewpoint of total atmospheric energy. Increased overall water vapor in the earth's atmosphere could mean more clouds world-wide, even though an overall warmer atmosphere would accommodate more water vapor before condensation occurred. If more clouds were formed, more sunlight would be reflected back out to space, partially or maybe even fully offsetting the warming effects of increased water vapor. Quantifying these possibilities was extremely difficult. Whether more clouds would actually occur was not known. Even if more clouds were to occur, the types of clouds would also be important because different types of clouds reflected sunlight differently.

Paul knew that the only way to determine the existence or extent of a multiplier effect was through temperature measurements and modeling. When describing this empirical methodology to non-scientists, Paul often used an analogy to rain in a river basin.

A river basin got rainfall that was measured at many places in the basin. The rainfall in each place where measurements occurred, such as two inches of rain from one storm, was only one impact of the rain. A secondary impact was runoff if there was enough rain. That runoff then collected in streams and rivers. Many physical phenomena in the basin determined the amounts of water collected and whether those amounts would become dangerous as a flood. Soil and ground absorption, land slopes, streambeds, and amounts and kinds of foliage all influenced flood potential. Measuring the effects of each of these physical phenomena was nearly impossible.

To predict the secondary effects from measured rainfall, scientists used empirical models that tried to replicate historic run-offs and stream levels from their associated rainfall patterns. Each model at its inception relied on estimated formulas designed to match observed effects. Then the model was modified by using different formulas and estimates until the model's predictions closely matched historic run-offs and stream levels. The best models gave predictions that were close enough to what would actually occur from different amounts of rain to warn people whether and to what extent flooding was likely to occur.

So it was with climate models that tried to predict the effects of gaseous changes in the earth's atmosphere.

The most important recent gaseous changes had been increased concentrations of carbon dioxide. The initial effects of these increased concentrations could be measured as additional energy in the troposphere, which translated into warming. But that warming had an important secondary effect by increasing the average capacity of the air to contain water vapor. How much or whether these secondary increases in water vapor would further increase the energy in the atmosphere depended upon complex physical phenomena. The only way to discern these effects was to use empirical models to try to match atmospheric temperature changes that had occurred historically as carbon dioxide concentrations had increased.

These empirical models also had to take into account other atmospheric changes. Increased or decreased concentrations of other greenhouse gases such as methane and nitrous oxides also increased or decreased the amount of energy in the atmosphere.

Aerosols played an important role as well. The most important aerosols were from volcanoes, whether from large eruptions or from multiple small eruptions over time. Aerosols also included increased low-altitude aerosols that came largely from the same human activities that had increased carbon dioxide concentrations. Extra aerosols mostly reflected sunlight, causing decreases in atmospheric energy, which counteracted the increases in atmospheric energy from increased carbon dioxide and other greenhouse gas concentrations.

Just like the models used to predict flooding in a river basin, each climate model at its inception relied on estimated formulas designed to match measured changes. The model was modified by using different formulas and estimates until estimated effects closely matched historic measured changes in atmospheric temperatures.

Had the predictions of these models been confirmed by the atmospheric temperatures that had been observed?

Paul knew that early models from the 1980s did not adequately take into account the cooling effects of aerosols, so their predictions of global atmospheric warming did not match what was observed in the following decade. Later models, however, did a much better job of predicting what was later observed. Indeed, a few models from the early twenty-first century were close to, but underestimated, the average atmospheric temperatures that ETOP had observed in the third decade of the twenty-first century.

It turned out that the greatest uncertainty was not in the models themselves, but in the projections about future greenhouse gas concentrations and aerosols produced by both volcanic eruptions and human activities. Those projections had to be made many years before actual atmospheric conditions were known, and aerosols in particular were impossible to predict with the accuracy needed for the models to portray with precision what later occurred.

Paul had come full circle, back to the observations of what had occurred in the earth's atmosphere in the last seventy years.

Clearly the concentrations of greenhouse gases other than water vapor had increased from seventy years ago, adding total energy to the earth's lower atmosphere. Local aerosol concentrations also had increased, subtracting some energy from the earth's atmosphere through increased reflection of sunlight. Water vapor and water had responded in complex ways to these changes.

Refining his thoughts from earlier, Paul recalled that ETOP's surface temperature measurements showed conclusively that the average temperature of the earth's atmosphere at the earth's surface had increased. Data compilations before ETOP also had observed increases after 1970. The rates of change detected by ETOP were about the same as the rates of change that had been calculated from those earlier methods in the time periods that ETOP did its measurements.

As Marilyn had explained to Karen Lewis, ETOP's refined system of world-wide measurements had removed uncertainties that had existed in the earlier compilations. But those uncertainties evidently had far less effect on the results compiled from the old methods than some critics had asserted. Paul was confident that the increases found in average atmospheric temperatures, including those compiled before ETOP, were real.

This was not the only real change that ETOP had found. ETOP's radiosondes and microwave sounding units also had detected mid-tropospheric changes during their twelve years of operation. According to these measurements, the average temperature of the earth's atmosphere in the mid-troposphere had increased as well, albeit less than the average atmospheric temperatures observed at the earth's surface. Equally important, ETOP's MSUs had revealed that the global average temperature of the lower stratosphere above the troposphere had declined. This is exactly what scientists had expected would occur if the troposphere warmed up by retaining more radiative heat from the earth's surface. The stratosphere would have to cool in order to maintain the balance between total radiation received from the sun and total radiation ultimately emitted by the earth back to space.

Paul knew that the temperature increases in the troposphere were especially important to weather dynamics. Being denser than the atmosphere above it, this lower atmosphere spawned all major weather features. Because total tropospheric energy greatly affected weather systems, a one degree Celsius temperature change in the troposphere represented potential for changes at the earth's surface that would include shifts in regional weather patterns, and ultimately shifts in regional climates.

Paul began to write his conclusions, but again was interrupted by tapping on his office door. This time he knew why. It was time to return to ETOP's satellite center.

CHAPTER 21

CYCLES

Paul arrived just in time.

Charles' computer screen for ETOP's Donner satellite read 2:58:10. Donner would be the first to reconnect its electronics to its solar panels, at least if its battery and reconnection mechanism worked as designed.

Marilyn was already there, transfixed by Charles's computer screen. The three-hour mark came and passed. Everyone knew that another two minutes were needed for Donner's electronic circuitry to charge and begin transmitting signals back to ETOP's receivers. At precisely 3:02:00, ETOP received a signal from Donner. It was back in operation.

During the next minute, ETOP's other three satellites also transmitted signals to ETOP's receiving stations. By 3:04:00, all satellites were again operational.

Few words were spoken. Everyone was more relieved than ecstatic. Numerous checks had yet to be conducted to be sure that no satellite had sustained damage, but so far everything appeared normal.

Paul and Marilyn left ETOP's satellite control center at the same time, nodding to each other, but little more. Both were still absorbed in their efforts to complete their investigations before they got together the following morning.

Paul returned to his office, sat back down at his desk, and started in yet again.

He wrote only a few words of his conclusion and stopped. "What about ...," he thought.

There was another, more elusive, set of atmospheric phenomena to consider.

He grabbed another piece of paper and wrote one word—"cycles."

He pulled back into his chair and closed his eyes, deep in thought. Only a few moments were needed. He opened his eyes, moved forward, and began jotting down more notes.

He wrote another word beneath "cycles," then grabbed another sheet of paper, repeated the word "cycles," and wrote a second word beneath it. He was now ready for details.

Paul began with the first new word he had written—"atmospheric."

Paul knew that tremendous advances had been made in the last two decades of the twentieth century to identify repetitive patterns of atmospheric weather related phenomena. These phenomena had cycles of several years, decades, or even centuries. The cyclical pattern of the El Nino-Southern Oscillation in the Pacific Ocean became known even to the general public. Other patterns, such as the North Atlantic Oscillation, Pacific-North American Teleconnection, and Tropical Atlantic Sea Surface Temperature Variability, were well-known to climatologists.

Could the rapid temperature increases observed around Greenland be caused by one of these natural cycles rather than by overall warming in the atmosphere?

Paul thought that the most likely candidate among these cycles was the North Atlantic Oscillation. This was a sea-level pattern that reflected the strength of an annual wintertime low atmospheric pressure in the northern North Atlantic Ocean around Iceland. When that low-pressure zone was strong, cold arctic air masses more frequently affected the northeastern seaboard of North America. Westerly winds also increased, pushing warmer air masses from the southern part of the North Atlantic Ocean to Western Europe in the winter. However, those warmer air masses would be blocked by the low-pressure zone around Iceland and thus would not contribute to warming at Greenland. This pattern of the North Atlantic Oscillation changed periodically, but not in a way that would enhance warming at Greenland.

Paul also remembered something peculiar about the pattern of the North Atlantic Oscillation during the last two decades of the twentieth century. It had occupied unusually persistent states that favored warming in Europe. Indeed, those states returned just a few years ago. These persistent states were inconsistent with warming at Greenland.

Another pattern in the tropics had been identified by the end of the twentieth century that appeared to coincide at least partly with the melting of glaciers in high tropical mountains. This unnamed pattern itself had been acting oddly in the last several decades. Its odd behavior also was inconsistent with the natural periodic cycle that previously had been identified.

Unusual behavior by these recognized natural weather cycles had to be explained. The only explanation that Paul could find was overall energy increases in the earth's troposphere. This meant that the unusual behaviors of these two natural weather cycles must only be the mechanisms that changed weather and potentially climates. They were not the underlying causes of those changes.

Paul jotted down a few more notes, wrote "no" at the top of this sheet. He turned to his second sheet of paper with the heading "cycles." Its second key word evoked a natural cycle, far removed from the earth, that had intrigued scientists for centuries. It was always a candidate for explaining anything odd that happened to the earth's climates. Paul had already considered a part of this natural cycle when he had examined possible changes in solar irradiance during the last seventy years.

The key word was "sunspots."

Sunspot recordings had been made on and off for two centuries beginning with their discovery by Galileo in 1610. Then in 1843, scientists had recognized that the sun had an average eleven-year sunspot cycle with greater and lesser sunspot activity. Later scientists had found from these recordings that the eleven-year sunspot cycle appeared to be part of longer natural solar cycles where the length of the cycle and maximum number of sunspots in each eleven-year cycle increased and decreased in some sort of solar rhythm.

Many researchers had used relative numbers of sunspots and their patterns over time as surrogates for the sun's irradiance to try to explain cooled and warmed climates that had occurred after 1610. These were climates in the Northern Hemisphere and especially in Europe where records had been kept that allowed changed climates to be identified and compared to sunspot numbers. The success of these efforts had been mixed.

Modern observations had shown correlation between sunspot peaks and irradiance maximums, but only because brighter regions called faculae had also peaked with sunspot peaks in the time period when observations had been made. Faculae, not sunspots, had accounted for the increased solar irradiance. In addition, variations in the sun's output had been shown not to be uniform for all wavelengths. Ultraviolet radiation had varied more than other wavelengths. All of these factors had complicated attempts to use historic sunspot data to represent actual changes in total solar irradiance and then to compare those changes to recorded climatic conditions.

Historic sunspot activity and climates aside, did 2032 coincide with maximum solar output under the sun's eleven-year output cycle? If it did, then maybe a short-term maximum solar output was working together with something else to create a short-term warming peak at Greenland.

Paul was not normally concerned with solar irradiance cycles, so he could not remember where the sun was in its current cycle. He did not want to go online or to find a text with that data either. He paused, looking at his globe.

Paul recalled an article on solar irradiance that he had read three months ago. He remembered that he would be turning seventy years old when the next peak occurred in the sun's eleven-year cycle. That would be 2035. The year 2032 was in the mid-range irradiance of the cycle. There was no short-term maximum solar output in 2032 other than the solar flare that had just occurred.

Paul also remembered from that article that the variance in solar irradiance between the peak and bottom of the solar cycle was tiny. At less than 0.1%, this variance was not even close to an amount that would be required to account for the global atmospheric warming that ETOP had measured.

Again, Paul wrote a few words on his latest sheet of paper to remind himself what he had considered. He then wrote "no" next to "sunspots."

Paul stood up and went to his window. He stretched his back while scanning the sky before him. It was azure blue, framed by white puffy clouds that were just beginning to turn golden as the sun neared the western horizon created by the Continental Divide of the Rocky Mountains.

Was he done? Not quite yet. One more possibility, although very remote, still existed. He returned to his desk, picked up his pen, and again wrote a single word on a new sheet of paper.

CHAPTER 22

THRESHOLDS

"Surprise."

Paul wondered how he could assess this possibility. After all, if he could think of a cause and effect, it would not be a surprise. Despite this logical trap, Paul knew that he had to try to think far beyond the most logical possibilities, even those that might initially seem very strange.

Historic experience had shown that surprises could occur in the earth's atmosphere and climates. Human activities that had affected atmospheric ozone in the twentieth century formed a sobering example of the unexpected.

Ozone at low altitudes in the troposphere acted like other greenhouse gases to warm the air by absorbing infrared radiation coming from the earth's surface. Ozone at high altitudes in the stratosphere primarily absorbed high-energy ultraviolet radiation coming directly from the sun. This reaction also created a warming effect, but, more importantly, also protected plant and animal life from the destructive effects of that radiation.

The surprise came from human activities that were seemingly unrelated to atmospheric ozone—the production and use of chlorofluorocarbons. In the 1970s some scientists had realized that chlorofluorocarbons could migrate up to the stratosphere. There they could react with and reduce the ozone layer, placing its beneficial effects at risk. These scientists had predicted gradual reductions in the amount of ozone in that layer world-wide. The surprise had occurred when a huge hole in the ozone layer had opened over Antarctica. This phenomenon was far more dangerous than the effects that had been predicted.

Even worse, the atmospheric concentrations of chlorofluorocarbons had only declined slightly after more than forty years despite strict treaty prohibitions in the twentieth century on their manufacture and use. The ozone-free zone remained at its maximum size even in 2032 because natural systems could not easily remove chlorofluorocarbons from the atmosphere.

Just as in the case of chlorofluorocarbons, if surprises were to occur from the increases in greenhouse gas concentrations that Paul had just considered, reversing those surprises would be impossible in the life span of human generations now alive unless some human mechanism could be created to reduce those concentrations. No natural mechanism was known that would reduce those concentrations in that time frame.

There was one kind of surprise that Paul could at least generally identify and that he feared most. That was a potential threshold of increased atmospheric energy that would cause a rapid shift in climates world-wide as the earth's weather systems rapidly adjusted to a new level of energy. Ice-core records showed that during the Ice Ages thresholds had existed after which rapid world-wide climate changes had occurred.

The risk of a threshold existed, but it was not possible to know in advance what that threshold would be. Nor was it possible to predict the precise climate shifts that would occur after a threshold was reached. Both would be surprises. The climate shifts could be very dangerous to human societies when they occurred, especially if they were part of global climate disruptions.

Paul stopped writing notes. He had gone through all of the possibilities he could think of. He looked again at the globe before him. It was getting late. The sun had set. A pink glow began to appear outside his window as golden puffy clouds were turning red. Soon they would all darken, as the last rays of sunlight were cut off by the earth's rotation. Although he was now fatigued, he felt that he had to try to reach some overall conclusions before his meeting with Marilyn tomorrow morning.

Paul reached out slowly to the first sheet of paper he had placed on his desk early this morning. He softly read aloud to himself the two questions that had prompted his simulated examination.

- Was the warmed atmospheric condition at Greenland in 2032 temporary or long-term?
- Did this warmed atmospheric condition signal a long-term change in regional climates of the United States?

The first question was easier to answer than the second.

By process of elimination, Paul found only one explanation for the rapid temperature rise at Greenland observed this year. Clearly the earth's troposphere as a whole was retaining significantly more energy in 2032 than it had retained seventy years ago. The elevated temperatures at Greenland were somehow a manifestation of that total energy increase. And that increase had been caused directly and indirectly by the well-documented increased concentrations of some greenhouse gases in the earth's atmosphere since the middle of the twentieth century. Exactly how that energy increase manifested itself at Greenland was a far more difficult question to answer, but it was not necessary to answer that question now. Only the effect of the energy increase was important.

So the warmed atmospheric condition at Greenland would be long-term unless the concentrations of greenhouse gases in the atmosphere could somehow be reduced. How likely was that possibility?

The build-up of greenhouse gases had occurred over more than seventy years of annual increases. Their concentrations were still increasing. When clearly increasing carbon dioxide concentrations had been documented after 1958, scientists had examined all possible sources for the increases. The same had been true for increasing methane and nitrous oxide concentrations.

Scientists in the middle of the twentieth century had known that natural systems produced huge amounts of carbon dioxide, with lesser amounts of methane and nitrous oxides. Perturbations in these natural systems were certainly possible reasons why the increased concentrations of these gases had occurred. One-by-one, possible natural causes had been eliminated as unsupported by observed facts.

Scientists now concluded that the only plausible explanations for all of the increases were human actions around the globe. These actions included the extensive burning of coal, gasoline, natural gas, and other fossil fuels and even old-growth forests in the case of carbon dioxide and leakages from the extraction of petroleum and natural gas in the case of methane. These activities produced so much additional carbon dioxide and methane that natural removal systems could not absorb their overload in the atmosphere.

These additions had disrupted the equilibriums that had existed just two hundred years ago with these gases. That was why their concentrations had increased. And the continuation of these activities on a massive scale assured that these concentrations would continue to increase. This meant that the higher temperatures at Greenland were not going to go away, and probably would soon increase further.

What about long-term changes in regional climates in the United States?

The warmed atmospheric condition around Greenland by itself would not signal rapid or long-term climate changes in the United States. More observations of related changes were needed to answer this question.

Maybe Marilyn had found that volcanic activity under the Greenland Ice Sheet contributed to the fresh water incursion that SMER had discovered south of Greenland. Then the changes around Greenland would have less global climatic significance. Paul expected to find out tomorrow morning.

CHAPTER 23

COMPARISONS

Marilyn, as usual, was prompt. Paul had left his office door open, so Marilyn walked right in, closed the door behind her, and sat in the chair in front of Paul's desk, next to his globe of the earth.

"Inspiration?" she commented, gesturing toward his globe.

Paul nodded affirmatively. Maybe they did know each other's idiosyncrasies too well.

"Well, Marilyn, what did you find out at NOAA?" asked Paul.

"Nothing that points to increased volcanic activity under the Greenland Ice Sheet," answered Marilyn. "I looked at two decades of NOAA photos. The photos this year show a lot of icebergs along Greenland's southern and eastern coasts—more than in other photos—but they are widely distributed. Only general melting of the ice sheet fits what I saw in the photos."

Paul winced, but was not surprised.

"What about you?" asked Marilyn.

"Not good news," began Paul. "Our land stations around Greenland show plus three decrees Celsius in the average annual temperature in just the last twelve years."

"Wow, that's a lot!" said Marilyn.

"You bet it is," responded Paul. He then summarized his notes from his mini-exam on what he thought could be causing these increases.

"Do you think that SMER's discovery of fresh water points to …?" Marilyn asked, but hesitated.

"Global climate disruptions?"

"Yes."

"Maybe so, but I hope not," said Paul.

Both Paul and Marilyn knew that global climate disruptions could cause regional climate changes in the United States and many other areas of the world as well.

Paul then told Marilyn about the two questions he had tried to answer when he considered whether local atmospheric warming had caused the fresh water incursions that SMER had discovered.

- Was the warmed atmospheric condition at Greenland in 2032 temporary or long-term?
- Did this warmed atmospheric condition signal a real change in the regional climates of the United States?

Now in the context of potential global climate disruptions, they both realized that these questions were too narrow. Together they conceived one new question that they would try to answer together.

- Had the concentrations of greenhouse gases in the atmosphere reached levels that would cause long-term atmospheric warming sufficient to change many climates around the world?

Paul and Marilyn knew that answering this question would be difficult. They also knew that climate models could not identify thresholds. But maybe the history of climate changes during recent Ice Ages would provide some guidance. They began their task by setting up a white board that Paul retrieved from his stash of presentation equipment located in a corner of his office.

"Let's look at the Ice Ages in the last one hundred thousand years," started Paul, as he wrote "100,000 years" on his white board. "We know that there were warm periods much like today's climates in between very cold periods," he added.

"And thresholds occurred where temperatures and climates changed very rapidly at the beginning and end of some of those warm periods," chimed in Marilyn.

"That's right," said Paul. "Just twelve thousand years ago the Younger Dryas cold event began and ended in less than twenty years. Let's look at atmospheric features that changed back then and also are changing now."

"I think that carbon dioxide concentrations would be one feature," said Marilyn.

"Agreed," said Paul as he wrote CO_2 on his white board.

"Atmospheric temperatures would be another," added Marilyn.

Paul wrote "temps" on his white board.

Paul and Marilyn both paused, trying to think of other features that could be compared to atmospheric changes that were occurring today. There were none that were significant.

"All right, let's look at carbon dioxide," said Paul. "Carbon dioxide concentrations rose and fell in a pattern similar to the rise and fall of atmospheric temperatures during the last one hundred thousand years," he commented, knowing that Marilyn would promptly correct common misunderstandings about this fact.

"Yes, but studies have shown that the increases in carbon dioxide concentrations followed rather than preceded the beginning of significant warming periods," said Marilyn. "We now know that changes in the earth's orbit around the sun increased the amount of sunlight hitting the earth. These changes interacted with changes in the earth's axis tilt and precession. The combination of these events caused the initial warming for the warm periods. Different combinations of these events caused the initial cooling that made ice sheets. That's why cooling and warming was periodic during the Ice Ages."

"That's right," commented Paul. "As oceans warmed up in the warm periods, they also released more dissolved carbon dioxide to the atmosphere. That extra carbon dioxide enhanced the warming already underway, but did not initially cause it."

"Plus the amounts of carbon dioxide in the atmosphere were always less back then than they are today," said Marilyn.

Paul and Marilyn did not need to say aloud what they both already knew.

Analysis of ice cores had revealed atmospheric carbon dioxide concentrations during the last eight hundred thousand years. During that long period, concentrations had been as low as 180 parts per million during severe Ice Ages and as high as 300 parts per million during warm periods.

The modern era was one of those warm periods. As late as 1800, the concentration of carbon dioxide in the atmosphere had been less than 300 parts per million. Then those concentrations had begun to increase slowly. Seventy years ago, the rate of increase had accelerated. Carbon dioxide concentrations had started at 315 parts per million in 1958 and were up to 440 parts per million in 2032. Human activities and not natural causes had created these increases.

"So, at least for carbon dioxide, Ice Ages history cannot help us spot a carbon dioxide threshold for global climate disruptions today," concluded Marilyn.

"Agreed," said Paul, writing "no" next to CO_2 on his white board. "Let's look at atmospheric temperature changes back then. Let's start with the coldest recent extreme about twenty thousand years ago. The warm-up from that period clearly provided a global climate rearrangement."

"That's when ice sheets covered much of Canada, Northern United States, Northern Europe, and Northern Siberia," right?" said Marilyn.

"That's it," responded Paul. "You know, the chemistry of air bubbles in ice core samples from back then shows that temperatures were almost twenty degrees Celsius colder than today. A warm-up of twenty degrees is far more than what we are seeing today. I think that the coldest extreme of the Ice Ages gives us no guidance. Let's look at the Younger Dryas cold period instead. That was not as cold as the extreme Ice Ages."

"Paul, I know that the end of the Younger Dryas led right into the modern warm period we are in today. But the average temperatures were still seven degrees Celsius colder than today. A warm-up of seven degrees is still a lot more than the two degree increase that we have seen in the last seventy years. If a seven degree warm-up is needed for a threshold to be crossed to a global climate rearrangement, then we are not close to that now."

"True enough," said Paul. "But I think that our looking back to the Ice Age temperature changes has a serious flaw. The temperature changes from cold extremes to warm periods obviously crossed thresholds that caused huge climate changes. But lesser temperature fluctuations also occurred within warm periods. Those fluctuations almost certainly crossed thresholds to lesser and shorter climate changes. Those changes are very difficult to measure precisely from the historic record.

"Even our modern warm period after the Younger Dryas has had significant temperature fluctuations. Suppose that our modern widespread agricultural operations had existed back then. Did those fluctuations cause climate changes that would have significantly impacted those operations? We just do not know."

"Are you saying that maybe, just maybe, the current temperature increases are getting us close to another threshold?" asked Marilyn.

"Basically, yes," answered Paul. "These temperature increases may be more important than they first appear. We cannot rule out the possibility that we are pushing close to a new threshold. If we are close to a threshold, massive regional climate changes around the world could occur within just a few years."

Paul and Marilyn stopped, taken aback by this possibility. They then looked again at the question that they had conceived.

- Had the concentrations of greenhouse gases in the atmosphere reached levels that would cause long-term atmospheric warming sufficient to change many climates around the world?

There was no certain answer to this question. Their reexamination of climates during the Ice Ages simply reconfirmed what they already knew—the newly changed chemistry of the earth's atmosphere, and the atmospheric temperatures and climates that it had produced and would produce, were in new territory. Global climate disruptions could well be underway that would change many regional US climates. Or climate disruptions could be many years away. They just would not know for sure until more secondary evidence was found.

Time did not allow for certainty. Severe crop shortages could occur in the United States in the next year or two. Decisions had to be made. The possibility of global climate disruptions was real enough to require action to try to counteract the underlying causes of the atmospheric warming now underway.

Paul and Marilyn had finished their tasks much faster than expected. Their mutual conclusion was so serious that they wanted to reconsider it before reporting it to Karen Lewis. A delay of a few more days would make no difference in assessing what to do next. Besides, the Thanksgiving holiday would soon be upon them. This break with their families might help them to have new ideas.

The Thanksgiving holiday came and went.

Neither Paul nor Marilyn had any new ideas that would change their somber conclusion. On Monday, November 29, 2032, they sent Karen Lewis a coded message.

CHAPTER 24

DILEMMA

While Paul Anderson and Marilyn Sawyer were trying to understand whether global climate disruptions were underway, other people were confronting the declines in United States crop production in 2032.

Just two weeks after Election Day, and shortly after the SMER data had been delivered to Paul and Marilyn, President Clark convened a full Cabinet meeting. With his reelection, all Cabinet members understood that they would be continuing in their appointed roles if they chose to do so. President Clark clearly had no desire to appoint anyone new. Instead, he wanted his Cabinet to begin making specific plans to accomplish the agenda that he had outlined generally during the election campaign.

President Clark had given each Cabinet member a succinct briefing paper two days before the meeting. In that paper, he provided point-by-point summaries of actions to be taken collectively and by each department. Those summaries also tagged those actions that would require new laws or funding adjustments from Congress. Many items concerned the new petroleum reality. None of these petroleum items was new to the Cabinet members, as all of the points had been debated during the election campaign.

After greeting all Cabinet members and gesturing for them to be seated around the large oval table in the Cabinet Room, President Clark also sat down at his central chair on one side of the table. He wasted no time. He worked his way quickly through the summaries, elaborating on each of his action topics as needed. Everyone was familiar, to greater or lesser degrees, with all of the action topics but one. This new topic was described simply as "US crop production." Unlike the other topics, no specific action plan was set forth beneath its topical heading. Its presence was a mystery to all Cabinet members except Bill Rand.

The president's comments on this mystery topic were brief but pointed. He said that US crop production reports for 2031 and 2032 had shown successive declines in all sectors. He attributed these declines to a rare combination of weather oddities in each agricultural region. Although he acknowledged that food prices would likely rise over the winter because of reduced harvests, he expressed confidence that global agricultural markets would supply any grain shortages that might seriously affect some US prices. He also asserted that the international prices of grains would remain low and that the total prices for imported grains would be favorable despite high transportation costs caused by high fuel prices under the new petroleum reality. President Clark said that Secretary of Agriculture Rand was working on proposals for incentives to American farmers to increase their crop production. All in all, he painted the US crop production decline as temporary, the effects of which would be relatively easy to negate.

Even though President Clark expressed optimism, he admonished all Cabinet members to keep this issue secret until Secretary Rand's proposals could be developed. President Clark did not tell the Cabinet members about the investigation that Vice President Van Waters was conducting.

Like the other Cabinet members, Secretary of State Melissa Straus was surprised to learn about the declines in US crop production. President Clark's comments alarmed rather than assuaged her. The United States had always been an exporter, not an importer, of grains, especially wheat. The possibility that the United States might have to depend on global grain markets to supply its needs for rice or even wheat was a totally new phenomenon. What if problems arose in the global grain markets? What if …?

Straus paled. She thought about that obscure State Department report that had been delivered to her office just a month ago when she returned from her diplomatic mission to France. She had read its synopsis from her staff. The report had compiled statements of high-ranking officials in a growing number of countries that questioned the wisdom of exporting basic agricultural goods, including grains. Straus realized that if those countries actually decided to restrict grain exports, then President Clark's assumption was incorrect. American companies may not be able to go into world markets to alleviate unlikely, but possible, grain shortages in the United States.

Straus remained silent for the remainder of the Cabinet meeting. In her mind, she was already rearranging her priorities for that day. Promptly after the meeting ended, she left the White House to return to her office in the Harry S Truman Building.

Straus' first order of business was to summon the assistant who had prepared the synopsis of the State Department report. She asked him bluntly what he thought about the probability that important grain producing nations would adopt, or even had, adopted policies against exporting grains in times of relative shortage. His answers were not comforting. He pointed to several specific parts of the report that considered that question. Straus knew that she must now read the entire report to reach her own conclusions. She began that very afternoon.

The report was every bit as dull as she had originally thought it would be. But its dullness did not hide the fact that its contents were troubling. Its author had examined public statements made here and there by governmental officials of numerous nations around the world about grains produced in their countries. Many officials had said that they would not export any grains in the future if they believed that their crop production was needed to supply adequate food for all of their nations' citizens.

This idea of export restrictions on grains was contrary to the open market philosophy that had dominated all international markets in the last four decades. That philosophy asserted that a global market for goods would be the best way to provide for the needs of every nation's citizens. Yet, here in 2032, many foreign officials were beginning to reject that philosophy, at least as far as it concerned grains.

The reasoning behind this new rejection was consistent, if not universal. The report cited governmental officials who had said that they had to keep domestic grains at home to protect their citizens. Simply put, they had asserted that international distribution of grains sometimes created prices that were beyond the means of many of their citizens. These officials had said that only cheap domestically grown crops could provide enough food for their people to avoid hunger or, in some cases, even starvation.

The report went beyond compiling these statements. It also examined whether widespread national policies that restricted exports of grains would really matter to the United States. The report concluded that they would not. For one, the global grain markets did not create mutual interdependencies such as those existing with some manufactured goods. For another, the United States was an exporter of grains, not an importer. It did not depend upon other nations to supply its most basic food needs.

The report also looked at impacts on other nations if restrictive export policies for grains became widespread. This analysis was more complex.

Citing publications that compiled crop production data around the world, the report said that most nations still relied primarily upon domestic crop production to meet their citizens' needs. Despite the global market philosophy and recent practice, the portion of crops used in the country or region of origin had remained at about eighty-five percent during the last two decades—the same as it had been during the last part of the twentieth century. This meant that only those nations that depended greatly upon imported grains to meet their citizens' basic needs would be affected by new restrictive export policies by other nations. According to the report, relatively few nations were in this category, although this small group included some nations with large populations.

More dangerous was the fact that just a handful of nations were major exporters of grains. If those nations somehow began to have declining production or adopted restrictive export policies, then the people in the importing nations with large populations would be in severe trouble.

Straus now saw an odd juxtaposition. President Clark optimistically dismissed possible adverse effects on Americans caused by declines in US crop production in future years because the United States could rely on robust global grain markets to make up any shortages. Conversely, this State Department report optimistically dismissed possible adverse effects on Americans caused by curtailed international grain markets because the United States had crop surpluses. The optimism of President Clark and the optimism of the State Department report each depended upon assumptions that the other factually challenged.

What if both assumptions proved to be false?

Straus began to realize that if US crop production continued to decline and global grain markets shrank, a genuine food shortage could occur in the United States.

How preposterous, she thought. The likelihood that either situation would occur by itself was minuscule. The likelihood that both situations would converge must be infinitesimal.

But what if these situations were probable?

After all, the president did introduce the possibility of shortages in domestic grain production. This idea would have been unthinkable just two years ago. Why did he say this? What did he know that he was not telling the Cabinet? Indeed, why would there be shortages at all in the United States? The United States had the best agricultural industry in the entire world. The president's brief mumbles about odd weather did not satisfy her.

The State Department report introduced the possibility that other nations might withhold their grains from global markets. This, too, would have been unthinkable two years ago. Yet this possibility was not just theoretical musing. It was drawn from actual statements of important governmental officials. If crop shortages occurred in the United States, would the United States not be able to make up its shortages from global markets? How about the impacts on those nations already dependent upon global markets and US grain surpluses to supply basic food needs of their citizens?

Straus could not begin to answer these questions by herself. But she knew that these questions had to be asked and answered. She also knew that she had unique information about global grain markets that President Clark did not have. She must both inform and confront the president. But when and how?

Straus had to fly to France the next morning to see Prime Minister Rousseau again about France's nuclear power plants. Because that meeting was so important, she was already scheduled to see both President Clark and Vice President Van Waters to discuss its results. She would have their undivided attention on Monday morning, November 22nd. That would be the time to reveal her unique knowledge about global grain markets. Maybe she could also find out the truth about US crop production.

Straus' meeting with Rousseau was far less confrontational than her meeting with him had been in October. Straus was less edgy this time because she had received help from nuclear power plant experts in the interim. She was better able to express specific concerns about France's new nuclear security systems. Rousseau was also less edgy. He had already confronted Straus about France's new policy on its nuclear power plants. He was also buoyed by the effective American-French exchange of documents from SMER and ETOP.

Despite the affable nature of Straus's meeting with Rousseau, when Straus saw President Clark and Vice President Van Waters again in the Oval Office, she had only bad news to convey. As they sat in a circle in the chairs in front of the president's desk, Straus reported that Rousseau had been cordial, but had remained adamant. France was fully committed to its revised policy on nuclear power plants. All of them would remain in service for the indefinite future.

The president and vice president were disappointed, but not surprised. They now hoped that France's new security measures would prove to be more effective against any clever attempt to steal fissionable material than the ill-fated Maginot line had been against the German invasion at the beginning of World War II.

The president and vice president stood up to thank Straus for her report and end their meeting, expecting her to take their cue. Instead, she remained seated.

"I need to discuss something else with you," said Straus firmly.

"What is it, Melissa?" asked President Clark, still standing.

"The declines in US crop production," she answered.

"My department has a report you need to know about. We have a small group that has free rein to analyze any trends that they can find that they think might have international policy implications. A month ago, their leader sent me one of their reports. Its author had collected and analyzed statements by officials in many nations about their export policies. He concluded that many nations were rethinking their policies on exporting grains. Absent huge surpluses, those nations would cease exports of wheat, rice, corn, and other grains. I think you can see what this means. If worldwide crop declines occur, grain exports from those nations could cease. Global markets in grains may shrivel."

"Shrivel?" asked President Clark, more as an exclamation than a question as he sat back down, focusing his attention on Straus.

"That's right," said Straus. She waited, seeing newly grim faces on both the president and vice president.

President Clark spoke next.

"So, if your report is correct and if US crop production does not meet our basic needs, are you saying that we might not be able to make up the difference from global markets?."

"That's right also," said Straus.

She waited again, seeing the president troubled by a scenario quite different than what he had told the Cabinet just last week. She knew then the question she had to ask.

"Mr. President," she said formally, "What is the truth about United States crop production?"

"Melissa, we're in a complicated and dangerous position," he said. "As I told the Cabinet members, our crop production this year was down. What I did not say was that it should not have been down. The acreage planted in the US actually increased this year because we released a lot of land from various conservation programs. Lois can tell you more about that decision. She is heading up our efforts to try to figure out why we have these declines and what to do about them."

"The problem actually began last year," said Van Waters. "One of Bill Rand's people discovered odd declines in last year's crop production. Bill was confident that her data were correct. That is why we agreed that he quietly release extra land for crops this year. In July this year, that same person spotted likely further declines in crop production for this year."

President Clark interrupted.

"When I heard about this, I thought that any declines would have been caused directly or indirectly by our new petroleum reality," he said. "So I asked Bill to devise a way to show that this had happened. He enlisted that same person for this task, a USDA assistant secretary named Karen Lewis. She was smarter than I was. She collected information from the USDA extension offices on many different possibilities, not just the direct and indirect effects of high petroleum prices. By the time she got all this information, US crop production declines were certain for this year, not just likely. She found that our new petroleum reality did not cause the declines. According to USDA field people, the declines were caused by universally odd weather."

"Universally odd weather? What does that mean?" asked Straus.

"It means that each agricultural region in the United States had weather far outside its norm," said Van Waters. "There was no consistent pattern. Although most areas were hotter and drier, some were much wetter. Karen Lewis did not rely only upon information from the USDA extension offices. She contacted experts at ETOP to get data about how abnormal the weather in 2032 had been."

"ETOP?" questioned Straus.

"Yes, ETOP," said Van Waters.

"Oh," said Straus. "So is there some connection here with the SMER information you wanted me to get from France?"

"There is indeed," answered Van Waters. "But that is a technical side of the problem. Let me tell you what Karen Lewis did. She first organized ETOP's weather data by agricultural region. She found that nearly every region of the United States had temperature and precipitation in 2032 that was outside ninety percent of previously measured temperatures and precipitation."

Straus' expression betrayed confusion. The vice president realized that she was getting far too technical. She quickly shifted to the conclusion that had been kept a tight secret thus far.

"If odd weather has caused our crop declines, and if even odder weather occurs next year, then we will have a real problem with domestic grain production," said Van Waters. "We could even have a general shortage of domestic food supplies in the United States."

"And my revelation to you just makes matters worse, doesn't it?" said Straus.

"You bet," said President Clark.

"But surely this year was just a fluke. What are the odds that next year will also be a fluke?" said Straus.

"That's what we are trying to figure out," said Van Waters. "We have met with Paul Anderson. He's the director of ETOP. We gave him the SMER data you got from France. He thinks that the SMER data may help answer that question."

"SMER again," thought Straus to herself. Now she knew why the president and vice president insisted on her finding out about SMER when she saw Prime Minister Rousseau a month ago. She was already involved in trying to solve this new problem without even knowing it.

"So, when will you know?" asked Straus.

"We're not sure," answered Van Waters. "I told Anderson to contact Karen Lewis by December 1ˢᵗ. Maybe we will know by then; maybe not. So it may be a few days, a few weeks, or longer before we know. If

ETOP concludes that next year is likely to be like this year or worse, we will have to create a plan, and in a hurry. At this point, we are keeping the investigation both narrow and secret. As you put it, we are hoping that this year was just a fluke."

"We will tell the entire Cabinet about this situation once we have better grasp of it," said President Clark. "In the meantime, keep it secret, as we have done."

Straus nodded. She was at once both disheartened by the bad news about crop production and pleased about her role in finding out about SMER to help identify what was happening.

CHAPTER 25

CABINET

A week after Secretary of State Straus had confronted the president and vice president, Karen Lewis received Paul and Marilyn's coded message. Translated, it meant that the SMER data revealed a long-term problem affecting crop production in the United States. The message also said that they wanted to see the vice president right away.

Paul and Marilyn's message was transmitted quickly up line, from Lewis to Rand and from Rand to Vice President Van Waters. The vice president told President Clark in person. The president decided that he needed to learn first hand what long-term problem Anderson was going to tell them about.

Just three days later, on December 2, 2032, President Clark, Vice President Van Waters, Bill Rand, Paul Anderson, Marilyn Sawyer, and Karen Lewis met around a rectangular table in a conference room of the Executive Office Building. Paul needed only a few words to describe the problem.

He first summarized what the SMER data revealed, focusing on the extraordinary amount of fresh water that SMER had discovered a few months ago. He then described his and Marilyn's investigation about why so much fresh water had occurred. He finally introduced the idea of a climate threshold, after which there would be global climate disruptions. He said that the SMER discovery could signal that a threshold had been reached when rapid climate shifts could occur throughout Western Europe, in the United States, and in other parts of the world. Huge changes could occur in just ten to twenty years. During any transition, neither the interim nor the ending local climates would be predictable. Some could lie within recent historic experiences; others could be vastly different.

No one had to be told that major climate uncertainties could wreak havoc on crop production in many areas of the world, including highly productive areas in the United States.

Paul and Marilyn expected their conclusions to be a shock to everyone present. They did not expect to be shocked in return.

After Paul finished his summary, Vice President Van Waters revealed the conclusions in the State Department report that Melissa Straus had presented to her and the president. She said that global grain markets could also be reaching a threshold where massive reductions could occur in the amounts of different grains in those markets. The existing safety net for the United States and other nations might disappear even more quickly than global climate shifts might occur.

The convergence of facts was clear. A food shortage in the United States was indeed possible, even as early as next year. Now solutions were needed, not investigations.

President Clark did what any politician would do. He decided to create a "crop production" task force to deal with the declines in US crop production and potential food shortages. Having already asked Vice President Van Waters to handle this problem, he appointed her as its chairman. He wanted everyone in the room to be part of the task force—Van Waters, Rand and Lewis from the USDA, and Anderson and Sawyer from ETOP. Anticipating a need for other expertise, President Clark gave Van Waters authority to add whomever else she believed could help them reach sound decisions.

No one was eager, but everyone was willing, to serve on the task force. They knew that the potential grain shortages, if they actually occurred, could trigger a need to make huge changes in governmental policies just to meet the basic food needs of all Americans.

President Clark then imposed an unusual restriction on the task force. The task force had to maintain absolute secrecy. Even its existence would be secret. The president said that he did not want American and other world citizens to become alarmed. He said clearly that he wanted sound solutions, not public consternation.

After setting up the task force, President Clark had one more action item. He said that he must now tell his Cabinet the full truth about the crop production problem and this new task force. He expected disbelief, or at least skepticism, within the Cabinet. He asked Bill Rand to prepare clear descriptions of the declines in US crop production in 2032 and his department's conclusions that odd weather, not other potential causes, explained what had happened. He also asked Paul Anderson to prepare a formal presentation about potential climate changes.

The Cabinet meeting on December 14, 2032 would long be remembered by those present. Seated around the large oval table inside the Cabinet Room in the White House were President James Clark, Vice President Lois Van Waters, the chairman of the Joint Chiefs of Staff, and the full Cabinet. Paul Anderson would be invited into the meeting only when the president decided that his contribution was needed. Paul remained on call in a private area of the Executive Office Building next door.

Cabinet meetings usually covered a variety of subjects. This, however, was no usual Cabinet meeting. President Clark began the meeting with a jolt.

"We have one subject to deal with today," he said. "The United States might have a food shortage next year."

Disbelief reigned in silence as everyone listened intently to the president's next carefully chosen words.

"As far fetched as this may seem," the president continued, "our crop production data for this year show a declining trend. We are not alone. Crop production in the European Union, Russia, India, and China also shows declining trends. If these trends continue, no large nation in the world will have a surplus beyond domestic needs next year. Some large nations may not even meet their domestic needs. And this situation could be worse in 2034. We also have reason to believe that most other nations will keep at home whatever successful crops they have. Despite the global economy that we have had for the past many decades, it looks like all of us are going to be entirely on our own for most grains."

All of the Cabinet members were skeptical, but again they remained silent. They knew that President Clark was a cautious person who would not say something so serious without having facts to support what he said. They did not have to wait to begin hearing those facts.

As planned, President Clark asked Secretary of Agriculture Rand to describe his data on US crop production. Rand stood up and went to his prearranged place at a computer projector found next to the president at the midpoint of the table. A large screen had been placed opposite the president. Using multiple graphs for different categories of products and different regions of the United States, Rand painted an unmistakable picture.

US crop production had universally declined in 2032. Even 2031 had shown declines, but these had not been large enough to raise serious concerns. Viewed with the declines of 2032, especially taking into account the expanded acreage under production, 2031 looked like a stepping stone to the poor results that occurred in 2032. If these trends continued in 2033 and 2034, even more significant declines would occur. Those declines possibly could be enough to create shortages in multiple US crops.

Rand also showed crop production figures for the European Union. They revealed declines similar to those in the United States. Rand noted that, within the European Union, production in Great Britain and France had declined the most. Production in a few smaller countries had not declined at all, but these results were nowhere near enough to counterbalance declines in the larger countries. Rand said that similar figures existed for Russia, China, and India, although they were more difficult to get and interpret.

After initial disbelief, one question was obvious on each face in the room. Why was this happening? President Clark stated this question openly as a prelude to the next part of Rand's presentation.

In response, Rand first described the various theories based on the new petroleum reality. Everyone knew that sharp rises in petroleum prices had occurred after December 2030. As this was a worldwide condition, some Cabinet members had initially locked onto this as a plausible cause of the decline in worldwide crop production. Beginning with the theory based on reduced fertilizer usage, Rand showed why each theory stumbled against known facts.

Rand then turned to various theories based on the monocultural nature of many crops. By the term "monocultural," he meant that the crops came from the same genetic seed pool. This practice had become especially common after genetic engineering of some food plants had first been successful near the end of the twentieth century. Some scientists had suggested that monocultural crops were more susceptible to specific plant diseases or destructive insect species because both could easily spread worldwide. Again, one by one, Rand showed that no common plant disease or destructive insect species had been identified in all or even a significant portion of the crops where declines had occurred. He also noted that no theory relying on monocultural crops fit the declines in the European Union because the EU had consistently restricted the use of genetically altered seeds. Yet those countries had crop declines similar to those in the United States.

Facial expressions of skepticism began to be replaced by expressions of frustration. Surely, some idea of the cause must exist that matched these facts. As previously arranged with President Clark, Rand now gave his personal theory of the cause. He stated it simply as local climate changes.

Rand and Clark knew that this cold statement would satisfy no one. They needed to learn its factual context. At last, the time had come for the president to ask Paul Anderson to join them.

As Paul entered the Cabinet Room, he was struck by the formidable array of people who were gathered there. When they all looked directly at him, he felt as if he had accidentally crashed a private club meeting. President Clark quickly broke through Paul's awkwardness by introducing each person assembled around the table. As the group settled down from their introductions, Paul replaced Secretary Rand at the computer projector. Paul and Rand had made a practice presentation on the previous Friday using similar equipment in Rand's office. At least this part of the experience was familiar to him.

Paul's presentation was purposely succinct. He began by describing what ETOP was and how it measured atmospheric temperatures, atmospheric gas concentrations, and other atmospheric features around the world. He then showed average atmospheric temperatures at the earth's surface as measured by ETOP since 2020, as well as temperatures back to 1900 that had been computed using prior methodologies. He said that ETOP's data were the most reliable, even though they were the most recent and covered the shortest period of time.

For the last twelve years, ETOP's data showed a clear increase of 0.2 degrees Celsius in the average atmospheric temperature at the earth's surface. Prior methodologies showed a much greater total increase since 1980, albeit over a longer period of time. Whatever one thought of the accuracy of the prior methodologies, they generally concurred with ETOP's measurements where there was overlap. Paul said that this gave some comfort about their accuracy before ETOP came on line.

Paul then showed the carbon dioxide, methane, nitrous oxide, and other greenhouse gas concentrations in the earth's atmosphere over time. Bringing the data on temperatures and greenhouse gases together, he showed a graph with results from several ETOP models that predicted average atmospheric temperatures based on assumed future concentrations of these gases and levels of aerosols in the atmosphere.

"Our model's predicted temperatures are very close to the temperatures that have been observed when actual gas concentrations have been reached and aerosols are as projected," said Paul. "These temperature changes reflect readjustments in the earth's total atmospheric energy at its surface. They appear to be only small changes, but when they occur on a global level these energy readjustments can change local climates. And local climate changes can occur rapidly."

As pre-arranged, Paul then deferred to Secretary Rand.

"The crop production data that we have are consistent with only one idea—that local climate changes are causing odd weather conditions that adversely affect production," said Rand. "If we really are having local climate changes, poor growing conditions will continue and maybe even get worse."

At this point, President Clark stepped in. He gave everyone an opportunity to ask questions. Most questions reflected a genuine concern that real food shortages might occur in the United States next year if present trends continued. A few questions probed Rand's theory that local climate changes were causing the declines in US crop production. Only Jeffrey Green, the secretary of defense, probed into the information that Paul had presented.

"Your graph on carbon dioxide concentrations in the atmosphere shows increases every year," stated Green. "Granted, some years had greater increases than others, especially before 2000, but never did the concentrations remain constant or decrease."

"That's right," said Paul.

"So why does your ETOP temperature graph show up and down temperatures each year and even a stretch of decreased global temperatures beginning in 2022?" asked Green.

"Good observations," said Paul. "The three year decrease starting in 2022 was caused by aerosols from a huge volcanic eruption. The volcano known as Soufrière erupted violently at the end of 2021. Soufrière is on the island of St. Vincent in the Caribbean. A similar eruption occurred in June 1991 in the Philippines. You may recall that the eruption of Mount Pinatubo destroyed Clark Air Force Base. If you look at the graph made from earlier methodologies used to calculate average atmospheric temperatures, temperature declines also occurred after that eruption during 1991 to 1993. The up and down feature of average annual temperatures reflects mostly natural variations in background volcanic aerosols. It also reflects periodic major weather producing features such as El Niño in the Pacific Ocean. Despite annual ups and downs and a few relatively flat periods, note that the decades-long trend shows increasing average atmospheric temperatures at the earth's surface."

"I don't want to get too technical here, but why do aerosols make a difference?" asked Green.

"The basic idea is straight-forward," answered Paul.

"Aerosols are small particles found in the atmosphere. Volcanic eruptions spew large amounts of aerosols into the atmosphere, especially sulfur dioxide. Many of these aerosols are pushed all the way into the earth's stratosphere. These aerosols get distributed widely around the earth. While they are in the stratosphere, they reflect more sunlight than would normally be reflected. The earth's lower atmosphere cools because less sunlight gets through to warm the earth's surface."

"OK, I've got one more question," said Green. "How big is a 'huge' volcanic eruption? Try to give me some idea in terms we can all understand."

"Volcano experts use several kinds of size measurements when ranking eruptions," said Paul. "The amount of tephra ejected is one measurement. The term 'tephra' means all of the material that is blown away from the ground. Another measurement is the estimated amount of sulfur dioxide aerosols that are blown into the stratosphere. That is the most meaningful comparative measurement for effects on the earth's atmospheric temperature. But probably the most useful comparison for you is the explosive power of the main eruption. Some observers estimated that the main eruption of Mount Pinatubo was a blast of more than forty megatons. Soufrière was even bigger, maybe seventy megatons. Does that help?"

"Yes," answered Green simply, as he jotted two notes down for himself.

Paul answered a few more questions. President Clark then excused him from the Cabinet meeting.

After Paul left the meeting, President Clark told each secretary to begin creating plans within his or her department to deal with possible food shortages next year. He also said that he had appointed Vice President Van Waters to chair a crop production task force that he had created to investigate what could be done to prevent further declines in US crop production. The president then identified the initial members of the crop production task force. Finally, he told the Cabinet members that the task force and the concern about future crop production issue had to remain secret, at least for now.

Initial grumbling gave way to the realization that the problem now facing the United States was unprecedented and extremely difficult to solve. No one wanted to reveal it and be forced to answer questions that could not now be answered.

While President Clark ended the Cabinet meeting, Paul remained in the hallway just outside the door to the Cabinet Room. Paul could not believe how tired he was for such a small amount of time in the Cabinet Room. But he could not leave the White House now. He had to see Vice President Van Waters as soon as possible.

CHAPTER 26

IDEA

Vice President Van Waters left the Cabinet meeting quickly after it ended. Paul Anderson intercepted her just after she exited the Cabinet Room. He asked if he could see her now in private. Seeing his grim expression, she agreed.

Within a few minutes, Paul and the vice president were seated facing each other in the comfortable chairs in front of the desk in her office in the West Wing of the White House. The door had been closed for maximum privacy.

"What's up?" asked Van Waters.

"Secretary Green's question during the meeting gave me a new idea," said Paul. "It might affect whom you choose for the crop production task force."

"Idea? What idea?" said Van Waters.

"Let me start with two observations," began Paul.

"First, there is no known way to reduce the increased concentrations of carbon dioxide, methane, and chlorofluorocarbons in the atmosphere in the next few years. These concentrations took decades to build up. Removal will take decades as well, even if we figure out ways to remove them in large amounts.

"Second, uncertainties about the new local weather regimes will make alternative crop planning very difficult. Reliance on alternative crops also assumes that new seeds, equipment, and knowledge can be transferred quickly to a huge number of farmers in many regions where crops are grown. It will take a long time to overcome the inertia in existing crop patterns.

"I have an idea for a temporary solution that could be effective quickly. It is based on phenomena that were evident in the atmospheric temperature graphs that I just showed the president's Cabinet."

Paul then described what he had in mind.

Van Waters quickly grasped Paul's concept. But a good concept was not necessarily doable. Neither Paul nor she knew whether the United States had its key element. At least the vice president could find out.

But first she had to tell President Clark about Paul's idea. The president must know what she wanted to investigate. Even vice presidents rarely treaded into those top-secret waters. At least she was uniquely qualified to do so.

Vice President Van Waters was an 1998 graduate of the United States Air Force Academy. When she had been nominated to the Academy, she had been determined to show all doubters among her high school classmates that she had what it took to be a first rate cadet and pilot. By the time she had graduated from the Air Force Academy, there were no doubters, only admirers. She had continued her pilot training in the Air Force, and had served with distinction as a fighter pilot in the Iraq war. Eventually, she had changed roles in the Air Force to be a tactical planner. After twenty years, she had retired from the Air Force, looking forward to spending more time with her husband of fifteen years.

She had soon learned that she enjoyed political issues and had too much energy to be satisfied being on the sidelines. She had been considered a throw-away candidate in her congressional district when she had opted to challenge the incumbent. But a combination of changing demographics and an overblown scandal caused by the incumbent's personal behavior had allowed her to claim a narrow victory.

In Congress, Van Waters had been lucky to receive her first choice committee assignment as a freshman—the House Armed Services Committee. She had made the best of this opportunity. She had quickly gained the respect of her colleagues, not only for her previous knowledge of the military through her Air Force experience, but also for her diligence in learning about all military issues facing Congress. Her knowledge and diligence had been respected back home in her district as well. Voters had rewarded her with two more terms in large victories.

President Clark had surprised everyone when he had chosen Lois Van Waters for his running mate in the 2028 presidential election. At that time, she had been in political life for less than six years, all in the United States Congress. But President Clark had believed that her previous experience in the military and in the House Armed Services Committee would be a great asset to him and the country. He also had believed that she had the toughness, intelligence, and good sense he wanted. His confidence in her abilities had been justified many times over in the four years since his election.

Now, President Clark had given Van Waters the hardest task she had yet faced as vice president. While President Clark had to continue to focus his efforts on dealing with the new petroleum reality, she had to focus her efforts on dealing with potential food shortages in the United States.

Having only just begun to assess this intractable problem, Van Waters was glad that Paul had come up with a new idea that might lead to preventing shortages, even if only temporarily.

When she told President Clark about Paul's idea, he was amazed at its boldness. He respected Paul for being courageous enough to suggest it. President Clark knew that his vice president was the best person to find out whether Paul's idea was even possible.

President Clark told the secretary of defense, Jeffrey Green, and chairman of the Joint Chiefs of Staff, Admiral John Crowell, that he wanted Vice President Van Waters to talk to General Wayne Meyer about top-secret information. Both were invited to attend any meeting she had with General Meyer. Green and Crowell later agreed that only Crowell would do so.

When General Meyer received a call from Admiral Crowell to set a time for the vice president to see him, he was delighted that he would see her again. General Meyer recalled testifying several times before the House Armed Services Committee when she was present as a member of that committee. She had asked excellent and fair questions every time. He was greatly impressed with her intelligence and commitment.

As the result of her prominent role on that committee, Van Waters's distinguished record while an officer in the United States Air Force had become well known in the highest ranks of the military. Her knowledge of military tactics was reputed to be phenomenal. The top ranking officers in the Pentagon respected no one in the executive branch of the government more than Vice President Lois Van Waters.

Van Waters arrived at the Pentagon ten minutes before her scheduled meeting with General Meyer on December 17, 2032. Even as vice president, she had to allow time to go through the last level of security that surrounded General Meyer and his staff. General Meyer's aide met her just after she passed through the first level of security.

Several minutes later, as Van Waters approached General Meyer's office, she could feel that his staff was watching every step she took. None of them had ever seen a president or vice president in this area of the Pentagon. As they watched her, they were also greatly impressed. The vice president had a distinct military gait, and carried herself with great confidence. *No nonsense*, they correctly thought.

When Van Waters entered General Meyer's office, two crisply uniformed men arose simultaneously. Admiral Crowell had arrived a few minutes earlier, so he and General Meyer could both greet the vice president. Protocol would be exact during her visit.

"Good afternoon, Ms. Vice President," General Meyer stated clearly. "Welcome to the Pentagon." He extended his hand, expecting and receiving a firm handshake in return.

"It's good to see you again," responded Van Waters, showing that she also remembered seeing General Meyer at congressional hearings. "And it's good to see you also, Admiral Crowell," she added, moving her eyes to him and giving him a firm handshake as well.

"And you as well," responded Crowell.

They all seated themselves comfortably in the chairs that General Meyer had arranged in a circle in the open space within his office. General Meyer offered Van Waters a beverage, but she declined. The two distinguished military men then waited to learn why the vice president had come.

"I need to ask you about our thermonuclear bombs," said Van Waters bluntly. This was hardly a surprise, as General Meyer's sole, but huge, responsibility was oversight of all nuclear weapons controlled by the United States. What followed, however, was wholly unexpected.

"Let me preface my real question," said Van Waters. "I know that the last nuclear bombs we built had relatively small yields, maybe less than one megaton each. I also know that many bombs were destroyed under the nuclear disarmament treaties. But do we have any really big bombs left, say with a yield of more than ten megatons?"

That's an odd question, thought both General Meyer and Admiral Crowell. Even General Meyer, who knew the nuclear weapons of the

United States better than anyone else, had to think back a long way to know what to say.

"We identify our nuclear weapons by purpose and use rather than yield, so give me a few moments to think about what we have," answered General Meyer. He knew that the really big bombs were old and had not figured in strategic military planning for many years before he became involved in the nuclear weapons section of the Pentagon.

As he paused, Van Waters expressed her own ideas about what might be available.

"I know that the Castle Bravo test in 1954 was about fifteen megatons," she said. "That's the biggest bomb that has been publicly disclosed. Do we have any bombs based on that design?"

General Meyer and Admiral Crowell again glanced at each other, knowing now that the vice president had indeed done her homework.

"As for Castle Bravo, the answer is no," said General Meyer. "As for other big bombs, the answer is yes. I think we have three of them."

"What size?" asked Van Waters.

"One is about twelve megatons, and the other two are about twenty megatons," answered General Meyer. "They are very old. I think they were built before 1960."

"Are they operational?" asked Van Waters.

Operational? thought General Meyer and Admiral Crowell. *What was the vice president after here?* Their concerned faces became immediately apparent to Van Waters.

"Don't worry, gentlemen, I am not trying to rethink our long standing defense strategy. We are not going to start rattling huge nuclear weapons as our sword to deal with nations that threaten us." She then began to describe why she came.

"General Meyer, you need to know something that is just as top secret at this time as your nuclear arsenal," she began. "Admiral Crowell already knows this. You see, there is now evidence that the United States might have a food shortage as early as next year."

"Food shortage?" blurted General Meyer spontaneously in disbelief.

"That's pretty much the reaction the president got when he told the Cabinet about this possibility," said Van Waters. "At that meeting, Bill Rand revealed the most recent statistics on US crop production from his Department of Agriculture. If the trend from last year through this year continues into next year, and then again into 2034, a national food shortage is definitely possible."

Van Waters paused.

"I'm still in shock," said General Meyer. "Who would ever guess that might happen here. Are the right people really sure that this is a real possibility?"

"Unfortunately, yes," answered Van Waters.

"At the Cabinet meeting, Rand also suggested that the declining crop production in the United States was caused by local climate changes. As Admiral Crowell knows, the president appointed me to lead a small task force to investigate whether Rand is right, and if so, whether anything can be done about it."

By now, General Meyer had regained his composure. "I'm having a hard time connecting this to large thermonuclear bombs," he said.

"Understandably, it's not obvious," Van Waters continued. "During the same Cabinet meeting and at the president's request, a scientist summarized what was known about changes in the earth's average atmospheric temperature in the last hundred or so years. He said that the average temperature had increased significantly since 1980. Increases in the last twelve years had been especially rapid. He explained that these increases showed a significant change in the earth's atmospheric energy. And that change could cause global climate disruptions. Those in turn could be causing the local climate changes that Rand suggested were responsible for declines in US crop production.

"The scientist also talked about what various computer models predict for future temperatures and local climates. His presentation included graphs showing that the average atmospheric temperature has not increased steadily every year. At least twice in the last fifty years, two or three year periods have occurred where the earth's average temperature noticeably dropped. Secretary Green asked the scientist about this. He said that these declines had been caused by aerosols from a huge volcanic eruption at the beginning of each of those two periods."

General Meyer and Admiral Crowell remained attentive, but were still unable to see where Vice President Van Waters was heading with her description. She continued undeterred.

"Secretary Green asked the scientist to describe what he meant by a 'huge volcanic eruption'. He said that one useful measurement was an eruption's estimated explosive power. He then described in megatons the two big eruptions that had caused average atmospheric temperatures to drop for a few years.

"After the Cabinet meeting, the scientist asked to see me in private. He said that he had been thinking about our dilemma. He said that he had been hoping for a big volcanic eruption right now. Then maybe our crop production would get back to normal, at least for a few years while everyone could figure out longer-term solutions.

"He then told me that one word that he had used in his answer to Green's question suddenly had clicked with him. The word was 'megaton.' He said that he remembered that thermonuclear bombs were also measured in megatons. That led him to thinking that maybe a big bomb could create a lot of aerosols or even an artificial volcanic eruption that would then have the same cooling effects as a natural volcanic eruption. That's why I wanted to see you. We want to find out whether we have any really big bombs anymore. If we do, then we can investigate his ideas further to see if they make any real sense."

General Meyer and Admiral Crowell were both relieved that the president and vice president really did have no plan to resurrect deterrence by nuclear bomb threats as a part of United States foreign policy. General Meyer, in particular, quickly became both intrigued by and skeptical of these new ideas that Van Waters had described. He remembered some secret underground nuclear tests that would contain useful information about the explosive power needed to blow apart volcanic rock.

"Do you know whether this scientist prefers using a bomb to make aerosols or to open up a natural volcano, allowing it to throw aerosols into the air?" asked General Meyer.

"Now you are getting beyond me," replied Van Waters. "I don't know. At this point, I just want to know whether we have big bombs."

"When I said that we had three big bombs," answered General Meyer, "I thought that you were asking about bombs that could be delivered today. We actually have quite a few more big bombs that are in obsolete delivery shells. The twenty-megaton bombs would be the most numerous. I think we may have more than thirty of these. We never made a monster bomb like the sixty-megaton bomb the Soviet Union tested in 1961."

"Before you get too far down this road, someone will have to reexamine our nuclear test ban treaties," interjected Admiral Crowell.

"Yes, I know that could be a problem," said Van Waters. "But I think we first need to figure out whether this idea has any hope of success. Your people know the capabilities of these bombs. They need to get together with some volcano experts. You will have to find them because they will have to qualify for top-secret security clearance. Maybe you can find a good one who already has that clearance."

"I think we can do all of this," said Admiral Crowell confidently, also secretly glad that this task would be done by military people who were accustomed to tight secrecy. "We'll get going immediately," he added.

"One other person must be involved," said Van Waters.

"Who's that?" asked Admiral Crowell, with a tone of concern about who that might be.

"Dr. Paul Anderson," replied Van Waters. "He's already been qualified for top level security clearance." Admiral Crowell nodded agreement at this name. General Meyer wondered what they knew that he did not, but he refrained from asking because the vice president clearly was preparing to leave.

Van Waters stood up abruptly, thanked the two men, and left General Meyer's office, knowing that the urgency of the situation was well understood by Admiral Crowell without her having to emphasize it.

After the vice president was out of sight down the hall, General Meyer closed the door to his office and looked squarely at Admiral Crowell.

"Who is Dr. Paul Anderson?" he asked.

"The scientist who came to the Cabinet meeting the vice president mentioned," said Admiral Crowell. "He is the director of the Earth Temperature Observation Project. He is also a member of the vice president's crop production task force."

CHAPTER 27

TEAM

Despite his outward confidence in the presence of Vice President Van Waters, Admiral Crowell knew that finding the right people to evaluate Paul Anderson's idea would not be easy, especially in the short time available. But he also knew that General Meyer was superbly skilled at assembling first rate teams on short notice. This whole investigation would now be General Meyer's project even though he was skeptical about its core idea. Admiral Crowell targeted the end of January as the time to have this team selected.

A true professional, General Meyer wasted no time in getting started. Immediately after Admiral Crowell left his office, he summoned his top aide to his office to begin making assignments.

Since Van Waters wanted Anderson as part of his team, General Meyer decided to be sure that Anderson's high level security clearance was warranted. General Meyer told his aide that, no matter who recommended Anderson or how well a previous security investigation had been done, he wanted a new investigation to be sure that Anderson was not a risk to reveal important military secrets.

Next, General Meyer directed that his aide find a person to search the Pentagon's database of security clearances to find everyone who was an expert on volcanoes. Although General Meyer understood very well that this type of expertise was not normally connected with national security, still, he thought that if he could find competent experts who already had clearance, he could accelerate evaluation of the idea that Van Waters had described.

The final item on his initial agenda was the easiest, and maybe the most important. He had to select an expert on old thermonuclear bombs who knew intimately all of their explosive characteristics. General Meyer smiled with satisfaction as he looked in his computer directory for the correct telephone number at the Fermi National Accelerator Laboratory.

It was no accident that the Joint Chiefs of Staff had long supported wide ranging research in atomic physics. General Meyer and others before him had continually urged this policy. They knew that, in the long run, the only way to have enough people knowledgeable about nuclear weapons was to have a large pool of physicists who were working regularly with atomic and subatomic particles. This policy would now pay off again. General Meyer knew that he could enlist Dr. Kristin Brown, formerly a civilian member of his division and now a senior scientist at the Fermi National Accelerator Laboratory.

The second security investigation of Paul Anderson proceeded quickly and without any glitch. This investigation confirmed the investigation that had been done for Vice President Van Waters. Interviews with present and past colleagues, neighbors, and friends painted an enviable picture of a person with high integrity and strong loyalty to his family and his country. In spite of the complete security report on Anderson and the vice president's insistence, General Meyer felt that he needed one more step. He still wanted to meet Anderson face to face before requesting Anderson to join his team, even though the idea that his team would be evaluating had been Anderson's idea in the first place.

General Meyer's aide arranged for him to see Anderson at ETOP, ostensibly to learn about military implications of the climate changes that ETOP was investigating.

Other military officers had visited ETOP before for the same stated purpose, so Paul did not suspect General Meyer's real intentions in wanting to visit him.

General Meyer arrived unobtrusively at ETOP on January 5, 2033. Although he wore his uniform, his military car was just like any civilian's car and he sat in its front seat as his driver had wound their way over the roads to ETOP.

In his usual style, Paul warmly greeted General Meyer just inside the front entrance door of ETOP's headquarters building.

There was no hiding that fact that a very special person had come to visit Paul. Not only General Meyer's uniform, but his tough appearance spoke of military authority. Although slightly shorter than Paul, General Meyer still looked like he had been lifting weights in training for a combat mission. Although in his fifty-sixth year, his naturally jet-black hair had yet to show any gray strands.

Paul promptly led General Meyer to the small conference room where Paul had previously arranged a short presentation to show him. No one else was present, as the aide for General Meyer who had arranged their meeting had clearly requested a meeting only with Paul.

General Meyer let Paul begin his presentation so that he could size him up. Within ten minutes, he knew that Paul was just the kind of person he wanted on his team.

"Let's now look at ETOP's measurements of atmospheric temperatures," said Paul as he clicked a graph onto a screen at the other end of the table where Paul and General Meyer were seated. "Here are the average temperatures at the earth's surface in the last twelve years."

"I see that the average temperature bounced up and down some from year to year, even though the trend was up," said General Meyer. "That is, except for three years around 2021. Looks like it dropped quite a lot in the first of those years."

Paul was surprised that General Meyer had spotted that feature and its precise dates so quickly.

"What volcano caused that temporary decline?" added General Meyer.

"How did you know that?" asked Paul, now even more surprised and feeling that General Meyer knew a lot more than he was letting on.

"I did not really come here to learn about ETOP's data," confessed General Meyer. "I came here to ask you to join a team I am leading. Vice President Van Waters recommended you."

"What team?" blurted Paul, feeling somewhat used and flattered at the same time. Then he knew.

"The team on my idea?" he asked, his heart pounding.

"You're quick," responded General Meyer. "We can't talk about it here. I will tell you what you want to know when you come to my office in the Pentagon."

Paul's expression told what he was thinking. *The Pentagon? I can't get in the Pentagon! What is the general thinking?*

General Meyer had expected Paul's reaction. "You're right about your recent national security clearance from Vice President Van Waters. It's high level, all right, but not enough to get you into my area of the Pentagon. We have done our own investigation. You sure have a lot of people who respect you. You now have another level of national security clearance. Here's a chip card. This, and your hand print, can be used to verify your clearance. Come in the Mall Entrance. I'll have one of my aides meet you there."

"When?" asked Paul.

"Tomorrow at 1:00 p.m.," replied General Meyer. "I want to get you involved right away."

"I'll rearrange my schedule and get a plane for this evening," said Paul. He then escorted General Meyer to the ETOP lobby. As he watched General Meyer leave ETOP's building and walk along the pathway through ETOP's security gate, he felt excited and apprehensive at the same time. Was his idea really sound or too risky? Had he opened a Pandora's box?

Paul had never been to the Pentagon before. He had driven by it several years ago while vacationing in Washington, D.C., but he had never been really close to it. As he approached the Pentagon after exiting the Pentagon metro station, its enormous size became truly daunting.

Just as General Meyer had said, Paul's chip card allowed the security officers to identify him at the Mall Entrance. General Meyer's chief aide met him just beyond the detector that Paul had to pass through. Much to his surprise, both he and the aide had to pass through two more security posts on their way to General Meyer's office. Paul began to realize just how unusual his security clearance must be.

"Welcome to the inner sanctum," said General Meyer light heartedly when Paul was escorted into his office. He gestured to Paul to sit across from him in one of two chairs in front of his desk. "We're going to be working closely together, so you had better know who I am and what I normally do here. I already know a lot about you."

General Meyer then described his role as the person most directly responsible for all nuclear weapons of the United States. He emphasized that Paul was now in the most secure of all secure places in the Pentagon.

After his description, General Meyer remotely turned on a large flat screen television located on the wall to Paul's right. He then showed Paul movies of tests of several thermonuclear bombs as a way to introduce

Paul to the bombs the United States had in its arsenal. One of those was the Castle Bravo test in the Pacific that Vice President Van Waters had mentioned in her initial meeting with General Meyer and Admiral Crowell.

"Let me state it as simply as I can," began General Meyer. "Castle Bravo was about fifteen megatons. I understand that you want to use a big bomb to create aerosols and to kick those aerosols into the stratosphere. The aerosols would then reduce average temperatures and postpone local climate changes. The goal would be to minimize the risk of food shortages. Am I correct?"

"Yes," answered Paul.

"Our project is to figure out whether this is feasible with our existing bombs. We need your help. What's the basis for your idea?"

Paul then described how scientists had discovered in the early 1990s that sulfur dioxide and other aerosols from big volcanic eruptions measurably cooled the earth's atmosphere.

"Of course, big eruptions can occur at any time and have done so historically," Paul continued. "Smaller volcanic eruptions have produced background aerosols in varying degrees that also have had cooling effects. We also now have regional hazes that create local cooling effects on the atmosphere. These hazes are comprised of sulfur dioxide and other aerosols that have come mostly from burning coal and other fossil fuels. These hazes partially offset the warming effects of increased carbon dioxide concentrations in the atmosphere that those same sources have largely caused.

"To counterbalance atmospheric warming, a few people have suggested that maybe large amounts of sulfur dioxide could be made and cast regularly into the upper atmosphere. This idea has been rejected because the quantities needed are far too large. Also, proper distribution, both horizontal and vertical, would be very difficult to achieve. Besides, sulfur dioxide in the lower atmosphere has many negative effects as well. For example, its absorption in water droplets can create acidic rain.

"If we can use a big bomb to create a lot of aerosols and simultaneously push them into the stratosphere, then maybe we can replicate the kind of cooling that volcanic eruptions achieve."

Paul's descriptions made General Meyer even more skeptical of Paul's idea.

"Do you really think that a big bomb by itself could create enough aerosols to make any difference?" he asked.

"No, I don't," answered Paul. "In fact, I think that we may have to figure out how to use a bomb to unleash an artificial volcanic eruption. It's the only way I know to get large amounts of aerosols into the stratosphere for world-wide results.

"What I also like about creating an artificial volcanic eruption is that it would be much like events with which we have had experience. The eruptions of Soufrière in 2021 and Mount Pinatubo in 1991 created serious problems in some regions, but not world-wide catastrophes. They both showed that high altitude aerosols generally, including sulfur dioxide, can have a big impact."

"So you do think your idea has real promise, don't you?" stated General Meyer.

"Maybe," said Paul. "I know the characteristics of the aerosols we want to have, but someone else will have to figure out whether a bomb can produce them. Also, the amounts needed are huge. A natural volcanic eruption throws aerosols into the atmosphere for days, not just one explosion. Of course, even if an artificial volcanic eruption can be created, its effects would only be temporary."

"Yes, I understand that," said General Meyer. "We have enough bombs to do more if needed."

General Meyer had intuitively sensed what Paul already knew. Increased concentrations of carbon dioxide and other greenhouse gases had built up over many years. They could not be reduced in just a few years or even a few decades. Humans first had to stop the activities that continued to add those gases to the atmosphere in large quantities. Enormous infrastructures had to be created so that substitutes for fossil fuel burning could be used sooner rather than later in a massive way. Humanity needed many years, maybe many decades, to change current economic patterns in order to stop adding greenhouse gases to the atmosphere. Far more time would be needed actually to remove those gases, whether by natural systems or by some as yet undeveloped human intervention. Many artificial volcanic eruptions would be needed to reduce or at least stabilize the average atmospheric temperature over those years.

"Let me shift ground," said General Meyer. "I have already chosen a bomb expert for our team. Her name is Kristin Brown. She is now at the Fermi National Accelerator Laboratory. She used to work here on all of our thermonuclear weapons. She knows more about our big bombs than anyone else. The other person we need is a vulcanologist. I have names of three who already have security clearance. I would like to choose one of them, if possible. Here, maybe you know them."

General Meyer handed Paul a copy of his list that contained three names along with brief resumes following each name. Paul looked over the list.

"Here's the person you want," said Paul, putting his finger on the third name listed. "Jacob Kahn."

"Jacob Kahn," repeated General Meyer aloud as he reread Kahn's resume on his copy of the list. "Why him?"

"I know that his specialty is stratovolcanic volcanoes," said Paul. "Those have the big, explosive eruptions that throw the largest amounts of aerosols into the stratosphere. Soufrière and Mount Pinatubo were stratovolcanic eruptions. So were Mount Vesuvius and Krakatau, two of the most famous eruptions in history. You may remember that the Mount Vesuvius eruption buried the Roman city of Pompeii back in 79 A.D. Krakatau was much more recent. Its eruption in 1883 was literally an explosion that could be heard three thousand miles away. It not only destroyed most of Krakatau Island in southwest Indonesia, its aerosols also created spectacular sunsets for years afterward as far away as Europe.

"Dr. Kahn has studied all of these. I also know that he was one of the American scientists at St. Vincent Island when Soufrière erupted in 2021. He's had close contact with something very much like what you want to create."

"Sounds like our person," said General Meyer decisively. "Do you know him?"

"We met once, but I can't say that I know him," answered Paul.

"All right, I will have one of my aides contact him," said General Meyer, anticipating a preliminary meeting with Jacob Kahn just as he had done with Paul.

"Admiral Crowell wants our team together by the end of January," said General Meyer. Now with you and Kristin Brown on the team, we just need Jacob Kahn and we can get moving."

Paul could see that General Meyer was starting to conclude their meeting so he quickly interjected.

"I think we need another person," he said.

"Oh? Who?" asked General Meyer.

"Someone who can assess the impacts on plant and animal life. We can project the effects of reduced sunlight on average atmospheric temperature. But that is just one result of an artificial volcanic eruption. The aerosols also have peculiar chemical compositions. With a nuclear bomb, radiation will be a factor as well. The effects of all of these must be considered. We do not want to make a bad situation worse."

"Indeed we don't," responded General Meyer. "Do you know someone who fits your description?"

"I think so," said Paul.

"Who?"

"Her name is Karen Lewis," answered Paul. "She's also on Vice President Van Waters's crop production task force, so she already has security clearance. I just recently met her. She's the one who first spotted the declines in US crop production. She seems to be very intelligent and creative."

General Meyer already felt that he could trust Paul's judgment. He promptly decided that Karen Lewis should be added to his team, subject to his meeting her personally and her passing another security investigation by his people.

"I'll call you for our first meeting after the other team members have been committed to our project," said General Meyer. "I want everyone to come prepared with facts and ideas. You are really the key person here to figure out exactly what we need in the atmosphere to have enough impact."

Paul nodded agreement. He knew what he needed to do.

The meeting then concluded. General Meyer's aide led Paul through the Pentagon's security maze back to the Pentagon's Mall Entrance.

During the next three weeks, General Meyer and his staff accomplished all of the tasks that were needed to have his new team committed by the end of January. General Meyer's initial meeting with Jacob Kahn confirmed what Paul had said about this superb scientist. In a later meeting at the Pentagon, General Meyer told Kahn about Paul's idea to try to create artificial volcanic eruptions. Kahn readily agreed to join the team. He immediately began analyzing how an artificial volcanic eruption could be achieved.

The second security clearance check on Karen Lewis was just as quick, and smooth, as the second security clearance check on Paul had been. General Meyer's initial meeting with her also confirmed what Paul had said about her. After her meeting with General Meyer at the Pentagon, she began thinking about the effects various aerosols could have on plants and animals.

At last, on January 26, 2033, General Meyer brought the team together in a conference room at the Pentagon to begin their project as a unit. The group achieved excellent rapport at this first meeting, allowing a quick start on evaluating Paul's idea.

Much to General Meyer's surprise, in less than a month, the experts on his team concluded that creating an artificial volcanic eruption was indeed possible. Although Paul's initial concept was sound, a number of important modifications were needed. Everyone's expertise played a role in the team's making those modifications.

Jacob Kahn confirmed Paul's notion that the thermonuclear bomb should be used to unleash an existing volcano rather than to create aerosols by itself. Even the great explosive power of a thermonuclear bomb could not match the explosive power and enormous amount of aerosols created by a big volcanic eruption. He thought that using a natural volcano also gave them the best chance to predict correctly the size of the aerosols that would be created.

Paul favored this approach for the same reason. He knew that proper aerosol size was critical to achieve adequate sunlight reflection and temperature reduction.

Karen Lewis also agreed, mostly because the aerosols would be similar to the aerosols from historic eruptions. Their effects would be much more predictable than the effects of aerosols created by a thermonuclear bomb alone. And, she thought, fewer bombs meant less scattered nuclear radiation.

Kristin Brown's analysis before the meeting showed that two bombs rather than one would be needed for each artificial volcanic eruption. Deep underground tests in the 1970s had proved that one bomb could fracture a column of solid rock, but not break through the surface. She said that one bomb could be used to fracture rock that lay above a magma chamber, but a second bomb would be needed to disperse that rock so that the magma could explode freely into an eruption.

Jacob Kahn concurred with this approach. He knew that it would be nearly impossible to find a magma chamber that already had built up enough pressure to blow away the fractured rock cover by itself. That was the equivalent of finding a stratovolcano that was just then going to have a massive natural explosive eruption. Unfortunately, they still would have to find a magma chamber with enough natural pressure to blast large amounts of aerosols high into the atmosphere once the bombs fractured and dispersed its rock cap. Otherwise, the bombs could just release lava flows or nothing at all.

General Meyer reported these overall conclusions to Admiral Crowell and Vice President Van Waters in early March 2033. Both of them were pleased at how quickly General Meyer's team had evaluated Paul Anderson's idea for an artificial volcanic eruption. Despite optimism, everyone also recognized that success with this unique approach was not guaranteed. Indeed, General Meyer continued to quietly express his skepticism to both Crowell and Van Waters.

CHAPTER 28

QUANDARIES

While General Meyer had been assembling his team, Vice President Van Waters's crop production task force had been active trying to come up with other ideas.

Van Waters had added three people to her task force, all of whom were scientists. The new members had brought expertise in farming, energy, and logistics. Paul Anderson and Karen Lewis had remained on the task force, but had assumed no roles beyond attending meetings so that they could concentrate on Paul's idea to create artificial volcanic eruptions. Marilyn Sawyer had become the primary climate expert for the task force. She also had become the acting director of ETOP while Paul was committed full-time to General Meyer's team.

The crop production task force had met in secrecy once every two weeks since its inception in early December 2032. The task force had engaged a number of people to collect information that the task force could evaluate as a whole. This had been an awkward process. The task force had to keep secret the real purpose for its data collection, while still revealing enough information to get the data it wanted, all on short notice. Keeping the purpose secret had been a real challenge because much of the information the task force needed was available only from agencies, universities, and businesses that had very public operations.

By March 2033, the task force faced several quandaries.

The information received from ETOP through Marilyn had convinced everyone that ETOP's data on average atmospheric temperatures were sound. Clearly these temperatures had increased in the last twelve years.

The task force also had become convinced that weather information in 2032 from all crop-producing regions of the Northern Hemisphere showed consistently odd conditions in 2032. Examined in retrospect, the weather in 2031 had been a hint of the odd conditions that had occurred in 2032. The task force as a whole at first could not decide whether these odd weather patterns also were something new or just rare variations within longer statistical averages.

Finally, the task force had become convinced that the data on US crop production in 2032 correctly showed real universal declines. But no task force member was yet willing to conclude that the observed odd weather patterns alone had caused these declines. Each person searched to discover other causes beyond those investigated by the USDA under Secretary Bill Rand.

Despite their efforts to find other causes for declines in US crop production, especially causes that could be removed easily with proper attention and expenditures, no idea fit the facts except the odd weather scenario. And the only causes that fit the odd weather scenario were local climate changes resulting from an increased average atmospheric temperature.

This process led the task force to a discouraging conclusion. If the odd weather was solely responsible for overall declines in crop production, and the odd weather was caused by an increased average atmospheric temperature, then prospects for improving crop production were poor.

The initial difficulty was that no one knew enough about the new weather regimes to be able to adjust crops to match these new weather patterns. Plus the inertia in the current system was immense. Huge investments had been made by many individuals and companies in equipment designed for specific crops in specific locations. In addition to this physical inertia and equally important, individual farmers were accustomed to dealing with particular crops and weather regimes, creating a kind of psychological inertia. Many years would be needed for conversion, even if existing agricultural areas remained viable for new crops. Proper new crops had to be identified promptly and seeds for the new crops made available.

The task force also found that the touted beneficial effects on plant growth from increased carbon dioxide concentrations in the atmosphere were very small in the context of current crop yields. To the extent a carbon dioxide enhancement effect existed for different kinds of annual crops, the effect was essentially instantaneous. Its benefits were already incorporated in the production of annual crops such as wheat, rice, and corn throughout the world. As Rand's data on US and world-wide crop production showed, those benefits must have been less significant than the adverse effects of odd weather, especially the rainfall changes that had occurred in major agricultural regions. Otherwise, total crop production would have increased rather than decreased under the influence of greater carbon dioxide concentrations.

Any carbon dioxide enhancement effect was also already incorporated in the growth of food-producing trees, bushes, and vines. Beneficial effects on some kinds of these plants were evident, but complex. Different kinds of plants in forests and plantations responded differently to increasing carbon dioxide concentrations. Competition among different plants was occurring but was poorly understood. As with annual crops, production data for the fruits and other foods coming from these plants showed that changing weather was overriding potential benefits of faster or larger growth from increased carbon dioxide concentrations. This was true even for those plants that had shown some increased yields under doubled carbon dioxide concentrations in test conditions where soil, moisture, and wind had been controlled.

The crop production task force grudgingly recognized that the only real way to avoid food shortages was to reduce the average atmospheric temperature in the hope that historic local climates would return. The long-term key to accomplishing this goal was to reduce the concentrations of carbon dioxide, methane, and other greenhouse gases in the earth's atmosphere. The first step to achieving this goal would be to stop immediately all human production of all of those gases. Unfortunately, even if this were possible, the average atmospheric temperature would still increase, not decrease.

The task force understood very well that the full effects of current concentrations of these gases in the atmosphere had not yet occurred. The earth's average atmospheric temperature could continue to rise for many years as the oceans adjusted to their temperature equilibriums with the increased energy trapped daily by the existing greenhouse gases. The only long-term way to reduce the average temperature was to stop nearly all human production of greenhouse gases and simultaneously to increase sources for absorbing both gases. These actions could not be taken in just a few years or even a generation.

Only one potential solution for relief in the next few years presented itself. That was Paul Anderson's idea to create a series of artificial volcanic eruptions.

This conclusion frustrated every task force member. They could imagine the reaction in Congress to this idea. Maybe a big volcanic eruption such as Soufrière or Mount Pinatubo would be welcome right now. But to create volcanic eruptions, especially really big ones? Had the vice president and her task force let their hopes carry away their good sense?

Congress would need time to adjust to such a radical, almost mythical, idea. As of March 2033, not even one volcano had been selected for this project. Indeed, maybe no satisfactory volcano would ever be found. Certainly a specific site had to be chosen to give the idea some reality.

But time was short. The crop production task force concluded that, if current trends continued, the decline in US crop production in 2033 might be discomforting, in 2034 might be serious, and in 2035 might be critical to everyone in the United States. Prospects for other nations were far worse if world-wide trends continued.

Despite accepting Anderson's idea, the crop production task force remained cautious. Although they were prepared to accept a thorough investigation of his concept, including selection and preparation of a first site, they were not yet ready to recommend its activation. Everyone on the task force wanted to be sure that the trend of declining crop production actually continued through 2033, and maybe even through 2034, before this drastic, and risky, measure was tried. But they also knew and recommended that all preparations would have to be done by the fall of 2034 so that an artificial volcanic eruption could be attempted then if really needed. Even a one-year delay could be catastrophically late.

The task force also identified some strategic problems with Anderson's idea that had to be overcome.

The United States first had to deal with the series of treaties signed over the last seventy years that had been designed to eliminate all nuclear explosions that might create any radiation fall-out in the earth's atmosphere. At the time these were negotiated and agreed upon, no one had imagined that nuclear bombs could have a uniquely useful non-military purpose such as Anderson's idea. Maybe the treaty terms would allow for his idea; maybe not. Vice President Van Waters asked several treaty experts to reexamine all of these treaties to see what was and was not permissible without changing any treaty's terms.

The United States also had to deal with a general abhorrence of all nuclear weapons, especially within the American and European publics. The idea of using a nuclear weapon for a peaceful purpose was foreign to all previous experience and thinking. Huge citizen opposition was possible. The task force concluded that the only way to minimize this kind of opposition was to have a sound and easily explained project that would not be operational unless genuine food shortages were imminent.

Everyone on the task force agreed that these two problems demanded even greater secrecy for this project than previously adopted, at least at the beginning. The task force did not want opposition, whether domestic or foreign, to develop so fast that this only known hope for reprieve would be stopped before it could be fully evaluated and developed.

The task force also identified an important exception to this extreme secrecy—the nations that had thermonuclear weapons had to be informed about the US crop production task force and Anderson's idea. This exception arose from the simple fact that these nations had the most critical piece of Anderson's idea. When it became clear within any one of these nations that a national food shortage appeared imminent, someone within that nation might also think of Anderson's idea.

One risk of two nations pursuing this idea without the knowledge of the other was an expensive duplication of efforts. But a far more dangerous risk was simultaneous creation of two artificial volcanic eruptions. This risk was more probable than might first appear because there would likely be a preferred time of year and conditions when a volcanic eruption should be created for its most predictable and effective results.

The combined effects of two volcanic eruptions at nearly the same time would be very difficult to predict. They could even collectively cast so many aerosols into the upper atmosphere that average atmospheric temperature would drop well below temperatures that existed in the twentieth century. Important regions could have odd weather typical of much colder world climate regimes. Total world crop production could decline just as much or more under these conditions than it would under the warming conditions that the crop production task force was now trying to counteract.

International cooperation was also needed because the best locations to create artificial volcanic eruptions were not yet known. Any nation whose boundaries encompassed known zones of stratovolcanoes could have the best sites. And every nation would have to be involved whose citizens lived in an area where significant fallout of volcanic ash from an artificial volcanic eruption was likely.

This was clearly an instance where international cooperation, not competition, was required. Unfortunately, keeping the project secret under these conditions would be difficult. Consultations with national representatives would have to be conducted very carefully.

The crop production task force finally decided to recommend that technological and diplomatic efforts be undertaken simultaneously. The time was too short to sequence these efforts.

Vice President Van Waters gave her task force's recommendations and proposed plan to President Clark at the end of March, 2033. He was pleased with the task force's thoroughness, clarity, and promptness. He agreed with every point presented and made only a few timing modifications.

First, he decided that all efforts to contact other nations about the US project would be postponed until probable sites for the artificial volcanic eruptions had been determined. Otherwise, discussions with other leaders would be too theoretical and more subject to misunderstanding.

Then President Clark decided that Congress should be told sooner rather than later about the task force's proposed plan, despite the enhanced risk of leaks to the public that this presented. In this way, he could start building congressional confidence in the plan from its very beginning. That confidence, in turn, would hopefully assure adequate funding for it.

Before going to Congress, President Clark knew that he first had to tell his Cabinet members about the plan. After all, they had been working hard to create programs to deal with possible food shortages in 2033 and later years. Even those most skeptical about the crop projections had recognized the potential gravity of these new circumstances. All Cabinet members deserved to know as soon as possible that some hope for reprieve did exist, however bizarre it might seem.

CHAPTER 29

ANALYSIS

"That's our plan," said Vice President Van Waters as she completed her summary at the president's Cabinet meeting on April 12, 2033.

Silence followed, as each Cabinet member tried to absorb what Van Waters had said. Most thought that the plan was bold. Some thought that its chances for success were minuscule. Fortunately, no one thought that it was crazy.

Everyone recognized that if the general public learned about the plan without having the factual background that the Cabinet members had received, some people might very well think that the plan was crazy and raise strong opposition to it. With almost no discussion, all Cabinet members agreed that secrecy had to be maintained until it was clear that an artificial volcanic eruption had to be created to try to alleviate real food shortages.

President Clark then told his Cabinet members that he and the vice president would also be taking this plan to Congress within two weeks. He also told them that he would instruct Secretary of State Straus to contact other nations about the plan, but only after Congress had approved the plan and General Meyer's team had selected the areas or even actual sites where the artificial volcanic eruptions would be attempted.

The president and vice president knew that they needed a short name for their plan before presenting it to Congress or someone there would concoct a name they may not like. Two weeks before the Cabinet meeting, they had decided to call it "Operation Vulcan."

President Clark revealed Operation Vulcan to Congress on April 21, 2033 in a joint, closed door session in the cavernous chambers of the House of Representatives. Before this session, he had invited the top congressional leaders from both major parties to the White House to discuss the plan.

Prolonged or rancorous debate never materialized. By now, the crop production reports from 2032 were well known. Congress had already spent more than a year dealing with dislocations caused by the new petroleum reality. Members of Congress already knew how nasty worldwide distribution problems could be under petroleum shortages. Worldwide grain shortages would surely create even greater distribution problems. Nations could be expected to look to their own needs first as shortages developed. Secretary of State Straus confirmed this probability in strong terms during the discussion in the joint, closed door session.

Congress swiftly approved Operation Vulcan. Senators and Congressmen uniformly viewed Operation Vulcan as sensible insurance for the possibility, or probability, that crop production in the United States would continue to decline. They also knew that their approval was limited at this time to the overall concept and early detailed investigation. Actual implementation would require more funding and further congressional review.

Even if all elements were in place to create an artificial volcanic eruption, Congress had a final check-point because the president agreed that no attempt to create an artificial volcanic eruption would occur without specific congressional approval. All agreed that an eruption would not be triggered unless severe grain shortages actually developed in both the United States and world markets. To have a measurable initial criterion, Congress arbitrarily decided that "severe" meant that large numbers of people in both markets were forced to rely on less than two thirds of their grain consumption in 2032.

President Clark presented a strong case that secrecy was needed to allow the investigation to be unencumbered by ill-informed opposition. Members of Congress agreed. Not a single leak about Operation Vulcan occurred. The public would not learn about it until President Clark revealed it at the end of 2033.

Even before the first joint session of Congress in April 2033, President Clark had entrusted Operation Vulcan entirely to Vice President Van Waters. She, in turn, had further entrusted its details to General

Meyer, while she and her crop production task force maintained overall responsibility. General Meyer organized Operation Vulcan in functional divisions, each headed by a scientist or military officer. Collectively, the divisional leaders were now called the "Vulcan Team," headed by General Wayne Meyer. The scientists who were division leaders were all drawn from the team that he had assembled in January. Paul Anderson, Kristin Brown, Karen Lewis, and Jacob Kahn each headed a division. Because of secrecy needs, much of the lower level work would be done by military personnel.

Vice President Van Waters's crop production task force remained in place, albeit largely inactive while Operation Vulcan proceeded ahead.

The Vulcan Team reported regularly to Vice President Van Waters. Despite General Meyer's lead role, Paul Anderson had the most difficult role as the person who decided when, or if, conditions were right to set off the volcanic eruption. Each of the other directors had their spheres of responsibility based on his or her expertise. All directors had their own staffs assigned to assist them, and in the case of General Meyer, the military establishment of the United States as well.

The Vulcan Team worked quickly.

Jacob Kahn's division identified areas around the world where appropriate sites might exist for a first artificial volcanic eruption. Past stratovolcanic activity was the most important feature for a potential site. His staff created a summary report that included maps showing the location of each area and descriptions of past stratovolcanic events in each area. The report also estimated the potential for future stratovolcanic events, both those occurring naturally and those that could be created artificially.

Everyone knew that this compilation was only a first step. What might be a perfect site from a volcanic perspective might be wholly unsuitable from the perspectives of damage control and international politics. That was why General Meyer assembled the Vulcan Team at the Pentagon on April 28, 2033, a week after the president had revealed Operation Vulcan to Congress. The team had to decide which factors would be paramount to each area with potential sites.

In what had become a regular format for the Vulcan Team, all members gathered in a designated conference room next to General Meyer's office. They sat comfortably in lightweight wooden chairs placed around a circular table made of cherry wood. The table was large enough to accommodate several more people than the five members of the Vulcan Team. General Meyer always occupied the chair that looked directly toward the entrance door to the conference room. On the wall behind him was a screen that was available for presentations from a portable projector.

General Meyer opened the meeting with little fanfare.

"Let's reexamine where we have been looking at possible sites," said General Meyer. "Jacob's summary has shown us regions where stratovolcanic eruptions have occurred within the last two hundred years. I want him to cover each of them briefly so that we can all comment or ask questions."

"As you know, we are looking only at the Northern Hemisphere," began Jacob. "Most of the large agricultural regions are in the northern temperate latitudes. We want to reduce not only the overall global temperature, but also regional temperatures where that might help crop production. With that in mind, look first at the Pacific Ocean. Almost every location along the edge of the Pacific Tectonic Plate has had a stratovolcanic eruption in the last century. All of these sectors are possibilities."

Jacob then directed his laser pointer to a large world map displayed on the screen behind General Meyer's seat. He moved its beam in an arc around the edges of the North Pacific Ocean, beginning with Indonesia, then moving north through the Philippines, Japan, and Russia's Kamchitka Peninsula, then east through Alaska's Aleutian Islands, and finally south along the West Coast of the United States, Mexico, and Central America.

"Another active sector is the Lesser Antilles islands, here, at the eastern edge of the Caribbean Sea," Jacob added. "Soufrière was here," he said, pointing to the island of St. Vincent. "Hot spots exist also in southern Italy. Mount Etna and Mount Vesuvius are there. Other active volcanic regions exist, but they have not had recent stratovolcanic eruptions. Hawaii and the Great Rift Valley in Africa are examples."

Jacob had barely finished when a barrage of comments and questions began.

"Lots of these places have large populations nearby," observed Karen Lewis. "We can't very well destroy cities with an artificial volcanic eruption."

"The prevailing jet stream from the west will push the volcanic ash to the east," added Paul. "Cities hundreds of miles to the east of a volcanic eruption can have direct damage from mounds of ash."

"Are you both saying that these areas are not suitable?" interjected General Meyer, as he directed his laser pointer first to the West Coasts of the United States and Mexico and then to Italy.

"Basically, yes, as far as I am concerned," said Paul. "You can add most of Indonesia and Japan as well. I'm not sure about the Philippines. It sure is an attractive possibility. Mount Pinatubo taught us how the aerosols would be distributed. We would not be guessing so much if we created volcanic eruptions there. We also learned a lot from Soufrière. Those islands in the Lesser Antilles all have open ocean to the east. I think these could be good sites."

"The Kamchitka Peninsula has lots of active volcanic sites and is sparsely populated," said Jacob. "It also has open ocean to the east. How about those sites?"

"I don't like the idea of exploding nuclear weapons in any other nation's territory," said Kristin Brown. "I don't want anyone snooping around. I'm most interested in the Aleutian Islands. At least the United States controls them. Are they active enough?"

General Meyer nodded agreement and looked to Jacob for an answer.

"There definitely are some sites there that have been active," he said. "Each island has a unique history. We would have to examine those histories to be sure. The Alaska Peninsula also has been active. One of the largest eruptions in the twentieth century occurred in the summer of 1912 at Katmai and Novarupta."

"Aren't the Aleutian Islands too far north?" asked Karen. "I don't see how we can get good aerosol distribution from there." Her question and comment were directed to Paul.

"Hmm. You know, I think the Aleutian Islands are located just right," said Paul. "The winter jet streams usually swing through them and dip into the Great Plains of the United States. Plus, winter jet streams have nearly double the intensity of summer jet streams. If we create a volcanic eruption when the winter jet stream is in place, aerosols from there should cool the Midwest so that more snow falls. That will increase overall moisture there, including summer rains. Also, these northern aerosols should cool Greenland. Fresh water from the Greenland Ice Sheet will be a tremendous problem for Western Europe."

Everyone looked at each other with mild astonishment that this obvious choice could be found so easily. They knew what now must be done.

During the next several months, the Vulcan Team's staff examined the Aleutian Islands and Alaska Peninsula in great detail. They looked for at least ten sites to permit a twenty to thirty year program. They also looked for the first site that gave the best opportunity to duplicate the effects of the Soufrière eruption in the Caribbean more than a decade ago.

Jacob Kahn's staff first conducted exhaustive research into existing archives of photographs, maps, and reports about these areas. Compilations of previous volcanic eruptions and seismic activity also proved to be helpful. A surprisingly large amount of information was available without having to make field trips to each island. Luckily, shortly after World War II ended, the Department of Army, then known as the War Department, had asked the United States Geological Survey to undertake a program of volcano investigations in the Aleutian Islands and on the Alaska Peninsula. Although that work was now more than eighty years old, it still formed an excellent reference to the volcanic character of the area.

In the early 1970s, the United States had even detonated thermonuclear bombs deep in one of the Aleutian Islands. The classified information from those tests, especially the test at Amchitka in November 1971, gave the Vulcan Team valuable information about how geologic formations common to the area would react to large explosions.

However, this archives research could only go so far. Field trips were needed in the summer of 2033 to assess the current status of each previously active volcano. These trips were potentially very dangerous. The Vulcan Team was looking for the easiest volcanoes to trigger, so field groups visited the most active sites in the Aleutian Islands and on the Alaska Peninsula. No one knew when a volcanic site would erupt. Even without an eruption, hot gases or lava were often present where the field group had to make its measurements.

Fortunately, the Vulcan Team found an excellent tool to expedite each field trip and to add enormously important information to the arsenal of data being collected. That tool was newly refined three-dimensional seismic technology that had been developed by the petroleum industry to search for petroleum at depths never before examined. It was easily adopted to locate large magma chambers, if any existed beneath an old volcano.

Locating a magma chamber below a volcano was only a first step. Channels had to exist from the magma chamber up to the volcanic cone. These were much harder to find. A balance also had to exist between magma pushing into these channels and any volcanic rock covering them. If the volcanic rock had too many fissures, magma could escape regularly as lava flows. With these flows, insufficient pressure would build up in the magma chamber to create an explosive eruption. If the volcanic rock was too thick and solid, the thermonuclear bombs available might not be powerful enough to remove or even fracture the rock cover. If most of the rock cover was not removed, magma might not explode through the remaining rock to give an eruption.

The Vulcan Team's efforts to find volcanoes that met all of these criteria were complicated by the short time available to examine each potential site. When seismic tests had located a magma chamber beneath a volcano, sometimes time was too short to conduct refined seismic testing to try to locate magma channels extending upward into the volcano's cone. The Vulcan Team then had to revert back to the unique known history of each volcano to help make its decisions.

At the beginning of August 2033, the Vulcan Team was ready to narrow its potential choices. The team selected five volcanoes as the best potential sites, but one stood out among the rest. The team chose Mount Gareloi on Gareloi Island as the best site for its first artificial volcanic eruption. Seismic tests in July 2033 had identified what was believed to be a very large magma chamber about ten miles below Mount Gareloi.

Mount Gareloi's largest recent eruption had occurred in 1929. This eruption had been nowhere near as big as the eruptions of Soufrière or Mount Pinatubo, so the Vulcan Team believed that potentially great magma pressure had not yet been released.

This idea was supported by a small eruption of Mount Gareloi that had occurred in 1980. Little was known about it because its discovery then had been pure luck. A stratospheric air sample collected by a balloon over Alaska had revealed an unusual amount of sulfur dioxide.

Sleuth work and satellite photographs had allowed this sulfur dioxide to be traced to Mount Gareloi. The 1980 eruption made the Vulcan Team believe that Gareloi remained continually on the brink of further eruptions. The team thought that removing part of Mount Gareloi would allow its magma chamber to release the large amount of aerosols they wanted.

The Vulcan Team also discovered a problem that showed the wisdom of President Clark's decision to get congressional support early in this process. Gareloi Island, as well as other preferred sites, was located in the Aleutian Island Wilderness. Nothing could be constructed or destroyed there without a change in the law that established that wilderness. The Vulcan Team recommended that President Clark approach Congress immediately for a waiver of the Aleutian Island Wilderness status for Gareloi Island. Largely for this reason, the Vulcan Team quickly adopted a nondescriptive code name for this first artificial volcanic eruption. It would be called simply "Project Prime."

At the end of August 2033, President Clark called another secret joint session of Congress. He described the current status of Operation Vulcan and specifically Project Prime. By now, further declines in US crop production appeared likely. Within a month, Congress voted overwhelmingly to waive the wilderness designation of Gareloi Island and neighboring islands as well. Project Prime's last legal obstacle had been overcome.

Secrecy for Operation Vulcan and Project Prime remained paramount until Project Prime was closer to reality. Secrecy was becoming more and more difficult to maintain as more and more people had to be told about Operation Vulcan. But the biggest threat to secrecy came from a different direction.

The deal that Secretary Straus had negotiated with Prime Minister Rousseau a year earlier for SMER data contemplated periodic exchanges of information beyond the initial exchange. SMER had continued its annual measurements in the northern North Atlantic Ocean south of Greenland. An undercover American research ship known only to the United States and France joined in this effort with its own methodology.

France kept its promise by providing the latest SMER measurements to the United States via Secretary Straus almost as soon as the Ministry of Agriculture got them from Marie Leclerc's team on SMER's ship. The

United States also promptly gave France via Prime Minister Rousseau the measurements made by scientists on its research ship.

In addition, ETOP regularly updated its climate projections using its latest data, the North Atlantic data collected by SMER, and other data collected by the US research ship. The United States kept its promise by providing those projections promptly to France. These exchanges were straight-forward, but the number of people who knew about the fresh water anomaly kept expanding.

A unique secrecy challenge also came from the personal friendship between Karen Lewis and Marie Leclerc. Karen, of course, knew about SMER's discoveries and Marie's role in making them. Marie, on the other hand, did not know that Karen knew about SMER's findings. More importantly, Marie also did not know about Karen's roles with the US crop production task force and Operation Vulcan or even the very existence of those endeavors. Somehow, Karen had to avoid her annual September rendezvous with Marie in 2033 without arousing suspicions and without jeopardizing her friendship with Marie.

Fortunately for Karen, Marie also was leery about having her rendezvous with Karen in 2033. Marie believed that she again had to keep SMER's discoveries secret from Karen. Last year's visit by Karen in Nantes had been awkward enough with Marie uncharacteristically having to avoid all mention of her summer adventures on SMER's ship. Marie thought that another visit like that would strain her friendship with Karen and maybe even arouse unwanted suspicions.

In mid-August, Karen sent Marie an e-mail in which she said that unexpected work commitments probably would prevent her from hosting Marie at Karen's home this year. Marie was relieved to get this news. Marie replied that she understood Karen's predicament and said that she had similar problems with SMER this year. As an alternative to keep family connections, Karen and Marie arranged for Karen's daughter, Nicole, and Marie's daughter, Annette, to spend a week together in Paris in mid-September.

While this mini-drama between Karen and Marie played out and while Congress was considering the bill that it eventually adopted to waive the wilderness designation of Gareloi Island, General Meyer jump-started Project Prime.

He had organized a military-style landing operation with the Army Corps of Engineers even before the Vulcan Team finally chose

Gareloi Island for Project Prime. He had already staged personnel and equipment at the Adak Naval Base when the Vulcan Team made its final selection in August. Immediately thereafter, ships left Adak to begin preparations at Gareloi.

September proved to be an ideal month for construction. A temporary dock on the northern side of Gareloi came first. Grading of land and installation of pre-fabricated barracks and the five steel operations buildings followed as more ships arrived from Seattle with those materials. The Corps of Engineers alone used more that a thousand personnel and many pieces of equipment to accomplish these tasks. Air Force personnel added to the total once barracks had been prepared. As many as fourteen hundred people were on the island at one time.

The personnel at Gareloi Island would soon be ready to begin the unique work that was needed to accomplish the Gareloi Solution. Many technical obstacles had yet to be overcome. But at least Project Prime was under way.

A lone person began to step back from the frenetic pace of creating Project Prime. She began to question the wisdom of the entire endeavor.

CHAPTER 30

CAUTION

As a military tactician, Vice President Van Waters was accustomed to examining not only what was right with a plan of attack, but also what could go wrong with it. She did not know enough about the science behind Operation Vulcan to be able to identify specifically what could go wrong, but her instincts required her to have someone else identify all risks very clearly. To that end, at the beginning of September, she sent a secret memorandum to the Vulcan Team with one simple question: "Are we trying to do something that creates greater risks of harm than what we are trying to prevent?"

The answer to this question would occupy the Vulcan Team throughout the month. The issue came to a head on September 29, 2033, just one week before the data on US crop production in 2033 would become public knowledge.

At Vice President Van Waters's request, General Meyer assembled the entire Vulcan Team at the Pentagon to give her their conclusions. After the Vulcan Team had arrived in their designated conference room, Van Waters joined them. Greetings were brief. She sat down in the chair between General Meyer and Paul Anderson.

General Meyer asked Paul to lead the scientific discussion. Paul began by placing the vice president's question into a framework to be analyzed by the Vulcan Team's scientists.

"Soufrière and Mount Pinatubo give us the guidance," said Paul. "We have four variables to match properly in order to reduce the average atmospheric temperature in the amount we want. You all know that these variables are aerosol size, aerosol composition, total tephra, and aerosol dispersion. We need to understand what can go wrong with each of these variables and how that will affect the new climate regimes we are trying to reverse."

Largely for Vice President Van Waters's benefit, Paul then recounted more specifically the criteria that each variable had to meet.

"We need to have aerosols with an effective average radius less than two micrometers," said Paul. "Otherwise, their warming effects will exceed their cooling effects. Average radii of less than one micrometer are much preferred.

"We also need a high proportion of the aerosols to be sulfur dioxide. When sulfur dioxide particles reach the cold stratosphere they react with water droplets there to form tiny droplets of sulfuric acid. These are the droplets that most effectively reflect incoming sunlight.

"The total amount of tephra has to be huge. Based on the eruptions of Soufrière and Pinatubo, we need at least ten cubic kilometers of pulverized material.

"Finally, we need the material to be blown high into the stratosphere. Only there will it well distributed by high altitude jet streams. Without good distribution, the global cooling effect we want will not be achieved."

Stating what was needed was relatively straight-forward. Identifying what could go wrong, and how, was much more difficult. The team members had analyzed these criteria, and other possible problems, with their best staff scientists. Every expertise was needed to sort through what was possible or probable.

After his introductory comments, Paul asked each team member to provide succinct statements of his or her conclusions. Karen Lewis would go first.

"My job has been made much easier by our decision to trigger a volcanic eruption rather than to make aerosols only from thermonuclear bombs," said Karen. "The aerosols will not be much different than aerosols produced by natural eruptions that have occurred. These aerosols have been studied extensively by many scientists. We will have a problem with crops only if the quantities are much greater than predicted. Even if they are much greater, most of the low-level ash will fall out on open ocean or a few Aleutian Islands, so no major agricultural area will be directly affected by falling ash. Ocean currents will quickly disperse the ash and the islands do not have crops on them. The biggest risk will come from a sustained eruption that pushes a lot more aerosols into the stratosphere than we want. We don't want excessive cooling any more than the warming we are trying to counteract."

"How about you, Kristin?" asked Paul.

"I'm just beginning to appreciate the enormity of natural volcanic eruptions," began Kristin. "The real questions here are going to be for you and Jacob. We have a fixed amount of deuterium in our thermonuclear bombs. Deep underground tests in the 1970s allowed us to develop formulas for how much rock will be fractured for each megaton of explosive power in one bomb. We used those formulas to figure out the size of the bombs we need at Gareloi Island. Still, we have never exploded two bombs in tandem before now. Using two bombs may give some multiplier effect we are not aware of."

"Multiplier effect?" asked Paul, startled. He had not heard about a possible multiplier effect before, nor had any other member of the Vulcan Team.

"Probably not as bad as you might think," said Kristin in response. "I have to give you some history here. The US scientists who made the Castle Bravo thermonuclear bomb in the early 1950s predicted its power to be five megatons. Its actual destructive power was fifteen megatons. In retrospect, they found a nuclear fusion reaction that they had not predicted.

"The Soviets also misjudged the effects of one of their early thermonuclear bombs. Their error was not in predicting its explosive power, but in misunderstanding its tandem effects with the atmospheric conditions prevailing when they set it off. Shock waves traveled much further than predicted. Some people were killed, including a child in a small settlement that they thought was far outside the danger zone. They later figured out that a temperature inversion had magnified the expected force of the shock wave.

"Our two bombs in tandem will also be an experiment, so something unexpected could happen as well."

Paul's mind again was jarred when he heard Kristin say the word "experiment." She was saying that the best minds in the world in the 1940s and 1950s, those brilliant physicists who created atomic and then thermonuclear bombs, misjudged what would happen from their experiments by underestimating the great power they were unleashing. Yet, here in 2033, the entire earth was in the middle of an experiment on a far greater scale because of changes in the chemistry of the earth's atmosphere, also caused by human choices.

Questions flashed in Paul's mind.

Have all of us misjudged what would happen from these chemical changes in the atmosphere? What reactions or effects have we missed? Have we underestimated the complexity of climatic patterns and their susceptibility to rapid shifts? How can we risk creating another influence on those patterns by trying to trigger a huge volcanic eruption? The only thing certain is uncertainty. Are we really beyond knowing only that what we know is that we do not know? Yet, how can we not try to do something? If we really are crossing a threshold to global climate disruptions, the consequences of this reality are far too great to ignore. Millions of human lives hang in the balance.

"Having said this," Kristin continued, "I think that any possible multiplier effect would not create a calamity. As I already said, we have a fixed amount of deuterium in our bombs. Even at one hundred percent efficiency, I think the most these bombs can do is blow off the top four thousand feet of Mount Gareloi. Their direct contribution of small particles to the stratosphere will be small compared to the load of aerosols we want to get from the volcanic eruption we are trying to trigger. After all, we are trying to match the effects of Pinatubo or even Soufrière. Certainly no extra danger to crops would exist if our tandem bombs were even ten times stronger than we have predicted. I think our main risk with these bombs is that the two bomb combination will not work well. A failure of this sort would just mean a discouraging dud, not extra risk."

Paul and the other members of the Vulcan Team were visibly relieved with Kristin's conclusion. Still, Kristin's revelation had been a surprise. Vice President Van Waters had clearly done the right thing by forcing a reevaluation of Operation Vulcan. What other surprises would there be today?

Paul gave his analysis next, reserving Jacob Kahn for last, knowing that Jacob had the most difficult predictive task.

"Let's look first at the question of aerosol distribution," he said. "As I said earlier, we want very widespread distribution of aerosols in the stratosphere so that we really do have global cooling of the troposphere. That's why we have chosen to trigger the eruption when the powerful winter polar jet streams pass right over the Aleutian Islands. If we do not get the widespread distribution we want, the worst that can happen will be somewhat less sunlight in smaller regions of the Northern Hemisphere, especially North America. That really won't have much impact.

"Remember that the 1912 Katmai and Novarupta eruptions on the Alaska Peninsula occurred in June. Weaker summer jet streams did not give widespread distribution to the aerosols produced by these eruptions. The world-wide impacts from these eruptions were nowhere near as great as the impacts from the eruptions of Soufrière or Pinatubo, even though the amount of aerosols was nearly as large. Other historic examples also exist where large amounts of aerosols from a stratovolcanic eruption probably were not as widely distributed as aerosols from other eruptions having the same size."

"Now let's examine the aerosols themselves," continued Paul. "I agree with Karen that our analysis here has been made much easier by our decision to trigger a volcanic eruption rather than to make aerosols only from thermonuclear bombs. There is no reason to believe that the average aerosol radius will be larger than those from the Soufrière or Pinatubo eruptions.

"Some smaller eruptions have had aerosols with larger average radii. But that appears to be a function of their reduced explosive power. Of course, these eruptions created far fewer aerosols. If we have a reduced explosive eruption at Gareloi, the quantity of aerosols will also be reduced. Odd effects from these limited amounts of large aerosols simply will not happen.

"As for sulfur dioxide, only so much of this is possible as a proportion of the total aerosols. Even the highest proportions observed yet in big eruptions caused no unexpected harm. Mexico's El Chichon in 1982 is a good example. The sulfur dioxide question is one of total aerosols quantity, not quality."

"This brings us to you, doesn't it, Jacob," concluded Paul.

All eyes now focused on Jacob Kahn. Everyone was satisfied to this point that Operation Vulcan carried little additional risk to crops in the United States or world-wide.

"We have two very different kinds of risk regarding the quantity of aerosols blown up into the stratosphere," began Jacob. "One of these is obvious. We cannot know for sure the total amount of aerosols that Gareloi will eject during its eruption, or even if we can trigger an eruption at all. Remember that the main magma chamber is ten miles below the island. Despite the seismic data we have, it's very hard for us to judge how big it is, what its sources of magma are, and what eruptive pressures exist there.

"History has to be our best guide here. Gareloi Island was formed over time by many eruptions. The same is true all along the Aleutian Arc. Katmai and Novarupta had large amounts of aerosols and some big explosions, but none were anywhere near as big as Tambora in 1815. We now have lots of data about Gareloi. Nothing indicates that Gareloi is another Tambora just waiting to explode in an enormous eruption. If anything, our greatest problem with Gareloi is that it will not produce enough aerosols to do what we want.

"Of course, if we do get the amount of aerosols that we want, Karen correctly pointed out that low-level ash could fall on nearby islands. They are mostly uninhabited, so I think that potential damage to structures on these islands would be minimal."

Noting expressions of relief, Jacob paused a few moments before continuing. "The other kind of risk is potentially more dangerous," he began slowly. "It is always possible that another major eruption somewhere else will occur within a few months of our Gareloi eruption. We can do nothing to stop this. If Gareloi does what we hope, but then is joined by another eruption as big as Soufrière, we could have the excessive cooling that Kristin mentioned. Maybe we could even have a volcanic winter in the summer, at least in the Northern Hemisphere. Paul and I have discussed this possibility."

"That's right," interjected Paul. "This definitely could happen if the second eruption is further south than Gareloi, but still in the Northern Hemisphere. Then aerosols from the two eruptions would be very widespread in the stratosphere over North America. The total effect could be similar to Tambora, even if the total amount of aerosols is much less. A big eruption close to Gareloi could be a problem as well if it occurred when the jet stream could disperse aerosols as widely as we want from our Gareloi eruption."

"I am calling this a possibility, not a probability," said Jacob. "Big eruptions like Soufrière are very rare. On the average, they occur only once every fifty or more years. Furthermore, careful monitoring of all stratovolcanic areas up to the date of our Gareloi eruption should uncover any volcano that is giving signs of an impending explosion. We can then postpone Project Prime to see whether nature will do the job for us. This gives us another level of protection to reduce the probability of two big volcanic eruptions close in time."

Paul was about to give a summary conclusion for the Vulcan Team to consider as a group, but Jacob was not yet finished.

"There is another potential effect we have to consider," Jacob continued. "It is unrelated to aerosols. As we all know, Mount Gareloi rises right up out of the Bering Sea. A major eruption there could create local earthquakes. More important, it could dump lots of material quickly into the sea as a landslide. Either could create a tsunami. As you know, historic tsunamis have killed many people. They are dangerous to people mostly because they occur without warning.

"Here, we will know exactly when a tsunami might occur, so advance warnings should eliminate the danger to people. Property damage is another story. We cannot avoid that if a tsunami occurs. An enormous tsunami like the one that occurred in Southeast Asia in 2004 is extremely unlikely. Any earthquake generated by the eruption will be small and local as an after-effect of the eruption rather than its cause. As for a landslide, the water displacement will probably fan out as the tsunami travels away from Gareloi. The main risk will be to the islands around Gareloi. They are sparsely settled, so property damage should be small."

"We will be prepared to reimburse property damage from any tsunami," interjected Vice President Van Waters quickly. "We will also reimburse any property damage from ash falling on nearby islands."

Paul could see that Van Waters was becoming satisfied that the risks of harm from Project Prime were far less than its potential benefits. He thought that the meeting had revealed all of the major adverse risks that everyone could think of. Paul asked if anyone had any questions to ask any of the other team members. No one did. As he looked back at the vice president, he saw that he did not need to express a summary conclusion for the group to consider.

"I think that our large scale risks are minimal," said Van Waters. "Usually we operate as a consensus, but this time I want a formal vote on the question whether we proceed with Project Prime."

Taking his cue from the vice president, General Meyer stepped in to conduct a formal vote by the Vulcan Team.

"Any further discussion before we vote?" he asked.

Van Waters and General Meyer purposely paused to look directly at each person in the room, one by one.

"Hearing none, all those in favor raise your hand," General Meyer then said. Every Vulcan Team member voted in favor of proceeding.

Paul agreed that Project Prime should move forward, but he felt compelled to add a caution to the confidence that was obviously increasing within Vice President Van Waters. He spoke up after the vote ended.

"Remember Ms. Vice President, even if we get the aerosols and cooling we want from Gareloi, we may not get a return to historic climate regimes," he said. "We think that this will happen, but we do not know for sure. Short-term cooling may not push us back across the threshold of rapid climate shifts that appear to be occurring. We want to be sure that you understand this part of Project Prime's risks."

"Yes, I know this," said Van Waters. "The president knows this as well. But we have no other option at this point. We will just have to hope for the best."

All nodded, acknowledging her statement. The meeting then concluded, with the vice president being the first to leave the conference room.

Later that day, Van Waters met with President Clark in the Oval Office to discuss Operation Vulcan and Project Prime. She told him about her question to the Vulcan Team, summarized the analyses by each team member, and reported their unanimous vote to proceed ahead.

President Clark was relieved that they had reached this conclusion. While the Vulcan Team had been concentrating on Project Prime, he knew that Van Waters's crop production task force had continued to monitor climate change indicators and to investigate other solutions.

The indicators in 2033 had all pointed in discouraging directions.

SMER's continued measurements of salinity in the northern North Atlantic Ocean, now augmented and confirmed by the undercover American research ship, showed that the Greenland Ice Sheet was discharging even greater amounts of fresh water in August and September 2033 than it had done in 2032. Although the fresh water discharged in 2032 ultimately did not reach the North Atlantic Drift, its effects on thermohaline circulation were beginning to be measurable. The extra amounts of fresh water in 2033 would just make matters worse.

ETOP's multiple measurements showed increased concentrations of carbon dioxide and methane in the earth's atmosphere. ETOP's compilations of average atmospheric temperatures at the earth's surface showed a rise in the average global temperature in 2033 that fit the upward trend of the last twelve years. Whatever had happened in 2032 was likely to happen again in 2033.

As for solutions, at least in the near-term, the crop production task force had found none other than Anderson's idea to create artificial volcanic eruptions. If the Vulcan Team had found this idea to be too risky, then there was no near-term solution to offer to American citizens and the world's people.

President Clark knew that the reports on US crop production would soon be disclosed publicly. No amount of rhetoric could hide that fact that production was down to levels on a per capita basis that were nearly as poor as crop production during the Great Depression of the twentieth century. Although an overall shortage in the United States would not yet exist, the numbers were uncomfortably close to that status. The downward trend was alarming.

Knowing that a potential short-term solution was at hand, even if it had to be kept secret from the public for awhile, allowed the president to be upbeat about future crop production for the United States in the next few years.

The international food situation was worse. Low crop yields existed in almost every nation. The predictions in Secretary Straus's State Department report had been accurate. Many nations were restricting exports of basic grains such as wheat, rice, and corn in an effort to keep food at home for their own citizens. These policies were also having adverse effects on nations whose own crops were inadequate to feed their people. Fortunately, some other nations carved out exceptions from their no-export policies for those nations, or at least for those nations that could afford to buy grains at new high prices. The nations that could not afford the new high prices were out of luck except for some donations from the United States and Canada. A monumental international supply crisis for grains loomed ahead.

Under these circumstances, every nation was examining what could be done to increase crop yields. The time had now come to reveal Operation Vulcan to the other nations of the world that had thermonuclear bombs and to important US trading partners as well.

CHAPTER 31

TRUTH

In October 2033, President Clark, Vice President Van Waters, and Secretary of State Straus collectively decided which governments should be told about Operation Vulcan and in what order. Top-level meetings would occur first with Canada and Mexico, the United States's neighbors and trading partners in NAFTA, even though neither nation was in the nuclear club of nations able to create a project like Operation Vulcan. Support for, or at least no opposition to, Operation Vulcan was especially important with Canada because its western provinces would be affected by falling volcanic ash from Project Prime.

Secretary Straus would next travel to Europe ostensibly for discussions about petroleum prices under the new petroleum reality. She would first see Prime Minister Rousseau, honoring the close coordination between the United States and France that had followed the SMER disclosures in 2032. His reaction would help her set a tone for discussions with the other European nuclear powers, Great Britain and Russia, as well as major European trading nations such as Germany.

Discussions with the nuclear nations of India, Pakistan, and China would be next, followed by discussions with other important Asian trading partners such as Japan and South Korea. The nuclear nation North Korea would be notified only when Operation Vulcan was revealed publicly. Straus would have arduous and potentially contentious trips.

Over a period of four weeks ending on November 18, 2033, Straus accomplished her diplomatic tasks. Fortunately, no other nuclear nation had begun plans for a project like Operation Vulcan.

No leader she visited had objected to Operation Vulcan based on existing nuclear weapons treaties. Straus had encouraged this lack of objection by giving each leader a summary analysis of all the treaties showing that the treaties permit the way that bombs would be used in Operation Vulcan. Probably more persuasive, each leader recognized that something had to be done to try to alleviate world-wide grain shortages. Operation Vulcan was at least a serious attempt to achieve that goal. By agreement with each nation's leaders, secrecy would be maintained until President Clark described Operation Vulcan publicly sometime in the coming months. Straus received a positive reception to the United States' efforts everywhere except in India.

Even there, India's prime minister agreed that Operation Vulcan made sense at this time. But she also sharply criticized the United States for having ignored warning signs three decades ago. She was particularly adamant that the United States bore most of the responsibility for the crop production problems now faced by India and most other nations of the world.

According to her, the United States government had failed to acknowledge both the existence of climate changes and the contribution of the industrialized nations to those changes. She said that these failures had led people in developing nations, including her own, to copy the United States in using the same technologies for their economic expansions as the United States had used historically. China in particular had followed the technological approach of the United States.

India's prime minister further asserted that this combination of procrastination and copying had caused two insidious effects.

One effect was to increase even more rapidly the amount of carbon dioxide and other greenhouse gases in the atmosphere due to increased emissions by all nations. She pointed specifically at the United States as historically and even then the largest emitter per capita in the world. The United States had also been the largest emitter nation in total amounts until overtaken by China at the early part of the twenty-first century.

The other effect was to delay development of alternative technologies that could be used on a truly massive scale to replace those technologies that created troublesome emissions in the first place. She said that the industrialized nations not only had the best resources to try to develop new technologies, but also had the moral obligation to do so as the primary historic generators of the emissions that now were causing climate changes. She asserted that these nations should have devoted necessary resources to this purpose long ago. In a bold accusation, she said that the United States had squandered a chance to be a hero, but instead had chosen to be a villain.

As Straus would learn later, India's prime minister was presenting a viewpoint that was held by many nations outside the nuclear club. This viewpoint would complicate finding solutions to the declining global trade in grains that was occurring in 2033.

By the beginning of December 2033, a world-wide decline in crop production had become painfully obvious. It had come suddenly upon the United States and the world at large in just two years. On top of the new petroleum reality, the American public had awakened to a new food reality of high prices and, in some cases, actual shortages. Americans were not happy about it. They expected their government to do something.

President Clark had planned to deal with this new food reality at length in his upcoming State of the Union address in January 2034. Public consternation preempted that plan. President Clark was forced to reveal Operation Vulcan in a special address before Congress in December 2033.

More than any other time in his presidency, even the onset of the new petroleum reality, President Clark consulted with and relied upon others to help him develop his speech to Congress, the American people, and a world-wide audience.

Vice President Van Waters shared her new-found expertise about the science involved with Operation Vulcan and Project Prime. She also ensured that the president had direct access to each member of the Vulcan Team. Both the expertise and caution of these individuals gave President Clark comfort in what the Vulcan Team was doing.

Secretary of Agriculture Rand described in detail for President Clark the difficulties in dealing with odd weather regimes. He arranged for the president to meet with some of the best experts in his department, in agricultural businesses, and in academe, while still maintaining the secrecy of Operation Vulcan. With respect to annual crops, these meetings revealed that no magical solution with new kinds of seeds was at hand. The uncertainty about what the new weather regimes were or would be, or even whether there were or would be new weather regimes, paralyzed any action to change seeds for traditional crops or to change the kinds of crops altogether. For food that came from perennial plants, such as fruit trees and grape vines, the long lead time to change the plants caused growers automatically to deny that any new weather regimes had arrived.

Secretary of State Straus was valuable to President Clark in two very different ways. She first reminded him about the reactions to Operation Vulcan that she had received during her trips to visit key world leaders in October and November. Later communications with some of those leaders added to the mix of reactions. This information helped President Clark to describe the crop shortage problem, as well as potential relief through Operation Vulcan, in ways that would be most palatable to other peoples of the world.

Straus also helped the president by informing those key leaders about President Clark's upcoming speech. They, as well as he, had to be prepared to deal with a firestorm of controversy that might follow his revelation of Operation Vulcan. For this reason, Straus also directed the United States ambassador to the United Nations to reveal Operation Vulcan in the Security Council meeting that preceded the president's address by only two days.

As a final step before his address, President Clark met with the top congressional leaders from both parties. They were not surprised when he told them that he believed the time had come to remove the cloak of secrecy from Operation Vulcan. They readily concurred that this was the proper time to do so. They said that most senators and representatives were anxious to show their constituents that something was being done about this new problem of high food prices and food shortages.

These leaders agreed to use their strong influence to assure that no information about Operation Vulcan would leak out from Congress before the president's address. Although a few representatives chafed at this restriction, they quickly realized that they did not know enough to respond sensibly to questions if they were the first to reveal Operation Vulcan. None of them wanted to be embarrassed by his or her lack of knowledge.

Thursday evening, December 15, 2033, arrived sooner than President Clark might have wanted, but he was well prepared to face the nation and the world.

Any public joint session of the United States Senate and House of Representatives was an impressive occasion, and this was no exception. President Clark was greeted warmly, even by members of the opposing party, as he walked to the front of the House chambers. The buzz of anticipation was even greater than at the previous year's State of the Union address, when the president had to talk about the new petroleum reality. Shockingly, the most technologically advanced nation on earth was now facing a problem at the most basic level of human need. How would it provide adequate food for every citizen?

President Clark began his address in a traditional way. He first recognized the leaders of the Senate and House and the members of his Cabinet. But he then greeted not only "my fellow Americans," but also "all peoples of the world," in a clear effort to engage his entire audience.

President Clark was candid.

"As you know, we have been dealing with the new petroleum reality during the last two years. We have been finding solutions to the problems that this has created.

"At the same time, another difficult situation was creeping up on us and our fellow citizens of the world. This year, crop production in the United States dropped a lot. We are not alone. Crop production in all but a handful of nations also dropped a lot.

"For many decades, the United States has produced grains well beyond the needs of our own citizens. Those surpluses have allowed us to be a leading exporter of grains to those nations whose people urgently needed that food. This year was much different. US exports declined. Worldwide, some other nations even stopped all of their previous grain exports. These changes have caused US and world grain and food prices to escalate.

"High prices have been an inconvenience for many Americans and a difficult problem for some. They have been an immense problem for many other people in the world. Only the generosity of our citizens, through your elected representatives, allowed us still to send basic grain supplies to our historic customer nations. We prevented many potential catastrophes. But catastrophes will be harder to avoid if the downward trend in crop production continues. Food shortages might also occur here."

President Clark paused, letting the gravity of this problem sink in to all who were watching and listening. He then began speaking more slowly, almost like a college professor, rather than a politician.

"Why has this happened?," he asked. "More important, what can be done about it?"

He paused again. The House chamber was deathly silent.

"The answer to my first question is now clear. Every agricultural region in the US experienced very odd weather during the growing season.

"Let me give you a few examples. California and the West Coast were much wetter than normal. Many crops there simply washed away or drowned in supersaturated fields. This was just the opposite of the severe and long drought that affected California in the early part of this century. The Midwest was much drier than normal. Most crops there were stunted by their lack of water. The South was much hotter than normal. Citrus trees had fewer blossoms and produced less fruit.

"Never in our records has every region of the country experienced very odd weather for that region. Even the Dust Bowl years of the 1930s did not match what we had this year. Back then, large portions of the United States experienced drought. But other regions had decent weather for growing crops. This was not so this year.

"What has happened in the rest of the world? The answer is the same. Odd weather conditions occurred in most major agricultural regions. There were no consistent patterns other than the fact that the conditions were very unusual and sometimes record setting. Some regions were too wet, some were too dry, most were too hot, and a few were too cold.

"Europe provides a good example. Southern Europe, around the Mediterranean Sea, was much warmer and drier than normal. Northern Europe, especially France and Great Britain, was much colder than normal. Traditional crops throughout these regions did not fare well.

"No one knows for sure why all of these odd conditions have occurred.

"A few scientists think that these odd conditions are just rare occurrences within normal statistical ranges for each region. However, some of these same scientists are also saying that the historic probability of so many of these odd conditions in the same year is exceedingly low.

"Other scientists think that what has occurred is the beginning of new climate regimes for these regions. They attribute these changes to what they call an overall increase in global atmospheric energy. For many years, we have been hearing about this kind of increase as 'global warming.' This is shorthand for what scientists measure as an increase in average atmospheric temperature. Data collected by our own Earth Temperature Observation Project show that the average annual atmospheric temperature has bounced up and down somewhat from year to year, but the trend has definitely been upward for the last decade. Data from other researchers show an upward trend for the last five decades.

"Warmer temperatures alone, however, are not the most important story. Far more important is what increased atmospheric temperatures mean to the climate of a specific region. A number of scientists are now saying that we probably are at a threshold where rapid shifts in local climates are occurring. They base this idea on evidence of changes that occurred thousands of years ago. Back then, very rapid shifts in climates occurred from time to time. What do I mean by 'rapid?' I mean just a decade or two.

"This administration will proceed cautiously in evaluating these scientific opinions. But we will not stand idly by if something can be done to provide greater certainty for our crop production.

"We believe that next year is a crucial year for evaluating the scientific theories. If we have the same set of abnormalities next year as we have had this year, then the theory of new climate regimes is probably correct."

President Clark could see grim faces throughout the House chambers, even among those who knew the most about Operation Vulcan.

"We have been evaluating what to do if that theory is correct. It will be impossible to make sweeping changes in crops in just a few years to match new climates. To buy time, we have devised a way to temporarily reduce the average atmospheric temperature. If successful, we believe that this reduction will create a return to the climate regimes of the twentieth century for a few years while we try to figure out long-term solutions. We have named this effort Operation Vulcan.

"The basic idea of Operation Vulcan is simple. We know that in the past big volcanic eruptions have thrown a lot of aerosols into the upper atmosphere. Good examples are the eruptions of Soufrière in the Caribbean in 2021 and Mount Pinatubo in the Philippines in 1991. Material from these eruptions obscured the sun so long that the average atmospheric temperature dropped for a few years. Operation Vulcan is designed to trigger volcanic eruptions to do just that.

"The first artificial eruption has been designated for October 2034 at a remote island in Alaska. We have named it Project Prime. The trigger will be two thermonuclear bombs that are exploded underground. Technical details will be revealed tomorrow and are not important here.

"We have many safeguards surrounding Project Prime and Operation Vulcan. We will not attempt an artificial volcanic eruption unless world-wide crop production next year is even worse than this year. It must also be worse because of very odd weather that follows the same pattern as this year. If so, an overheated atmosphere is almost certainly the cause. Then Operation Vulcan can be placed in action to try to cool the atmosphere.

"No other nation in the world will be attempting a similar project. We have cleared this with the leaders of all nations that have thermonuclear bombs. This ensures that there will be no conflicting attempts to cool the atmosphere in this way.

"We will use an elaborate monitoring system to identify potential large volcanic eruptions that could occur naturally around the time of our artificial eruption. Maybe nature will do its own job of cooling the earth's atmosphere for awhile. Our main purpose here is to avoid the combined effects of two very large volcanic eruptions."

President Clark paused again, preparing to end his special address with a warning and a promise.

"Hopefully, we can cool the atmosphere with an artificial volcanic eruption. That does not guarantee that good growing conditions will occur in all agricultural regions. Historic statistical variability of weather will still apply. Nevertheless, we do expect most regions to have normal weather. That should permit enough good crops to prevent serious grain shortages next year and for a few later years as well."

The president paused again.

"We must all recognize that Project Prime, and Operation Vulcan, are only temporary solutions.

"We will begin immediately to evaluate what can be done as long-term solutions. I will be asking Congress to greatly increase funding for research to examine all aspects of this problem. We will be working with the United Nations and with other nations to draw on their unique expertise to find and assess all potential solutions. We will be sharing information with other nations. This is a world-wide problem that requires cooperation among all nations. I pledge to all

Americans and citizens of the world that we will dedicate our resources to understanding this problem and to solving it in the best way possible for all of humanity.

"God bless you and God bless the United States of America."

With such a serious and sudden ending, members of Congress momentarily hesitated in applauding President Clark. Protocol quickly overcame hesitation. The president received a standing ovation for his candor and forthright approach. Despite the enthusiasm, he and the assembled senators and representatives knew that a great deal of effort, creativity, and good luck would be needed to accomplish successfully what the president had outlined in his address.

The American and world publics reacted swiftly to President Clark's speech. For most people, optimism overcame shock.

When technical details revealed Gareloi Island as the location for Project Prime, American media adopted a new name for this project—the Gareloi Solution. Even President Clark began to use this term. At first, the Vulcan Team continued to refer to their first project as Project Prime, in stubborn adherence to the fact that, at most, this project could only be the beginning of a long-term solution to the problem of global climate disruptions. Soon, however, even the Vulcan Team succumbed to labeling their first project "the Gareloi Solution."

For its part, Congress dealt immediately with President Clark's proposals. Even before the president's State of the Union address one month later in January 2034, Congress funded a host of major research initiatives directed toward understanding and solving the declines in crop production in the United States and elsewhere. Speedy legislation had not been observed like this in Congress since the follow-up to the September 11, 2001 terrorist attacks on the United States.

Even under expedited legislating, everyone recognized that research was needed for two fundamentally different approaches to solving the food shortage problem for the long-term—adaptation and reversal. Adaptation assumed that the atmospheric concentrations of greenhouse gases would continue to increase and that people would have to adapt to whatever new climate regimes those increases would cause. Reversal assumed that the climatic changes being caused by existing greenhouse gas concentrations could be reversed so that historic climate regimes would return.

The adaptation approach would devote resources to changing both crops and growing methods to adapt to new climate regimes. This approach was complicated by a general uncertainty about what the new climate regimes were or would be. The changes experienced in 2032 and 2033 had not been foreseen. At least they had now been identified. But no one knew whether these changes reflected new climate regimes or whether they were merely transitional changes on the way to other climate regimes.

Adaptation also relied on two additional assumptions—first, that most existing agricultural regions would still be suitable for some useful and valuable food crops under the new climate regimes and second, that other locations would be available for planting crops to make up for those regions that were no longer suitable. The second assumption would prove to be shaky in 2034.

World-wide, increased population during and after the latter part of the twentieth century had caused all of the best agricultural lands to be used already. The same pressures had caused marginal or poor crop lands to be used as well. In some areas, tropical rain forests or other vegetation had been cleared for crops, only to discover that topsoil was thin and could support crops for only a few years. In other areas, good cropland that had existed in the middle of the twentieth century had been overrun by urban expansion, making it no longer available to produce food.

Another difficulty with the adaptation approach also quickly became apparent. The migration strategy that had been used by human ancestors to adapt to climate changes was no longer available. Both a shortage of potential new food-producing locations and fiercely protected national boundaries restricted vast numbers of people to their home nations. Even though individuals and small groups of humans were the most mobile animals on earth, human societies were not.

The adaptation approach also resigned many natural ecosystems to vast changes over extremely short periods, at least in biological terms, with the demise of many species of plants and animals.

All of these ecosystem changes would affect humans as well as the ecosystems themselves. Many people relied directly on existing ecosystems for their sustenance. Many more people relied indirectly on existing ecosystems for essential food and fresh water. So the adaptation approach to solve the food shortage problem by itself was much more complicated, risky, and difficult than it first appeared.

On the other hand, the reversal approach also had its own difficulties. Reversal required devoting resources to trying to change local climates back to those that existed generally in the twentieth century. The whole idea was so daunting as to seem impossible.

The reversal approach first required an end to annual increases in the atmospheric concentrations of greenhouse gases such as carbon dioxide and methane that resulted from human activities. Nearly every person on the planet contributed every day to these increases, individually in a small way, but collectively in an enormous way. Changing those human activities would be impossible without good substitutes that would provide the same benefits that these activities provided and that would be available on a massive scale large enough to end those activities.

The reversal approach faced yet another difficulty. As Vice President Van Waters' crop production task force had learned, even ending the activities that had caused increased atmospheric concentrations of greenhouse gases would not be enough. The concentrations of carbon dioxide, methane, and some other gases had to be reduced to levels that would reduce the average atmospheric temperature. Decades or even centuries would be needed for natural systems to absorb the existing overloads. This meant that methods to absorb rapidly the excess carbon dioxide and other gases on a huge scale also had to be developed. No one knew how to do this or even if it could be done.

The relative permanence of the increased greenhouse gases in the atmosphere also could lead to an uncomfortable psychological difficulty for many people and their governments. People and their governments were accustomed to dealing with short-term causes and effects. Once the cause ceased, so would its effects. This was not true for the greatly increased atmospheric concentrations of carbon dioxide and other gases that now existed. Serious frustration was likely to occur when major efforts to change had no immediate effects on those concentrations.

Debates between advocates of an adoption approach and advocates of a reversal approach to solving this new food shortage problem played out in Congress and in public opinion as well. Ultimately, a majority in Congress did not choose sides in these debates. Congress provided huge funds for both the adaptation and reversal approaches. Congress cut back on many governmental services to provide these emergency funds.

Congress also made no effort to restrict the research subjects because no one knew what research might be most productive. The most immediate need, of course, was to minimize current and upcoming food shortages. Only the Gareloi Solution and an ongoing Operation Vulcan provided hope for that need.

CHAPTER 32

DETOUR

General Meyer's jump-started preparation now paid off. By the time President Clark addressed the nation and world in December 2033, the Vulcan Team had conceived and put into motion its plan for placing the two twenty megaton bombs at Gareloi Island.

The planning for the upper bomb, now code named Alpha, had been simple. In October, crews had used traditional machines and explosives to bore a tunnel into the northeastern slope of Mount Gareloi to a point just 3,000 feet below its summit. The bomb itself would be deployed using techniques developed during many underground tests in the 1960s and 1970s.

Planning for the lower bomb, now code named Omega, had been much more difficult. The Vulcan Team first had to find a magma channel extending up to Mount Gareloi from the large magma chamber located far below the Bering Sea's floor.

In their initial examination of Mount Gareloi, Jacob Kahn's group had done a series of refined seismic tests that had mapped possibilities, but had not found a channel. Fortunately, further tests in September had found what appeared to be the tip of a magma channel located just 10,000 feet below Mount Gareloi's summit. Kahn had thought that the lower bomb could most effectively be placed about 2,000 feet above this channel.

Knowing where to go was much easier than getting there. Underground temperatures at a depth of 8,000 feet normally exceeded eighty degrees Celsius. Temperatures close to the magma channel would be much higher, probably exceeding two hundred degrees Celsius.

In early 2034, Kahn's group enlisted United States and Canadian tunneling experts to try to solve this problem. In less than six months, they created a robotic drilling machine that was built from new materials able to withstand temperatures even above four hundred degrees Celsius. While this machine was being built, crews had used traditional machines and explosives to start making the first part of the lower tunnel beginning one hundred yards west of the portal of the upper tunnel.

Crews in the lower tunnel reached rock with greatly elevated temperatures by early March 2034. With great expectations, they then deployed the robotic machine. No one was disappointed. The machine was an immense success. In just three months, the machine bored a tunnel nearly eight feet in diameter down to a point four hundred feet from the projected location for the deployment of Omega above the magma channel. Unfortunately, this was as deep as they dared to go. At the tunnel's end, the temperature rose sharply to more than three hundred degrees Celsius, much hotter than they had anticipated.

This extra high temperature created a new challenge. Everyone knew that even the high temperatures that had been projected would have made Omega's deployment the most dangerous operation of the Gareloi Solution other than detonation of the two thermonuclear bombs. A bomb could not be exposed to three hundred degree temperatures very long. At the very least, high temperatures could make a bomb inoperative. A bomb could also collapse and release in a small space all of the poisonous Plutonium in the atomic bomb that was its trigger. If this were to occur before Omega was detonated, concentrated Plutonium vapors at the tunnel's portal would be very difficult to prevent. A Plutonium release could poison people on the island and would also make the tunnel unusable for deploying another bomb in its place.

Now they encountered temperatures more than a hundred degrees hotter than had been predicted. The Vulcan Team had little choice but to test Omega's deployment device under these new conditions. This device rolled quickly down the tunnel by remote control so that the bomb would be exposed to high temperatures only a short time. Its distinctive feature was a new refrigeration unit that relied on phased evaporation of water kept in tanks on the device. The water's staged vaporization would keep the bomb cool until it was triggered.

The Vulcan Team tested Omega's refrigeration unit in late June. Disaster struck. The device exploded when its water evaporated so quickly that its vent pipes could not handle all of the steam.

The Vulcan Team clearly had a problem to solve. Omega, the lower bomb, was essential to success, or at least that is what Kristin Brown, Jacob Kahn, and their fellow experts thought. The team had used water for cooling in Omega's original deployment device in part to maintain the tunnel's usability if the device failed during testing. That very feature had saved the Gareloi Solution for 2034. The damage to the tunnel from the explosion of the cooling system on the deployment device had been minimal. The steam that had caused the explosion had simply spread into the rest of the tunnel, where it had condensed as water as it had approached the tunnel's entrance. Unfortunately, the Vulcan Team now knew that the amount of water needed would require any similar device to be far too large to fit in the tunnel. They had to create a new design.

As the group responsible for the integrity of the thermonuclear bombs, Kristin Brown's division had created Omega's deployment device. After its failure, she enlisted additional scientists and industry refrigeration experts to come up with new designs for devices that could be completed in less than two months. With such a short time period, modifications to existing devices seemed to be the only feasible solutions.

Although Kristin's division had examined available industry refrigeration units before they had created their special device, they conducted another industry search again. They found nothing directly suitable, although they created some sketches of possible redesigns of two units.

While the industry search was under way, other people looked at modifying the design of the cooling system on the deployment device that had failed. Mostly, they considered using another substance in place of the water. Every known coolant was examined. Even the most promising coolants had some flaw.

Kristin shared with Paul her frustration after just two weeks into her division's search for new design ideas. She complained to him about each of the alternatives that people were considering, describing the ideas and the flaws in their practicality. She even showed him the sketches of two industry refrigeration units that they had found and tried to modify. One of the sketches included an electrical power cord that would extend from the portal to the device and would be laid out as the device moved quickly down the tunnel. The cord was so heavily insulated that it looked like a hose.

A hose?

Paul had an idea.

Paul knew that the original cooling system had failed because the amount of water used to cool it was inadequate. All of the water had evaporated too quickly into steam. Everyone knew that inadequate release of that steam is what caused the explosion. One easy fix was to enlarge the vents on the cooling device so that pressure could not build up. But the device still could not carry enough water to provide cooling long enough to protect the bomb.

Paul realized that if a continuous stream of water was available for continuous evaporation, the bomb could be cooled indefinitely. Could a water hose be laid down just like the electric power line in the sketch? If so, then a continuous flow of water through a hose could cool the bomb. Then the bomb could also be moved more slowly into place and stabilized with less urgency.

Paul described his idea to Kristin. She understood his concept immediately. Neither of them had any idea whether any water hose existed that could withstand the heat in the tunnel, could insulate the water from that heat, and could be laid out quickly over more than two miles as the bomb moved down the tunnel. Kristin, however, was determined to find out.

July passed and then August.

At the end of August, the Vulcan Team breathed a sigh of relief. Kristin's division had solved the problem of protecting Omega when placed at the end of its tunnel amidst heat from the magma channel nearby. The solution came from Paul's idea to use a continuous flow of water. A flexible water hose had been found that could withstand both the heat and rough treatment from quick layout in the tunnel. Five tests had been conducted successfully using a new deployment device with its new cooling system.

The anti-shock feature of Omega's deployment device was the only part of the device that could not be tested on site in the lower tunnel. This feature was designed to protect Omega from the shock wave made by Alpha's detonation just one second earlier. It had been tested in Nevada using ordinary explosives. Although no one knew how it would respond to the much larger and sharper shock wave created by Alpha, they had done all they could do to test it. Everyone was optimistic and some were confident that it would protect Omega.

The Gareloi Solution was ready if needed.

While the Vulcan Team struggled with technological problems, the world's farmers struggled with other problems.

In early 2034, most farmers in the Northern Hemisphere had planted their regular annual crops. They had remained optimistic that the bad weather of 2033 was just a statistical anomaly, despite what scientists and the President of the United States had been telling them. Those farmers who had wanted to change crops had been frustrated by the lack of knowledge about what their new regional weather regimes would be. Few farmers also had proper equipment to plant and harvest wholly different crops. Modified seeds of existing crops that were tailored to altered conditions had not yet been created and maybe were not possible. As Bill Rand had told President Clark two years before, the inertia in the agricultural system was immense.

Throughout 2034, all agricultural regions of the United States again experienced the kind of odd weather conditions that had occurred the year before. But this year the oddities were even more extreme.

ETOP's measurements showed that other major agricultural regions of the world were also having odd weather conditions that were like those which had occurred in 2033.

Significant food shortages in the United States were now very likely. For the United States, the food shortages would be discomforting. For some other parts of the world, they could be devastating.

This new food reality shattered the decades old goal of the United Nations to reduce the number of people in the world suffering from perpetual hunger. From a high of more than a billion people in 2005, some success had been achieved by reducing this number to less than a half billion people by 2032. Now, in 2034, the number of people suffering from hunger was rising rapidly. Far worse, hundreds of millions of people were now facing potential starvation, not just perpetual hunger.

Anger and despair rose side by side.

Demonstrations occurred daily in capital cities around the world. Most were peaceful; some were not. Many foreign governments hastily created new laws designed to assure that food would be distributed equitably among their citizens. The success of these laws was spotty at best. Other foreign governments allowed market prices to determine initially who got food, with governmental purchases being used to distribute food directly among the nation's poorest citizens. Some nations simply had inadequate food supplies for all of their citizens.

The amount of grains in reserve throughout the world had fallen from the normal five hundred million tons at the end of 2030 to just two hundred million tons at the end August 2034. This was less than a thirty day supply at the current rate of world-wide consumption. And that reserve was unevenly distributed among nations and peoples.

Hateful anger by the have-nots against the haves was inevitable. Terrorist acts increased exponentially against the wealthy industrialized nations of the world, whose food supplies, although marginal by their standards, far surpassed those of other peoples. Resources devoted to dealing with terrorist acts and threats exceeded even the resources devoted to the war on terrorism in the early years of the twenty-first century.

In the United States, most people were frustrated and some people were angry, but few people became violent. Americans were still far better off than most other people in the world. To the extent finger pointing arose, it was directed against decisions made more than two decades ago.

Critics asked why politicians then had ignored warning signs. Had they learned nothing from Hurricane Katrina back in 2005 and from other unusual and destructive weather events that occurred later? Why had they failed to devote significant resources to defend the United States against risks from the response of climates to obvious changes in the composition of the earth's atmosphere? Now that early failure created an urgent need for much larger resources to enhance food production and also to bolster national defense against an increasingly unsettled and angry world population.

Procrastination was no longer an option available to American politicians. The American public wanted something done now. President Clark obliged. He called for another joint session of Congress two days after Labor Day 2034. His address was short and direct, ending with words few were anxious to hear.

"The Constitution requires a declaration of war to be approved by the Senate. In a real sense, we now need a declaration of war against future food shortages. Operation Vulcan is our military strength. Project Prime, what we all now call 'the Gareloi Solution,' is our first battle. I ask your approval to begin this war."

Congress so obliged that very day.

CHAPTER 33

MISSION

General Meyer visited Gareloi Island frequently to critique all progress on the Gareloi Solution. As expected, he was present again with the arrival of Alpha and Omega on September 28, 2034.

Paul returned from his hike to attend a briefing in Building 2 that would include everyone on the island with major responsibilities for the Gareloi Solution. The entire Vulcan Team except Karen Lewis would be present along with three military officers. Karen remained in Washington, DC, at the special station that had been created to rapidly assemble data on aerosol distribution that would be collected from monitors scattered around the world.

This briefing was the first of two briefings designed to determine whether all conditions were met for Alpha and Omega to be detonated. The second briefing would be held on the day before the trigger date for the volcanic eruption, now set for October 7th.

Paul was the first to arrive at the briefing room. The room was rather small, with only basic chairs, temporary tables at its sides, and portable visual aids equipment. No one was deceived by its apparent throwback to the style of a small classroom in an earlier era with all chairs facing the wall opposite the entrance. What was occurring on this small island may be the most ambitious, sophisticated, and dangerous project ever attempted by humankind.

General Meyer, Kristin Brown, Jacob Kahn, and the three military officers arrived a few minutes later. Unlike the conference room used by the Vulcan Team in the Pentagon, here the briefing room was designed to hold up to twenty people. Even with a small group such as the Vulcan

Team, each person stood at the front of the rows of chairs to give his or her report.

General Meyer gave a brief introduction that outlined the sequence of reports to be given. Kristin Brown went first.

Kristin reported that Alpha and Omega were ready for deployment, or at least as ready as they could be. This whole operation had tested everyone's knowledge about these weapons in a way that no one could have anticipated when they had been designed and made during the Cold War of the twentieth century.

Jacob Kahn gave his final assessment on the location and size of the magma chamber below Mount Gareloi and the magma channel leading up onto the mountain. If Alpha and Omega fractured and removed the rock cap as expected, plenty of aerosols should be released in the classic pattern of a stratovolcano.

The three military officers next confirmed their preparations.

The first officer described how Gareloi Island would be evacuated just before and during the morning that Alpha and Omega were to be detonated.

The second officer described efforts being made to protect the operation from outside interference and simultaneously to protect people from getting into the danger zone of the operation. Naval vessels were keeping all ships and boats at least twenty miles from Gareloi. Commercial flights between the United States and the Orient had been rerouted permanently two months earlier without fanfare to avoid the Aleutian Chain of islands.

The third officer described the success that wildlife experts under his command had achieved. They had trapped, transported, and released all of the wild animals that they could find on Gareloi Island, especially its endangered blue foxes.

Paul Anderson gave the last report. He said that the jet stream had shifted to its average winter pattern. Its velocity was much greater than just two months ago. Paul reminded everyone that this combination was the pattern that they needed to disperse properly the aerosols that they hoped would come from their artificial volcanic eruption. However, he also emphasized that weather was an uncertainty that remained. A powerful front or storm could displace the jet stream or could disrupt proper dispersal of aerosols into the jet stream if it struck Gareloi Island at the same time as their artificial volcanic eruption.

Despite the weather uncertainty, confidence abounded. Every known contingency had been dealt with and all problems overcome, at least those over which the Vulcan Team had control. Everyone expected the briefing on October 6th to be a formality simply to confirm details.

October 6th arrived swiftly. It was a cold, gray day typical of the Aleutian Islands in October. Fog had shrouded Gareloi Island each morning for the last two days, followed by light misty rain. This weather was no impediment to the Vulcan Team's plans to detonate Alpha and Omega the following morning.

A final briefing was scheduled for 2:00 p.m. Except for General Meyer, the Vulcan Team and three military officers arrived and were seated a few minutes early. At precisely 2:00 p.m., General Meyer entered the room with Allison Smith. As a show of respect to this new person in the group, all those present stood up. General Meyer introduced her to each member of the Vulcan Team with a crisp summary of the member's background and role in the Gareloi Solution.

Everyone knew why Smith was there. Since the mid-1960s, all nuclear warheads of the United States had required two unlocking procedures for arming. One was held by the commander in charge and the other was held by the president's envoy. Allison Smith was that envoy. Alpha and Omega could not be detonated without the unique information carried to the island by her.

Unlike other briefings, this time General Meyer remained in front of the room while others were seated. He ticked quickly through his checklist of questions. Only one item raised any uncertainty.

"Paul, do we have suitable weather?" he asked.

"We are watching a developing cold front," answered Paul. "It's now over the Anadyrskoye Plateau in the eastern end of Siberia. I do not expect it to be a problem for tomorrow, but we will be watching its status throughout the night."

General Meyer asked a few more questions and then gave everyone an opportunity to inquire further. No one needed to do so in these final hours. Everyone was ready to leave, but General Meyer did not move. He clearly had prepared to say something more. He began speaking in a resolute tone rarely heard from him.

"We all know that tomorrow is a critical day for our country and humanity'" he said. "If the Gareloi Solution succeeds, physical events will be placed in motion that will affect every person on the earth. We believe that these events will help return us to familiar systems and circumstances to the benefit of all people and nations."

Not much new here. Paul had heard similar statements from General Meyer and others many times. He had even made them himself. What followed, however, was quite different.

"Even though we have not tested a large thermonuclear bomb since the 1970s, we are confident that Alpha and Omega will detonate as designed. Of course, everyone here has seen movies of the Castle Bravo test in 1954. At fifteen megatons, that is close to the explosive power of Alpha and Omega. The Russians have generously shared information about larger Soviet tests in the 1950s and early 1960s. They even showed us film of the monster sixty megaton bomb that they exploded in 1961.

"But you all know that no scientist, soldier, or politician now alive has seen the explosion of a large thermonuclear bomb. Movies cannot begin to create the sense of respect, awe, and fear reflected in recorded observations by the people who actually saw these events. Some surprises occurred with almost every one of the early tests.

"As you know, tomorrow we have planned an entirely new and more awesome event. Record your observations and thoughts. If we are successful, posterity will mark tomorrow as the beginning of a new age in human destiny just as surely as Alamagordo, New Mexico marked the beginning of the atomic age in human conflict. God help us that it all works just as we have predicted it will."

General Meyer then promptly left the briefing room with Allison Smith and Kristin Davis to discuss the final arming procedures for Alpha and Omega.

General Meyer's somber words impacted everyone present. The remaining Vulcan Team members and military officers were transfixed momentarily, reflecting upon what he had said.

Potential risks had been a major part of the debate in the decisions to create Operation Vulcan and specifically the Gareloi Solution. Nevertheless, once creating artificial volcanic eruptions had become a national priority, everyone connected with Operation Vulcan had focused on the tasks and evaluations needed to make its first project a success. Certainly each person in the Vulcan Team had thought and even talked about Operation Vulcan's inherent risks. This was especially true when Vice President Van Waters had raised her cautionary question a year ago. But never had these risks been stated within the group in the blunt way just done by General Meyer.

Paul was affected more than the others. He remained motionless, almost in a trance. Ever since he had learned about declining US crop production and possible US food shortages, he had devoted his life to understanding what could be causing this to occur and how to remove that cause. He had conceived the critical idea to provide relief and had helped move his idea to reality. That idea would be tested in just seventeen hours. He had felt exhilarated and proud as the day had begun.

But now, other emotions intervened. Paul remembered that he had spent the last two years trying to solve a problem that he had spent more than thirty years of his professional career trying to prevent. Despite many warnings, clear scientific evidence, and sound analyses, he had been unable to influence enough people to try to move away from historic ways of doing things. Those historic ways had continued to change the composition of the earth's atmosphere. Even thirty years ago, it had been an atmosphere that had no precedent in the last eight hundred thousand years. A shake-up of some kind had become inevitable. For a few minutes, his failure to prevent the current problem saddened and even angered him.

Paul's thoughts ran quickly to the present. *The risks that General Meyer had summarized were real. What if the Gareloi Solution fails? What then? No one had another solution. The lives of tens of millions, maybe hundreds of millions of people hung in the balance. If only enough people had seen this potential problem decades ago, maybe …*

"Paul, are you all right?" asked Jacob, jogging Paul from his thoughts.

"I'm OK," responded Paul. "Just thinking about what lies ahead."

Jacob sensed otherwise, but remained silent.

Paul and Jacob then left the briefing room and walked outside the building. The sky had darkened. Mist had become even colder than when he had entered the building less than two hours ago. He looked around. The operations base on Gareloi Island seemed even more out of place than before, now that it was largely abandoned.

Everyone but the Vulcan Team and personnel needed for the deployment of Alpha and Omega had left yesterday on naval ships. Most were bound for Adak. Some regular military personnel who had worked on the Gareloi Solution remained on a naval ship stationed twenty miles northwest of Gareloi. These fifty men and women had been selected by lot to observe the explosions at zero hour.

The Vulcan Team and deployment personnel were scheduled to leave Gareloi just two hours before zero hour tomorrow morning to assume positions next to this other ship. A third ship would join them carrying representatives from the United Nations and the world's media, very different from the secrecy that surrounded the beginning of the atomic age. All were hoping to be able to see and transmit world-wide images of the world's first artificial volcanic eruption. At least thirty other naval vessels would remain stationed around Gareloi to assure that no unauthorized ships or boats would come too close to the island.

Paul decided to take one last look at the Vulcan Team's preparations, all of which would be obliterated tomorrow morning. He first walked to the openings of each of the tunnels located just one hundred yards apart on the northeast slopes of Mount Gareloi.

Although these tunnels looked like old mines with new tracks running into them, a closer look revealed sheathed fiberoptic cables running along their sides. These cables would carry the critical information needed to trigger Alpha and Omega in precise sequence. Because a fiberoptic cable could not withstand the heat near the magma channel at the end of the lower tunnel for Omega, the cable ended at a transmitter one thousand feet from the final placement of Omega. The coded information would have to be carried the last thousand feet by radio waves.

Paul next walked to Building 5, the deployment building. As a Vulcan Team member, he was among the few non-essential personnel who were allowed to see Alpha and Omega up close. Even on this remote island, General Meyer had set up a security checkpoint at the entrance of this building. After passing the checkpoint, Paul entered Building 5. Looking like a large rectangular metal box from the outside, on the inside Building 5 looked more like a high school gymnasium than the heart of an arming facility for thermonuclear bombs.

Alpha and Omega were already in their deployment devices located on opposite sides of the floor. Paul was again astounded at the small size of these bombs. They had originally been designed to be as compact as possible so that they could be delivered by missiles or planes as weapons of war. At least now these bombs would be used for peaceful purposes,

Paul thought. Still, the power and risks inherent in their use was almost overwhelming.

After just a few minutes looking over the deployment activity, Paul turned around, exited Building 5, and walked back to Building 2. He knew that he would have to spend a long night there.

Paul's remaining tasks were easy in concept, but difficult in practice. He had to advise General Meyer whether local weather conditions and upper atmospheric winds were proper for success. Although General Meyer had the ultimate authority to postpone zero hour, he would rely almost solely on Paul's opinion whether to proceed or not.

In the last two years, the upper atmospheric winds in the Northern Hemisphere had been charted much more carefully than ever before. This new information showed that shifts from the summer pattern to the winter pattern usually occurred steadily within a one month period of time, with the winter pattern being in place normally by the end of September. However, the winter pattern varied from day to day, and even more from week to week, especially the intensity and location of the polar jet stream.

Luckily, the latest results from this morning's balloon and satellite measurements showed that the average winter pattern they wanted was in place. Sulfur dioxide and other aerosols from the Gareloi eruption should be transported over the Midwestern United States and back out to Greenland before again circling the Northern Hemisphere, including important parts of Russia.

Paul first examined the most recent reports from his team on upper atmospheric conditions. No problems here, he thought, as a computer simulation based on 4:00 p.m. data showed exactly the high altitude wind patterns that they expected and wanted.

Usually the local weather on Gareloi Island could be predicted accurately enough about twelve hours in advance unless a sharp weather front was approaching. As he had told the Vulcan Team several hours ago, a cold front was developing over eastern Siberia. What was its current status?

The latest afternoon reports on local weather were troublesome. The cold front had become stronger and had begun to move toward Gareloi. Paul could now see his long night would also be mostly a sleepless night.

Paul began his routine of checking every two hours the latest satellite data on the cold front. These data could only reveal its general strength and location. Despite these limitations, as nighttime continued, these data became encouraging.

At 4:00 a.m. on October 7th, reports from two naval ships stationed four hundred miles north of Gareloi Island confirmed what Paul had hoped. The cold front had not yet reached these ships. The front had stalled over the northern Bering Sea. Paul spoke briefly with General Meyer, stating simply that the Gareloi Solution was a go.

Alpha had been armed last night just two hours after Paul had seen it in Building 5. It had been moved to its detonation place in the tunnel within an hour after being armed.

Allison Smith and General Meyer waited until 6:00 a.m. to arm Omega. It had already been placed in its deployment device and moved to the lower tunnel's portal. Arming took only six minutes. At 6:15 a.m., the deployment crew activated systems to move Omega to its detonation location. Omega was in place before 7:00 a.m. Its deployment device was working as planned.

Shortly after 8:00 a.m., the last members of the deployment group boarded a small naval ship at the temporary dock on the northern side of Gareloi Island. Paul and the other Vulcan Team members joined General Meyer on the ship's bridge. They all looked back at Gareloi as the ship left the dock.

Mount Gareloi loomed over 5,000 feet above them against a dark gray background of clouds that had not yet been illuminated by the rising sun. Mount Gareloi would soon be blown apart to less than a third of its current height. The sheer magnitude of material expected from the ensuing eruption would guarantee that the project's base would be destroyed by the weight of rocks and ash falling upon it.

The twenty mile voyage to their observation location northwest of Gareloi Island was too swift. A common mixture of tension, anticipation, and fear was much easier to control while the ship was moving. As the ship became stationary, with idling motors exactly opposing the sea current, all of these emotions welled up in everyone as they stared toward Mount Gareloi during its last hour. At first a light fog made Mount Gareloi barely visible from this distance. Then, unexpectedly, this early morning fog lifted as if told to do so by a movie director. The northwestern side of Mount Gareloi presented itself against a dark blue sky.

Everyone had black glasses to wear in case light from Alpha's explosion pierced the volcanic rock that would be torn apart by Alpha's shock waves. General Meyer's aide had distributed these glasses as they had boarded ship almost two hours ago. Zero hour of 10:00 a.m. was nearly upon them.

Kristin Brown conducted the countdown. At thirty seconds before zero hour, she started a second-by-second count. Deathly silence had already overtaken the ship. At twenty seconds, two nearby ships sent flares skyward as a final warning to all ships in case the countdown communication had broken down. At ten seconds, General Meyer ordered everyone to cover their eyes with their glasses. At five seconds, Kristin raised and sharpened her voice in an unconscious emphasis of what was to come.

"Five. Four. Three. Two. One. Detonate."

The longest second anyone had ever experienced passed with nothing happening at Mount Gareloi. Then bright streams of light momentarily pierced its upper flanks. The top 3,000 feet of the mountain bulged and split apart. Just as it appeared that the mountain might settle back down, a second surge blew off the whole mountaintop, scattering it in all directions.

Within a minute, an enormous gray roiling cloud rose along a three mile wide crater with sides now only 2,000 feet above sea level. At thirty minutes, this cloud reached over 90,000 feet into the sky. Its top began to move southeastward. The first artificial volcanic eruption in history had been born.

In spite of initial euphoria, Paul and the other members of the Vulcan Team knew that great uncertainty still lay ahead. To be most effective, the average particles had to be about one micron in diameter. Although typically that was the size produced by natural stratovolcanic volcanoes such as Gareloi, no one knew whether an artificial volcanic eruption would behave the same as a natural one. Also, the total mass of aerosols injected into the stratosphere should lie within a particular range, no more and no less.

On the next day, Gareloi continued to spew volcanic ash and sulfur dioxide high into the stratosphere. Satellite cameras traced the path of the first aerosols ejected. They had spread out along their predicted path. Paul examined the initial data on particle size from first samples.

The average size was 0.9 microns and particle size distribution fit the expected bell curve, exactly as desired.

Paul also read the report from Jacob Kahn's vulcanology group. They estimated that if Mount Gareloi continued to erupt, on and off, just as it had done in the first twenty-four hours, five days would be needed for the volcano to eject the mass of particles they wanted. This goal had been modeled after the Mount Pinatubo eruption in 1991 in the Philippines. Its major eruption had occurred on June 15, but contributing eruptions had occurred for seven days, on and off. Like Gareloi, Pinatubo was located along the Pacific fault line, so everyone was optimistic that a similar eruptive pattern would occur here.

On October 12, 2034, the Gareloi eruption subsided. It had ejected into the upper atmosphere almost the exact amount of aerosols desired. Paul and the Vulcan Team were amazed and delighted. Now the upcoming winter and summer would prove whether this calculated gamble would produce the climatic conditions desired in the next three years for the United States, Europe, Russia, and other regions.

The world's news media and commentators heaped praise upon the Gareloi Solution and the Vulcan Team. Despite early criticism, they exclaimed the brilliance of the plan and its marvelous execution. Optimism was high that this perfect eruption would give the perfect result. Already, talk of the second man-made volcanic eruption in 2037 was common, at least among the American media and American politicians.

The Vulcan Team was more cautious.

CHAPTER 34

NATURE

An artificial volcanic eruption was new in human history. President Clark honored the Vulcan Team for this unique achievement in a White House ceremony on Tuesday, November 28, 2034.

The weekend before, celebrations had been held around the country to coincide with Thanksgiving. Despite the winter food hardships looming ahead, optimism rebounded as farmers in the United States and around the Northern Hemisphere began planning next year's crops.

The Vulcan Team had long planned to come together at regular intervals after the eruption of Mount Gareloi. They wanted to assess regularly the progress of the projected cooling and climatic reversion that the Gareloi Solution was designed to create. They also needed to begin preparations for the next stage of Operation Vulcan. The November 28 ceremony at the White House automatically collected the team in one place, so they met again in the Pentagon the next morning.

Just seven days earlier, the original agenda had been modified to include a new topic to deal with information that had just come to light.

On November 20th, Paul had received a telephone call from a friend at the National Earthquake Information Center in Golden, Colorado. He had told Paul that the center's seismographs had detected a small earthquake very close to Gareloi Island. Normally, this would not be of much interest in that earthquake-prone area. But this earthquake had been over ten miles deep. Paul had recognized immediately that its epicenter could have been near or at the magma chamber of Mount Gareloi. Paul had remembered what Jacob Kahn had told him about magma chambers. Jacob had said that on rare occasions they filled up very rapidly after a main eruption occurred, setting the stage for a new eruption in the near future.

When Paul had told everyone on the Vulcan Team about this small earthquake, initially, no one, even Jacob Kahn, had been very concerned about it. Tremors after a volcanic eruption were common. Nevertheless, the team had decided to discuss at its upcoming meeting the possibilities that this earthquake might foreshadow.

The entire Vulcan Team was present. Even Vice President Van Waters was there because she wanted the latest information to report back to President Clark.

After covering the original agenda, General Meyer asked Jacob to address what had now been dubbed "Paul's tremor." Jacob said that the probability of another large eruption at Gareloi Island was low. He described why that was so, emphasizing the fact that the eruption they had triggered had released pent-up energy from the magma chamber beneath the island. But he also cautioned that stratovolcanic eruptions historically had been unpredictable. Another eruption could not be ruled out as a possibility.

Given this possibility, however slim, Paul reminded everyone about the importance of the jet stream's location if another eruption was to occur. He said that the winter jet stream that passed by the Aleutian Islands was irregular, moving north or south from its average winter location in response to upper air disturbances from cold fronts. He also said that, as of two days ago, the winter jet stream had shifted as far south as it ever did in the winter. If an eruption were to occur now, the aerosols would be distributed differently than the aerosols from the eruption they had triggered on October 7th. This meant that the combined impacts of the two eruptions would be far greater than if the jet stream had remained in the pattern that had existed on October 7th. A really large volcanic eruption now could double the cooling effect from the eruption they had triggered.

Everyone already knew that the only well-documented analog to so many aerosols in the stratosphere had been the eruption of Tambora in 1815. No one wanted a repeat of a volcanic winter in the summer such as that which followed Tambora, especially now when global grain reserves were at their lowest level in many decades.

Questions about these new possibilities had hardly begun when General Meyer felt his silent emergency cell phone. He looked at its message and pressed a button. He excused himself, stood up and walked quickly around the table to the conference room door. The room became silent. What message could cause General Meyer to break from the meeting?

General Meyer opened the door, revealing his aide standing at attention. His aid handed General Meyer a folded piece of paper. While still standing in front of the open doorway, General Meyer opened the piece of paper and read its contents. His face became ashen. He then nodded to his aide, and closed the door slowly while turning to face the Vulcan Team. He spoke softly as he looked directly at each person in the room, one-by-one.

"Our observers near Gareloi Island report a huge eruption of Mount Gareloi. They say that it is even more spectacular than the one we triggered on October 7th."

General Meyer paused. He then spoke again, slightly turning his head from side to side with resigned frustration.

"It looks like nature has dealt the next card."

APPENDIXES
AND NOTES

INTRODUCTION TO
APPENDIXES AND NOTES

The Gareloi Solution is fiction. The characters and specific future events are imaginary. The subject and risks portrayed, however, are not fiction. Historic events before 2016 and scientific descriptions are as accurate as my research and understanding could make them. Ten appendixes provide additional information on some of the relevant facts. The notes provide references to underlying fact sources.

"What we know is that we do not know" is not just a statement for literary impact. Broad-based predictions are possible for increased atmospheric temperatures that are caused by projected changes in the composition of the earth's atmosphere. But we do not know exactly what regional and local climate changes will accompany increased atmospheric temperatures. I think that these changes are not knowable before they occur. If changes in the composition of the earth's atmosphere continue to occur in the ways that they have occurred in the last twenty years, rapid regional climate changes and even global climate disruptions are at least possible in the next two decades.

Hopefully, our short window of opportunity to try to avoid potential global climate disruptions has not closed. A wait and see strategy consigns all of humanity to an uncontrolled global experiment. Yet no magic solutions exist today that people will adopt on the huge scale required. I believe that only extensive and varied research and implementation can stop this dangerous experiment. My hope for all humanity is that no person now alive will have to contend with rapid regional climate changes and maybe global climate disruptions with consequences such as those portrayed in *The Gareloi Solution*.

Donald E. Phillipson

APPENDIX 1

Atmospheric carbon dioxide concentrations from year 1000 to year 2014 (Common Era)

Carbon dioxide concentrations in the earth's atmosphere remained relatively stable during the 800 years preceding the early 1800s at about 280 parts per million (ppm). Concentrations increased slowly from the 1800s until the late 1950s. In succeeding decades, concentrations increased at greater rates from less than 320 ppm in 1958 to 400 ppm in 2014.

The two figures in this appendix show atmospheric carbon dioxide concentrations in two different ways.

Figure 1A is the typical depiction of increases in atmospheric carbon dioxide concentrations used by the Earth Systems Research Laboratory of the National Oceanic and Atmospheric Administration (NOAA) and others. It shows most precisely the changes observed from 1958 to 2014 in measurements made at the Mauna Loa Observatory on the Big Island of Hawaii. The saw tooth line in this figure shows actual measurements—the annual up and down pattern is caused primarily by lesser and greater absorption of carbon dioxide by the land-based plants of the Northern Hemisphere during different seasons. The solid line within the saw tooth line represents the seasonally corrected data. The y-axis in this figure starts at 310 ppm.

Figure 1B is adapted from figure 1A, but its y-axis starts at -0- ppm. The relatively steady atmospheric carbon dioxide concentration that existed in the 800 years before the 1800s (280 ppm) is shown as a reference. Although odd in appearance, figure 1B illustrates the proportional increases of carbon dioxide concentrations that have occurred since the early 1800s. By 2014, atmospheric carbon dioxide concentrations were more than 40% larger than they had been in 1800 (1.4 times as large in 2014 as in 1800).

Source for figure 1A:

Figure 1A is a copy of the figure created by the NOAA Earth Systems Research Laboratory and shown at http://www.esrl.noaa.gov/ccgg/trends/ (February 2015). These data are consistent with data shown in Stocker et al., *Climate Change 2013: The Physical Science Basis* (IPCC report), 166 (figure 2.1—figure 2.1 includes South Pole measurements).

Source for text and figure 1B:

Figure 1A above; Houghton et al., *Climate Change 2001: The Scientific Basis* (IPCC report), 201 (figure 3.2); and Stocker et al., *Climate Change 2013: The Physical Science Basis* (IPCC report), 485 (figure 6.7). The data for the centuries preceding 1900 are measurements of carbon dioxide in air bubbles found in ice cores drilled at locations in Antarctica and Greenland.

Figure 1A. Atmospheric carbon dioxide concentrations from 1958 to 2014 in parts per million using 310 ppm as the reference base

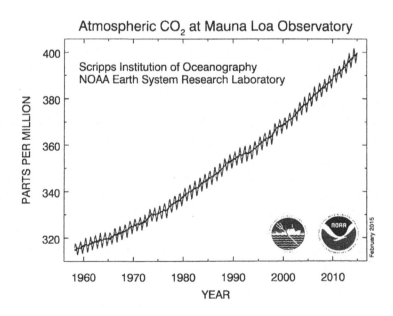

Figure 1B. Atmospheric carbon dioxide concentrations from 1958 to 2014 in parts per million using -0- ppm as the reference base

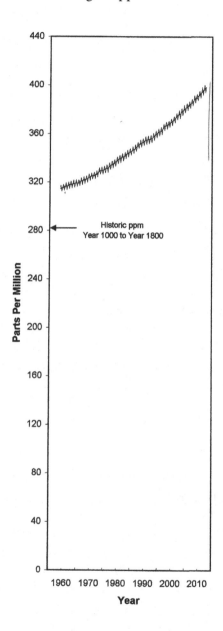

APPENDIX 2

Atmospheric methane concentrations from year 1000 to year 2014 (Common Era)

Methane concentrations in the earth's atmosphere remained relatively stable during the 800 years preceding the early 1800s at about 700 parts per billion (ppb). Concentrations increased significantly in the twentieth century. Methane concentrations have continued to increase in the twenty-first century, albeit at a lesser rate.

As of 2014, the atmospheric methane concentration had more than doubled from 1800. Note that methane's concentration is in parts per *billion* as compared to carbon dioxide's concentration in parts per *million*. Although carbon dioxide's concentration is about 400 times methane's concentration, methane is a stronger greenhouse gas, so its contribution to heating the earth's atmosphere is more significant than this 400 to 1 ratio would suggest.

The two figures in this appendix show atmospheric methane concentrations in two different ways.

Figure 2A is the typical depiction of increases in atmospheric methane concentrations used by the Earth Systems Research Laboratory of the National Oceanic and Atmospheric Administration (NOAA) and others. It shows most precisely the changes observed from 1983 to 2014 in measurements made from the NOAA global air sampling network. The saw tooth line in this figure shows actual measurements—the annual up and down pattern is caused by greater and lesser releases of methane by decomposition of land-based organic matter in the Northern Hemisphere during different seasons. The solid line within the saw tooth line represents the seasonally corrected data. The y-axis in this figure starts at 1550 ppb. This shortened time frame for methane measurements shows that modern measurements do not always extend back as far as we would like.

Figure 2B is adapted from figure 2A, but its y-axis starts at -0- ppb. The relatively steady atmospheric methane concentration that existed in the 800 years before the 1800s (750 ppb) is shown as a reference. Although odd in appearance, figure 2B illustrates the proportional increases of methane concentrations since the early 1800s. Except for temporary flattening from 1999 to 2006, the rates of increase that occurred during the 1983 to 2014 time period were similar to the rates of increase that occurred in the previous decades of the twentieth century (both rates of increase being approximately 100 ppb per decade). The effect of these rates of increase in the last 110 years and more modest increases in the previous century was to create atmospheric methane concentrations in 2014 that were 140% greater in 2014 than they had been in 1800 (2.4 times as large in 2014 as in 1800).

Source for figure 2A:

Figure 2A is a copy of the figure for methane created by the NOAA Earth Systems Research Laboratory and shown at http://www.esrl.noaa.gov/gmd/aggi/aggi.html (February 2015). These data are consistent with data shown in Stocker et al., *Climate Change 2013: The Physical Science Basis* (IPCC report), 167 (figure 2.2—figure 2.2 includes South Pole measurements).

Source for text and figure 2B:

Figure 2A above; Houghton et al., *Climate Change 2001: The Scientific Basis* (IPCC report), 249 (figure 4.1); and Stocker et al., *Climate Change 2013: The Physical Science Basis* (IPCC report), 485 (figure 6.7). The data for the centuries preceding 1900 are measurements of methane in air bubbles found in ice cores drilled at locations in Antarctica and Greenland.

Figure 2A. Atmospheric methane concentrations from 1983 to 2014 in parts per billion using 1550 ppb as the reference base

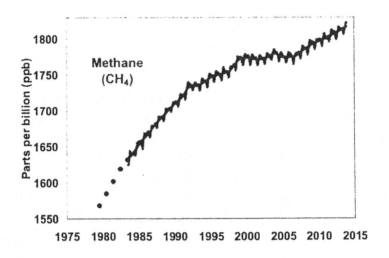

Figure 2B. Atmospheric methane concentrations from 1983 to 2014 in parts per billion using -0- ppb as the reference base

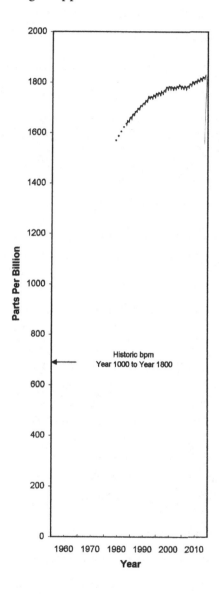

APPENDIX 3

Atmospheric nitrous oxide concentrations from year 1000 to year 2014 (Common Era)

Nitrous oxide concentrations in the earth's atmosphere remained relatively stable during the 800 years preceding the early 1800s at about 270 parts per billion. Concentrations began to increase in the nineteenth century.

Nitrous oxide's rate of increasing concentration has been much less in percentage terms than carbon dioxide's or methane's rate of increase. As of 2014, its atmospheric concentration was about 20% greater than its atmospheric concentration in 1800. As with methane, note that nitrous oxide concentrations are in parts per *billion* (ppb).

Figure 3 is the typical depiction of increases in atmospheric nitrous oxide concentrations used by the Earth Systems Research Laboratory of the National Oceanic and Atmospheric Administration (NOAA) and others. It shows most precisely the changes observed from 1979 to 2014 in measurements made from the NOAA global air sampling network. The y-axis in this figure starts at 295 ppb.

Source for text and figure 3:
Figure 3 is a copy of the figure for nitrous oxides created by the NOAA Earth Systems Research Laboratory and shown at http://www. esrl.noaa.gov/gmd/aggi/aggi.html (February 2015). These data are consistent with data shown in Houghton et al., *Climate Change 2001: The Scientific Basis* (IPCC report), 253 (figure 4.2) and in Stocker et al., *Climate Change 2013: The Physical Science Basis* (IPCC report), 485 (figure 6.7).

Figure 3. Atmospheric nitrous oxide concentrations from 1979 to 2014 in parts per billion using 295 ppb as the reference base

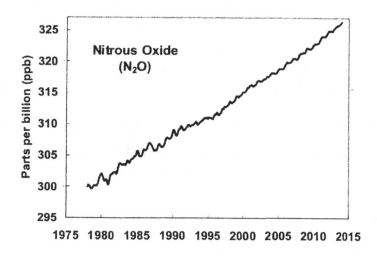

APPENDIX 4

Sources of increased amounts of selected greenhouse gases in the earth's atmosphere

Some people contend that only natural processes have caused most, if not all, of the observed increases in atmospheric concentrations of trace greenhouse gases. They cite atmospheric conditions that existed millions of years ago as proof that natural processes could be responsible for these increases.

In this context, this appendix considers the human contribution to increases in the atmospheric concentrations of four kinds of trace gases. In ascending order of their importance as greenhouse gases in the earth's atmosphere, they are (1) nitrous oxides, (2) chlorofluorocarbons, (3) methane, and (4) carbon dioxide.

This ranking is based on the radiative forcing of each kind of gas that was calculated for the NOAA Annual Greenhouse Gas Index by the Earth System Research Laboratory of the National Oceanic and Atmospheric Administration. See ESRL/NOAA data at http://www.esrl.noaa.gov/gmd/ccgg/aggi.html (January 2016).

The ESRL/NOAA website includes a colored graph that shows the relative contribution over time of each major greenhouse gas other than water vapor to "radiative climate forcing" in watts per square meter. This forcing is a measurement of atmospheric warming caused by the absorption of heat radiation by each gas without taking into account secondary effects from that absorption or warming.

An important secondary effect of this atmospheric warming is to increase the average atmospheric concentrations of water vapor. Water vapor is the most important greenhouse gas, but its role in global warming is complex because increased water vapor also forms increased clouds that can act to decrease warming.

(1) Nitrous oxides

Natural sources of nitrous oxides exist, especially soils where incomplete nitrification by leguminous plants has occurred (e.g. peas and beans). Significant amounts of nitrous oxides also are produced by such human activities as the use of nitrate and ammonium fertilizers and the high temperature burning of fossil fuels and some biomass. This latter source exists because air is 78% nitrogen and 21% oxygen. High heat causes some of the nitrogen and oxygen to react to form nitrous oxides. The increased concentration of nitrous oxides in the earth's atmosphere compared to two hundred years ago is consistent with estimates of human sources and reflects some natural absorption of the nitrous oxides that have come from human sources. Wayne, *Chemistry of Atmospheres, Third Edition*, 25, 232–34; Houghton et al., *Climate Change 2001: The Scientific Basis* (IPCC report), 251–53; Stocker et al., *Climate Change 2013: The Physical Science Basis* (IPCC report), 1401–2.

(2) Chlorofluorocarbons

Almost no chlorofluorocarbons exist in nature, so chlorofluorocarbon concentrations in the earth's atmosphere have been caused solely by human manufacture of these chemicals.

Chlorofluorocarbons are important as greenhouse gases, but even more important as gases that affect the ozone layer in the stratosphere. The ozone layer reduces the amount of ultraviolet radiation from the sun that hits the earth's surface. In the late twentieth century scientists discovered a hole in the ozone layer above Antarctica. Chlorofluorcarbons that had migrated up to the stratosphere had reacted with ozone in a way that had fully depleted the ozone layer at that location.

Atmospheric chlorofluorocarbon concentrations have mostly reached a steady state because late twentieth century treaties have restricted the use of chlorofluorocarbons. Chlorofluorcarbons are stable gases with few natural destructive mechanisms. Thus, as a greenhouse gas, chlorofluorocarbons play a nearly constant role at the present time and probably will play a nearly constant role for many more decades or even centuries. The ozone hole above Antarctica continues to occur although it is no longer expanding. Wayne, *Chemistry of Atmospheres,*

Third Edition, 216–20; Bigg, *Oceans and Climate*, 26, 219–20; Houghton et al., *Climate Change 2001: The Scientific Basis* (IPCC report), 255; Stocker et al., *Climate Change 2013: The Physical Science Basis* (IPCC report), 168–70, 678, 1402–3; "Alumna Profile: Susan Solomon: Atmospheric Chemistry, Help the Earth Heal Itself."

(3) Methane

Methane is produced and released into the atmosphere by natural anaerobic processes such as rotting vegetation in wetlands. Human activities also release methane into the atmosphere. An example is methane that escapes into the air when petroleum or coal is extracted from the ground. The increased concentration of methane in the earth's atmosphere compared to two hundred years ago is consistent with estimates of human sources and reflects some natural absorption of the methane that has come from human sources. Wayne, *Chemistry of Atmospheres, Third Edition*, 21–23; Houghton et al., *Climate Change 2001: The Scientific Basis* (IPCC report), 248–51; Stocker et al., *Climate Change 2013: The Physical Science Basis* (IPCC report), 1401–2.

(4) Carbon dioxide

Many large natural processes produce carbon dioxide, thereby adding carbon dioxide to the atmosphere. Other large natural processes remove carbon dioxide from the atmosphere.

Human activities also add carbon dioxide to the atmosphere, such as fossil fuel burning and cement production. Some human activities add carbon dioxide to the atmosphere by reducing natural carbon dioxide removal mechanisms such as dense tropical forests. Few regular human activities remove carbon dioxide from the atmosphere.

Warming oceans also add carbon dioxide to the atmosphere by releasing more dissolved carbon dioxide (colder oceans can hold more carbon dioxide), but these extra releases are much smaller than the additions of carbon dioxide resulting from direct human activities.

Carbon dioxide that has been added to the atmosphere as the result of human activities has overwhelmed the equilibrium between natural carbon dioxide production and natural carbon dioxide removal. This is the primary reason why atmospheric carbon dioxide concentrations have increased to levels far higher than the highest levels measured for the last 800,000 years. The increased concentration of carbon dioxide now found in the earth's atmosphere compared to two hundred years ago is consistent with estimates of human sources and the effects of other human activities. Houghton et al., *Climate Change 2001: The Scientific Basis* (IPCC report), 204–8; Stocker et al., *Climate Change 2013: The Physical Science Basis* (IPCC report), 1401–2.

Assessment

Some people try to diminish the importance of human activities in contributing to increased concentrations of these four greenhouse gases by comparing the human contributions to ongoing natural processes. These comparisons are particularly prevalent for carbon dioxide.

For example, some people claim that human produced carbon dioxide is not important because it is far less than the amount of carbon dioxide produced by natural systems or the amount of carbon dioxide already dissolved in ocean water. Human produced carbon dioxide is indeed far less than the carbon dioxide produced by natural systems. However, the claim that human produced carbon dioxide is unimportant fails to recognize that the human contribution has disrupted the equilibrium among natural systems. That disruption is why atmospheric carbon dioxide concentrations are now much higher than any concentrations that have occurred in the last 800,000 years.

APPENDIX 5

Comparative annual average atmospheric temperatures at the earth's surface from 1880 to 2014

The comparative annual average atmospheric temperatures at the earth's surface have been calculated using available data from a variety of sources, including meteorological stations and ships traversing the oceans. Original data sources are more numerous, more widespread, and probably more accurate after World War II than before and during World War II.

Changes in average atmospheric temperatures at the earth's surface over long historic periods reflect predominantly an interplay of changes in (1) atmospheric greenhouse gas concentrations (greater concentrations will increase temperatures), (2) atmospheric aerosols, especially from volcanic activity (greater amounts will decrease temperatures), (3) surface reflectivity (greater reflectivity will decrease temperatures), (4) solar irradiance (greater irradiance will increase temperatures), and (5) periodic global weather causing systems such as the El Niño/Southern Oscillation phenomenon.

Source for text: Philander, *Is the Temperature Rising?*, 32–40, 139–50; Stocker et al., *Climate Change 2013: The Physical Science Basis* (IPCC report), 392–93.

Source for figure 5: Figure 5 is a copy of the figure for global land and ocean temperature anomalies found at http://www.ncdc.noaa.gov/cag

from the NOAA National Climate Data Center (Timescale: 12-Month; Month: December; Start Year: 1880; End Year: 2015). The reference -0- is the twentieth century average. These data are consistent with Stocker et al., *Climate Change 2013: The Physical Science Basis* (IPCC report), 193 (figure 2.20).

Figure 5. Comparative annual average atmospheric temperatures at the earth's surface from 1880 to 2014 (land and ocean)

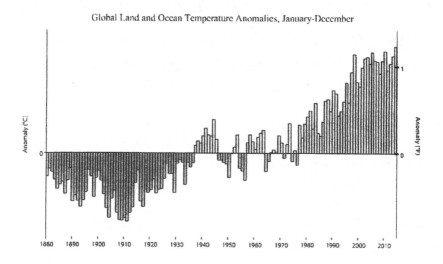

APPENDIX 6

Comparative average temperatures of the mid-troposphere from 1978 to 2002 as determined from microwave sounding units on satellites

The text of *The Gareloi Solution* describes how microwave sounding units (MSUs) on satellites can measure the temperature of parts of the earth's atmosphere at certain altitude zones (chapter 7 [History] and chapter 19 [Satellites]).

Briefly stated, five factors allow MSUs to determine these temperatures:

(1) Oxygen is present in a uniform concentration throughout the atmosphere (20.9%).

(2) Oxygen absorbs some infrared radiation (heat) and re-emits radiation at unique microwave frequencies.

(3) Oxygen emits much more microwave radiation at the unique frequencies when oxygen is at certain pressures, and four of those pressures correspond to altitude zones in the earth's atmosphere.

(4) The "brightness" (strength) of oxygen's microwave emissions also corresponds to oxygen's temperature.

(5) An MSU on a satellite can detect and measure the brightness of atmospheric oxygen within range of the MSU.

MSUs on satellites have measured the brightness of the microwave emission from atmospheric oxygen at four channels of frequencies. Channel 2 is 53.74 GHz, which corresponds to the mid-troposphere (roughly 13,000 to 23,000 feet above sea level). Linking these "brightness" data from one satellite to another has been a challenge.

The Mears et al. article in 2003 illustrates the difficulty in using MSUs to measure the earth's average atmospheric temperature at the mid-troposphere. The analysis by Mears et al. of the same data used by earlier authors (Spencer and Christy) yielded an increase in the average temperature of the mid-troposphere over both land and ocean during the time period 1978 to 2002. On the other hand, the Spencer and Christy analysis yielded essentially no change. Most of the difference occurs during 1985-1987 when one particular satellite was active. At about the same time as Mears et al., Vinikov and Grody also reanalyzed the satellite data. Their reanalysis yielded a greater increase in the mid-troposphere temperature than Mears et al. Comparing the authors, we have Mears et al. with +0.097 degrees Kelvin per decade, Spencer and Christy with essentially no change, and Vinnikov and Grody with +0.220 degrees Kelvin per decade for the time period 1978 to 2002.

These different data analyses are important because the disconnect between atmospheric temperatures derived from measurements by MSUs in the 1990s (no warming) and temperatures derived from compilations of atmospheric temperatures recorded at the earth's surface (warming) led some people to contend that the earth's atmosphere was actually not warming. These people then asserted that compilations of atmospheric temperatures at the earth's surface were erroneous.

Recent analyses of measurements by satellite sensors (e.g. microwave sounding units and advanced microwave sounding units) show two results. First, certain analytic uncertainties prevent sound conclusions about warming or cooling in the mid-troposphere (channel 2 brightness). Second, other analyses are consistent in concluding that the stratosphere has cooled since the mid-twentieth century up to 2012 (the last year of the data) (channel 4 brightness). Cooling of the stratosphere is consistent with warming in the lower troposphere because otherwise the total energy received from the sun and total energy transmitted back out to space from the earth would be out of balance.

Source for text:

Mears, Schabel, and Wentz, "A Reanalysis of the MSU Channel 2 Tropospheric Temperature Record," 3650–64; Spencer and Christy, "Precise Monitoring of Global Temperature Trends from Satellites,"

1558–62; Vinnikov and Grody, "Global Warming Trend of Mean Tropospheric Temperature Observed by Satellites," 269–72. The latest analyses are summarized in Stocker et al., *Climate Change 2013: The Physical Science Basis* (IPCC report), 194–97.

Source for figure 6:

Figure 6 is figure 12 in Mears, Schabel, and Wentz, "A Reanalysis of the MSU Channel 2 Tropospheric Temperature Record," 3660. (Used with permission of the American Meteorological Society)

Figure 6. Comparative average temperatures of the mid-troposphere from 1978 to 2002 as determined from satellite microwave sounding units (see detailed description below)

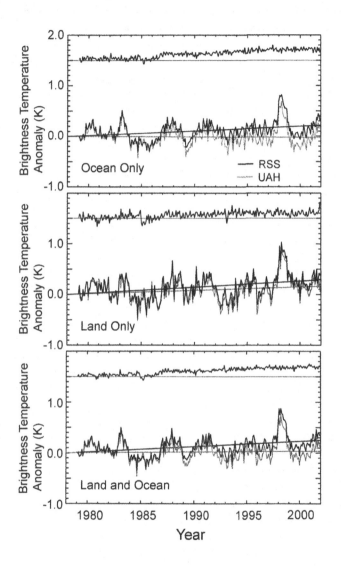

Figure 6 shows trends in global MSU channel 2 brightness, which reflects relative temperature. (a) Ocean-only global time series. In the pair of traces, the black trace (generally the upper trace) is the monthly time series found by Mears et al. (RSS), while the gray trace (generally the lower trace) corresponds to the ocean-only time series from Christy and Spencer, version 5.0 (UAH). The black line (upper line around 0.0) is a linear fit to the Mears et al. time series, and a gray line (lower line around 0.0) is a fit to the Christy and Spencer time series. The top trace shows a difference time series (RSS minus UAH, UAH being the straight line) offset by +1.5 degrees Kelvin. (b) Same as in (a) except for land-only observations. (c) Same as in (a) except for land and ocean data combined. [This description is the description of figure 12 in the Mears et al. article.]

APPENDIX 7

Total solar irradiance from 1978 to 2012

Solar irradiance is the incident flow of energy received by the earth from the sun per unit area. Total solar irradiance in the thirty-four years from 1978 to 2012, as measured by satellite radiometers, reflects tiny daily variations and tiny periodic variations over time, but no clear trend of increased total solar irradiance. Thus, increased total solar irradiance cannot be the cause of observed temperature increases in the atmosphere during that time period.

Some people point to the sun's eleven-year cycle of irradiance variation as a factor in recent atmospheric warming. However, as illustrated in the Gray et al. article cited below, the difference between maximum and minimum solar power available to the earth during the eleven year cycle is only about 0.17 watts per square meter. This amount of warming compares to 1.60 watts per square meter attributed to increased greenhouse gas concentrations. As a proportion of the 239 watts per square meter of solar power, the warming from the solar cycle difference is 0.07% of the solar power and the warming from increased greenhouse gas concentrations is 0.67% of the solar power.

Source for text:

Gueymard, "The Sun's Total and Spectral Irradiance," 423–53 (see especially figure 1 for the time period 1978 to 2003). Stocker et al., *Climate Change 2013: The Physical Science Basis* (IPCC report), 688–89 (figure 8.10), 392–93; Gray et al., "Solar Influences on Climate," 2, 6–9.

APPENDIX 8

Atmospheric carbon dioxide concentrations during the Ice Ages

Atmospheric carbon dioxide concentrations in the last 800,000 years varied as enormous ice sheets changed atmospheric dynamics. These concentrations did not exceed 300 parts per million (ppm) until the twentieth century. They were sometimes even less than 200 ppm. The data for the Ice Ages and centuries preceding 1900 are measurements of carbon dioxide in air bubbles found in ice cores drilled at locations in Antarctica.

Source for text and figure 8:

Figure 8 is adopted from the figure created by the National Oceanic and Atmospheric Administration and found at http://www.climate. gov/news-features/understanding-climate/2013-state-climate-carbon-dioxide-tops-400-ppm (February 2015). The NOAA figure uses 150 ppm as the reference base rather than the -0- ppm reference base used in figure 8. These data are consistent with National Research Council, Committee on Global Change Research, *Global Environmental Change: Research Pathways*, 241 (figure 6.1), Houghton et al., *Climate Change 2001: The Scientific Basis* (IPCC report), 201–3 (figure 3.2), and Solomon et al., *Climate Change 2007: The Physical Science Basis* (IPCC report), 444 (figure 6.3).

Figure 8. Atmospheric carbon dioxide concentrations during the Ice Ages and up to the present in parts per million

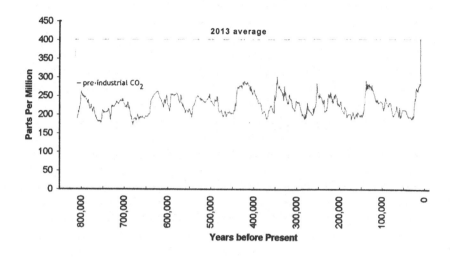

APPENDIX 9

Contribution of changed carbon dioxide concentrations to changed atmospheric temperatures at the earth's surface during recent Ice Ages

Relying on a graph prepared by Crowley, the National Research Council noted some correlation between inferred atmospheric temperature changes and carbon dioxide concentrations during the last 160,000 years, which included several Ice Ages. During that long period, atmospheric carbon dioxide concentrations varied from about 180 parts per million (ppm) to about 300 ppm. When compared to atmospheric temperature changes during the same time period, the carbon dioxide concentrations usually increased *after* or sometimes along with the most significant temperature increases. Thus, increases in carbon dioxide concentrations may have enhanced temperature increases that already were underway, but they did not initiate the temperature increases.

Carbon dioxide concentrations were measurements of carbon dioxide in air bubbles found in ice cores drilled at locations in Antarctica and Greenland. Global surface temperatures were inferred from changes in the proportion of heavy water in the ice cores (water containing the hydrogen isotope deuterium).

Source for text:

National Research Council, Committee on Global Change Research, *Global Environmental Change: Research Pathways*, 241; Crowley and North, *Paleoclimatology*, 121. See also Bigg, *Oceans and Climate*, 187–89 and Stocker et al., *Climate Change 2013: The Physical Science Basis* (IPCC report), 399.

APPENDIX 10

Is "peak oil" a myth?

"Peak oil" production occurs when the physical production capacity of the sources of petroleum available to supply demand peaks and then begins to decline.

Reaching "peak oil" production is not the same as running out of petroleum. Production is the rate at which petroleum can be extracted from conventional wells and other sources. Even when large reserves of petroleum remain in a proven oil field, shale oil formation, or other source, the rate of extraction is limited by the geologic structures in which the petroleum is found. Thus a production peak can occur even when large reserves of petroleum are known to exist. [See Alleklett, "Oil: A Bumpy Road Ahead," 12.]

United States Peak Oil

In 1956, the American geologist M. King Hubbert predicted that petroleum production in the United States would peak in the early 1970s. He was right. US petroleum production peaked in 1970 and began to fall thereafter.

Hubbert's methodology worked well in the conditions surrounding US petroleum production in the mid-twentieth century. Petroleum came solely from conventional sources, namely free flowing petroleum located in underground formations accessible by wells, known as oil fields. Extensive experience with these sources gave Hubbert two key data for his methodology—well capacities relative to known oil field reserves and logical estimates of total discoverable petroleum reserves.

With respect to well capacities, the oil import quota system existing at that time limited the role of foreign petroleum, so the vast majority of petroleum available for use in the United States came from domestic wells. [See Trade Expansion Act of 1962, 76 Stat. 877, § 232, October 11, 1962 (authority given to the president to limit petroleum imports if they threaten US security).] Except in Texas, competing domestic producers maximized production from their wells to meet US demand, which gave a realistic measure of their production capacity. In Texas, the Texas Railroad Commission regulated wells to a percentage of their capacity to maintain prices, a system that required realistic estimates of their production capacity. Together, these factors provided good estimates of the maximum production possible from all proven oil fields.

Hubbert also could estimate (to some extent guess) the amount of conventional petroleum that would be discovered in the United States. Exploration had already developed enough information about underground formations throughout the United States to make his estimates at least plausible.

Using these data, Hubbert then made estimates of future production from proven oil fields and from estimated future discoveries. These estimates led to his prediction. [See Deffeyes, *Hubbert's Peak*, 1–5.]

World Peak Oil

World-wide petroleum production after the mid-1970s and especially in the early twenty-first century has differed in several ways from United States production in the mid-twentieth century.

Although petroleum is sold in international markets, the Organization of Petroleum Exporting Countries (OPEC) has changed supply dynamics by substantially holding back production from time to time for political, market control, and price reasons. International sanctions against petroleum-rich nations such as Iraq and Libya in the late twentieth and early twenty-first centuries also reduced world-wide production capacity available to supply demand. Some countries such as Saudi Arabia also have kept their production capacity secret. Unlike petroleum production in the United States in the mid-twentieth century, a true public picture of physical production capacity from all active world-wide conventional sources does not exist.

An estimate of ultimate world-wide conventional petroleum reserves also is uncertain. Regarding proven oil fields, nations announce their own known reserves, but some of these estimates are highly questionable. For example, in the late 1980s, some OPEC nations abruptly increased their announced petroleum reserves. Whether these were simply updates of old estimates or wishful thinking is unknown. Other potential sources such as underwater formations in the Arctic probably exist but their extent and feasible production capacity are uncertain. [See Deffeyes, *Hubbert's Peak*, 4–7, 146–49.]

Further complicating the world-wide peak oil picture is the emergence into world markets of petroleum that comes from unconventional sources. Principally, these other sources are now shale oil (especially in the United States) and tar sands (especially in Canada). Recent high prices have allowed the use of relatively expensive technologies to access these sources. Thus, at certain price points, these sources of petroleum have to be added to the world-wide physical production capacity and ultimately recoverable petroleum reserves when determining whether or when peak oil production will occur.

As illustrated by experience in the United States, estimates for the future production capacity of unconventional petroleum sources can be elusive.

Case Study: Shale Oil in the United States

The US Energy Information Administration publishes an "Annual Energy Outlook." The Annual Energy Outlook 2014 contains a report under Issues in Focus that states "the projected trends in oil production vary tremendously in the alternative cases" due to significant "uncertainty in the resource and technology assumptions." Those technology assumptions include estimated ultimate recovery from shale oil wells and the characteristics of production decline curves for those wells. The production decline curves, for example, vary widely across different shale oil formations and even different wells in the same formation.

This report includes projected US crude oil production from both conventional and unconventional sources under high oil and gas resource assumptions and under low oil and gas resource assumptions. Illustrating the tremendous variance in projected trends, production under the high assumptions case is double the production under the low assumptions case. The low assumptions case projects total US crude oil production in 2030 that is roughly the same as production in the mid-1990s. This is considerably less than production in 2013 that reflects the shale oil boom achieved through the use of hydraulic fracturing technology. [See Van Wagener, "U.S. Tight Oil Production."]

Conclusion: Is "Peak Oil" a Myth?

Peak oil clearly was not a myth for the United States in the mid-twentieth century. In my opinion, viewed solely from the supply side, peak oil also is not a myth for the world-wide petroleum market because petroleum sources are finite and the ability to produce petroleum from those sources has geologic and other physical limitations. Technologies that become economically feasible under high prices may increase total production beyond traditional estimates that rely mostly on conventional petroleum sources, but eventually a production limit will be reached.

Whether that production limit will create severe economic dislocation, however, depends upon whether world-wide demand for petroleum exceeds that limit. In the twentieth century, demand for petroleum continued to rise with population growth and economic growth. If that rise continues in the twenty-first century, then a disruptive peak oil phenomenon will occur if that demand exceeds the petroleum production limit.

In the fiction of *The Gareloi Solution*, demand for petroleum continues and a disruptive peak oil phenomenon occurs in 2030. However, disruptive "peak oil" is not inevitable. As the petroleum glut in the mid-2010s has demonstrated, the real production limit may be larger than many analysts have predicted. In addition, if petroleum demand flattens or even decreases (for example, if alternatives are developed and used on a large scale), then a disruptive peak oil phenomenon could be delayed for many decades and maybe even altogether.

NOTES

Introduction

Each note contains the beginning and ending words of the sentence to which the note refers. The page number is the place where the end of that sentence occurs. Where the sentence is found at the end of a paragraph, context may dictate that the note supports the content of the full paragraph, not just the sentence referenced.

Chapter 2

6. **Before the turn...before 2010.** Deffeyes, *Hubbert's Peak*, 146.
7. **Except for...twenty-first century.** Deffeyes, *Hubbert's Peak*, 1–13, 133–158.
8. **Whatever the reason...previous year.** See appendix 10: Is "peak oil" a myth?
8. **By then...prevent shortages.** See appendix 10, paragraph entitled "Case Study: Shale Oil in the United States."

Chapter 4

23. **Their interest had...early 1990s.** National Research Council, Committee on Global Change Research, *Global Environmental Change: Research Pathways*, 302.
24. **This warm current...would suggest.** Whipple, *Restless Oceans*, 48–49; Bigg, *Oceans and Climate*, 148–50.
24. **Many French citizens...become scarce.** Ritchie, *Encyclopedia of Earthquakes and Volcanoes*, 166–67; Simkin and Siebert, *Volcanoes of the World, Second Edition*, 7–8.
25. **Duvall had said...year 2000.** Krabill et al., "Rapid Thinning of Parts of the Southern Greenland Ice Sheet," 1522–24.

25. **Other scientists...five years.** Krabill et al., "Greenland Ice Sheet: High-Elevation Balance and Peripheral Thinning," 428–30; Thomas et al., "Mass Balance of the Greenland Ice Sheet at High Elevations," 426–28.

25. **Later studies...few decades.** Stocker et al., *Climate Change 2013: The Physical Science Basis* (IPCC report), 349–51, 355–57.

28. **Precise satellite...numerous places.** Philander, *Is the Temperature Rising?*, 135.

28. **When mapped...near the surface.** Philander, *Is the Temperature Rising?*, 140.

29. **SMER also...years of observations.** Models suggest that increased precipitation in northern latitudes will occur if the average temperature of the lower atmosphere rises. This increase would reduce the salinity of the North Atlantic Ocean. National Research Council, Committee on Abrupt Climate Change, *Abrupt Climate Change: Inevitable Surprises*, 114.

30. **That could have...to disperse.** National Research Council, Committee on Abrupt Climate Change, *Abrupt Climate Change: Inevitable Surprises*, 114–15.

30. **The Amazon River...its mouth.** Goulding, Barthem, and Ferreira, *Smithsonian Atlas of the Amazon*, 29.

Chapter 5

33. **A combination of...earth's rotation.** Bigg, *Oceans and Climate*, 16–19, 66–70; Philander, *Is the Temperature Rising?*, 128, 134.

33. **It occurred...Drift partly filled.** National Research Council, Committee on Abrupt Climate Change, *Abrupt Climate Change: Inevitable Surprises*, 76–78, 108–111; Houghton et al., *Climate Change 1995: The Science of Climate Change* (IPCC report), 212–13; Houghton et al., *Climate Change 2001: The Scientific Basis* (IPCC report), 436–37.

34. **All of these...by the current.** Bigg, *Oceans and Climate*, 18, 216 (salt water is more dense than less salty water); Philander, *Is the Temperature Rising?*, 130–34.

34. **This whole network...thermohaline circulation.** Bigg, *Oceans and Climate*, 16–19; Philander, *Is the Temperature Rising?*, 130–34.

34. **Should this effect...even stop.** Philander, *Is the Temperature Rising?*, 130–34; National Research Council, Committee on Abrupt Climate Change, *Abrupt Climate Change: Inevitable Surprises* 89–106.

35. **Even though North...around the world.** Bigg, *Oceans and Climate*, 16–17, 191.

35. **When that had...five thousand years.** Bigg, *Oceans and Climate*, 189–92; National Research Council, Committee on Global Change Research, *Global Environmental Change: Research Pathways*, 242–49.

38. **"Back in 1997...earth's atmosphere.** Kyoto Protocol, Article 3.

38. **That event showed…social unrest.** Ritchie, *Encyclopedia of Earthquakes and Volcanoes*, 166–67. (Cooling from the Tambora volcanic eruption in 1815 caused crop failures and food shortages in France that created anarchy and starvation in 1816.)

Chapter 6

48. **Agribusiness…at that time.** Changnon, *El Niño, 1997–1998*, 109–35.
50. **We cannot match…simplifying conditions.** National Research Council, Committee on Global Change Research, *Global Environmental Change: Research Pathways*, 445–516; National Research Council, Committee on Abrupt Climate Change, *Abrupt Climate Change: Inevitable Surprises*, 7.
50. **They do differ…future conditions."** Stott and Kettleborough, "Origins and Estimates of Uncertainty in Predictions of Twenty-first Century Temperature Rise," 723–26.

Chapter 7

53. **ETOP would…from then.** Since about 1957, standard launch times for weather balloons have been 0000 (midnight) and 1200 (noon) UTC (Coordinated Universal Time). Lazante, Klein, and Seidel, "Temporal Homogenization of Monthly Radiosonde Temperature Data, Part I: Methodology," 226.
54. **But it applied only to industrialized nations.** The Kyoto Protocol committed industrialized nations to reduce their aggregate emissions of greenhouse gases to amounts below their 1990 levels. Kyoto Protocol, Article 3.
54. **The Paris Agreement…ambitious reductions.** Paris Agreement, Article 4.1. It states:

> In order to achieve the long-term temperature goal set out in Article 2, Parties aim to reach global peaking of greenhouse gas emissions as soon as possible, recognizing that peaking will take longer for developing country Parties, and to undertake rapid reductions thereafter in accordance with best available science, so as to achieve a balance between anthropogenic emissions by sources and removals by sinks of greenhouse gases in the second half of this century, on the basis of equity, and in the context of sustainable development and efforts to eradicate poverty.

The temperature goal set out in Article 2.1 is to hold "the increase in the global average temperature to well below 2 °C above pre-industrial levels and to pursue efforts to limit the temperature increase to 1.5 °C above pre-industrial levels."

55. **The expressed reason …Kyoto's requirements.** Vig and Faure, *Green Giants? Environmental Policies*, 208.

56. **They identified regional…variety of ways.** For example, in 2003 the Pentagon asked two private consultants to consider potential global impacts of abrupt climate change on US national security. Burns, Robert, "Pentagon Study Looks at Global Climate."

Chapter 8

60. **The radiosonde…balloon's flight.** Lazante, Klein, and Seidel, "Temporal Homogenization of Monthly Radiosonde Temperature Data, Part I: Methodology," 224–25.

60. **"That way we…place to place.** Before the fictional ETOP, radiosonde launches used a variety of instruments and procedures because launches were done independently by each nation in the radiosonde network. Lazante, Klein, and Seidel, "Temporal Homogenization of Monthly Radiosonde Temperature Data, Part I: Methodology," 225.

61. **"That five thousand…said Paul.** Philander, *Is the Temperature Rising?*, 119. (Seven hundred were launched at midnight and seven hundred were launched at noon Greenwich Mean Time.)

61. **These failures prevented…the averages.** Houghton et al., *Climate Change 1995: The Science of Climate Change* (IPCC report), 147.

63. **This dual uniformity…over many years.** Spencer and Christy, "Precise Monitoring of Global Temperature Trends from Satellites," 1558; Philander, *Is the Temperature Rising?*, 36. (The concentration of oxygen in the Earth's atmosphere is 20.9%.)

63. **This amount of radiation…unique wavelength.** Spencer and Christy, "Precise Monitoring of Global Temperature Trends from Satellites," 1558–59.

63. **This was a zone…above sea level.** Guyot, *Physics of the Environment and Climate*, 221–22.

63. **When a microwave…altitude zone.** Spencer and Christy, "Precise Monitoring of Global Temperature Trends from Satellites," 1558–59; Mears, Schabel, and Wentz, "A Reanalysis of the MSU Channel 2 Tropospheric Temperature Record," 3650–52.

63. **Because oxygen…same place.** Spencer and Christy, "Precise Monitoring of Global Temperature Trends from Satellites," 1558–59; Mears, Schabel, and Wentz, "A Reanalysis of the MSU Channel 2 Tropospheric Temperature Record," 3650–52.

64. **Few gaps in coverage exist.** Some angles of measurements were not made because of their strong impact on instrument life. Vinnikov and Grody, "Global Warming Trend of Mean Tropospheric Temperature Observed by Satellites," 271.

64. **They did not agree...surface stations.** Balling, "Geographical Analysis of Differences in Trends between Nearsurface and Satellite-based Temperature Measurements," 2939–41; Spencer and Christy, "Precise Monitoring of Global Temperature Trends from Satellites," 1558–59; Mears, Schabel, and Wentz, "A Reanalysis of the MSU Channel 2 Tropospheric Temperature Record," 3650–52.

64. **Later calculations...contained uncertainties.** See appendix 6.

66. **The years-long drought...under this standard.** "California Drought."

66. **Huge rainfall...weather as well.** Salter and Zagier, "Rescue Crews Assist with Evacuations in Midwest Flooding;" Salter, "Flooding Forcing Evacuations, Traffic Troubles in Missouri;" "Some Key Numbers after Historic Illinois, Missouri Flooding."

Chapter 9

69. **Marilyn said...meteorological programs.** Houghton et al., *Climate Change 2001: The Scientific Basis* (IPCC report), 3, 105–17; Stocker et al., *Climate Change 2013: The Physical Science Basis* (IPCC report), 165, 187–89 (land temperatures), 189–92 (sea surface temperatures), 192–94 (land and surface temperatures).

70. **The WMO had set...place to place.** See website of the World Meteorlogical Organization under "About Us"—"Vision and Mission," http://www.wmo.int.

70. **The biggest gaps...Southern Hemisphere.** Houghton et al., *Climate Change 1995: The Science of Climate Change* (IPCC report), 147 (radiosondes).

71. **Marilyn said...urban heating effect.** Houghton et al., *Climate Change 2001: The Scientific Basis* (IPCC report), 105–10; Stocker et al., *Climate Change 2013: The Physical Science Basis* (IPCC report), 188–89.

71. **At most...measured trend.** Houghton et al., *Climate Change 2001: The Scientific Basis* (IPCC report), 105–6; Stocker et al., *Climate Change 2013: The Physical Science Basis* (IPCC report), 189.

72. **Again, scientists...minimize them.** Hoyt and Shatten, *Role of the Sun in Climate Change*, 85–86.

75. **We have less...not as good.** See National Research Council, Committee on Abrupt Climate Change, *Abrupt Climate Change: Inevitable Surprises*, 46.

77. **While there...back to space.** Bigg, *Oceans and Climate*, 22. (Solar radiation at Mauna Loa observatory decreased ten percent for a year after Mount Pinatubo erupted.)

77. **The earth's atmosphere…the stratosphere.** McCormick, Thomason, and Trepte, "Atmospheric Effects of the Mt. Pinatubo Eruption," 399–404.

77. **It's on Saint Vincent Island.** Philpott, *Caribbean Sunseekers: St. Vincent and Grenadines*, 12, 79; Simkin and Siebert, *Volcanoes of the World, Second Edition*, 150.

77. **Pinatubo was…revised models.** McCormick, Thomason, and Trepte, "Atmospheric Effects of the Mt. Pinatubo Eruption," 404.

Chapter 10

79. **They reflect some…other regions.** National Research Council, Committee on Global Change Research, *Global Environmental Change: Research Pathways*, 137–40 (Plate 5); Doran et al., "Antarctic Climate Cooling and Terrestrial Ecosystem Response," 517–20.

82. **"Secondary indications," said Paul.** E.g. Hoyt and Shatten, *Role of the Sun in Climate Change*, 153–64.

82. **"Starting before the 1990s…were shrinking.** See Houghton et al., *Climate Change 2001: The Scientific Basis* (IPCC report), 127–29. Globally, the glacial mass has continued to shrink in each of the last five decades. Stocker et al., *Climate Change 2013: The Physical Science Basis* (IPCC report), 338–42.

82. **"And then around 2000…added Paul.** See Houghton et al., *Climate Change 2001: The Scientific Basis* (IPCC report), 124–25. The overall trend for the extent of Arctic sea ice remains downward, but with annual variations. Stocker et al., *Climate Change 2013: The Physical Science Basis* (IPCC report), 323–26.

82. **Northern permafrost…has been monitored.** See Houghton et al., *Climate Change 2001: The Scientific Basis* (IPCC report), 127; Stocker et al., *Climate Change 2013: The Physical Science Basis* (IPCC report), 362–64.

83. **Many bears…sea going prey.** See Churchill, "The Big Meltdown," 52–56.

83. **"The polar bear story…said Paul.** McCarthy, James J., et al., *Climate Change 2001: Impacts, Adaptation, and Vulnerability* (IPCC report), 239, 354–55.

83. **These will clearly…are found."** Hoyt and Shatten, *Role of the Sun in Climate Change*, 153–56 (insects); Parmesan and Yohe, "A Globally Coherent Fingerprint of Climate Change Impacts across Natural Systems," 37–42 (multiple species); Root et al., "Fingerprints of Global Warming on Wild Animals and Plants," 57–60 (multiple species).

83. **"What appears…have changed."** Field et al., *Climate Change 2014: Impacts, Adaptation, and Vulnerability—Part A: Global and Sectoral Aspects* (IPCC report), 303–6.

83. **"If insect pests...the first time."** Field et al., *Climate Change 2014: Impacts, Adaptation, and Vulnerability—Part A: Global and Sectoral Aspects* (IPCC report), 1054.

83. **Of course, increased...stricken areas.** McCarthy, James J., et al., *Climate Change 2001: Impacts, Adaptation, and Vulnerability* (IPCC report), 926–27; Dlugolecki, "An Insurer's Perspective," and Nutter, "A Reinsurer's Perspective," in *Climate Change and the Financial Sector*, edited by Jeremy Leggett, 64–81 and 82–90.

Chapter 12

100. **Although floods...increased crops.** Changnon, *El Niño, 1997–1998*, 160–61.

100. **Even then, lost production...remaining regions.** Sidey, "The Big Dry," 12–15; "Heatstroke," *Time*, 51; Rosenzweig and Hillel, *Climate Change and the Global Harvest*, 5.

100. **Droughts...nation's crops.** *Crop Prospects and Food Situation—No. 4 November 2006*, 3.

101. **The United States...of the 1930s.** Yancey, *Life During the Dust Bowl*, 12.

Chapter 13

106. **The stage...Anti-Cult's plan.** France, Russia, and Japan recycle their spent nuclear fuel rods. The United States opted for a one use approach. Haeberlin, *A Case for Nuclear-Generated Electricity*, 170–71.

107. **Everyone had known...sinister purpose.** Haeberlin, *A Case for Nuclear-Generated Electricity*, 165–73.

108. **Nuclear experts...power plant's reactor.** Haeberlin, *A Case for Nuclear-Generated Electricity*, 168–70.

108. **Eventually...convicted of treason.** None were executed, as France abolished the death penalty in 1981. Brunner, *Time Almanac 2002*, 713.

110. **Even though nuclear...nuclear program.** Haeberlin, *A Case for Nuclear-Generated Electricity*, 165–69.

110. **The Chernobyl incident...a catastrophe.** Brunner, *Time Almanac, 2002*, 618. (An explosion and fire occurred in April 1986 at the Chernobyl Power Plant near Kiev, Ukraine, which was part of the Soviet Union in 1986.)

110. **France had then...these plants.** Haeberlin, *A Case for Nuclear-Generated Electricity*, 274.

110. **In addition...waste disposal.** Haeberlin, *A Case for Nuclear-Generated Electricity*, 274–75. (Nuclear power provided 19.8% of the United States' electricity in

2000. Percentages do not tell the whole story. The United States and France ranked respectively first and second in the world in terms of the total amount of electricity generated by nuclear power in 2000. The total for the United States was nearly twice the total for France.)

113. **Spent fuel rods…recycling facility.** Haeberlin, *A Case for Nuclear-Generated Electricity*, 170–71.

114. **In contrast…custom designed.** Haeberlin, *A Case for Nuclear-Generated Electricity*, 287.

Chapter 14

118. **But the proportion…was still small.** Berenstein, *Alternative Energy—Facts, Statistics, and Issues*, 49. (In 1999, wind turbines produced less than 1% of the electricity generated in the United States. Including hydroelectric and geothermal power as renewable sources, all renewable sources produced less than 10% of the electricity generated in the United States in 1999. By 2013, this US percentage for all renewable sources had risen only to 13%. "Net Generation by Energy Source: Total (All Sectors).")

119. **"Melissa, you Americans…said Rousseau.** Vig and Faure, *Green Giants? Environmental Policies*, 207–208, 212–17.

119. **"Yet the United States…in 2001.** Vig and Faure, *Green Giants? Environmental Policies*, 208.

120. **I know that…potential new sources.** *Budget of the U.S. Government, Fiscal Year 2005*, 391–95. ($635 million for the president's coal research initiative; $375 million for renewable energy and efficiency research); Berenstein, *Alternative Energy—Facts, Statistics, and Issues*, 39–43; McSlarrow, *Statement at Hearing on Proposed Fiscal Year 2005 Budget Request for the Department of Energy.* (Testimony on *proposed* Fiscal Year 2005 budget for the US Department of Energy allocated $447 million to coal burning power plant research and $375 million to renewable energy and efficiency research.)

Chapter 15

127. **Changes have to…normal variations.** Bryant, *Climate Process and Change*, 5–7.

128. **The so-called natural…existed in 1900.** National Research Council, Committee on Abrupt Climate Change, *Global Environmental Change: Research Pathways*, 127–29.

128. **We are trying…not fully understand.** Bryant, *Climate Process and Change*, 9–13.

128. **Concentrations of carbon dioxide…than today.** See appendix 8.

129. **They delay…extra energy.** Bigg, *Oceans and Climate*, 14, 43–45; Whipple, *Restless Oceans*, 76–78.

129. **Others believe…much longer.** Hoyt and Shatten, *Role of the Sun in Climate Change*, 96, 105, 166 (four to five years); Stocker et al., *Climate Change 2013: The Physical Science Basis* (IPCC report), 266 (ten years or more).

129. **In other words…could occur.** National Research Council, Committee on Global Change Research, *Global Environmental Change: Research Pathways*, 311; National Research Council, Committee on Abrupt Climate Change, *Abrupt Climate Change: Inevitable Surprises*, 163–64.

130. **Just one CFC…ozone molecules.** Philander, *Is the Temperature Rising?*, 183–90; National Research Council, Committee on Global Change Research, *Global Environmental Change: Research Pathways*, 194–95.

130. **That is why…signed in 1987.** Philander, *Is the Temperature Rising?*, 183.

130. **It's caused by…working together.** Philander, *Is the Temperature Rising?*, 183–90.

130. **"For example…recent Ice Ages.** National Research Council, Committee on Global Change Research, *Global Environmental Change: Research Pathways*, 132–33, 240–49.

130. **We believe…local changes.** National Research Council, Committee on Global Change Research, *Global Environmental Change: Research Pathways*, 132–33, 237–49; National Research Council, Committee on Abrupt Climate Change, *Abrupt Climate Change: Inevitable Surprises*, 24–36.

130. **The Somali Current…each six months.** Philander, *Is the Temperature Rising?*, 140; Whipple, *Restless Oceans*, 91.

Chapter 17

143. **Or the water…faster than normal.** National Research Council, Committee on Global Change Research, *Abrupt Climate Change: Inevitable Surprises*, 78–80; Krabill et al., "Rapid Thinning of Parts of the Southern Greenland Ice Sheet," 1524.

143. **Unlike volcanic activity…over large areas.** See Krabill et al., "Rapid Thinning of Parts of the Southern Greenland Ice Sheet," 1522–24; Krabill et al., "Greenland Ice Sheet: High-Elevation Balance and Peripheral Thinning," 428–30.

144. **Paul and Marilyn…Ice Ages.** National Research Council, Committee on Global Change Research, *Global Environmental Change: Research Pathways*, 132, 242–43; National Research Council, Committee on Abrupt Climate Change, *Abrupt Climate Change: Inevitable Surprises*, 24–27.

144. **Three decades ago…the planet.** Observations indicated that Greenland as a whole did not have surface temperature increases in the 1980s and 1990s. Krabill et al., "Greenland Ice Sheet: High-Elevation Balance and Peripheral Thinning," 429.

144. **Greenland could…other regions.** Some of the largest surface atmospheric temperature increases in the last twenty-five years of the twentieth century occurred in Northern Canada and Siberia. Houghton et al., *Climate Change 2001: The Scientific Basis* (IPCC report), 117 (figure 2.10). These areas remained sparsely populated, so the urban heating effect could not be a direct cause of these increases.

145. **Western Europe…recorded history.** Bigg, *Oceans and Climate*, 190–91; National Research Council, Committee on Abrupt Climate Change, *Abrupt Climate Change: Inevitable Surprises*, 89–106, 108–111.

Chapter 18

146. **Oceans covered…"Blue Planet."** Bigg, *Oceans and Climate*, 12.

147. **They had created…and Maine.** Bigg, *Oceans and Climate*, 189–90.

148. **As shown to Karen…not every year.** See appendix 5.

148. **The 1998 high point…time period.** See appendix 5.

149. **The amount of upper…and Soufrière.** See appendix 5 (surface temperatures); Stocker et al., *Climate Change 2013: The Physical Science Basis* (IPCC report), 61–63, 691–93 (for effect of volcanic aerosols, see figure 8.13).

149. **This brown haze…earth's surface.** Tran, "Regional Brown Cloud Termed Global Danger."

149. **Whether or not…modern times.** See appendix 5.

150. **By 1998…million in 2014.** See appendix 1.

150. **Now, in 2032…per million.** 440 ppm is a linear extrapolation from figure 1A in appendix 1.

150. **Measurements of…than in 1958.** See appendixes 2 and 3.

151. **Only in the twenty-first…ambient aerosols.** Stocker et al., *Climate Change 2013: The Physical Science Basis* (IPCC report), 391.

151. **Very simply, more…other fossil fuels.** Bigg, *Oceans and Climate*, 222–24; Houghton et al., *Climate Change 2001: The Scientific Basis* (IPCC report), 299–306; Stocker et al., *Climate Change 2013: The Physical Science Basis* (IPCC report), 596.

151. **Especially important…twentieth century.** Tran, "Regional Brown Cloud Termed Global Danger."

151. **Some of these low-altitude…reflecting sunlight.** National Research Council, Committee on Global Change Research, *Global Environmental Change: Research Pathways*, 227–31.

151. **Reflection occurred…forming clouds.** Philander, *Is the Temperature Rising?*, 82; see generally Stocker et al., *Climate Change 2013: The Physical Science Basis* (IPCC report), 576.

151. **Increased amounts…not well understood.** Houghton et al., *Climate Change 2001: The Scientific Basis* (IPCC report), 299; Stocker et al., *Climate Change 2013: The Physical Science Basis* (IPCC report), 616, 685.

151. **These trails…earth's surface.** Solomon et al., *Climate Change 2007: The Physical Science Basis* (IPCC report), 186–88.

152. **Paul first looked…labeled irradiance.** See appendix 7.

152. **Many scientists used to…even centuries.** Hoyt and Shatten, *Role of the Sun in Climate Change*, 48–49.

152. **A roughly eleven-year…been identified.** Gueymard, "The Sun's Total and Spectral Irradiance," 426; Hoyt and Shatten, *Role of the Sun in Climate Change*, 61–63.

152. **They called this irradiance the "solar constant."** Gray et al, "Solar Influences on Climate," 9 (figure 5(a)); Gueymard, "The Sun's Total and Spectral Irradiance," 425–27; Hoyt and Shatten, *Role of the Sun in Climate Change*, 11, 48; see appendix 7.

152. **These observations…had been available.** See appendix 7.

152. **Especially when combined…last one million years.** Philander, *Is the Temperature Rising?*, 179–82; National Research Council, Committee on Global Change Research, *Global Environmental Change: Research Pathways*, 240–41; Bigg, *Oceans and Climate*, 28–30.

153. **They would not be…hundred years.** Bigg, *Oceans and Climate*, 28–30.

153. **Scientists called…surface reflectivity.** Philander, *Is the Temperature Rising?*, 33–34.

153. **These great increases…out to space.** Bigg, *Oceans and Climate*, 19; National Research Council, Committee on Global Change Research, *Global Environmental Change: Research Pathways*, 242.

153. **Arctic sea ice had decreased, but Antarctic sea ice had increased.** Stocker et al., *Climate Change 2013: The Physical Science Basis* (IPCC report), 323–35.

154. **This set of changes…create crops.** Ruddiman, "How Did Humans First Alter Global Climate?," 50.

154. **Nevertheless, even…surface reflectivity.** Houghton et al., *Climate Change 2001: The Scientific Basis* (IPCC report), 441–44; Stocker et al., *Climate Change*

2013: The Physical Science Basis (IPCC report), 686–88; Bigg, *Oceans and Climate*, 230.

Chapter 19

155. **These very large solar…satellite useless.** Jaroff, "Stormy Weather," 64–66.

156. **To avoid this…huge solar flare.** Jaroff, "Stormy Weather," 64–66.

156. **Unfortunately, no cover…had occurred.** All electromagnetic radiation travels at the speed of light in a vacuum such as space. *International Encyclopedia of Science and Technology*, 123.

156. **In turn, that time…to the earth.** Simple calculation. The average distance of the earth from the sun is 149.6 million kilometers. Light travels at 300,000 kilometers per second, so the time for light to travel from the sun to the earth is 8.31 minutes. Data Source: *International Encyclopedia of Science and Technology*, 217, 221.

157. **The first use…in 1978.** Spencer and Christy, "Precise Monitoring of Global Temperature Trends from Satellites," 1558.

157. **The original purpose…weather predictions.** Mears, Schabel, and Wentz, "A Reanalysis of the MSU Channel 2 Tropospheric Temperature Record," 3650.

157. **Sometimes two functioning…sometimes only one.** Mears, Schabel, and Wentz, "A Reanalysis of the MSU Channel 2 Tropospheric Temperature Record," 3652–53, 3658.

157. **Yet in order to…on different satellites.** Mears, Schabel, and Wentz, "A Reanalysis of the MSU Channel 2 Tropospheric Temperature Record," 3663–64.

158. **The MSUs detected…at each position.** Mears, Schabel, and Wentz, "A Reanalysis of the MSU Channel 2 Tropospheric Temperature Record," 3652.

158. **Comparing atmospheric temperatures…were made.** Mears, Schabel, and Wentz, "A Reanalysis of the MSU Channel 2 Tropospheric Temperature Record," 3650–64.

158. **This factor, known…the same satellites.** Mears, Schabel, and Wentz, "A Reanalysis of the MSU Channel 2 Tropospheric Temperature Record," 3653–55.

Chapter 20

162. **The ultraviolet portion…upper atmosphere.** Bigg, *Oceans and Climate*, 4–6, 11–12; Philander, *Is the Temperature Rising?*, 35–36, 40.

162. **Based on the amount…have an atmosphere.** Bigg, *Oceans and Climate*, 4; Philander, *Is the Temperature Rising?*, 35 (15° C.).

162. **This absorption increased…of these molecules.** Bigg, *Oceans and Climate*, 7–11.

163. **This was thirty-three…greenhouse gases.** Bigg, *Oceans and Climate*, 4 (16° C.); Philander, *Is the Temperature Rising?*, 34–36.

163. **The gases that did act…trace gases.** Bryant, *Climate Process and Change*, 118–19; Philander, *Is the Temperature Rising?*, 35–36.

163. **Compared to the total…water was minuscule.** Wayne, *Chemistry of Atmospheres, Third Edition*, 5 (Fresh water in lakes and rivers comprises only 0.6% of the Earth's water.)

163. **Water vapor…greenhouse gas.** Bigg, *Oceans and Climate*, 10–11; Philander, *Is the Temperature Rising?*, 51–52.

163. **They had been in…had been possible.** Bigg, *Oceans and Climate*, 21–22.

163. **But by the time Congress…thousand years.** National Research Council, Committee on Global Change Research, *Global Environmental Change: Research Pathways*, 239, 215–22.

164. **From a base level…twentieth century.** See appendix 4.

164. **The increased concentrations…earth's atmosphere.** See appendix 4.

164. **On balance, carbon dioxide…did methane.** Bigg, *Oceans and Climate*, 10–11.

164. **Their concentrations…in Hawaii.** Wayne, *Chemistry of Atmospheres, Third Edition*, 1–3, 51–53, 57–58; Philander, *Is the Temperature Rising?*, 31 (80% of the atmosphere's mass lies within ten kilometers above sea level.)

165. **More water vapor…surrounding air.** Philander, *Is the Temperature Rising?*, 51–52; Wayne, *Chemistry of Atmospheres, Third Edition*, 683.

165. **By sheer size…this equilibrium.** Philander, *Is the Temperature Rising?*, 78–84.

165. **If that total energy…would increase.** Wayne, *Chemistry of Atmospheres, Third Edition*, 683; see Philander, *Is the Temperature Rising?*, 78–84, 161–62.

165. **By itself, increased…typical greenhouse gas.** Bigg, *Oceans and Climate*, 26.

165. **Water vapor's condensation…atmospheric energy.** Philander, *Is the Temperature Rising?*, 76–88.

165. **Increased overall water vapor…condensation occurred.** Bigg, *Oceans and Climate*, 225–27.

166. **Even if more clouds…sunlight differently.** Bigg, *Oceans and Climate*, 226–27; Philander, *Is the Temperature Rising?*, 87–88. Some people have postulated that the increased water vapor in the atmosphere that is caused by increased atmospheric heat resulting from increased concentrations of greenhouse gases will produce increased clouds world-wide that will exactly counterbalance the increased atmospheric heat from greenhouse gases by reflecting more sunlight back out to space. With this exact counterbalance, the earth's atmosphere will

not warm at all and climates will not change. If this exact counterbalance effect were to exist, it should occur for events that add energy to the atmosphere (creating more world-wide clouds) and also events that subtract energy from the atmosphere (creating less world-wide clouds). Volcanic eruptions are events that subtract energy from the atmosphere by blocking sunlight. Atmospheric cooling has consistently followed major volcanic eruptions, so a postulated diminution in world-wide clouds does not counterbalance the cooling effect from the volcanic eruption. This result shows that the postulated exact counterbalance effect from changes in clouds does not exist, at least for short term reduced atmospheric energy. See McCormick, Thomason, and Trepte, "Atmospheric Effects of the Mt. Pinatubo Eruption," 399–404. (Atmospheric cooling occurred after the eruption of Mount Pinatubo in 1991.)

167. **Paul knew that…following decade.** Houghton et al., *Climate Change 1995: The Science of Climate Change* (IPCC report), 235; Houghton et al., *Climate Change 2001: The Scientific Basis* (IPCC report), 781–82.

168. **Clearly the concentrations…lower atmosphere.** National Research Council, Committee on Global Change Research, *Global Environmental Change: Research Pathways*, 180, 239.

168. **Data compilations…after 1970.** See appendix 5.

168. **The stratosphere…back to space.** Stocker et al., *Climate Change 2013: The Physical Science Basis* (IPCC report), 194–201; Wayne, *Chemistry of Atmospheres, Third Edition*, 57.

168. **Being denser…weather features.** Guyot, *Physics of the Environment and Climate*, 221–22.

169. **Because total tropospheric…regional climates.** See Wayne, *Chemistry of Atmospheres, Third Edition*, 45–95.

Chapter 21

171. **Other patterns…well-known to climatologists.** National Research Council, Committee on Global Change Research, *Global Environmental Change: Research Pathways*, 87–90, 141–47.

171. **Westerly winds…in the winter.** National Research Council, Committee on Global Change Research, *Global Environmental Change: Research Pathways*, 141; Bigg, *Oceans and Climate*, 149–50.

171. **It had occupied…in Europe.** National Research Council, Committee on Global Change Research, *Global Environmental Change: Research Pathways*, 138, 142.

172. **Another pattern…tropical mountains.** National Research Council, Committee on Global Change Research, *Global Environmental Change: Research Pathways*, 145–47.

172. **Unusual behavior…to be explained.** National Research Council, Committee on Global Change Research, *Global Environmental Change: Research Pathways*, 137–40.

172. **Sunspot recordings…in 1610.** Hoyt and Shatten, *Role of the Sun in Climate Change*, 14–34.

172. **Then in 1843…sunspot activity.** Hoyt and Shatten, *Role of the Sun in Climate Change*, 34–35.

172. **Later scientists…solar rhythm.** Hoyt and Shatten, *Role of the Sun in Climate Change*, 173–87.

172. **The success of these efforts had been mixed.** Hoyt and Shatten, *Role of the Sun in Climate Change*, 172–202; see Nesme-Ribes et al, "Solar Dynamics and Its Impact on Solar Irradiance and the Terrestrial Climate," 18,923–35 and Wigley and Raper, "Climatic Change Due to Solar Irradiance Changes," 2169–72.

173. **Faculae…solar irradiance.** Gray et al, "Solar Influences on Climate," 2–3.

173. **Ultaviolet radiation…other wavelengths.** Hoyt and Shatten, *Role of the Sun in Climate Change*, 67–68.

173. **All of these factors…climatic conditions.** Hoyt and Shatten, *Role of the Sun in Climate Change*, 48, 58–67.

173. **At less than 0.1%…ETOP had measured.** Stocker et al., *Climate Change 2013: The Physical Science Basis* (IPCC report), 689 (figure 8.10). Assuming a consistent eleven-year cycle from a peak solar irradiance in 2002, later peak solar irradiances would occur in 2013, 2024, and 2035 due to the eleven-year cycle. See Gray et al., "Solar Influences on Climate," 2–3.

Chapter 22

174. **Ozone…earth's surface.** Philander, *Is the Temperature Rising?*, 50.

174. **This reaction also…that radiation.** Bigg, *Oceans and Climate*, 4–6; Philander, *Is the Temperature Rising?*, 183–86.

175. **This phenomenon…had been predicted.** Philander, *Is the Temperature Rising?*, 183–86; Wayne, *Chemistry of Atmospheres, Third Edition*, 232–62.

175. **Even worse…manufacture and use.** Montreal Protocol; Stocker et al., *Climate Change 2013: The Physical Science Basis* (IPCC report), 168–70, 678; "Alumna Profile: Susan Solomon."

175. **The ozone-free zone…atmosphere.** Stocker et al., *Climate Change 2013: The Physical Science Basis* (IPCC report), 731 (lifetimes).

175. **No natural mechanism…time frame.** Stager, "Tales of a Warmer Planet;" Stocker et al., *Climate Change 2013: The Physical Science Basis* (IPCC report), 1106–7.

175. **Ice-core records…had occurred.** Bigg, *Oceans and Climate*, 189–90.

176. **Scientists in the middle…nitrous oxides.** See Bigg, *Oceans and Climate*, 21–22.

176. **These actions included…case of methane.** See appendix 4.

177. **And the continuation…continue to increase.** See appendixes 1 and 2.

Chapter 23

179. **"Just twelve thousand years…twenty years.** National Research Council, Committee on Global Change Research, *Global Environmental Change: Research Pathways*, 132, 242–48; National Research Council, Committee on Abrupt Climate Change, *Abrupt Climate Change: Inevitable Surprises*, 24–36.

180. **"Yes, but studies…said Marilyn.** See appendix 9.

180. **"We now know…hitting the earth.** National Research Council, Committee on Global Change Research, *Global Environmental Change: Research Pathways*, 241.

180. **That's why cooling…Ice Ages."** Bigg, *Oceans and Climate*, 28–31; Philander, *Is the Temperature Rising?*, 170–82.

180. **"As oceans warmed up…to the atmosphere.** Bigg, *Oceans and Climate*, 87; Philander, *Is the Temperature Rising?*, 128.

180. **During that long period…warm periods.** See appendix 8.

181. **Carbon dioxide concentrations…in 2032.** National Research Council, Committee on Global Change Research, *Global Environmental Change: Research Pathways*, 57–58 (figure 2.8.a). 440 ppm is a linear extrapolation from figure 1A in appendix 1.

181. **Let's start with…twenty thousand years ago.** National Research Council, Committee on Global Change Research, *Global Environmental Change: Research Pathways*, 242–43.

181. **"That's when ice sheets…said Marilyn.** Bigg, *Oceans and Climate*, 19.

181. **"You know, the chemistry…colder than today.** National Research Council, Committee on Global Change Research, *Global Environmental Change: Research Pathways*, 242–49; Philander, *Is the Temperature Rising?*, 177; National Research Council, Committee on Global Change Research, *Global Environmental Change: Research Pathways*, 242.

181. **But the average temperatures...colder than today.** National Research Council, Committee on Global Change Research, *Global Environmental Change: Research Pathways*, 242–48.

181. **A warm-up of...last seventy years.** See appendix 5.

181. **"Even our modern...temperature fluctuations.** Bigg, *Oceans and Climate*, 30–31 (figure 1.28).

Chapter 24

186. **For another, the United States...not an importer.** Rosenzweig and Hillel, *Climate Change and the Global Harvest*, 212.

186. **Despite the global market...twentieth century.** Rosenzweig and Hillel, *Climate Change and the Global Harvest*, 217–18; Reeder, *Industry and Trade Summary: Grain (Cereals)*, 46; *Crop Prospects 2006*, 4 (table 2).

186. **More dangerous...exporters of grains.** Reeder, *Industry and Trade Summary: Grain (Cereals)*, 46–49, A–38 (table A–46). For example, in 1999/2000, just five nations supplied 87% of the wheat exports in the international market, led by the United States, which alone supplied 28% of the total market.

Chapter 25

192. **Huge changes...to twenty years.** National Research Council, Committee on Global Change Research, *Global Environmental Change: Research Pathways*, 242.

196. **He also noted...genetically altered seeds.** Vig and Faure, *Green Giants? Environmental Policies*, 25–42.

197. **Soufrière is...in the Caribbean.** Simkin and Siebert, *Volcanoes of the World, Second Edition*, 151; Philpott, *Caribbean Sunseekers: St. Vincent and Grenadines*, 14, 79.

198. **You may recall...Air Force Base.** Ritchie, *Encyclopedia of Earthquakes and Volcanoes*, 14, 177.

198. **Despite annual ups...earth's surface.** See appendix 5.

198. **The earth's lower atmosphere...earth's surface."** McCormick, Thomason, and Trepte, "Atmospheric Effects of the Mt. Pinatubo Eruption," 399–404.

198. **"The amount of tephra ejected is one measurement.** Simkin and Siebert, *Volcanoes of the World, Second Edition*, 25.

198. **That is the most meaningful...atmospheric temperature.** Simkin and Siebert, *Volcanoes of the World, Second Edition*, 24.

198. **Some observers estimated…forty megatons.** Dane, "Science: Pinatubo's Toll," 102–3. (Mount Pinatubo's main eruption was estimated at 2,000 to 3,000 Hiroshima bombs.); Glasstone and Dolan, *Effects of Nuclear Weapons, Third Edition*, 6. (The Hiroshima bomb was estimated at 20 kilotons, so Pinatubo would have been 40 to 60 megatons. A megaton is the explosive energy released when one million tons of TNT [trinitrotoluene] explodes.)

Chapter 26

204. **"I know that the Castle Bravo…she said.** Rhodes, *Dark Sun*, 478–79 (plate 82), 541.

206. **He remembered some secret…to blow apart volcanic rock.** *Geologic and Hydrologic Effects of the Cannikin Underground Nuclear Explosion.*

206. **We never made…tested in 1961."** Seaborg, *Kennedy, Khruschev and the Test Ban*, 112, 114; Sakharov, *Memoirs*, trans. Lourie, 218–21.

206. **"Before you get too far…Admiral Crowell.** Seaborg, *Kennedy, Khruschev and the Test Ban*, 254–82; Sakharov, *Memoirs*, trans. Lourie, 229–32; Treaty Banning Nuclear Weapons Tests (1963).

Chapter 27

212. **One of those was…Admiral Crowell.** Rhodes, *Dark Sun*, 478–79 (plate 82), 541–42.

212. **These hazes partially…largely caused.** Bryant, *Climate Process and Change*, 55, 128–30; Wayne, *Chemistry of Atmospheres, Third Edition*, 403–8 (sources of sulfur dioxide); National Research Council, Committee on Global Change Research, *Global Environmental Change: Research Pathways*, 227–31.

212. **For example, its absorption…create acidic rain.** Wayne, *Chemistry of Atmospheres, Third Edition*, 409–22.

213. **Far more time…human intervention.** Stager, "Tales of a Warmer Planet."

214. **You may remember…in 79 A.D.** Ritchie, *Encyclopedia of Earthquakes and Volcanoes*, 245.

214. **It not only destroyed…as Europe.** Simkin and Siebert, *Volcanoes of the World, Second Edition*, 22; Ritchie, *Encyclopedia of Earthquakes and Volcanoes*, 122–24.

216. **Deep underground tests…the surface.** *Geologic and Hydrologic Effects of the Cannikin Underground Nuclear Explosion.*

216. **She said that…into an eruption.** Glasstone and Dolan, *Effects of Nuclear Weapons, Third Edition*, 253–57.

Chapter 28

219. **The initial difficulty…weather patterns.** Annual crops are the most flexible food source. Trying to match other food sources such as fruit trees and grape vines with uncertain future climate regimes would be even more difficult.

219. **In addition to this…psychological inertia.** El Niño 1997-1998 in the United States showed that the agricultural sector was less likely to respond to the El Niño warnings than some other economic sectors. See Changnon, *El Niño, 1997–1998*, 22–23, 121–122, 130–134.

220. **Its benefits were…throughout the world.** Plant species use different photosynthetic mechanisms, known as C3 or C4 pathways. Research in controlled greenhouses has shown that C3 plants (e.g. wheat, rice, and soybeans) are generally more responsive to carbon dioxide enrichment than C4 plants (e.g. corn and sugarcane). Many weeds are C3 plants, so the net effect of carbon dioxide enrichment is unclear. In addition, plant responses to carbon dioxide enrichment do not necessarily increase total nutritional value of the food crop. Rosenzweig and Hillel, *Climate Change and the Global Harvest*, 71–74; see also Field et al., *Climate Change 2014: Impacts, Adaptation, and Vulnerability—Part A: Global and Sectoral Aspects* (IPCC report), 493, 496.

220. **Otherwise, total crop production…concentrations.** Contrast the example in *The Skeptical Environmentalist* where simplified extrapolation of some tests of doubled carbon dioxide concentrations under controlled conditions assumes direct application to real world agriculture or natural forests. Lomborg, *The Skeptical Environmentalist*, 299.

220. **Competition among…poorly understood.** Rosenzweig and Hillel, *Climate Change and the Global Harvest*, 70–86.

220. **This was true even…been controlled.** McCarthy, James J., et al., *Climate Change 2001: Impacts, Adaptation, and Vulnerability* (IPCC report), 254–58.

220. **The earth's average…greenhouse gases.** Bigg, *Oceans and Climate*, 14, 43–45.

221. **These actions could not…a generation.** Bigg, *Oceans and Climate*, 95. (The oceans act as a drag on atmospheric carbon dioxide increases and also as a drag on atmospheric carbon dioxide decreases.)

221. **The United States first…earth's atmosphere.** E.g. Treaty Banning Nuclear Weapons Tests (1963); see Seaborg, *Kennedy, Khruschev and the Test Ban*.

Chapter 29

227. **He moved its beam...Central America.** Simkin and Siebert, *Volcanoes of the World, Second Edition*, cover page.

227. **Hawaii and...are examples.** Simkin and Siebert, *Volcanoes of the World, Second Edition*, 44–125.

228. **One of the largest...Novarupta."** Ritchie, *Encyclopedia of Earthquakes and Volcanoes*, 117.

228. **Plus, winter jet streams...summer jet streams.** Bryant, *Climate Process and Change*, 35–39; Guyot, *Physics of the Environment and Climate*, 271–72.

229. **Luckily, shortly after...Alaska Peninsula.** Coats, *Geologic Reconnaissance of Gareloi Island, Aleutian Islands, Alaska*, preface.

229. **In the early 1970s...Aleutian Islands.** *Geologic and Hydrologic Effects of the Cannikin Underground Nuclear Explosion.*

230. **The team chose...volcanic eruption.** United States Geological Survey Maps, Alaska Topographic Series: *Gareloi Island, Alaska, 1954, Rev. 1983.*

230. **Mount Gareloi's...in 1929.** Simkin and Siebert, *Volcanoes of the World, Second Edition*, 113; Coats, *Geologic Reconnaissance of Gareloi Island, Aleutian Islands, Alaska.*

230. **This idea...occurred in 1980.** Sedlacek, Mroz, and Heiken, "Stratospheric Sulfate from the Gareloi Eruption, 1980," 761–64.

231. **Gareloi Island...Wilderness.** United States Geological Survey Maps, Alaska Topographic Series: *Gareloi Island, Alaska, 1954, Rev. 1983.* Alaska National Interest Lands Conservation Act, Pub.L.No. 96-487, 94 Stat. 2371 (1980).

Chapter 30

235. **Average radii...much preferred.** Bigg, *Oceans and Climate*, 214; McCormick, Thomason, and Trepte, "Atmospheric Effects of the Mt. Pinatubo Eruption," 401.

235. **These are the...incoming sunlight.** Simkin and Siebert, *Volcanoes of the World, Second Edition*, 24; McCormick, Thomason, and Trepte, "Atmospheric Effects of the Mt. Pinatubo Eruption," 399–404. (The eruption of El Chichon in Mexico in 1982 had about the same explosive power as the eruption of Mount St. Helens in the United States in 1980, but produced ten times as much sulfur dioxide in a far larger aerosol cloud with much greater atmospheric effects.)

235. **Based on the eruptions...pulverized material.** Simkin and Siebert, *Volcanoes of the World, Second Edition*, 83. (Total tephra from Mount Pinatubo exceeded ten cubic kilometers.)

236. **Deep underground tests…in one bomb.** *Geologic and Hydrologic Effects of the Cannikin Underground Nuclear Explosion*; Glasstone and Dolan, *Effects of Nuclear Weapons, Third Edition*, 253–62.

236. **In retrospect…had not predicted.** Rhodes, *Dark Sun*, 541.

236. **They later figured out…shock wave.** Sakharov, *Memoirs*, trans. Lourie, 190–94.

237. **Even at one hundred percent…Mount Gareloi.** Glasstone and Dolan, *Effects of Nuclear Weapons, Third Edition*, 253–62. (This text describes a formula for approximating the crater size that would be created by an atomic or thermonuclear bomb with known explosive power.)

237. **That's why we…Aleutian Islands.** Guyot, *Physics of the Environment and Climate*, 271–72.

238. **Weaker summer jet…these eruptions.** Guyot, *Physics of the Environment and Climate*, 271–72. Not all large volcanic eruptions in recorded history have clearly caused global atmospheric cooling, perhaps because of reduced aerosol distribution. See Hoyt and Shatten, *Role of the Sun in Climate Change*, 204–9.

238. **The world-wide impacts…nearly as large.** Ritchie, *Encyclopedia of Earthquakes and Volcanoes*, 86–87; Simkin and Siebert, *Volcanoes of the World, Second Edition*, 117.

238. **Other historic examples…same size.** The 1831 eruption of Babuyon Claro (Luzon Island, The Philippines) could be an example of a large eruption having minimal world-wide distribution of tephra. Simkin and Siebert, *Volcanoes of the World, Second Edition*, 83.

238. **Mexico's El Chichon in 1982 is a good example.** Simkin and Siebert, *Volcanoes of the World, Second Edition*, 24.

239. **Katmai and Novarupta…Tambora in 1815.** Simkin and Siebert, *Volcanoes of the World, Second Edition*, 117, 74.

240. **Either could create a tsunami.** A tsunami is a powerful, fast-moving water perturbance that can push huge amounts of water onto what would normally be dry land. The Krakatau eruption in 1883 created tsunamis up to 120 feet high along the coasts of Java and Sumatra. Simkin and Siebert, *Volcanoes of the World, Second Edition*, 22; Ritchie, *Encyclopedia of Earthquakes and Volcanoes*, 123.

240. **An enormous tsunami…unlikely.** On December 26, 2004, a 750 mile long displacement between the Burma and Indian tectonic plates in the Indian Ocean created a powerful and broad tsunami. More than 200,000 people died. Property damage to coastal communities all around the Indian Ocean was enormous. "Tsunami," *Time*, 32.

Chapter 31

244. **The United States…twenty-first century.** In the year 2000, the United States had 4.6% of the world's population. That same year, the United States consumed 26% of the fossil fuels that were consumed world-wide. Thus, the United States contributed about one fourth of all the carbon dioxide added to the Earth's atmosphere from the consumption of fossil fuels in 2000. (Amounts calculated from data in Boyle, Everett, and Ramage, eds., *Energy Systems and Sustainability*, 67 [Table 2.2], 70 [Table 2.3], 79 [Figure 2.13].)

252. **In some areas, tropical…a few years.** Whitmore, *Introduction to Tropical Rain Forests*, 133–48, 164–78.

252. **In other areas…to produce food.** Example: the Silicon Valley area south of San Francisco.

Chapter 32

255. **Underground temperatures…degrees Celsius.** Deffeyes, *Hubbert's Peak*, 21.

259. **From a high of…people by 2032.** Sachs, "The End of Poverty," 42–54.

260. **This was less than…world-wide consumption.** The text uses the term "grains," whereas the UN uses the term "cereals." "Cereals" are wheat, rice, and coarse grains such as corn. At the end of 2006, cereal stocks were at 403 million tons. World-wide use in 2006 was 2,060 million tons. The world stocks-to-use ratio was 19.5 percent, which was a historic low that represents about 71 days of reserve at the 2006 rate of use. Both production shortfalls and increased use accounted for this result. Cereals production improved in later years, reaching 2,542 million tons in 2014. Use increased as well, but not as much as production, so cereal stocks rose to 631 million tons at the end of 2014 (a 25 percent stocks-to-use ratio, giving a reserve of about 91 days). *Crop Prospects and Food Situation—No. 4 November 2006*, 4–5; *Crop Prospects and Food Situation—No. 1 March 2015*, 8.

260. **Had they learned…occurred later.** Hurricane Katrina struck the Gulf Coast of Louisiana, Mississippi, and Alabama on Monday, August 29, 2005. It completely destroyed many communities. Putrid water flooded most of the city of New Orleans when protective levees broke.

Chapter 33

263. **Its velocity was...two months ago.** Guyot, *Physics of the Environment and Climate*, 271–72.

265. **At fifteen megatons...Omega.** Rhodes, *Dark Sun*, 541–42.

265. **They even showed...in 1961.** Sakharov, *Memoirs*, trans. Lourie, 218–21; Seaborg, *Kennedy, Khruschev and the Test Ban*, 112, 114.

265. **Some surprises occurred...early tests.** Rhodes, *Dark Sun*, 541–42; Sakharov, *Memoirs*, trans. Lourie, 188–94.

265. **If we are successful...in human conflict.** McKain, *Making and Using the Atomic Bomb*, 105–6, 113.

266. **Even thirty years ago...thousand years.** See appendix 8; National Research Council, Committee on Global Change Research, *Global Environmental Change: Research Pathways*, 239, 215–22.

268. **Luckily, the latest...was in place.** Guyot, *Physics of the Environment and Climate*, 271–72.

271. **Its major eruption...on and off.** Ritchie, *Encyclopedia of Earthquakes and Volcanoes*, 266.

Chapter 34

273. **He said that...from cold fronts.** Guyot, *Physics of the Environment and Climate*, 272.

BIBLIOGRAPHY

Intergovernmental Panel on Climate Change

Reports by the United Nations' Intergovernmental Panel on Climate Change have been published approximately each six years. They summarize and provide references to a huge number of peer-reviewed articles that have appeared in publications around the world.

The volumes that describe the reported science about climate change and impacts of climate change provide information far beyond the IPCC's summary findings. Those summary findings are widely reported in the media in even briefer form than presented in the IPCC documents.

The IPCC volumes that provided specific information used in *The Gareloi Solution* are listed here by publication date rather than by the name of the lead editor. These volumes also are listed in the "other references" alphabetically by the name of the lead editor.

1995 IPCC Report on Scientific Basis

Houghton, J. T., L. G. Meira Filho, B. A. Callander, N. Harris, A. Kattenberg, and K. Maskell eds. *Climate Change 1995: The Science of Climate Change: Contribution of Working Group I to the Second Assessment Report of the Intergovernmental Panel on Climate Change.* Cambridge, UK and New York: Cambridge University Press, 1996.

2001 IPCC Report on Scientific Basis

Houghton, J. T., Y. Ding, D. J. Griggs, M. Noguer, P. J. van der Linden, X. Dai, K. Maskell, and C. A. Johnson eds. *Climate Change 2001:*

The Scientific Basis, Contribution of Working Group I to the Third Assessment Report of the Intergovernmental Panel on Climate Change. Cambridge, UK and New York: Cambridge University Press, 2001.

2001 IPCC Report on Impacts

McCarthy, James J., Osvaldo F. Canziani, Neil A. Leary, David J. Dokken, and Kasey S. White eds. *Climate Change 2001: Impacts, Adaptation, and Vulnerability, Contribution of Working Group II to the Third Assessment Report of the Intergovernmental Panel on Climate Change.* Cambridge, UK, New York, Oakleigh VIC Australia, Madrid, and Cape Town, 2001.

2007 IPCC Report on Scientific Basis

Solomon, Susan, Dahe Qin, Martin Manning, Melinda Marquis, Kristen Averyt, Melinda M. B. Tignor, Henry LeRoy Miller, Jr., and Zhenlin Chen eds. *Climate Change 2007: The Physical Science Basis, Contribution of Working Group I to the Fourth Assessment Report of the Intergovernmental Panel on Climate Change.* Cambridge, UK and New York: Cambridge University Press, 2007.

2013 IPCC Report on Scientific Basis

Stocker, Thomas F., Dahe Qin, Gian-Kasper Plattner, Melinda M. B. Tignor, Simon K. Allen, Judith Boschung, Alexander Nauels, Yu Xia, Vincent Bex, and Pauline M. Midgley eds. *Climate Change 2013: The Physical Science Basis, Contribution of Working Group I to the Fifth Assessment Report of the Intergovernmental Panel on Climate Change.* Cambridge, UK and New York: Cambridge University Press, 2014.

2014 IPCC Report on Impacts, Adaptation, and Vulnerability

Field, Christopher B., Vicente R. Barros, David Jon Dokken, Katharine J. Mach, Michael D. Mastrandrea, T. Eren Bilir, Monalisa Chatterjee, Kristie L. Ebi, Yuka Otsuki Estrada, Robert C. Genova, Betelhem Girma, Eric S. Kissel, Andrew N. Levy, Sandy MacCracken, Patricia

R. Mastrandrea, and Leslie L. White eds. *Climate Change 2014: Impacts, Adaptation, and Vulnerability—Part A: Global and Sectoral Aspects, Working Group II Contribution to the Fifth Assessment Report of the Intergovernmental Panel on Climate Change.* New York: Cambridge University Press, 2014.

Other References

Afghanistan, Lifting the Veil. Upper Saddle River, NJ: Prentice Hall, 2002.

Alaska National Interest Lands Conservation Act, Pub.L.No. 96-487, 94 Stat 2371 (1980).

Alleklett, Kjell. "Oil: A Bumpy Road Ahead." *World Watch* 19, no. 1 (January/February 2006): 10–12.

"Alumna Profile: Susan Solomon: Atmospheric Chemistry, Help the Earth Heal Itself." *News Journal, College of Chemistry. University of California, Berkeley* 13, no. 2 (Fall 2005): 24–25.

Balling, Robert C., Jr. "Geographical Analysis of Differences in Trends between Nearsurface and Satellite-based Temperature Measurements." *Geophysical Research Letters* 23, no. 21 (October 15, 1996): 2939–41.

Berenstein, Paula. *Alternative Energy—Facts, Statistics, and Issues.* Westport, CT: Oryx, 2001.

Bigg, Grant R. *The Oceans and Climate.* Cambridge, UK: Cambridge University Press, 1996.

Boyle, Godfrey, Bob Everett, and Janet Ramage, eds. *Energy Systems and Sustainability.* Oxford, UK: Oxford University Press in association with The Open University, 2003.

Brunner, Borgna, ed. *Time Almanac 2002.* Boston: Information Please, 2001.

Bryant, Edward. *Climate Process and Change.* Cambridge, UK: Cambridge University Press, 1997.

Budget of the U.S. Government, Fiscal Year 2005. Washington, DC: The White House, 2013. http/www.whitehouse.gov/omb/budget.

Burns, Robert. "Pentagon Study Looks at Global Climate." The Associated Press, February 26, 2004.

"California Drought." United States Geological Survey, January 2016. http://ca.water.usgs.gov/data/drought/.

Changnon, Stanley A. *El Niño, 1997–1998, The Climate Event of the Century.* New York: Oxford University Press, 2000.

Chasan, Daniel Jack. "Will the Dunes March Once Again?" *Smithsonian* 28, no. 9 (December 1997): 70–79.

Chase, T. N., R. A. Pielke Sr., T. G. F. Kittel, R. R. Nemani, and S. W. Running. "Simulated Impacts of Historical Land Cover Changes on Global Climate in Northern Winter." *Climate Dynamics* 16 (2000): 93–105.

Churchill, Eugene Linden. "The Big Meltdown." *Time*, September 4, 2000: 52–56.

Cragg, Dan. *Guide to Military Installations, 5th Edition.* Mechanicsburg, PA: Stackpole Books, 1997.

Coats, Robert A. *Geologic Reconnaissance of Gareloi Island, Aleutian Islands, Alaska.* Bulletin 1028-J, United States Geological Survey. Washington, DC: Government Printing Office, 1959.

Crop Prospects and Food Situation—No. 4 November 2006. Food and Agriculture Organization of the United Nations, 2006. http://www.fao.org/docrep/009/j8123e/j8123e03.htm.

Crop Prospects and Food Situation—No. 1 March 2015. Food and Agriculture Organization of the United Nations, 2015. http://www.fao.org/glews/english/cpfs/14410e/14410E.html.

Crowley, Thomas J. and Gerald R. North. *Paleoclimatology.* New York: Oxford University Press, 1991.

Dane, Abe. "Science: Pinatubo's Toll." *Popular Mechanics*, December, 1991: 102–3.

Deffeyes, Kenneth S. *Hubbert's Peak: The Impending World Oil Shortage.* Princeton, NJ: Princeton University Press, 2003.

Dlugolecki, Andrew. "An Insurer's Perspective." In *Climate Change and the Financial Sector: The Emerging Threat—The Solar Solution*, edited by Jeremy Leggett, 64–81. Munich: Gerling Akademie Verlag, 1996.

Doran, Peter T., John C. Priscu, W. Berry Lyons, John E. Walsh, Andrew G. Fountain, Diane M. McKnight, Daryl L. Moorhead et al. "Antarctic Climate Cooling and Terrestrial Ecosystem Response." *Nature*, January 2002: 517–20.

Earth Science Research Laboratory of the National Oceanic and Atmospheric Administration. Facts at http://www.esrl.noaa.gov.

Feddema, Johannes J., Keith W. Oleson, Gordon B. Bonan, Linda O. Mearns, Lawrence E. Buja, Gerald A. Meehl, and Warren M. Washington. "The Importance of Land-Cover Change in Simulating Future Climates." *Science*, December 9, 2005: 1674–78.

Field, Christopher B., Vicente R. Barros, David Jon Dokken, Katharine J. Mach, Michael D. Mastrandrea, T. Eren Bilir, Monalisa Chatterjee, Kristie L. Ebi, Yuka Otsuki Estrada, Robert C. Genova, Betelhem Girma, Eric S. Kissel, Andrew N. Levy, Sandy MacCracken, Patricia R. Mastrandrea, and Leslie L. White eds. *Climate Change 2014: Impacts, Adaptation, and Vulnerability—Part A: Global and Sectoral Aspects, Working Group II Contribution to the Fifth Assessment Report of the Intergovernmental Panel on Climate Change.* New York: Cambridge University Press, 2014.

Gareloi Island photographs, 1946. Lakewood, CO: United States Geological Survey (documents located at Lakewood Federal Center, Colorado).

Geologic and Hydrologic Effects of the Cannikin Underground Nuclear Explosion, Amchitka Island, Aleutian Islands, Alaska. USGS 474-148. Denver, CO: United States Geological Survey, June 1972.

Gilbert, Jeremy and Colin Campbell. "What We Know and What We Think We Know." *Proceedings, Denver World Oil Conference, ASPO-USA, November 10-11, 2005.* http://www.aspo-usa.com.

Gillett, Nathan P. and David W. Thompson. "Simulation of Recent Southern Hemisphere Climate Change." *Science*, October 10, 2003: 273–75.

Glasstone, Samuel and Philip Dolan. *The Effects of Nuclear Weapons, Third Edition.* Washington, DC: United States Department of Defense and United States Department of Energy, 1977.

Global Climate Change, A Better Path Forward. Irving, TX: Exxon Mobil Corporation, 2000.

Goulding, Michael, Ronaldo Barthem, and Efram Ferreira. *The Smithsonian Atlas of the Amazon.* Washington, DC: Smithsonian Books, 2003.

Gray, L.J., J. Beer, M. Geller, J.D. Haigh, M. Lockwood, K. Matthes, U. Cubasch, D. Fleitmann, G. Harrison, L. Hood, J. Luterbacher, G.A. Meehl, D. Shindell, B. van Geel, and W. White, "Solar Influences on Climate." *Reviews of Geophysics* 48 (2010): 4001–53.

Gueymard, Christian A. "The Sun's Total and Spectral Irradiance for Solar Energy Applications and Solar Radiation Models." *Solar Energy* 76, no. 4 (2004): 423–53.

Gurney, Kevin Robert, Rachel M. Law, A. Scott Denning, Peter J. Rayner, David Baker, Phillippe Bousquet, Lori Bruhwiler et al. "Towards Robust Regional Estimates of CO_2 Sources and Sinks Using Atmospheric Transport Models." *Nature*, February 7, 2002: 626–29.

Guyot, Gérard. *Physics of the Environment and Climate.* Chichester, West Sussex, UK: John Wiley & Sons, 1998.

Haeberlin, Scott W. *A Case for Nuclear-Generated Electricity.* Columbus, OH: Batelle Press, 2004.

Handbook of Chemistry and Physics, 39th Edition. Cleveland: Chemical Rubber Publishing, 1957.

Hansen, James E. and Andrew A. Lacis. "Sun and Dust Versus Greenhouse Gases: An Assessment of Their Relative Roles in Global Climate Change." *Nature*, August 23, 1990: 713–19.

"Heatstroke." *Time*, September 5, 1988: 51.

Hegerl, Gabriele C., and John M. Wallace. "Influence of Patterns of Climate Variability on the Difference between Satellite and Surface Temperature Trends." *Journal of Climate* 15, Issue 17 (September 1, 2002): 2412–27.

Houghton, J. T., L. G. Meira Filho, B. A. Callander, N. Harris, A. Kattenberg, and K. Maskell eds. *Climate Change 1995: The Science of Climate Change: Contribution of Working Group I to the Second Assessment Report of the Intergovernmental Panel on Climate Change.* Cambridge, UK and New York: Cambridge University Press, 1996.

Houghton, J. T., Y. Ding, D. J. Griggs, M. Noguer, P. J. van der Linden, X. Dai, K. Maskell, and C. A. Johnson eds. *Climate Change 2001: The Scientific Basis, Contribution of Working Group I to the Third Assessment Report of the Intergovernmental Panel on Climate Change.* Cambridge, UK and New York: Cambridge University Press, 2001.

Hoyt, Douglas V. and Kenneth H. Shatten. *The Role of the Sun in Climate Change.* New York: Oxford University Press, 1997.

The International Encyclopedia of Science and Technology. New York: Oxford University Press, 1999.

Jaroff, Leon. "Stormy Weather." *Time*, February 14, 2000, 64–66.

Jones, P. D. "Recent Warming in Global Temperature Series." *Geophysical Research Letters* 21, no. 12 (June 15, 1994): 1149–52.

Karoly, David J., Karl Braganza, Peter A. Stott, Julie M. Arblaster, Gerald A. Meehl, Anthony J. Broccoli, and Keith W., Dixon. "Detection of a Human Influence on North American Climate." *Science*, November 14, 2003: 1200–3.

Kiester, Edwin, Jr. "Water, Water, Everywhere." *Smithsonian*, August 1977: 34–44.

Kolesnikova, Maria and Luzi Ann Javier. "Russia Bars Exports of Grain for Rest of 2010." *The Denver Post*, August 6, 2010, Sec. B, 8B (from *Bloomberg News*).

Krabill, W., E. Frederick, S. Manizade, C. Martin, J. Sonntag, R. Swift, R. Thomas, W. Wright, and J. Yungel. "Rapid Thinning of Parts of the Southern Greenland Ice Sheet." *Science*, March 5, 1999: 1522–24.

Krabill, W., W. Abdalati, E. Frederick, S. Manizade, C. Martin, J. Sonntag, R. Swift, R. Thomas, W. Wright, and J. Yungel. "Greenland Ice Sheet: High-Elevation Balance and Peripheral Thinning." *Science*, July 21, 2000: 428–30.

Krüger, Christoph. *Volcanoes.* New York: G. P. Putnam's Sons, 1971.

Kyoto Protocol to the United Nations Framework Convention on Climate Change. 1997. http://unfccc.int/kyoto_protocol/items/2830.php.

Lazante, John R., Stephen A. Klein, and Dian J. Seidel. "Temporal Homogenization of Monthly Radiosonde Temperature Data, Part I: Methodology." *Journal of Climate* 16, January 15, 2003: 224–40.

Lazante, John R., Stephen A. Klein, and Dian J. Seidel. "Temporal Homogenization of Monthly Radiosonde Temperature Data, Part II: Trends, Sensitivities, and MSU Comparison." *Journal of Climate* 16, January 15, 2003: 241–62.

Lean, Judith, Juerg Beer, and Raymond Bradley. "Reconstruction of Solar Irradiance Since 1610: Implications for Climate Change." *Geophysical Research Letters* 22, no. 23 (December 1, 1995): 3195–98.

Leggett, Jeremy, ed. *Climate Change and the Financial Sector: The Emerging Threat—The Solar Solution.* Munich: Gerling Akademie Verlag, 1996.

Lemley, Brad. "The New Ice Age." *Discover,* September 2002: 34–41.

Limited Test Ban Treaty (see Treaty Banning Nuclear Weapons Tests …).

Lomborg, Bjorn. *The Skeptical Environmentalist: Measuring the Real State of the World.* New York: Cambridge University Press, 2001.

McCarthy, James J., Osvaldo F. Canziani, Neil A. Leary, David J. Dokken, and Kasey S. White eds. *Climate Change 2001: Impacts, Adaptation, and Vulnerability, Contribution of Working Group II to the Third Assessment Report of the Intergovernmental Panel on Climate Change.* Cambridge, UK, New York, Oakleigh VIC Australia, Madrid, and Cape Town, 2001.

McCormick, M. Patrick, Larry W. Thomason, and Charles R. Trepte. "Atmospheric Effects of the Mt. Pinatubo Eruption." *Nature,* February 2, 1995: 399–404.

McKain, Mark, ed. *Making and Using the Atomic Bomb.* Farmington Hills, MI: Greenhaven, 2003.

McPhaden, Michael J, and Dongxiao Zhang. "Slowdown of the Meridional Overturning Circulation in the Upper Pacific Ocean. *Nature,* February 7, 2002: 603–7.

McSlarrow, Kyle E. (Deputy Secretary, Department of Energy). *Statement at Hearing on Proposed Fiscal Year 2005 Budget Request for the Department of Energy.* United States Senate Committee on Energy and Natural Resources, February 10, 2004.

Mears, Carl A., Matthias C. Schabel, and Frank J. Wentz. "A Reanalysis of the MSU Channel 2 Tropospheric Temperature Record." *Journal of Climate* 16, November 16, 2003: 3650–664.

Michaels, Patrick J. *Carbon Dioxide, A Satanic Gas?* Testimony before the Subcommittee on National Economic Growth, Natural Resources and Regulatory Affairs, United States House of Representatives, October 6, 1999 (available from the Cato Institute at http://www.cato.org/publications/congressional-testimony/carbon-dioxide-satanic-gas).

Montreal Protocol on Substances that Deplete the Ozone Layer. 1987. http://ozone.unep.org/new_site/en/montreal_protocol.php (see also http://ozone.unep.org generally for information on the Montreal Protocol from the Ozone Secretariat, United Nations Environment Programme).

National Climate Data Center of the National Oceanic and Atmospheric Administration. Facts at http://www.ncdc.noaa.gov/cag, February 2015.

National Oceanic and Atmospheric Administration. Facts at http://www.cmdl.noaa.gov and at http://www.climate.gov.

National Research Council, Committee on Global Change Research. *Global Environmental Change: Research Pathways for the Next Decade.* Washington, DC: National Academy Press, 1999.

National Research Council, Committee on Abrupt Climate Change. *Abrupt Climate Change: Inevitable Surprises.* Washington, DC: National Academy Press, 2002.

Nesme-Ribes, E., E. N. Ferreira, R. Sadourny, H. Le Treut, and Z. X. Li. "Solar Dynamics and Its Impact on Solar Irradiance and the Terrestrial Climate." *Journal of Geophysical Research* 98, no. A11 (November 1, 1993): 18,923–35.

"Net Generation by Energy Source: Total (All Sectors)." Table 3.1.A, Electricity, Electric Power Annual, U.S. Energy Information Administration, 2016. http://www.eia.gov/electricity/annual/html/ epa_03_01a.html.

NOAA Annual Greenhouse Gas Index. Earth System Research Laboratory of the National Oceanic and Atmospheric Administration. http:// www.esrl.noaa.gov/gmd/ccgg/aggi.html, January 2016 and http:// www.esrl.noaa.gov/gmd/aggi/aggi.html, February 2015.

Nutter, Franklin W. "A Reinsurer's Perspective." *Climate Change and the Financial Sector: The Emerging Threat—The Solar Solution*, edited by Jeremy Leggett, 82–90. Munich: Gerling Akademie Verlag, 1996.

Paris Agreement under the United Nations Framework Convention on Climate Change, December 2015. http://unfcc.int/resource/ docs/201.

Parmesan, Camille, and Gary Yohe. "A Globally Coherent Fingerprint of Climate Change Impacts across Natural Systems." *Nature*, January 2, 2003: 37–42.

"Peak Oil." *World Watch* 19, no. 1 (January/February 2006).

Philander, S. George. *Is the Temperature Rising? The Uncertain Science of Global Warming*. Princeton, NJ: Princeton University Press, 1998.

Philpott, Don. *Caribbean Sunseekers: St. Vincent and Grenadines.* Lincolnwood, IL: Passport Books, 1996.

Pielke, Roger A., Sr. "The U.S. National Climate Change Assessment: Do the Climate Models Project a Useful Picture of Regional Climate?"

Witness testimony, Committee on Energy and Commerce, United States House of Representatives July 25, 2002.

Prata, A. J., D. M. O'Brien, W. I. Rose, and S. Self. "Global, Long-Term Sulphur Dioxide Measurements from TOVS Data: A New Tool for Studying Explosive Volcanism and Climate" in *Volcanism and the Earth's Atmosphere* ed. Alan Robock and Clive Oppenheiver, Geophysical Monograph 139. Washington, DC: American Geophysical Union, 2003, 75–92.

Reeder, John. *Industry and Trade Summary: Grain (Cereals).* USITC Publication 3350. Washington, DC: Office of Industries, U.S. International Trade Commission, September 2000.

Reilly, J. M. "Climate Change and Agriculture: The State of the Scientific Knowledge (Guest Editorial)." *Climate Change* 43, no. 4 (December 1999): 645–50.

Rhodes, Richard. *Dark Sun: The Making of the Hydrogen Bomb.* New York: Simon & Schuster, 1995.

Ritchie, David. *The Encyclopedia of Earthquakes and Volcanoes.* New York: Facts on File, 1994.

Robock, Alan and Clive Oppenheimer, eds. *Volcanism and the Earth's Atmosphere.* Geophysical Monograph 139. American Geophysical Union, 2003.

Root, Terry L., Jeff T. Price, Kimberly R. Hall, Stephen H Schneider, Cynthia Rosenzweig, and J. Alan Pounds. "Fingerprints of Global Warming on Wild Animals and Plants." *Nature*, January 2, 2003: 57–60.

Rosenzweig, C. "Potential Impacts of Climate Change on Citrus and Potato Production in the U.S." *Agricultural Systems* 52 (1996): 455–79.

Rosenzweig, Cynthia, and Daniel Hillel. *Climate Change and the Global Harvest.* New York: Oxford University Press, 1998.

Ruddiman, William F. "How Did Humans First Alter Global Climate?" *Scientific American*, March 2005: 46–53.

Sachs, Jeffrey D. "The End of Poverty." *Time*, March 14, 2015: 42–54.

Sakharov, Andrei. *Memoirs.* Translated by Richard Lourie. New York: Alfred A. Knopf, 1990.

Salter, Jim. "Flooding Forcing Evacuations, Traffic Troubles in Missouri." The Associated Press, December 31, 2015.

Salter, Jim and Alan Scher Zagier. "Rescue Crews Assist with Evacuations in Midwest Flooding." The Associated Press, December 30, 2015.

Saunders, Fenella. "Chaotic Warnings from the Last Ice Age." *Discover*, June 2002: 14.

Seaborg, Glenn Theodore. *Kennedy, Khruschev and the Test Ban.* Berkeley, CA: University of California Press, 1981.

Sedlacek, W. A., E. J. Mroz, and G. Heiken. "Stratospheric Sulfate from the Gareloi Eruption, 1980: Contribution to the 'Ambient' Aerosol by a Poorly Documented Volcanic Eruption." *Geophysical Research Letters* 8, no. 7 (July 1981): 761–64.

Senate Resolution No. 98, 105th Cong., July 25, 1997.

Shepley, James R. and Clay Blair, Jr. *The Hydrogen Bomb: The Men, The Menace, The Mechanism.* New York: David McKay, 1954.

Sidey, Hugh. "The Big Dry." *Time*, July 4, 1988: 12–15.

Simkin, Tom, and Lee Siebert. *Volcanoes of the World, Second Edition: A Regional Directory, Gazetteer, and Chronology of Volcanism during the Last 10,000 Years.* Tucson, AZ: GeoScience Press, published in association with The Smithsonian Institution, 1994.

Solomon, Susan, Dahe Qin, Martin Manning, Melinda Marquis, Kristen Averyt, Melinda M. B. Tignor, Henry LeRoy Miller, Jr., and Zhenlin Chen eds. *Climate Change 2007: The Physical Science Basis, Contribution of Working Group I to the Fourth Assessment Report of the Intergovernmental Panel on Climate Change.* Cambridge, UK and New York: Cambridge University Press, 2007.

"Some Key Numbers after Historic Illinois, Missouri Flooding." The Associated Press, January 4, 2016.

Spencer, Roy W. and John R. Christy. "Precise Monitoring of Global Temperature Trends from Satellites." *Science*, March 30, 1990: 1558–62.

Stager, Curt. "Tales of a Warmer Planet." *The New York Times*, November 29, 2015, SR 4–5.

Starke, Linda, ed. *Vital Signs 2003, The Trends That Are Shaping Our Future.* New York and London: W.W. Norton & Company, 2003. (The Worldwatch Institute, in Cooperation with the United Nations Environment Programme.).

Stocker, Thomas F., Dahe Qin, Gian-Kasper Plattner, Melinda M. B. Tignor, Simon K. Allen, Judith Boschung, Alexander Nauels, Yu Xia, Vincent Bex, and Pauline M. Midgley eds. *Climate Change 2013: The Physical Science Basis, Contribution of Working Group I to the Fifth Assessment Report of the Intergovernmental Panel on Climate Change.* Cambridge, UK and New York: Cambridge University Press, 2014.

Stott, Peter A. and J. A. Kettleborough. "Origins and Estimates of Uncertainty in Predictions of Twenty-first Century Temperature Rise." *Nature*, April 18, 2002: 723–26.

Thomas, R., T., Akins, B. Csatho, M. Fahnestock, P. Gogineni, C. Kim, and J. Sonntag. "Mass Balance of the Greenland Ice Sheet at High Elevations." *Science*, July 21, 2000: 426–28.

Trade Expansion Act of 1962, Pub. L. No. 87–794, 76 Stat. 872.

Tran, Tini. "Regional Brown Cloud Termed Global Danger." *Rocky Mountain News*, November 14, 2008, 28 (from *The Associated Press*).

Treaty Banning Nuclear Weapon Tests in the Atmosphere, in Outer Space and Under Water, U.S.-U.K.-U.S.S.R., August 5, 1963, 14 U.S.T. 1313. (aka Limited Test Ban Treaty of 1963).

"Tsunami." *Time*, January 10, 2005 (Special Report): 30–39.

United States Geological Survey Maps, Alaska Topographic Series:
Adak, Alaska, 1957, Rev. 1983
Atka, Alaska, 1959, Rev. 1983
Gareloi Island, Alaska, 1954, Rev. 1983

United States Geological Survey Maps, AMS Series.
Gareloi Island, Alaska, 1952 [AMS Series]

Van Wagener, Dana. "U.S. Tight Oil Production: Alternative Supply Projections and an Overview of EIA's Analysis of Well-Level Data Aggregated to the County Level." In *Annual Energy Outlook 2014* (Issues in Focus). Washington, DC: U.S. Energy Information Administration, 2014. http://www.eia.gov/forecasts/aeo/tight_oil.cfm.

Vig, Norman J. and Michael G. Faure, eds. *Green Giants? Environmental Policies of the United States and the European Union.* Cambridge, MA: MIT Press, 2004.

Vinnikov, Konstantin Y. and Norman C. Grody. "Global Warming Trend of Mean Tropospheric Temperature Observed by Satellites." *Science*, October 10, 2003: 269–72.

Wayne, Richard P. *Chemistry of Atmospheres, Third Edition.* Oxford, UK: Oxford University Press, 2000.

Whipple, A. B. C. *Restless Oceans.* Alexandria, VA: Time-Life Books, 1983.

Whitmore, T. C. *An Introduction to Tropical Rain Forests.* New York: Oxford University Press, 1990.

Wigley, T. M. L. and S. C. B. Raper. "Climatic Change Due to Solar Irradiance Changes." *Geophysical Research Letters* 17, no. 12 (November 1990): 2169–72.

Winsor, P. "Arctic Sea Ice Thickness Remained Constant during the 1990s." *Geophysical Research Letters* 28, no. 6 (March 15, 2001): 1039–41.

Wolff, Eric W. "Whither Antarctic Sea Ice?" *Science*, November 14, 2003: 1164.

World Meteorological Organization. Information at http://www.wmo.int.

Yancey, Diane. *Life During the Dust Bowl.* Farmington Hills, MI: Lucent Books, 2004.

INDEX

Printed in the United States
By Bookmasters